A SCIENTIFIC ROMANCE

BOOKS BY RONALD WRIGHT

Fiction
*A Scientific Romance*

History
*Stolen Continents*

Travel
*Time Among the Maya*
*On Fiji Islands*
*Cut Stones and Crossroads: A Journey in Peru*

Essays
*Home and Away*

# A SCIENTIFIC ROMANCE

—— a novel ——

# RONALD WRIGHT

ALFRED A. KNOPF CANADA

Published by Alfred A. Knopf Canada
Copyright © 1997 by Ronald Wright

All rights reserved under International and
Pan American Copyright Conventions. Published in Canada
by Alfred A. Knopf Canada, Toronto, in 1997. Distributed
by Random House of Canada Limited, Toronto.

Canadian Cataloguing in Publication Data
Wright, Ronald
A scientific romance
ISBN 0-676-97056-7
I. Title.
PS8595.R62S34 1997    C813'.54    C96-932149-X
PR9199.3.W74S34 1997

Pages 311–312 constitute a continuation of the copyright page.

Printed and bound in the United States of America
First Edition

For Janice
And for Max

What did the victims matter that the machine destroyed on its way? Wasn't it bound for the future, heedless of spilt blood?

— Zola, *La Bête Humaine*, 1894

If you are the dreamer, I am what you dream.
But when you want to wake, I am your wish,
and I grow strong with all magnificence
and turn myself into a star's vast silence
above the strange and distant city, Time.

— Rilke, *The Book of Hours*, 1905

# CONTENTS

Part I

THE WELLS DEVICE

## —1—

Dear Bird:

A message in a bottle. Well, a disk in a jar. Hope you find it all right. Should be easy enough to spot, bobbing in my wake. For your eyes first but not necessarily your eyes only. Do what you like. Think of this as a little gift of intellectual property to go with the other things I've left. You'll be hearing from my solicitors (an ill phrase for you, I shouldn't wonder) but fear not, they bring tidings of material gain. The flat mainly.

Some of what follows may be stuff you know, but I thought it best to leave a fullish account in case you need it for evidence or publication. Forgive the bits about you, about Anita. You're the only one of us left now, Bird. I've forgiven you, and I'm sure Anita did. Perhaps you haven't forgiven us. That's up to you. Bear with me if one or two things seem wrong or unfair; you may as well know how I see (saw?) things. I'm trying to be an honest ghost.

Some of what I've told you since reappearing in your life isn't exactly right. I've brought you here to the Thames marshes on expectations that won't be fulfilled. All that work for nothing but a disappearing act. Well, not quite; you'll have my worldly goods.

*To my good friend Charles Gordon Parker.* I still wonder about the name. Was your mother really watching Charlton Heston in

*Khartoum* on the night you were conceived? Or was she a bop fanatic, as you told Anita? (And who was listening to bop in Millwall in 1967?) Anyway, you could hardly be less like Charlton Heston, and I mean that as a compliment. It takes more than a cheesy smile to catch a woman like Anita. And more than your music to keep her as long as you did, despite what you used to think. Anita may have been crazy about jazz, but we both knew she had a tin ear. *Between you and me, Dave* — you said to me once — *I sometimes wonder if she can tell Buddy De Franco from Acker Bilk.* Jazz for her was an accessory, like that ridiculous pipe. While for you it was the only thing you never joked about.

I didn't know she'd given you the pipe. I saw it land with your handful of earth. That was a fine thing to do, Bird. Anita believed in an afterlife (doesn't every Egyptologist?). I can see her there beside Osiris, fugging up the underworld with Borkhum Riff.

Odd how we spent our whole first year at Cambridge without bumping into one another. We must have attended some of the same lectures (if you ever attended any); we must have danced at the same dances, got drunk in the same pubs. We all liked the Rose when we felt genteel and the Loco when we didn't. But it took that crummy summer job flogging Old Master lithographs door to door for the South African with the rusty Jag. Forgotten the guy's name, but I remember his pep talk in the car that cold June night in — what, 1986? — the night we met. The immense policeman pulling us up: *Is this your vehicle, sir?* His torchlight on moth-eaten steel and poultices of fibreglass. *Reckon that'll take my weight, sir?* And the South African in his poshest voice, weedy with Capetown vowels no matter how hard he cultivated: *Be my guist, officer.*

The Jag bouncing under the weight of the law. Anita bouncing between us in the back, so slim and light, her face ochre in the streetlamps, sitting upright on her splendid mane, which seemed in the sodium glare like incandescent iron. You dark, trim, and sleek in your leather jacket and tie, poised like a kingfisher.

*Devid meet Anita and Bird—Charlie Parker, his real name believe it or not, and he ectually blows a tolerable alto sax. My con artist of the week! Learn from success, Devid. Bird's tidy. Bird's clean. Charming. Maybe not as charming as the lovely Anita here, but close. Not a fucking hairy like you. No offence, man. Just my training style.*

I caught him in the mirror, grinning to himself because the Jag didn't break and the copper let us off, saying *Mind how you go*, and we had to bite our tongues. Or more likely he was trying to catch Anita's eye. Her large eyes with fine dark rings around those irises that could be blue or green or grey. Seascape eyes, our northern sea, not her reefs and palms.

*You've got to make the punters lahk you, Devid. Develop a role. Watch Bird. What are we tonight, Bird? Poor art student earning an honest crust? A little bit arty's okay—goes with the image, makes you interesting to the wife. But not a dishonourable discharge from the Mixican army. Leave the poncho at home next time. Doesn't suit a big blond joker like you anyway. People might wonder what you've got on underneath.*

Fourteen years ago, Bird; and the images are still brighter, I'll bet, than any of those lithographs we sold. But I must get on with what I owe you: an explanation, an apology. You're going to walk out of the King Canute, down to the boat with a jug of bitter in your hand and two Scotch eggs in your pocket, and look over the water to my "human torpedo," and what are you going to see? The fata morgana, St. Elmo's fire, corposants jiving on the waves? I'm not exactly sure. But you'll see enough to know that what you're about to read is the truth. I hope you remembered to keep the camcorder running. With that you'll stand a chance of getting someone to believe you.

This business in which you've been obliged to take part began, in a way, the summer after we graduated and you left. I decided to stay on in archaeology, go for a Ph.D. That June I turned twenty-one and came into my parents' estate, the proceeds from the farm. Not riches (because of debts) but enough to follow a university career.

I suppose the main motive for staying on was Anita's staying on. But I'd also been truly bitten, on Clive Skeffington's dig at Alexandria, by what she called her gnawing rat. She meant a sleek, inquisitive, tenacious creature—the Rat of the Chinese calendar, perhaps—who burrows into the skeleton of time to answer Gauguin's questions: *What are we? Where do we come from? Where are we going?*

Only Anita carried on with Egypt, as you probably know. Skef's efforts failed to dislodge you from your Classics, and that salty dust gave me a sweeter tooth—for mossy statues by warm seas, or florid temples in a dripping forest. I remember you at the Pyramids when we first arrived: *All that sweat. A mountain of slave-sweat piled up for eternity. So many lives spent only to negotiate with death.* And Anita: *Come off it, love. You can spoil anything that way.* You were right, though. Ancient Egypt is a bore on the subject of mortality: no theatres, no gymnasia, no ball-courts, scarcely a palace or a fort; but enough tombs and funeral rites to last the human race forever.

It was Easter Island I wanted, or Angkor, Kuelap, Copán— anywhere far from the centres of our world. But they would have taken me too far from her, and who gets funding, let alone per- mission, to work in places like that now? Over the years I have made it to some of them, though to visit, not dig (I've become keen on trees and birds). And of course they're no longer quite as adver- tised. *Son et lumière* has been installed, there are five-star hotels just off camera, and the "enveloping jungle" is confined inside the fence like a rare beast.

So what could I do? What could I substitute for stone colossi on a lonely island? What besides those Yogi Bear faces frowning at the Pacific would draw me through another four years' paperchase? The answer surprised me. It came one sunny afternoon in the garden of that riverside pub near your old rooms on Jesus Green (the George? — the one where a rugby club tried to see how long man could live on beer alone). You'd left town in disgrace by then. Anita was working quietly, recuperating — forgive me for bringing it up — from the May Ball incident. Her wrist had healed but she still cried and rambled in her sleep, more than she knew.

I was in a deckchair, soaking up ale and sunlight, watching tourists on the water, idly listening to what I thought was an English conversation I couldn't quite overhear. It turned out to be Dutch — you know how it sounds: *Would you like coffee or go snogging? Have five raw oysters in my pocket. Was that your mother or an Irish wolfhound?* At that moment a puntload of Germans, the musical type Anita used to call lagermorphs, burst into "Jerusalem" — *End did zoze feet* — putting me in mind of two old loves: literature and primitive machines. (Yet another love we shared, come to think of it, though my taste ran to Romantics and satanic mills rather than Cicero and dodgy old motorbikes.) I saw a way to make it work: industrial archaeology with a head of theoretical steam.

You may think that a poor substitute, a mere toe in the oceans of the past. But the strange half-modern world of the Victorians had always intrigued me. I wanted to see the mechanical dragons of the Coal Age as they were seen when they were *first* seen. What dreams and nightmares they inspired, what hopes and dreads and intimations.

My bookshelf filled with titles like *The Semiotics of Steam* and *The Early Locomotive: A Gendered Discourse.* I became au fait with the machine as metaphorical body: piston as penis (eighteenth century), railway as nervous system (nineteenth), brain as telephone exchange (early twentieth), mind as software (late twentieth), and on we go to the fraying border between humanity and artefact. I did like the hardware, though. The Victorians' iron monsters, like Easter Island statues, were monuments to unexamined truths. Or so it seemed that river afternoon.

"Ah!" said Anita. "Worship and dread of the machine." We were in her flat later the same day, having tea. This was the best of times between us — the summer of 1988, when you'd gone and she was mine as much as she would ever be. Her marine eyes turned glassy, as she dredged for helpful information.

"Dickens of course, *Hard Times*. And Zola. Laplace's demon might be worth a candle. And the thunder-and-lightning man. What *was* his name?" Her hand flew to her throat and fluttered like a pale moth about her locket, the one you gave her. "Crosse? Yes. Andrew Crosse. Friend of Kinglake's. Thought he'd created insect life by passing electricity through stone. Mary Shelley heard him lecture. Don't miss the rebellion of the tools in the *Popol Vuh*. And there's always my ancestor William, 'Astronomye is an hard thynge, and evil forto knowe. . . .' Damn! Forgotten. Something about geometry being sinful."

Her hand fluttered again, impatiently. She went to the window, began to fill her pipe, turned and smiled. "Sorcerye is the sovereyne book that to the sciences belongeth."

Was Anita really descended from Langland? I suppose she could have been. (How many Langlands are there?) She certainly had chunks of him by heart. The later things surprised me more. I'd imagined the Victorian age as a time of uncurdled certainties, but you can't think that after reading Butler, or Morris, or Richard Jefferies. And she sent me to H.G. Wells, scientist *manqué*, pupil of Huxley, tutor of A.A. Milne.

1895. Think of it! Wells brings out *The Time Machine*. The bascule jaws of Tower Bridge have been munching river fog for just one year. Night after night in Covent Garden, Mabel Moll is luring audiences to the Moth and Flame. Wilde's *Earnest* is a wild success, but he's having a bad year — prison with hard labour, manuscripts pinched from his Chelsea house. Across the Channel an elderly Jules Verne is seeing predictions from *Paris in the Twentieth Century*, turned down by his publisher thirty years before as too fantastic, take shape before his rheumy eyes. William Morris is near death, finishing *The Well at the World's End*. Groucho Marx is born in New York; and in Abilene, Kansas, Dwight D. Eisenhower begins first grade.

Anyway, they gave me the doctorate (*Mechanism as Meaning: A Portrait of the Engineer as a Young Man*—my thesis title), though it was a close call with Anita's leaving me halfway through. Then Skeffington found me a fellowship in Houston for '93-'95, which put off the matter of gainful employment and gave me a chance to do some travelling and birding in Latin America. I think he hoped Texas would help me get over her. Certainly he hadn't much use for my new field.

*Meaning and Gender and All That. Oh dear. Don't you think it's risky to be too modern, David? You might find yourself quite suddenly old-fashioned. The French themselves realize that Parisian theory is an art form; the Americans, poor lambs, take it seriously. What a shame you're too young to remember when gender was a property of foreign languages and we British just had sex.*

Skef's retired now, by the way. Same as ever last I saw him: fit, fussy, feisty, a beard like a nanny-goat's and the old eye still out for a pretty figure and the main chance. Has a new wife half his age and a nice little hobby-farm near Cherry Hinton. Strawberries, I think, and an acre or two of Christmas trees. He had a soft spot for you, Bird, despite your hasty departure. Skef was a lefty from before the flood, so a Cockney in Classics was right up his street. Go and see him, show him this, talk it over. I owe him an explanation too.

He thought I was all set for a teaching post after Houston— somewhere like LSE or MIT. But the jobs were drying up. I must have sent a hundred applications. Skef got so tired of cranking out testimonials that he told me to write them myself and forge his signature (not hard: it looks like the Arabic for Shell). I ended up a long way from Easter Island or the Maya cities—as a curator at that iron and nostalgia theme park they made out of St. Pancras station, the Museum of Motion. You'd like the early bikes: several Nortons, a Scott, and a rare 1919 BSA V-twin, our youngest exhibit (we're meant to be strictly pre–Great War). Mostly locomotives, of course, standing at the platforms like great cart-horses frozen to death in their stalls.

I could have told you most of this over a pint after Anita's funeral, but the talk didn't exactly flow then, did it? (I've been so evasive lately that secrecy's become a habit.) What follows I could not have told you until now.

Skeffington rang right after last Christmas. Out of the blue. We hadn't spoken since I'd moved back to London. I hadn't told him about the job. We were friends, but never easy — I'd always had the feeling he thought me a lightweight or a dilettante.

"David. Happy New Year! Happy Millennium!" He must have overdone the cognac; he'd forgotten I drop out around Christmas, prescribe myself a little avoidance therapy, a trip abroad. Usually Muslim countries or South America, anywhere that doesn't make a fuss over Saint Nick. I know I told him years ago about my parents' death — more than I'd revealed to anyone except Anita. Did I ever tell you that it happened on a Christmas Eve? It was 1978 — six months after my eleventh birthday. Not my parents' fault. They were careful about drink and driving; the other driver wasn't. More than twenty years ago now, but every December it comes back.

Normally I wouldn't have picked up the phone, but I was expecting a call from the airline. I'd just got back from the Red Sea and Jordanian had lost my bags.

"Where've you been hiding, David? Lucky thing your number hasn't changed. Nobody stays put these days. It's far too long since we saw each other." He talked about Sarah, the new wife (a trophy, he let me know) and I confessed about the museum. He said he'd always hoped I'd get over my infatuation with "gadgets and hot frogs" and devote my gifts to "the main problem in European protohistory." *His* main problem: the barbarian hiatus (since Alexandria his interests have wandered north).

"Think of it, David. Three or four centuries lost in the cracks between the fall of Rome and rise of Christendom. Wide-open field. Room for new blood. Beowulf and Arthur, Gildas and Nennius. Doesn't it tempt you?" Then he got to the point. "Still doing any work on Wells? I imagine you've already heard about this hoax?"

I hadn't a clue, but wasn't going to say so.

"I'm faxing you. You'll find it amusing. I didn't think anyone apart from you remembered Wells or cared about him. But it seems someone does. Perhaps a rival of yours. Let me know what you find out."

I picked it up a few minutes later at Paper Tigers, round the corner from my flat—a badly transmitted copy of what appeared to be a legal document, a sort of testament, bearing the stamp of Riddle and Barclay, Solicitors and Commissioners for Oaths, St. John's Wood, and the supposed autograph of a geriatric Herbert George Wells. It was dated May 2, 1946. (You'll find the original at home, along with an earlier draft of this letter. Top left drawer of the desk.)

TO BE OPENED ON DECEMBER 21st, 1999.

To Whom It May Concern:
I do not know what terms of address will be the norm in 1999, so allow me to proceed without formalities. My intention is that this document should find its way into the hands of someone familiar with my work. At the most, I am immodest enough to believe that my name and books will still be known, and that some promising young scholar will

be embarking on a career in the field of Wellsiana. At the least, I trust I'm a period curiosity, a flame still guttering in the minds of a few devotees of the literary debris of a century ago. Either way, I beg you to take seriously the preposterous tale you are about to hear, and I must insist that in return for being privy to these thoughts you will at least suspend your disbelief long enough to do what I ask at the end. (It is nothing dangerous, costly, or difficult.) If you can't promise me this, read no further and pass these pages to another.

You will of course be acquainted with my scientific romance, *The Time Machine*, in which a Traveller constructs a device which enables him to voyage into the future. It has no doubt struck you as a fable, a morality play upon the structure of society, upon our capacity as a species for good and evil, advancement and depravity. It is all that indeed. But unless my voyager has already returned (and I pray to a God in whom I do not believe that she has) and unless the secret is now common knowledge (which it may well be), I am sure nobody over twelve years old will have entertained for one moment the thought that such a voyage could actually have been made.

When the idea for *The Time Machine* first came to me I had little interest in the scientific detail of the proposition; it was merely a plot device, an armature on which to wind ideas. However, I thought it well to acquaint myself with the latest scientific thinking, so as not to write a tale that would embarrass me among the *cognoscenti*. I wrote to Nikola Tesla in the United States, newly famous for his discovery of the rotating magnetic field, invention of the alternating current motor, and other less orthodox research into electricity and radiation. Tesla was not merely a genius but a visionary to whom nothing seemed unlikely or impossible. He had, for example, plans to transmit power wirelessly over vast distances, and once proposed electrifying the whole Earth in order to communicate with the inhabitants of Mars, whom he believed to be the source of cosmic signals his equipment had detected.

I thought the idea of time travel would intrigue him. The great man answered me once courteously enough, but referred my further enquiries to a protégée, a young woman by the name of Tatiana Cherenkova, who, he assured me, was a brilliant mind destined to go far beyond his own accomplishments. "Already she is trespassing on secret lands beyond my reach," he wrote in his extravagant English, "already I see her radiance casting shadows on my feeble glow. I predict that this young woman will ignore precedent and startle civilization with her discoveries." I took this to be the hyperbole natural to Middle Europeans and suspected he was fobbing off a tiresome crank (I was then unknown beyond a small London circle) onto someone with time less valuable than his own.

Miss Cherenkova and I began to correspond. She told me much more than I needed to know about theories of time, electrical fields, gravitation, electromagnetic waves, and so forth. It became rather too much of a good thing, and I employed so little of it in my fantasy that I did not trouble to give her contribution public credit. I did however send her an autographed copy of the first edition, and the poor girl—for she was only twenty-three—wrote back in terms of the strongest gratitude and admiration. When Tesla came to London in 1897, about two years after *The Time Machine* was published, he brought her with him. Tatiana and I arranged to meet.

Now (and this is where my tale becomes increasingly difficult to write, even for eyes unborn) I and my second wife,

Amy Catherine Robbins—Jane, as I called her—had married in 1895. We were still very much in love. Yet I have never been able to resist the attraction of an exceptional mind in a tender female frame. In short, after a professional association of some months, Tania Cherenkova became my mistress. I found her a small house with a room where she could work—in a mews off the Brompton Road—and helped her in every way to continue her research, which took a new and unfortunate direction.

Still obsessed with my fantasy of time travel, she delved deeper and deeper into theories and practicalities surrounding it. I believe she picked Tesla's brains, without letting him know exactly what she was pursuing. One day she announced that she thought it could be done. It was, she told me, so much simpler than anyone had imagined. Indeed, she became haunted by the notion that someone else might succeed before she did. At first I was not very interested in her project, which I thought to be madness born of her infatuation with me and distance from Tesla's guiding hand, but I was still interested in her. I gave her money (the sudden success of my early novels made it easy to be generous). Tesla had put her in touch with Lord Rayleigh and others at the Royal Society, telling them she was another Madame Curie; and such she might indeed have been. They gave her the run of their laboratories and equipment. They even lent her the services of machinists and technicians.

Slowly I became drawn into the project myself. As I write these words, Man has just unleashed the awesome forces of the atom against his own kind. Yet nobody seems to have suspected that there was another path to atomic power, a simple path involving a few coils and jars and electrolytes in the presence of certain rare elements. She discovered this docile yet prodigious source of energy and employed it to drive what she called a "temporal displacement field generator"—her Time Machine. In view of where her discoveries led, I have kept silent about them ever since. But I must now break that silence in the hope she may still be alive.

Naturally, I never thought she would succeed. My motive for helping her was to spend time with her. Poor Jane suspected nothing. Indeed, I brought her to see the two of us hard at work in Tania's private laboratory. The scene of pure scientific enquiry was entirely persuasive. This idyll occupied me one or two days a week for more than a year. I would arrive at the mews with flowers and wine, we would work together on her cells and coils, and we would indulge our physical passion. The role of faithful assistant did not come easily to my nature, but I would also bring my work to her—drafts of new writings—for her penetrating and adoring eye. If you are a writer you will know that an author must have praise. It is a drug without which he cannot produce. (Jane also read all I wrote but, poor thing, the praise of an inferior mind is no praise at all.)

After about fifteen months the inevitable happened: I began to tire of Tania and her madcap scheme. I went less often to the mews. I became impatient with her disquisitions on the field generator, even with her praise for my own work. Now it was she who had become the crank. I began to withdraw both head and heart. I still saw her occasionally because I feared that if I stopped altogether she might expose our liaison to Jane or, worse, to the press.

The last of these occasions was New Year's Eve, 1899. It was the middle of the afternoon; Jane was taking her nap. Tania summoned me by telephone in the most urgent terms. I could see as soon as I arrived that she was distraught; her eyes burned with a manic excitement mixed with deep apprehension. She made me sit beside her on the cot in the laboratory, the scene of many adulterous pleasures. I'd brought no flowers this time, no wine, no writing for her approbation. "I've done it!" she said. "The field generator is built. Today will be its maiden voyage, and I shall be the maiden — for with this machine it may be possible to return to earlier states of one's being. Today I shall leave you, HG. I shall go back to my youth and innocence."

I knew then she had lost her reason. She herself had told me on several occasions that if time travel was possible at all, it could only be in a forward direction. To enter the past had to be impossible because of the obvious problem, now hackneyed by every writer of "science-fiction" (how I loathe that term), that a voyager could go back and kill his parents and so prevent himself being born, and so forth.

On that dreadful afternoon she told me she planned a first voyage of exactly one year — forward to December 31, 1900. If that was a success, she would return to the present for an instant, wave a last goodbye, and then go back to December 31 of 1897, her first winter here, when we were still nothing more than colleagues. She then planned to destroy the device, and that would be the end of the whole affair, with both man and machine. She would resume her work with Tesla in New York.

I reminded her that she herself had said it was impossible to regress in time. She smiled the smile of someone with a great secret.

"I no longer believe so. Time is not the constant I used to think it was. It is not linear in the way you imagine. A traveller in space distorts time. Time is dependent on speed and route. It is even possible, in theory, to arrive before you have left."

Of course I see now that she had anticipated some of the conclusions that Albert Einstein would publish in 1905. But at the time it sounded like the wildest gibberish. I begged her not to carry out her plan. I said I thought she needed a rest, time for reflection, away from London, away from me. She wouldn't hear of it. I implored her to send the machine empty, or put a dog in it, but she said I would have to kill her on the spot to prevent her going.

She then told me that she'd made certain provisions for her safety. The machine had some sort of fail-safe, settings that would override the operator's coordinates if there was an inconsistency in the calculations, or any mishap. She had set it to return automatically to this very spot, in exactly one century.

Why a century? I demanded to know, grasping her arm so fiercely that she winced. "Because one hundred years from now no one will remember you and me, no one will care about our *affaire*, and the march of science will have made these discoveries a commonplace. The people of 1999 will have no more trouble bringing me safely in than we would have stopping a runaway brougham." I contemplated striking her, knocking her out for her own good. But common sense stopped me. The machine couldn't possibly work, so why assault her? And if it *did* work—an ignoble voice told me—I should be rid of her! Suspicious circumstances, perhaps, but no *corpus delicti*. I could tell the police that, yes, through Tesla I had known her slightly; that lately she had seemed a little disturbed; that she had probably wandered off in a funk, or taken, as I had suggested she should, a spur-of-the-moment holiday.

I will not attempt to describe the machine, except to say it was an ugly thing, as massive and forbidding as an armoured car. If what I am writing means anything at all, you will soon see it for yourself. I pray you will also see her. She would have been a great woman of science had I not seduced her and then stood by while she cast herself into an unimaginable void. What I wouldn't give now — old, spent, and near my end — to take her place on that voyage!

The machine worked. That is to say, it vanished; but it did not reappear, though I waited in that room without sleep until the small hours. I returned exactly one year later, with identical results. I wrote a circumspect note to Tesla, telling him that Miss Cherenkova had disappeared without trace, that the London police feared she had fallen in the river or been the victim of a criminal attack, and asking him to let me know immediately if she should ever contact him. She never did. The only hope for her now is that she did indeed build in some sort of fail-safe. It seems quite likely that that was just a fib she told me — so I would let her go. But it is the only scrap of hope that remains from this tragic affair.

I have now carried this burden for half a century. I know I shall soon die. Were I to make this public now, it would be dismissed as the raving of a mind at the end of its tether, unable to distinguish fiction from reality, real life from the jejune fantasies of its youth. So I leave it to the end of the Millennium, when, if Man has held his present course without disaster, I assume the principles of her device will be well known. And if they are not, and if this story seems as unlikely in 1999 as it does in 1946, at least do me the kindness of extending the benefit of the doubt.

Go to No. 26, Midnapore Mews, SW3, or as close as you can to the site if it no longer exists. (I have confirmed, however, that it survived the Blitz.) Get there by six at the latest, and be prepared to stay until dawn. She left me at exactly 6.44 p.m., so in theory, taking into account the fact that 1900 was not a leap year, she should return in the first moments of the twenty-first century. You may think me mad if you like, but I beg you again to do what I ask, and to rescue, if such be possible, this unfortunate girl whom I so callously misused.

H. G. W., 13 Hanover Terrace,

[signature]

P.S. I need hardly add that retrieval of the machine will amply repay your efforts. The elucidation of its secrets could put you in the company of Einstein; and, if they are no longer secrets, at the very least it will be a priceless artefact in the gallery of science.

— 2 —

That sly appeal to self-interest was a nice touch—just what you'd expect from HG. The hoaxer had done some homework. The stuff on Tesla checked out too, up to a point. Tesla had certainly been an oddball, dabbling in everything mentioned and more besides, but there was no reference to a Tatiana Cherenkova in the sources I had at hand. Normally I would have left it there, passed it on to some other Wellsian I had a grudge against (several came to mind), but it was the holidays, a distraction was welcome, and who can resist playing Holmes? Directory Enquiries confirmed that Wells's solicitors were still in business at the same address, but all I got was *Thank you for ringing Riddle and Barclay. Your call is important to us....* I rang Skef back to find out how the document had reached him.

"Solicitor chap. Joseph Riddle. Grandson of the man Wells dealt with. Sounded quite genuine over the phone."

"But why approach you?"

"Oddly enough, he'd heard of your work. Computer search turned up one of your papers on Wells. What was it? 'Invisibility as Metaphor in the Life of. . . .' "

"Metonymy."

"Come again."

"'Invisibility as Metonymy in the Discourse of H.G. Wells,' *Meaning Quarterly*, number. . . ."

"Quite. Anyway, he knew you were the man for the job. He thought you were still at Cambridge. When he couldn't find you here the college passed him on to me."

"Anyone else seen this?"

"Not as far as I know, but there must be other copies floating around. All part of this millennium hysteria, I'd say. Has to be. Why else would Tania's return be timed for the first moments of the twenty-first century? My God, I'll be glad when it's over and done with in a few days."

Already it seems so passé, a midnight obsession one is ashamed of in the morning — though it isn't even a year ago — but then, of course, the whole world was twitching with a multiple chiliasm. Nostradamus outselling Jeffrey Archer, cattle mutilations in Wyoming, cargo cults in Melanesia, crop circles spreading like ringworm over the face of England, Aryan Christians expecting Rapture in the Rockies, the Righteous and Harmonious Fists terrorizing Hong Kong, apparitions of Finn MacCool in a dozen Dublin pubs. And mathematical pedants trying to spoil it all by insisting the millennium won't really begin until *next* January.

The document was suspiciously apt for the *Zeitgeist*.

Skef also suggested a rival scholar could be winding me up; he thought it might be fun to take the bait and run with it. A third possibility occurred to me: perhaps Wells himself *had* written this in his dotage — as self-parody or an oblique confession of how he'd treated the women in his life, for all his public feminism. It wasn't hard to see young Tania as Rebecca West or Amber Reeves.

Perhaps we'd stumbled on an authentic Wellsian metafiction (another word HG would certainly have hated).

It was the afternoon of December 29th. I looked up Midnapore Mews in the *A-Z*. There it was—just twenty minutes from my place in Chelsea. Did I tell you Uncle Phil died in '94? Never met him, did you? The Reverend Philip Wringham, Mother's elder brother and my legal guardian after her death until he ran foul of the law. (Usual trouble of vicars who mix the chrism and the jism.) Big-boned and fair like me, though he'd begun to lose his hair and the colour had leached from his moustache except where nicotine kept it yellow. I lived with him for six years, though I was away at school much of the time. He was only fifty-five. Galloping lung cancer—another pipe smoker, far worse than Anita, down through the dottle, match after match.

That's how I inherited the flat which you will soon be viewing. It's a bit gloomy, north-facing, which can get you down no end in winter, but big for London and comfortable in an Edwardian way, with a real fire and good malt. It was handy to have just as I was coming back from the States and looking for work, though unnerving to live there again—so many echoes of Phil and those years as a boy. It's never really stopped being his, never felt like mine. He lurks in the carpets and curtains, a sour transpiration on muggy summer nights; and in winter I hear the creak of him rising from his chair by the hearth. I still haven't redecorated or hung up half my pictures.

Whenever I'm away from London for more than a few days I see the flat again through child's eyes, through the tearless stare I believed was expected of me when he took me there twenty years ago. *You're a brave boy, Davy, I know you are.* So much bigger than it looks to a grown-up: rooms like public halls and the passage long as an alley, haunted by noises from watertanks and people you never met on the other sides of walls. A brassy smell at the threshold—his tobacco and his body, a bachelor smell you noticed when you walked in—and his terrifying hobbies, Bavarian automata, most crippled, a few still able to twitch an arm or roll an eye like dying soldiers, toys which enticed but were all the more odd and frightening for being a grown-up's toys, untouchable, unclean. The long passage always dark except for watery daylight from the well of the building, where pigeons roosted on fire-escapes. (I dreaded a fire less for the flames than for the thought of having to climb out onto those slimy iron ladders, which looked as if they'd buckle and pitch you four floors down among the dustbins like a broken doll yourself.) At the end of the passage the bathroom, its steady drip as sharp in the tiled darkness as a deathwatch beetle; and beyond that the room he kept for his Bunsen burner, his retorts and chemicals, peculiar smells like hospitals and undertakers' (a smell I knew); and the strange beast at the heart of his labyrinth, on a table under a black velvet drape: a Wimshurst machine, *circa* 1890, a device of counter-rotating discs and brushes, cranked by hand, generating insane amounts of static electricity.

It was said at Phil's trial that he used all this as lures and props in his seductions. I didn't testify—I was only seventeen—but I suspect they were on the right track. I've been meaning to haul the better stuff down to the museum.

The rest of the place is lined with books. Walls of theology, a half-decent stack of novels, ditto poetry (all pre-Eliot except for things I've added), and a little locked cabinet containing the only literature he seems to have consulted often. One-handed literature, Bird, dog-eared and foxed, some of it quite old, much of it quite nasty. Twelve-year-olds with ankles tied, Moroccan catamites, golden showers (sniffily described in court as undinism), you name it. No idea why the law didn't take all this away when he got caught with the altarboys, or why he didn't ditch it himself when he knew his lungs were gone. Denial perhaps. But then I haven't got rid of it either. Never made the time. Make sure you do. Sorry, wandering again.

There was a time when I enjoyed walking in London but lately it's become less pleasant—beggars plucking your arm, spitty harmonicas in your ear, would-be muggers loping behind you, and the dogshit escalating in calibre as people trade chihuahuas in for Dobermanns. The other day a woman in rags even offered me a baby. London, the last metropolis that worked!

Still, I decided on a recce—a good way to banish seasonal ghosts. Twilight was thickening into dusk. I passed below the dome of the Brompton Oratory, with its papal orb, and followed a narrow lane behind it, *A-Z* in hand, coming out after a few meanders on Midnapore Mews.

What was it I told you—the American collector's *pied-à-terre*? Well built, about 1860, nice brickwork on the architraves; quite a grand abode for grooms and horses in its day, and tony until recent years, though the block has been diced into a barcode by owners painting and redoing their façades.

None of this activity looked recent. One or two places still had a presentable car outside but many were empty, For Sale and To Let signs nailed on doors. Number 26 seemed to have been on the market for some time. The brass knocker was verdigrised, and a barn swallow flew out of a missing pane in the fanlight. A sign announced viewing by appointment through Lomas & Hennessy, Estate Agents. The house had escaped sixties modernization and eighties gentrification. Many of the old stable doors along the block were bricked up to make ateliers and foodie kitchens, but these were original, their long hinges bearing the maker's name— *COLLINGE, LAMBETH*—beneath a heavy rind of paint. No one had opened them in decades.

In front were two disintegrating concrete urns, once flower-boxes, filled with litter and dry weeds. I stood on the better one, peered in through a transom window. The room still had its stone flagging beneath scattered newspaper, empty jars, flattened tubes of paint. So this was where Tatiana Cherenkova had supposedly built her machine, where she and Wells had drunk wine and bonked each other on a narrow cot. The hoaxer had chosen well.

I tried the front door. Locked. But a small tail of wire was hanging from the fanlight. Someone *had* found this place, was perhaps still squatting here. A tug released the latch. I went in cautiously and called. Smells of damp wallpaper, drains, mice, hairspray. The carpet was gone from the stairs, leaving a narrow path of bare pine between verges of pea-green paint. In dust on the pine were footprints — slim, bare prints of a woman or child. Upstairs I found a bath with rust beards under the taps, and two bedrooms. One held a few stretchers and canvases (hideous abstract dribbles, sort of thing I associate with mental patients and Jackson Pollock). In the other was a foam pad, a sleeping bag, and cardboard boxes full of women's things: sequinned handbag, half-used lipsticks, black cardigan, discarded tights like fallen nests.

At the back a kitchen looking onto a tiny yard and high wall coped with broken glass. A cast-iron fireplace, a few wooden chairs held together with wire, a table made of plywood and crates; a wobbly pagoda of dishes and coffee mugs in the sink. On the table an open pot of jam, half a loaf, and a pile of lipsticked dog-ends in a saucer. Mice had had a go at the food — droppings and jam tracks all over the place. The squatter had moved in just before Christmas and gone away for the holidays. Or had she? Were squatter and hoaxer one and the same?

I left everything as I'd found it and went home to my own flat, which I may as well warn you isn't a lot better in the housekeeping department. You'll need to get Scrubbers in, Bird. I couldn't tell you the last time I vacuumed a floor or brushed the loo. It used to drive poor Anita to distraction when she and I lived together in that sunny place of hers on Belvoir Terrace (you'd been so tidy, she said, despite your Bohemian ways). I swear I made an effort. I'd do the dishes, scour the bath, trim the laurel, religiously put out the bins. Somehow she'd always find egg on a plate or a dust-ball in a corner (they call them *moutons* in Dominica). Small wonder she was such a good digger — she didn't miss a thing.

I remember when the three of us hired a car to see the battle-fields. The road out of Alexandria soft and oily in the sun, a mosaic of bottlecaps at every truck stop, paper and plastic blowing like tumbleweed across the desert, tins and tyre rinds all the way to El Alamein, and Anita saying, *Don't knock it, boys. Give it a few years and it's our bread and butter.* Archaeologists may commune with ghosts but we're also garbagemen. (Someone actually approached me not long ago to excavate a rubbish tip — a fresh one near Peter-borough — he'd thrown away a winning lottery ticket.)

For Anita digging was a devotional act, a way of cheating entropy, a raising of the dead and buried so thorough it was tanta-mount to blasphemy. Her pits were models, the walls precisely ver-tical, the strata geomantically acute, each find standing on its plinth of soil, numbered and flagged in her fine italic hand and brushed as clean as a tooth. Woe betide the living who intruded. I even began to feel sorry for the tourists who found their way to the site, cheery pink potato-faces looming over us, prodding at pot-sherds with their toes, knocking dirt onto Anita's spotless trowel-work. *You kids hope to learn something from them rocks?* She'd ignore them huffily for a while, then speak bad Arabic if she spoke at all. They'd look at you, Bird — you could pass for an Egyptian as long as you kept your mouth shut, but she and I certainly couldn't — they'd look at her, shake their heads, and shuffle off to their taxis obscurely insulted.

Two days later I went back to the mews at about the same time, taking a book, a slice of pizza, a torch, and a bottle of McGee's Yukon Thaw (an overproof Canadian rum I've become unwisely fond of) to see in the millennium and numb myself against the sense of foolishness and futility that I knew would overtake me as the evening wore on without results. I'd decided to do exactly what Wells asked. The competition wasn't stiff: millennium cele-brations hosted by Cliff Richard and Cilla Black, Hogmanay live from Glasgow, or *How I Won the Cold War*, a dramatization of Ronald Reagan's "memoirs."

Steady drizzle had fallen all afternoon. Mist flocked over the Thames in the evening chill and nibbled at the rooftops of the West End. I loitered down the street for a while to see if anyone was following the same instructions. The streetlamps began to fade, their saffron stains blotted by the pavement. I was inside a shrinking bubble in the fog, which seemed to absorb all sound except my breath and the scrape of the scarf on my chin. Traffic over on the Brompton Road died away. I could scarcely hear my own footfall.

Things had changed at Number 26: a ruddy glow lit the fan-light and a bass rhythm beat inside like a racing heart. I stood on an urn to peep in Tania's lab. The floor was strewn with mattresses and cushions, curiously inviting in the ruby light spilling across the flagstones from a passage door. The artist had returned and was throwing a party. At that moment silhouettes appeared and I dropped like a weasel. I should have bottled out — gone home, for-gotten the whole thing. But I'd already fortified myself with a swig or two and, what the hell, it was New Year's Eve. I rapped confi-dently on the front door, as if expected.

"Nina!" a deep voice yelled as the door swung open. "Anuvver of yer admirers." A girl wobbled out of the kitchen, out of incense and smoke. She came slowly along the passage, bobbing to the music, her long straight hair backlit by an overhead bulb wrapped in red paper. She seemed to have black hair, black lipstick, black eyes pooled in mascara, and she was nearly naked. Small gold rings pierced her nipples. She looked about sixteen. She spoke as if she'd taken me for someone she knew but couldn't place: "Welcome to my party." Her arm wrapped around my neck; she kissed me fiercely and smokily, our teeth colliding.

A voice said, "Get him in if he's coming and shut the fucking door."

Nina took my hand and led me to the kitchen. I opened my pack, waved the rum to shouts of approval, set it on the table with a bang. The room was lit by flames and packed with the sort of people you'd expect to find in a London squat: retro-freaks in headbands and those velvet jeans that were last in fashion when we were in nappies, three or four leathery Hell's Queers, and over by the sink a knot of Anglo Attitudes—wrinkled scalps tattooed with swastikas and flags—drinking from jam jars. A bit worrying, the Attitudes. So was a shaved Neanderthal skull reticulated with thin dark lines like the craquelure on a porcelain egg (a new one on me, presumably art school and *sui generis*). The women were harder to classify, as many of them had shed their clothes and were sitting in a circle by the grate. Attitudes were ransacking the place for firewood, breaking up chairs, wrenching timbers from a cupboard.

"Who are you, ven? Professor Prune?" It was Egg, his face in mine, his breath reeking of skunk and a bad liver. I suppose I did look a bit academic; no one else was in cords and a baggy sweater.

"David. Friend of Nina's. I'm early." That was silly, given that the party was already going, but my nerves were bad. "I'm looking for someone. Anyone been around here asking for Wells?"

"Wells who?"

"Never heard of him."

"You mean the owner?"

"You with the plod?"

"Nah. He means the fillum." An Irish voice. "*The Invisible Maan.*"

Egg said: "The Invisible-fuckin'-Man! If we peel the clothes off the prof here, reckon he'll vanish?" This provoked general laughter.

"If you want to stay, mate," said an Attitude, "you'll have to undress the part." He was tugging at my sweater. A large woman, Mother Earth type, unzipped my cords. In a few seconds I was stripped to my watch. "I know!" the woman said. She ran out of the room and came back with a bolt of paper towel, the heavy crêpe sort (they must have nicked it from a public loo). They began to wrap me, up one leg, down the other, like a mummy. I was thrown to the floor, turned over roughly, my face in spilt beer and drowned cigarettes. Someone said, "Leave his knob out."

"And his mouth. We might need his mouth."

"*I* might need my mouth." I kicked at a pale freak, thin chest and plucked-chicken arms speckled with red wounds like a Mexican Christ. "I might feel like breathing."

"All right, man. Take it light." A tall Jamaican girl.

Suddenly Nina was there, searching my face with her wobbly eyes. I know you like them young, Bird, but now she looked lost and fragile and possibly illegal. "Breathe out," she was saying. "Empty your lungs." She took a long pull on a pipe, put her lips on mine, inflated my chest. Then a hand over my mouth from behind. "Hold it, man. Don't fuckin' lose it."

A few people had begun settling in small circles on the cushions in Tania's lab — the party room. Nothing had started yet. A boom-box was thumping out the new Oedipus Wrecks. I lay back against the wall and let my mind wander. There was nothing to do but wait.

More people arrived; soon they forgot I was there. I parked myself in a dark corner with a jar of rum, drinking slowly, keeping an eye out for Wells scholars. It seemed possible that three or four *bêtes noires* of mine might turn up. Lansing Larouche, for one, the Texan of the runny nose, who always pokes his snout wherever mine's just been. Or Pučić, the post-everything literary *penseur* known in the trade as Deep Croat. No, Deep Croat wouldn't come; he was hardly a man of action. But James Clough might — nuts-and-bolts type from Manchester, a specialist in early underground trains. He'd take the Wells document at face value and turn up with an ambulance for Tania.

At least I'm well disguised, I thought. If Clough or Larouche shows up here he'll never spot me in this rig; I'm indeed the Invisible Man.

Bodies began drifting in from the kitchen. Soon there was a merry scene: daisy chains, sandwiches, people stacked up like mating toads, women on all fours, men pumping them at either end, and two or three complaisant slashers delicately inscribing each other with razor blades. The room filled with the sounds of a milking barn, the semen smell of unripe Brie. You would have been in there like a dirty shirt, Bird, but I worry about Henry IV. Is a fuck worth dying for? Nina didn't care, and everybody wanted Nina.

I watched, drank, deflected propositions, reached the foreshore of oblivion, the room rotating in an oceanic roar. My thoughts, insofar as I remember them, returned to the machine. *An ugly thing, as massive and forbidding as an armoured car.* "Wells" was maddeningly brief, but it sounded as though the contraption might do a lot of damage. What would happen if it *did* appear? Would we be crushed? Vaporized? What if it landed a bit off target, in the middle of another mass, a wall say? Would that set off a nuclear explosion? Shouldn't I be trying to get these people out?

Then I'd remember where I was. There may be nothing in physics to rule out time travel categorically, but nothing created from the technology of a hundred years ago, no matter how brilliant, could possibly have stolen a march on the entire twentieth century. There was no need to worry about revenant devices from 1899.

The rut had ended. I must have dozed. Bilious sodium light was draining from the transom windows onto oily bodies posed like victims of a massacre. A deep, low shock passed through the building, more felt than heard.

A tube train hurtling down its rusty bore.

But there was a strike; no trains were running. What if that chthonic boom was a harbinger?

Let me say, as shorthand for the indescribable, that I panicked. I don't mean I did anything rash. Quite the reverse: I was immobile. For a long time, so it seemed, I was pinned to the floor by an unseen weight, an incubus. With this gradually there came a certainty—fervid as a religious vision—certainty that the unthinkable was going to happen. I wrestled the weight off me—extraordinarily difficult, like forcing yourself to take a breath in a drowning dream. I must have hobbled to the kitchen, for I found myself there with mummy wrappings still around my legs. The fire had died down, embers had spilled over the floor (too damp to catch), but a glow from the grate lit the room.

About a third of the overproof rum remained. I seem to have had no doubt as to what to do. I splashed the spirit along the floor like an arsonist, backed away, tossed a match. Blue and orange flames licked down the passage to the doorway of Tania's lab. Glistening corpses came reluctantly to life. I spread more, called *Fire!* Bodies sprang up, snatched at clothes, made for the door, dragging those who couldn't move. I ran upstairs, brought Nina her things (even her artwork), told her I'd heard a siren. Soon they were all outside; there was a flurry of bicycles being unchained, of old cars coughing and grinding down the street.

My watch, which I usually keep a little fast, showed four minutes after midnight. I switched off the lights, bolted the front door, waited in the passage, hearing only a surge in my temples like waves on a shingle beach.

There isn't much to tell, and what there is is absurd—a Frankenstein's lab scene from Hammer Films. A cold phosphorescence drenched the room. Blue snakes hatched on the ceiling and began to ripple down the walls. I remember wondering if the rum had condensed there and caught fire again, if that could explain it.

Then the room seemed to be the target of a lightning strike. I was deafened by a sound I couldn't hear, a sound within me, a detonation in my head.

A ball of light or fire had formed in mid-air. The light grew, filling much of the room yet fading as it did so, resolving into something dark and bristly — a sphere like a sea-urchin, a flattened ball of copper spines, vivid one moment, insubstantial the next, hovering and spinning, slowing down. Horsewhips of light arced from the spikes to walls and floor with a sound of ripping canvas. This noise also oscillated, near, then far — like an old wireless wandering off signal — as if the thing couldn't quite anchor itself in space or time.

It seems to me now that my thoughts and actions must have been spurred by what is known as hysterical strength. I can find no other way to account for recognizing what to do, and doing it. As the sphere turned I saw coils and circuits mounted on exterior subframes like the handles of a goblet or a Roman lamp. Somehow a chair was in my hands; somehow I hurled it accurately at a loop of wire.

The sparking and pulsing ceased at once. The thing dropped to the flags with a sound like a jail door.

— 3 —

Messrs. Lomas & Hennessy, Estate Agents, worked out of a one-room office above a greengrocer's on Fulham Road. A suggestion of root vegetables hung about the stairs. Times had once been better: the clock and desk had come from larger premises, as had some good oak filing cabinets with brass handles. Neither agent was in; only a carbuncular youth wearing a grimy white shirt open at the neck beneath a black waistcoat. He pulled the file, frowned.

"I'm afraid the owners of Midnapore Mews are unreachable

at the moment, sir. So if you're in a rush, as you say, you can only accept or decline their terms."

"Perhaps I could contact them myself?"

"I'm afraid not, sir. All I have here is a numbered company in Grand Cayman. Mr. Lomas might know more, but he won't be back for another ten days."

"What do they want for the place?"

"Rent or buy?"

"I was thinking a one-year lease."

"Nineteen hundred and fifty per calendar month. Tenant pays all bills except rates." He looked up and smiled obsequiously. "Don't know the place myself. Must be rather nice."

"Not very. That's far too much." I paused, as if in doubt. "But I'll take it for now. Monthly basis. The location's important. I'll want to renegotiate as soon as possible."

Next I sent a fax to Skef:

Jan. 3, 2000

To:   Prof. C. V. Skeffington, The Bothy, Cherry Hinton.

From: David Lambert, Flat 5, 19 Oliphant Gardens, SW10

Happy New Millennium! 26 Midnapore Mews exists all right. Went there night before last as "Wells" asked. Big disappointment. Place empty and up for sale. I got in (someone had been dossing). Filthy damp and cold. No lights or water. Still, I stayed the appointed time, saw in the Era with a paperback and a bottle of rum. Went home about 3 a.m. Needless to say not a soul turned up — not even Clough. So much for our suspicions. It seems we're the butt of a practical joke. Better not breathe a word.

I don't suppose you want to waste any more time on this, but if the solicitor rings again, could you ask him to bike me the original document? (I'll pay.) I should at least be able to tell when it was written. Might be good for a footnote some-day if it turns out old HG himself was having us on.

I'll pop down for a visit soon. Until then,

Cheers,

David

I was now in lawful occupation of the mews, I'd thrown Skeffington off the scent, and there seemed little risk of being dis-turbed by a shady landlord in the Caymans. I celebrated with sushi at Yoshiwara's.

Let me try to reconstruct for you the machine's reappearance in Tania's lab that night. Understand that these events aren't clear to me, Bird, even now. Or rather, some parts are eidetically clear while others are altogether missing, like memories of a car crash.

I won't forget the quality of that sound pulsing and dying in the darkness like the last toll of a cathedral bell inside a tower. The Northern Lights were sparkling on my eyes, a shifting curtain of light beyond which I was blind. I was terrified I'd lost my sight (later I found that all circuits in the house and along the street had blown). I recall speaking in the darkness, just to hear my own voice: *All right. I'll make you a unicorn's bargain: I'll believe in you if you'll believe in me.*

I withdrew to the kitchen, groping along dank walls, thankful when my eyes made out a feeble glow in the grate. There were matches on the mantel. After a long time, so it seems, I went back to the front room and struck a light. The time machine was still there.

The next thought was Tania's rescue. At the top of the device was a hatch or porthole, secured by a spoked wheel. It wasn't easy, in my condition that night, to climb the spikes and balance there five feet from the floor. The wheel scorched my palms. A slight hiss of escaping pressure. I wasn't certain, because of the olio of human and electrical discharges already in the room, but the sphere seemed to exhale a fragrance — hot beeswax, coal fires, and a floral, feminine perfume. Not, thank God, the stink of death. The hatch came loose, swung upwards on a hinge. I called down, feeling both afraid and quite absurd. "Miss Cherenkova! Tania! Is anybody there?"

*Is anybody there?* Three or four times I must have asked that question: the question of seance. I got down, ransacked the kitchen for my torch, climbed back up laboriously. The beam shook so in my hand, amplifying fear, that it was difficult to make out objects in its path, but gradually it sketched what did indeed look like a late Victorian time capsule: a cross between a club car and a diving bell, deeply upholstered in button padding and burgundy leather. Around the wall several instruments and heavy switches — chronometer, potentiometer, other equipment I couldn't identify — all beautifully made of mahogany, ivory, and brass. (It's a shame I couldn't let you see inside, but you'd have guessed it was hardly a human torpedo.) Immediately below me was the pilot's seat, an affair of oak and nickel-plated knobs and hinges, resembling an antique dentist's chair, which is exactly what it turned out to be. This had grim leather straps for the waist, wrists, and ankles — like something a madhouse might have used. The seat was reclined, the belts unbuckled. Nobody was aboard.

Shock slowly gave way to curiosity. How long this took I can't say. A mass of dark material was heaped on the chair. A woman's clothing. Charcoal woollen coat with squirrel-fur trim; linen shirtwaist dress with leg-of-mutton sleeves, quite plain but in a striking heliotrope; and a pair of black laced boots, size five or six. About right for an 1890s bluestocking. I'd reached down and fished out these garments one by one, examining them as best I could with the torch; but the underwear — a fine cotton chemise and a rather frisky pair of silk drawers (a gift from Wells?) — was another matter. These were still warm and creased with the bodily presence of their owner, still sweet with her perfume. It was as if she had stepped out of them seconds ago.

A grey disc above me. A faint sound of tyres on wet asphalt. A taste of bile and undigested booze. I coughed, looked at my watch; I'd spent the first morning of the third millennium passed out inside the time machine.

Again the fear when I understood where I was, or appeared to be. Memories—scraps of memory—from the night before settled and lodged, one by one, like fragments of a torn-up letter fluttering from a high window. As my mind pieced these together, the very coherence of what I've just told you became cause for alarm. We weren't strangers to the occasional psychotropic substance, were we, Bird? But this was unlike any acid trip, any mental state I'd ever known. Terror lay in its realism, its juxtaposition of normal and impossible. I'd gone barking mad.

Eventually I crawled out, peeling a shin on one of the copper spikes, the pain welcome for the physical jolt. I found what was left of Nina's larder, swilled out a pan, revived the fire, made an instant coffee. The best coffee I've ever tasted. I pinched my cheek, snapped fingers in my ears, shone the torch into my eyes. I struck a match, inhaled phosphorus, held a finger in the flame. All senses seemed in working order. The only evidence I might be mad was what was in my memory and in that room. Now, I've been told more than once in my life that psychotic delusions always are utterly convincing. Perhaps this called for self-committal. But I have a horror of hospitals. I decided to keep the unicorn's bargain. The thing seemed real; I would act on the assumption that it was.

Like you, I'm not a trusting soul; my instinct was to hide. What else could I do? Call the press and announce that H.G. Wells's time machine had appeared on a foggy night in Brompton? I'd be banished to the realm of those middle-aged couples who are abducted from Iowa by spacecraft and forced to engage in carnal acts with aliens resembling Elvis and Jackie Kennedy. Or I'd receive a frosty visit from Old Etonians in good suits; experts would come, determine the machine was genuine, take it away. I'd be squeezed out, silenced, consigned by faceless authorities to the giggle farm. The device would become a state secret, and I'd end my days knitting doilies and sending unprinted letters to the *Times*.

A public demonstration voyage? Tempting, but the thought of Tania's warm and empty pupa on the dentist's chair was quite enough to put me off. *The pressure of the past*—Skef's favourite phrase kept rising in my mind. He was right about the weight of obligation that falls upon the archaeologist like a lavish, unexpected gift. You're afraid of breaking it; you feel you must do something with it, but you don't know what or how. *And there's only one chance to do it right, because excavation is destruction.*

For several days I didn't touch the machine except to search and photograph it thoroughly. I considered showing the images to someone and asking what was there, but abandoned this as I grew more wary and more confident that I was *compos mentis.*

Gradually the thing became familiar. Each morning as I lowered myself into the sphere my eyes would encounter the same rich colours—the deep red leather, the wood and brass, the Moghul pattern of the Axminster rug on the floor. Once I even reclined in the dentist's chair and lit one of Tania's cigarettes, blowing smoke rings up through the hatch. I forgot to mention those. Besides its own equipment and her clothes the machine had held nothing, no work notes or supplies, no personal belongings. The one exception was a silver cigarette case in a pocket of Tania's coat. Inside were a dozen Turkish smokes—expensive ones with black paper and gold bands, the tobacco moist and aromatic—and this poem, or part of a poem, on a folded sheet of blue writing paper:

And these again, these atoms, clustered stars
Of bezelled lightning, instantly conglobed
As passionate molecules, atomic pairs
In most material wedlock interfused
Insatiably, to throng in countless swarms,
Hive upon hive of radiancy insphered
And whirling through immensities of space.


Do you recognize those lines? (Anita would have, if they were ever published; what a memory she had for sources.) At first I thought they might be Wells's — though the handwriting isn't. Perhaps they're Tania's.

The difficulty of these first days was eased, in a way, by practical tasks — renting the mews, drawing a screen of secrecy around it and myself. The museum was the highest hurdle. I'd been due back at work on the fifth. My downstairs neighbour — Calixto Pool, a young Mexican in business studies — was kind enough to compose a letter, no questions asked, in oblique Spanish, purporting to be from a certain Señora Saavedra de Lambert of Asunción. I enclosed this with a translation and letter of my own begging the museum board for a leave of absence "because of a serious crisis involving my next of kin in Paraguay." I hinted at kidnapping, geriatric Nazis, drug cartels, regretting that in the interests of safety I couldn't be more specific. (Cali's a good bloke, by the way; give him an *abrazo* from me when you see him.)

The next step was to make Midnapore Mews secure. I painted out the transom windows and bolted a steel sheet inside the double doors; I installed locks, bars, alarms. Outside I assiduously maintained the air of dereliction, replacing cigarette packets and kebab wrappings in the barrels whenever they blew away. Sometimes I'd even scoop up dog turds and leave them on the step.

In the lab I fitted strong lighting and a work-bench, adding tools and computer gear as the need arose. I did a lot of reading, mainly Tesla and his contemporaries but also more recent developments in physics and electrical engineering (thankful for a couple of science A levels).

I still don't know how the machine works. I got about as far as a tribesman who strolls out of the bush and steals a car. He finds out that one pedal makes it go and another makes it stop. He masters steering-wheel and clutch. He even deduces that it drinks petrol. But he has no idea what an internal combustion engine is.

Tania's device somehow achieves displacement in time by producing an electrical plasma similar to ball lightning. Ball lightning's funny stuff—it bounces through buildings, materializes inside aeroplanes, falls into water and sets it boiling without being extinguished. Some physicists doubt these observations; others doubt their rules. Tesla was a self-taught genius who possessed, as he wrote, "the boldness of ignorance." He had no patience with establishment notions of what was possible or worthwhile. And he spent a lot of time on ball lightning—I've seen notes of his in which he claims to have produced it.

Wells never specified what drove the fictional machine, for all Tania's help. His Traveller merely pulled a lever to command what amounted to perpetual motion. The real machine, however baffling, abides by the Draconian laws of thermodynamics. The "distance" travelled is proportional to the energy available. The two cylinders attached by subframes to either side of the sphere contain a Tesla coil and its power source, the "jars and electrolytes" mentioned by Wells. At first I thought this was some sort of battery, but I now believe that Tania anticipated the recent discovery of cold fusion, whatever that may really be. (Governments are still spending serious money on the phenomenon, despite its knockers. Hitachi and Mitsubishi are heavily involved. Might be a good investment tip there, Bird.) Power is accumulated, calibrated, and fed into the coil—essentially a huge ignition coil capable of enormous voltages and frequencies. Even so, Tania's instruments show that the maximum range she envisaged was a thousand years—eternity's small change. She'd never have made it to AD 802701, the age of the Eloi and the Morlocks.

The technical notes are in my desk. You may think I didn't learn much, but it took months to get this far. I couldn't go to the flat except for raids in the small hours, or to any of my usual haunts, in case someone from the museum found out I was still in England. When I dropped out in January I withdrew a large part of my legacy in cash, but the pile dwindled fast. So obsessed was I with understanding the machine and finding its creator that I gave no thought to how I'd pick up the threads of life and career when I emerged. I was cut off from friends, colleagues, from everyone. Not that I have many friends in London. I seem to have lost the art of friendship, Bird—the late-night calls, impromptu visits, reckless confidences. One becomes too busy, too guarded, too self-conscious. Perhaps this is just growing up. Whatever the reason, I've made no new friends like you and Anita, which is why I brought you into this (albeit at the last minute and on false pretences). May it do you some good, old mate. May it make amends —for Anita, for neglect, for everything.

I was sleeping badly, eating junk: doner kebabs, boil-in-bag kippers, too much alcohol and chocolate. I was living like Carlos the Jackal. Or Tesla: "I do not think there is any thrill that can go through the human heart like that felt by the inventor as he sees some creation of the brain unfolding to success. . . . Such emotions make a man forget food, sleep, friends, love, everything."

Love. Women had come and gone in Chelsea but I hadn't thought of love in years. Anita spoiled me for other women. The ones before her and the ones since were always safe: older, married, foreigners passing through. Who could match Anita's mind, her looks, her learning, her compassion, her will; and above all her distance, the unlikely catalyst that made all the above combine into such a formidable alloy? Early in April I brought home a *Times* with dinner. It fell open at Deaths, and there she was.

> LANGLAND.—On April 2, peacefully after a long illness. ANITA HILARY FORBES Ph.D, Egyptologist, aged 32. Beloved only daughter of Gen. Malcolm Forbes Langland (Royal Highland Regiment, ret.) and the late Winifred Dolores (née Betancourt), of Malvern Hills, Dominica, West Indies. Funeral service at St. Osyth's Church, Mayfair, Friday April 7, 2.45 p.m., followed by burial at Kensal Green Cemetery. No flowers, please. Donations, if desired, to Oxfam, Survival International, Future Heritage.

A "long illness." Anita ill? And the implication of drawn-out suffering in that formula. Oh Bird, why weren't we *told*? She was never ill. Wouldn't be. Had no time for it. Had better things to be and do. The news gutted me. And—this is really silly, but I can say it now—I suppose all the time I'd been working on the machine I'd had somewhere in the depths of my mind the mad idea I might use it someday to go back into the past. Not for professional purposes; that didn't entice: too much like climbing Everest by helicopter, and who would really want to enter antiquity in all its filth and danger? I remember you saying that life expectancy in ancient Rome was only nineteen years. No, my notion was to turn the clock back just a bit, to try again with her. And a few years more, to keep my parents in on Christmas Eve. Silly, I know, but even Tania had dreams of life repair.

That Friday, you'll recall, was indecently fine though spring had been late: the sky clearer than it ever is in London, daffodils thrusting through the winter's litter, pavements ready to lift and burst with life. The walk had tired me, whether from grief or long hermitry in the mews. I was wearing dark glasses and an old black suit and homburg of Uncle Phil's (in case Skeffington turned up). I was hot. Somehow it hadn't occurred to me that you'd be there. But we could hardly avoid each other in a crowd that size, could we? Why so few? Why no husband, no lover, no more old friends? Only that strange elderly relative, three or four rumpled types who looked like colleagues from the British Museum (you can always tell archaeologists by the stoop, the stretched pockets, the eyes to the ground), a pair of suave Egyptian attachés, a small claque of tearful women from the hospice (not Anita's type at all), that ass of a vicar reciting Goldsmith—"And still the wonder grew / That one small head could carry all she knew"—and you.

People change and I'm bad with faces, especially after a dozen years. You weren't the colour I'd expected. Your skin had lost its finish like furniture left in the rain, and though you still had most of your hair the spring and sheen were gone. You'd been so proud of that colouring; I remember you claiming in Alexandria that you had Mohawk blood, a great-grandfather— how you accepted Skef's invitation to the dig not so much because his classical graffiti and inscriptions turned you on (they were hardly the Rosetta Stone), but to see the Nile, follow the route of the Mohawk canoemen brought from Montreal by Kitchener for the Sudan campaign.

I wasn't sure it was you until I saw the pipe hop discreetly from your hand like a small animal set free. And you saw that I saw, spotting me in that Verloc costume. It's always cruel to see time and gravity written on a face: you'd moved up a generation, and I (as you gently put it) was a dreadful sight. I couldn't keep myself from inhaling the scent of her grave—the first cut earth I'd smelt all year.

I'd hoped we might talk about Anita afterwards, but you had a way of turning monumentally silent and staring into your beer whenever I tacked towards the subject. There wasn't much you wanted to talk about in any area, was there? I am really sorry things haven't gone well for you these dozen years. I saw it in your back

—a vulture, not a kingfisher—I heard it in your voice. You'd had quite a vowel movement at Cambridge; now you were Cockney again, more so than ever, mutinous in glottal stops and diphthongs.

There's some air to clear, a sealed room that needs a draught. Anita. I want you to know I didn't take her from you, Bird. And I didn't keep her long (two years in all, a little less than you). It was her choice. Easy, you may think, to shift blame onto the dead. Hardly what a gentleman would do. But I've no motive except to let you know the truth. By the time you read these words I'll be as far from this world as she is.

Blame's the wrong word. Anita wasn't the sort who can be blamed. She answered only to herself, like a cat. On winter days she'd move like one, following the sun round her place, ending under a west window in the bathtub, book in hand, the sunset making a ginger halo of her hair. In anyone else such self-sufficiency would have been intolerable, but with her it was so natural that if she hadn't been that way she wouldn't have been the woman we both loved. Both *love*.

Skef has to take some of the blame—for the morale on his dig. I don't think you know what passed between Anita and me in Egypt after you left. This may come as a surprise, yet I feel I should tell you now because it may help you understand what happened later. I've always admired Skef and still count him a friend, but when he got out there in the desert, lord of his dig, it was as if he became possessed by a baleful genie. His sense of humour soured and dried up like a waterhole. He grew twitchy and obsessive, full of petty orders and one-sided conversations. It was really bad when he appeared for dinner in his galabiya—less T.E. Lawrence than a truculent shepherd from a nativity play.

Why did he have to be so tight with the food? Dig camps are emotionally incestuous enough—pressure-cookers bulging with jealousy and hormones—without keeping eight or nine young people on short rations. I remember our eyes landing on the bowl of falafel each night when Latif set it down beside the hissing lamp. We'd count how many there were, hoping the number was easily divisible, and watch each other like gunslingers as the rice and dubious meat went round the table. We were chronically starved, like Arab dogs. Add sexual tension to that and you've got trouble. Whenever I could I'd stuff myself on peanuts bought from the Bedouin girls; Anita would come to my room, bestow a sisterly kiss (so I thought), and say in her stage whisper, *I'm suffering from peanut envy.*

Nobody was surprised when you blew up at Skef and took off like that. He had it coming. Of course, none of us knew that you and Anita had also had a row. I was the only one she told, and not until some time after.

God knows I fought it, Bird: denied the very possibility of her love. It seemed so out of the question, so easy and safe to keep the status quo: you and Anita an item — a family to my orphan eyes — and I the staunch Pythagorean corner of the triangle, the family friend. Understand that to someone like me isolation is a natural state. You don't break it lightly, because you know it'll be so much harder to bear when it returns. You don't need to be an archaeologist to know that nothing lasts and nobody lives forever.

Did you guess how much I admired and envied you? Not only for Anita and your dear old Mum but for your brio and social ease, your East End wit and wits, your cool sense that the world owed you everything (I've always felt it's the other way round). I even envied your illegitimacy — so raffish, and one parent so much better than none. And I admired you above all for your music, which came up out of you like a flow of strange wealth from a dangerous, inexhaustible mine.

When the wind blew the right way during the afternoon siesta we'd hear you out among the dunes, weaving marvellous tapestries of sound. And when you left, the desert suddenly turned drab. I still see you at that expat bar, The Wise Monkeys, the night you brought your sax and got on stage with the bellydancer's combo, weaving Parker and Bichet through snake-charmer quarter-tones and flapping drums. Anita was so delighted and so proud of you that she glowed as if gently on fire inside, like a jack-o'-lantern, a light I'd never seen before in her Carrara skin. You even charmed the old snake who ran the place — Pierre? Piers? Anita dubbed him the Wise Manqué — whose living hung on those who came looking for the city of Durrell's *Quartet*, never to find it except framed on the walls of his bar. And I see you drunkenly beating on her door in the compound at two in the morning, blowing your horn and singing at the top of your voice, *I've got a bottle of wine and my arse is clean.* And she furious for days, but loving it, secretly loving it, your whiff of brimstone.

Like her, you also had compassion, a thing too personal to show. Anita told me what you did for Awad, the crewman whose daughter nearly died. No one else knew, and that was the way you wanted it. We'd already betrayed you when she told me that, but in every other way we were loyal, we always were. Let's not lose the good days, Bird. Let's not forget the Mediterranean sunsets from the Pharos site, and the calash into town — she loved the smell of horses — warm together on flea-ridden upholstery.

Skef opened the purse a smidgen wider after you left, but his moods and the diet still drove Anita and me into Alex for a feed whenever we got the chance. Evenings under the stuffed crocodiles and brass palm lamps, beer sliding down our throats, fingers salty with prawns, oily with broiled quail. And after dinner her pipe smoke drifting thickly across the sepia photographs of prewar Alex, the framed verses from Cavafy:

> A skin made of jasmine-petals on a night...
> An August evening...but was it August?
> I can barely reach it now, barely remember...
> Those eyes, the magnificent eyes....

Well, it *was* August, the last week of the dig. Only a false start, as I've said, a premature bloom in the hothouse air that expeditions breathe, though it would flower again. You'd been gone three or four weeks — by then you must have reached Khartoum. Even so I didn't see her set a course for me. I told myself that I was helping, helping the pair of you come to your senses. Yes, I was naive, but believe me when I say it was unimaginable till much too late. I no more expected Anita to want me than to be raised to the peerage. Later — in Cambridge, I mean — it would seem obvious all along, a slow collision between ships unable to steer aside.

A week before the dig ended, she and I walked into the desert to watch the sun go down from the German tank. Strange — afloat in all that Egyptian time, I think nothing affected me as much as the rust-red tank hulls stranded on the dunes like bits of crustacean, already clean and fleshless though men in living memory had burned alive in them like heretics. We were talking of going home. *England!* she said. *Curry and peas and motorways and smeary Turner skies. And months of the year without flowers, except the hanging baskets of Babylon. And Bird. What on earth am I going to do about dear Bird?* Neither of us saw the brown corkscrew on the horizon, twisting down from the sky. The khamsin season had been over for months.

The first warning was grit in our eyes. We turned from where the sun had just drowned in its own blood to look behind us and it was as if a black goat had been slaughtered and its body drained on the sky. It came so fast. We ran and ran — that tank must have been two miles from camp. Unable to keep our eyes open, we ran down bushes and tripped over stones. And once we felt soft things jerking beneath our feet — heard shrieks and cries of *Allah!* — and knew we'd run over the prone forms of Bedouin huddling under blankets in a wadi.

We got perhaps another half mile, then realized it was hopeless, that if we wanted to survive we had to do the same. Luckily we'd brought a blanket of our own to sit on because the metal of the tank could be so hot. We found a small gully, lay on our sides among some boulders, and spread the cotton above us. Even in our shelter the air was a powdered soup, unbearably hot, intruding everywhere, filling our ears like hourglasses, forming clay on the moistness of our mouths and nostrils. It was soon impossible to speak. I won't forget the smothering taste of it: old, salty, dead and yet alive, as if all Egypt's ten thousand years since the first seed was planted, the first animal yoked, and civilization began were in that dust. Ottoman, Arab, and Roman bones; Ptolemaic mummies, of people, cats, jackals; molecules of flesh and natron; New and Old Kingdom middens, predynastic floors; things of alabaster, faience, cloth, and clay; fossil pollen of plants that breathed and bloomed and hurtled through the verminous innards of goats and fellaheen and pharaohs. It was as if the earth into which we'd been delving all summer had risen up to bury us. And if the storm had lasted longer it might have done so, for the cotton sagged and pressed with its gathering load.

We heard later that the Bedouin we'd trampled had thought, in their fright, that we were djinn. Egyptians talked of the storm for weeks, taking it as an ill sign of changes in their land. From the pharaohs until a generation before, the Nile had flooded each year, spreading silt and water so predictably that they'd planted their fields by the calendar. But since the Aswan Dam had broken the ancient contract between river and people, the land was turning saline and the silt fell in Nubia, to be stolen by the wind: the gift of the Nile withdrawn by Egypt's gods because she'd tried to hoard it.

A change of temperature woke us. The heat had passed and chilly draughts found their way under the blanket like clear streams. We heaved the desert off, and the stars blazed in air so clear that the lights of Alexandria barely fogged the darkness. We began to sneeze and sing and laugh, beating dust from our clothes, examining wounds, drunk with freedom and release. And we stayed among the rocks, giddy as kittens, making gritty love till dawn.

The dig ended, and she and I went on that sightseeing trip the three of us had planned to do. She climbed every pylon, descended into every tomb, took expert turns at the helms of feluccas on the river, practising her Arabic, laughing off the men and boys who tried to jostle her and touch her hair with their fulminating mix of lust and awe whenever my attention strayed. (A man in Karnak offered me £3,000 for Anita; a man in Kom Ombo offered her £200 for me. They knew their market.) Fleas devoured us in Luxor, bedbugs in El Amarna, and in Memphis an American kid tried to flog us a mummy's leg for a ticket home.

It lasted a month, that early secret bloom, just the time we had before coming back to our last undergraduate year as if nothing had happened.

Her jokes let me know she wasn't serious. *After a row doesn't count. Lover away doesn't count. Out of the country doesn't count. So we're clear on three not-counts. When it comes to infidelity, travel does broaden the mind.* Anita wouldn't say what had caused the rift with you, feeling it would be disloyal to discuss it, which I suppose was a way of saying she hadn't given up on you.

Please take these revelations in the spirit intended, Bird. We mustn't quarrel over Anita's memory; we should celebrate having known her. But what did we really know? Did you meet any family, any friends outside our circle? I never did. All she ever told me was that she was the child of elderly parents, that they lived on their estate in Dominica — one of the old plantation clans. They never came to England; her mother wouldn't fly and her father's health couldn't take the climate any longer, not even for his annual pilgrimage to Lord's. When she wasn't up at Cambridge she stayed with a cousin, a retired publisher or something on Wimbledon Common. I never met this cousin, never asked to, never was asked. Presumably that creature at the church in tweeds was she or he —

an old covered wagon, hardly the sort you could approach and say, *I knew your cousin. We were lovers. How did she die?*

It always seemed out of the question to know more about Anita than she wanted you to know. When we first met I noticed how she asked all the questions. I'd feel pumped dry. I'd make up my mind to let her do the talking next time, but it seldom happened. She'd talk, and everything she said was worth listening to, but none of it was self-revelatory. Or if it was, it was insubstantial and didn't quite fit with other impressions, so you could never construct a coherent picture, though you'd never catch her in a contradiction. Her presence had to be enough — like an extraordinary artefact, provenance unknown.

I'm not sure I should tell you this — it seems too intimate, which is odd in itself when you hear what it is — but throughout the time we were lovers she never addressed me by my first name when we were alone. It was always *Mr. Lambert*, her campy joke. I think it began as her way of saying that our affair was between strangers, that the here and now didn't count, that we weren't betraying you. (It was also powerfully erotic, like having sex when dressed.) The day she called me David again I knew I'd lost her.

She left me and went back to Egypt in 1990. She was vague about the project and how long it would take her (something about digging with Germans). She never returned to Cambridge while I was there, or if she did I never saw her or heard a word. I went up to London to see her off, though it had ended between us a fortnight before. I still don't know exactly why; perhaps you do.

Over the years I wondered if the two of you had made it up, had even married perhaps. I sent letters to Luxor, to the Dakhla Oasis, to Heliopolis, to Aswan. Two postcards came. The first wounding, unworthy of her (though clever in a puerile way): a sunny Levantine beach, Israeli stamp, and one line: *Topless in Gaza, on the pill, with Dave.* Unsigned. I prefer to think "Dave" sent this, whoever *he* was. The second I believe was genuine Anita: the unfinished obelisk at Aswan, the largest stone ever attempted by the Egyptians, the one that was their match, cracked and prostrate in its quarried womb and tomb. And on the back, from the Book of the Dead, three words of Aten — *I am Yesterday* — in that green ink she liked.

## — 4 —

I went back to the cemetery with fresh flowers, and saw that some-one (you?) had left *Nymphaea* lotus and forget-me-nots, saw that a headstone had been been raised:

> Truth telleth that love is    the treacle of heaven
> May no sin on her be seen    who useth that spice

Only Anita could have chosen such an epitaph, or made so free with her ancestor's verse.

Her death had broken the spell of the machine, diminished its secret. I put my work on it aside to find out what I could about her illness. The vicar of St. Osyth's would reveal nothing, not even the undertaker's name, until I realized that he'd known Uncle Phil, quite possibly in the carnal sense. This loosened his tongue. The "funeral home" referred me to a doctor in Harley Street — a Dorothy Six, in case you want to try talking to her yourself. I say *try* because Dr. Six hasn't an obliging nature. "Who gave you my name?" was how our conversation began. "I can't possibly discuss patients with anyone. *Surely* you know that." She struck me as one of those brisk, contemptuous county matrons — the sort who were head girl and never got over it.

"I'm not asking you to trample your Hippocratic oath, doctor. There are medical reasons for my wanting to talk to you. Personal medical reasons."

"If you're saying what I *think* you're saying, it's up to your GP to contact me, or vice versa. An approach like this is most improper." She shifted piles of paper on her desk. She had mannish hands, large, muscular, a signet but no wedding ring. There were sailing photos on the wall, the doctor ruddy and keen in oilskins.

"I haven't got a GP. I haven't been to the doctor in years— not since I was living in Cambridge. And he's retired now."

She saw me (privately) the following Tuesday, at her surgery, a sunny Regency drawing-room with chintz curtains and a great marble sink in the corner. I told her I hadn't felt really well in months, and the symptoms—sleeplessness, diarrhoea, little stamina —seemed to be getting worse. All true enough. Then I began to ask about Anita, but she wasn't having that.

"I agreed to see you for a consultation."

"Well, if you won't tell me what she died of, will you at least tell me what she didn't? We were close. For years. If it was AIDS you have a duty to inform me. May I assume, then, that it wasn't?"

"Very well. I can tell you that Ms. Langland tested negative for HIV." Her eyes were tired and sad, as though they'd once been kind but the kindness had been exhausted by experience. I got up to leave but she insisted on examining me. Her manner seemed to be softening, curiosity overcoming her contempt. "I agreed to see you for a consultation, and a consultation you shall have. There *are* other things to look out for besides the ones in the newspapers. Now will you *please* get undressed and lie down over there."

She poked and prodded, listened, offered nothing more. Months of bad eating, overwork, and worry had taken a toll. She ordered tests: blood, urine, stool, tomography, the works. Found nothing. She got me eating, exercising, taking vitamins and minerals. Altogether she had me see her three times last spring.

With each visit Dr. Six opened up a little more. It seems that Anita returned to London from Egypt about a year ago—she'd been teaching at the American University in Cairo — underweight, very weak, and prone to catalepsy or cataplexy (an attack was never clinically observed). She was tested for three kinds of hepatitis, a dozen tropical diseases, and Henry, of course. They found nothing worse than a couple of small-time parasites, the usual myrmidons of Cleopatra's revenge. Yet Anita kept deteriorating until she could no longer care for herself. In November she went into that hospice. Five months later she was dead. At the end she weighed only sixty pounds. I'm sorry, Bird — it's as painful for me to write this as it must be for you to read it — but I thought you'd want to know. The worst is that she'd begun to lose her mind.

Dr. Six couldn't bring herself to admit she had no answers, not even the ghost of a diagnosis. (This was perhaps the main source of her grumpiness.) The best she could do was suggest that Anita might have had an unknown strain of HIV which doesn't show on current tests. Anita had told her about the transfusion she'd had that dreadful night of the May Ball. Blood wasn't entirely safe at the time, which means her death could be on our hands. Whose fault, Bird? Mine for knocking you down? Yours for the axe? Anita's for raising her arm? God, why did we have to behave like barbarians? I recall Anita's words when she came out of surgery and I apologized: *Forget it. Both of you. We human beings are all barbarians, and always will be.* But is that any excuse?

"Please understand," said Dr. Six, unusually expansive on my last visit, "that we live at a time when some illnesses — only a few, I should stress — seem to be appearing, mutating, and spreading a step ahead of detection and treatment. Unfortunately microbes evolve much more quickly than people do." She tapped a neat stack of medical journals on her desk. "The dose of penicillin needed to treat streptococcus A, for instance, has risen by more than two thousand times since penicillin was discovered — if it works at all. This is why I tend to be overly cautious nowadays when I see a patient presenting symptoms with unspecific aetiology. Ten years ago I'd have suspected nothing worse than chronic fatigue, mononucleosis, jaundice perhaps. . . . Those days are gone, I'm afraid. I want you to keep in touch. You're *so* much better than when I first saw you, and I'm ninety-*nine* per cent certain that it *is* only fatigue. But we *do* have to think now about that one per cent, don't we? I'd like very much for you to stay in touch."

This wasn't reassuring. I didn't feel *so* much better, and I was becoming wary of Dr. Six's emphases.

Two or three messages came from her in June and July asking me to ring. I didn't bother. I was immersed in the machine again, approaching the limit of what I could learn on my own. I'd decided to send off a brief report on my findings—pseudonymously—to one or two physicists who, in the flurry of debate over time theory in the science press last year, seemed to have open minds.

It must have been early in August when I woke up one morning and found I couldn't get out of bed. I couldn't tell whether the problem was mental or physical; I was simply immobilized, weak as a rag. It lasted twenty or thirty minutes. While I lay there I began to worry about small things I'd ignored: the runs again, dizzy spells, a cold that wouldn't go away. I'd been sleeping badly, woken by nightmares—often I'm bolted inside the machine, in darkness, trying to strike a light; the matches are wet, their heads break off, I drop the box, and so forth. This usually ends with my producing a dim flame, and I see a hideous figure in the dental chair, a mummy with vellum skin, red hair, and wormy sockets, a young woman like Anita, dead for a hundred years.

Over the months, as I worked alone, I'd fallen into the habit of talking to that missing woman—telling her my plans, my worries, how my days had gone. Sometimes on the edge of sleep I'd hear the glide of satin or detect a hyacinth fragrance in the room. There were days I half expected she'd appear, that my work would draw her back. The doorbell would ring and there she'd be, a strangely dressed young redhead on the step. *Mr. Lambert? My name is Tatiana Cherenkova. You don't know me but I used to live here. I believe I may have left something behind. May I come in?*

Thinking that the work might be to blame, perhaps radiation from computer screens or prolonged exposure to high voltage fields, I eventually returned Dr. Six's calls. She was "awfully glad" to hear from me. She sat me in a chair opposite her desk. She made a gable of her forearms, like a praying mantis; she touched her lips to her fingertips, stiffened abruptly, slapped her palms on the blotter.

"I haven't been as frank with you, David, as perhaps I should have been. I could have told you more about your friend, Ms. Langland. It's so difficult when the next-of-kin lives on the other side of the Atlantic. The father's. . . . I rang him once. And you told me you hadn't been close to Anita in years. So I didn't think I was in a position. . . ."

"Did you reach her cousin? Retired publisher or something. Lives in Wimbledon."

"Oh. I didn't know." The gable went up again. I regretted speaking. She seemed about to change her mind; then:

"Do you know anything about BSE?"

I kept quiet.

"Bovine spongiform encephalopathy. Mad cow disease."

"I've stopped eating steak-and-kidney pies."

"This still may be just a *scare*, which is one reason I hate discussing it. But evidence *is* mounting that the disease has jumped from animals to humans." She went into a long preamble, which I already knew, though not in such detail: scrapie, a degeneration of the brain originally confined to sheep, spread to cattle in the 1980s because someone had the bright idea of using sheep offal for cattle feed. It is possible that the population of this country became widely contaminated before measures were taken ten years ago; it's also possible that the measures were inadequate. Nobody can be sure because the incubation period in human beings may be as long as thirty years. Other carnivores fed on the nastier cuts of British beef have begun to die. First it was zoo animals: tigers, cheetahs, bears, wolves. Then domestic cats and dogs, including many fed on tinned petfood, which indicates that the pathogen is not destroyed by cooking. The possibility of other vectors — gelatin, milk, cheese, even the soil itself — can't be ruled out. In short, one of the jolliest tales of arrogance, greed, and stupidity since thalidomide.

"We probably won't know for certain whether we have a massive public health disaster in this country for another five or ten years." Dr. Six reconstructed her gable, caught herself, straightened, and began to inspect a picture near the washbasin, a photograph of a catamaran in high seas. "What I didn't tell you before is that I authorized the taking of some tissue samples from Ms. Langland's body. The laboratory results were inconclusive but worrying. Creutzfeldt-Jakob disease, CJD — that's what we call this condition in humans — isn't easy to detect. But there's some reason, only a *tiny* reason, to think she could have been infected."

She pushed a file across the desk. It contained coloured microscope images resembling William Morris wallpaper: thin-sections of poor Anita's brain. "The conclusions are unclear, David. Highly tentative. Three specialists have looked at these. One sees nothing abnormal; one isn't sure. That leaves only one who *thinks* he can see something. I'm afraid I can't judge the data for myself. Few people can. But I *can* tell you that some of her symptoms — emaciation in particular — are *not* typical of CJD."

"But she wasn't living here. Mad cow's a British problem. You told me she was in Egypt all those years."

"Mad cow is *mainly* a British problem. But we used to export cattle and beef all over the world. Expats often eat tinned pies and sausages from home. And I'm afraid Creutzfeldt-Jakob *is* found in its own right, so to speak, in North Africa. Libyans have a high incidence, apparently from eating sheep's eyes. In any case, she could have contracted it before she left England. But I must *stress* that there's no certain proof Anita had CJD, or—even if she *did*—that it was advanced enough to kill her."

Oh Bird, how could they be so vague? How could they diagnose it in cows and cats and not in her?

The good doctor coolly set out her replies like chessmen, unimpressive individually but amounting to a position I couldn't assail. The disease wasn't new. But it had been rare, either because not many sheep had it or not many people ate the wrong bits of the sheep, or because in earlier times people died of other things before CJD had time to get them. Nothing could have been done for Anita. The infectious agent is still unknown. It is thought to be a renegade protein, something never identified before. It's nasty, Bird. These little wigglies go munching through your grey cells like grubs in Gorgonzola. Spongiform means exactly that: your brain ends up as mush. Scrapie got its name because demented sheep rub themselves raw on fences. All over Britain, unseen maggots may be hatching and quarrying in our pulse: England done in by its roast beef.

"David. Do you see what I'm saying? You *appear* to be reporting some of the symptoms Anita reported in the early stages of *her* illness. I'd like you to have a new test that's just been developed. I think we should do a biopsy."

"You mean you want to drill a hole in my head and scoop out pieces of my brain."

It wasn't like that, she insisted, but I'd stopped listening. Since CJD is hard to detect, incurable, and untransmissible to other humans—except cannibals—I couldn't see the point in looking for it. Why should there be a connection between Anita's case and mine? Dr. Six argued that Anita and I had lived together during the late eighties, the time when contamination was most likely. No doubt we'd eaten the same meals. Wouldn't I rather *know*? I said I would not. I'd rather live in a fool's paradise for a few more years than with the certain prospect of a horrible death. If I had CJD, nearly everyone did. I told the doctor to drill her other patients for it. I'd worry when I started rubbing myself on fences.

I rented a numbered post-box, sent off copies of my report on the machine, and took a walking holiday in the Welsh mountains. It was lovely there in September: golden days, nights dusty with stars, morning hoar-frost crunching underfoot.

There were no urgent messages from the Rutherford or MIT when I got back. The only thing in the box was from the Institute of International Achievement, congratulating me on my nomination as World Intellectual of the Decade. All I had to do to receive a gold medal and personalized proclamation to this effect, was send £499 to.... Physicists weren't beating a path to my door. Fair enough. Would you answer a letter from a chap claiming to have a time machine in his garage?

I began putting in more hours at the library, hoping to turn up something on Tesla, Wells, or Tania. But I'd often find myself haunting the medical shelf, reading the same found-poems for the umpteenth time:

Creutzfeldt-Jakob...
Inevitably fatal,
affects adults in mid-life...
dementia and myoclonic seizures;
ends in
death.

Believed identical with *kuru*,
found among certain New Guinea tribes
who ritually consume
the brains
of their
dead.

On September 22nd, the equinox, when day and night are in balance throughout the world (I notice these things because my birthday falls on the June solstice), something again pinned me to the bed. It lasted longer than before. I could hear Mother's ormolu clock, each *sotto voce* stanza of clicks at the quarter-hour, its chimes turned off. Then I was released, limp and clammy as an empty wet-suit. It took me an hour to make a cup of tea.

Each slip and stumble, each act of clumsiness and careless-ness, is suspect now. I go out for something and forget what it is before I reach the Brompton Road. I find myself in Harrod's and can't remember why or how I got there. I read the same page three or four times without recognition till I come to the last line. Some days I eat two dinners, others none at all. I hear an idling car out-side, run to the window, but there's nothing there, only a tinnitus, an engine throbbing in my head. Or a maggot. The days of the week have become as alien and portentous as the Aztec calendar. Sun Day, Moon Day, Thor's Day: Which comes first and why? What do they mean? What powers measure out our loans of time? Earthquake, Vulture, and Death, for all I know. Imagine a day named Death!

These signs persuade me I am doomed: Messrs. Creutzfeldt and Jakob have possessed me. Tiny invaders are tunnelling from cell to cell, recruiting my own proteins to their cause like escapers setting off a prison riot. Perhaps they pullulate in all of us except a righteous coterie of vegans. Blessed are the tofu eaters, for they shall inherit the earth.

If this strikes you as fatalistic, Bird, or premature, remember that I am, and am not, myself. There are good days and bad; weeks of remission when I'm right again, and all the above seems fool-ish nonsense. But the bad days come back, they always do—days I'm frozen like a lizard in a sunless world, unable to stir. It's get-ting difficult to separate the me from the not-me. I seem obscurely responsible for the pains of the world; and the pains of the world inflame my private wounds. The machine, Tania's monumental absence, the news from China and Nigeria, Anita's death....

I went to the hospice where she died, I don't know why. Perhaps because I owed it to her to touch the banisters she touched, to breathe her air. Perhaps to flirt with death, once an abstraction, now my ardent suitor. Emily Chadwick House, a women's place. Laura Ashley curtains, stained glass, macramé, potted palms; and a face at the door, suspicious of man, the creature who'd condemned so many of them to this. They were all Henry cases, or so it is believed: Belsen cheeks, limbs like bats' limbs, eyes as wild as horses' in a burning barn. They were kind, they touched my hands, their eyes said they wanted me to hug them but I couldn't, afraid they'd crumple in my arms. Nor could I stand that hothouse, thick with disinfectant and the cabbage stink of ruptured bowels.

They gave me an envelope containing a photo overlooked when Anita's room was cleared. A photo I'd taken the day she left for Egypt all those years ago: Anita beside her favourite sculpture, the lion goddess Sekhmet at the British Museum: Sekhmet the Mighty, who drank and had a cruel streak.

The matron insisted I have lunch with her and some of those who could still wield a knife and fork. Haddock in milk. The way fish always is now: slender and juvenile, like a child tart. Remember *Teach a man to fish and you'll feed him for life*? Well, he's fished the ocean dead and his twelve-year-old daughter's selling blowjobs in Bombay.

I burst from that place into the afternoon, into lungfuls of cold wet air. At the end of the street, on a faded zebra crossing by a small park, went a man—a bellied, grey-bearded, bald old man. With a scarlet macaw strutting behind him. Honest. Three blowzy tailfeathers sweeping along the asphalt like a monarch's train. *Coom along Flaubert, you old booger*—a tipsy northern voice —*time to go home.* Flaubert had no rope or chain. He limped a little, his pincer feet unsuited to paving. Half his feathers gone, a crazy old boozer for company, a filthy city for a forest, an appearance no more respectable than his owner's, and lame to boot. But unbeaten — you could see that in his pirate's eye. He didn't give a stuff.

I decided then to buy a shooter. To have on hand. The thought of suicide makes for a calm passage across many a night. I'll not go gentle.

## — 5 —

I was going to leave it at that, say nothing more on the subject of health, let you draw your own conclusions. But yes, after the September attack I did allow a biopsy. The arguments for doing so were no better than before, but it's hard not to peep at fate when she lifts the curtain.

"You won't miss them," Dr. Six assured me with unwonted humour. "You lose more cells from a hangover." They showed me the drill — less grucsome than you'd think  and the same three haruspices who'd examined Anita's brain delivered their pronouncements on mine. This time they were less ambiguous: two yeas; one abstention.

Not a lot of room for doubt, or hope.

But room for an avalanche of memory. Now I was a victim too, and victimhood would bring redemption from survivor's guilt, would reconcile me with those frozen faces and unfinished conversations that rise up in dreams, with Mother and Father, with Merlin my puss who hated London and Phil and ran away, making the loss complete.

My first day home from months at school, that smell of home: roses and Ajax, a treacle tart in the oven, Mother's scent lingering in the bedroom cupboard where her mink has been (removed for my return), she singing while she lays the table. Off with the hated shoes and shorts and shirt and tie, into jeans and down to the blackberry tunnel—dark earth arched by rocketing brambles—to see if the rabbits are still there. To find a line of stumps, reeling and frayed and half uprooted, thorns feeble against steel.

Father's old green jersey with the leather elbows. Tears and futile blows against his knitted chest. He has me at arm's length, holding me off, tickled by the zeal of my rage, laughing sheepishly at her, saying what he always says: *Sorry, Davy. I know it's hard. Buck up, old chap. We were your age once. The simple truth of the matter is that brambles and rabbits are a blessed nuisance. When this place is yours you'll see that what I do is for the best. You'll thank me for it. A fellow can't have hedgerows breeding weeds and pests, just because they're pretty. He can't have brambles jamming up his combine. Can he now? No one can afford to thumb his nose at progress. If I did I'd end up like old Carrington down the lane. Hasn't got a pot to piss in.* I don't laugh. *You like the seaside, don't you Davy? You want a new bike? Somehow we have to earn the money to pay for things. The price of grain stands still for no man.* And I (kicking now): I hate you, I hate you, I hate you! You killed the bunnies, you cut down their home. You killed them. You did! I wish you were dead! I wish it was you who's dead.

Start on those memories; I don't need them any more. Nibble them from me first, it's all the same to you. Take the bad now; leave me alone a little with the good. Many such conversations have I had with my tiny anthropophagi. But memory keeps emerging from its burrow, ravenous after years of hibernation. I ride the Circle Line all day, day after day, line without end, Amen; a six-pack of lager in a paper bag, and empty seats around me even in rush-hour. I walk the mean streets—up Lavender Hill, through Brixton—asking for trouble I never receive, immortal because I'm already dead.

Death Row does concentrate the mind; it snaps the weary chain of life's decisions, absolves you from material consequence, gives *carte blanche*. To do what? Well, make your list: take a cruise to the ends of the earth, gamble everything on Far East futures, endow a chair at Cambridge, assassinate a politician, poison a polluter, die happy in a Jag or a bordello, found a guerrilla band, seek an audience with the pope and give him your views on birth control—I could go on. In my case it was fly the time machine, of course.

They say that in California there are freezers full of well-heeled stiffs awaiting resurrection of the body when a shiny future will repair their stricken hearts and lungs and wake them with a perfect smile. How long before there's a cure for what I have; for what Anita had; for what we all may have? Ten years? A century? It rather depends on one's idea of progress, but I can leave tomorrow and find out.

Or should I go back and start again? Keep the family in on Christmas Eve. Become a vegan. Warn Anita about the food in England, and the men.

But *can* you go back? I gave a lot of thought to this. My instincts were with Wells—that retrograde motion in time is a non-starter. Perhaps that was Tania's mistake. Perhaps she really did try to return to her life pre-Wells, transgressed some cosmic law that guards the hymen of the past, and what?—vanished, ceased to exist, dematerialized? (*died* seems too prosaic)—leaving her machine to bolt riderless to the millennium.

The future seemed much the better prospect: it would involve no violations of causality, no argument with mainstream physics. In his Special Theory of 1905, Einstein predicted that a shift into the future is not merely possible but inevitable for objects in low gravity or at high speeds. Atomic clocks have proved him right. Even at the infant pace of NASA spaceships, less time passes on board than down on earth. The higher the speed, the greater the shift. A traveller moving near the speed of light would return to a world that had aged hundreds or thousands of years in her absence.

My working hypothesis, for what it's worth, is that Tania's device somehow induces this effect: its temporal leaps are a kind of running on the spot. One thing is clear: very little time elapsed inside that capsule since it left the nineteenth century. It brought the sulphurous atmosphere of coal-fired London, yet no dust or tarnish. Tania's perfume was fresh, her clothing warm and newly laundered.

So to the future I shall go. And if I find a cure there and dare tempt fate once more, maybe then I'll try reverse — when I'm old in that future, with nothing left to lose — sail back to Anita, to my parents; restore truncated lives, rebuild my own. And in the wishful words of the Comanche Ghost Dance, *We shall live again.*

And if I fail? I fail. It'll be more stylish than a bullet.

All autumn I nailed together my one-man ark, finishing it a few days before I came to see you. The activity eased my mind and brought a lasting physical remission. I was no longer knocking out my brains over the mysteries of this antique; I was simply putting it back in order.

I'd not forgotten that the device had had trouble landing in the mews, that if I hadn't torn out a wire it might have dragged its anchor through the years. Tania's instruments were out on the bench. I decided, despite aesthetic misgivings, to replace them with digital technology. The job of her ponderous calculating machine — banks of brass gears and dials into which she'd programmed calendrical data — could be done by a laptop. The chronometer, good though it was, was no atomic clock. These upgrades would be expensive; I needed to raise some cash.

Not long after I took up the post at the museum, I'd received a catalogue and business card from one P.I. (Powie) Kraus, BA, of Brunel's Kingdom Antiques, Los Angeles, *Specialists in Scientific Victoriana.* (Powie's parents, in an access of mythopoeia, fancied descent from both Indians and Puritans; so it's Powhatan Increase Kraus in full, but he's touchy about it. You'll find his address at the flat, though as far as I know he isn't turned on by old bikes, and I already tried to flog him the Wimshurst machine—"a dime a dozen" in the States, apparently.) Powie had taken me to dinner at Claridge's, plied me with Bollinger till I was legless, bought me a room at the hotel.

"Underneath," I recall him saying, "there's no difference. English, American. It don't matter. We speak the same language." His hands, his mouth, even his ears were mobile, but the chameleon eyes never once left mine, never seemed to blink. The difference, I was thinking, is that you pronounce pianist like penis, and when Browning comes up in conversation you mean a pistol and we mean a poet.

"The language of art, David. You and me, we're connoisseurs." It rhymed with skewers. "You and me aren't lab technicians. We don't delve into the past to classify, to stash away in plexiglass cases for snot-nose kids who don't know Humphry Davy from Davy Crockett. We love these things. We care. We appreciate aesthetic value. We want to touch them. We want to *have* them. These things are like women for us—or boys, if you like boys. I'm broad-minded. Let me freshen your glass.

"I mean we hate to see Beauty off limits, kept hidden away by some dried-up academic asshole who don't treat her right. No offence. I think you know what I'm talking about. To my way of thinking, Dave, there's as much art in a genu-wine Harrison chronometer as in a Leonardo." Powie signalled for another bottle, ringing the empty like a bell. I couldn't help liking the rogue.

"Now all I'm asking you to do, Dave, is be my eyes and ears here in London England. Our field's a small one, see. Museum funds aren't limitless. Something real *primo* comes up. Unique, beautiful. A dark industrial jewel. Let's say you can't acquire it for the nation, your budget won't run to it. That's where I come in.

That's when I want you to pick up the phone. And I'll be grateful. I'll be truly grateful."

Just in case there was any doubt about the form Powie's gratitude might take, when I'd fled to my room two things were waiting on the bed: a cheque and an escort girl. I didn't cash the cheque.

I dug out Powie's card and rang him up. He was coming to England in mid-October; we agreed to meet late one night at the flat.

The moment he took the chronometer and calculating machine in his hands I saw I could name my price. "Where in heck didja find stuff in this kinda shape?" He was licking his lips and sucking breath until he began to lather like an old nag. "Like it was crafted yesterday!" He didn't expect an answer. No one's doing fakes that good. The man knows his period. He's also a careful observer. "Wouldja look at that, Dave," he said, passing me his jeweller's glass after a long inspection of the brass face of the calculator. It took me a while to make it out, but there, scratched into the clear lacquer coating on the metal, was a date in an italic Victorian hand: *AD 2500.*

Powie was too absorbed to notice my excitement.

I said I thought the instrument might have been used by an astronomer to plot eclipses and conjunctions—who else would need to run dates so far into the future? This seemed to satisfy him; he said he always liked a personal trace of the original owner. We looked for more dates or notes, found nothing, not even a month or day.

Wiring up the new equipment was easier than I'd expected— essentially like grafting electronic ignition and navigation onto a vintage aircraft. I programmed the laptop with three calendars: Gregorian, Julian Day Count, and—for insurance—Maya Long Count, which runs on a different arithmetic. Most calendars make the mistake of counting years or months, which always compounds some error. The day is the fundamental particle of earthly time. Wells knew this: his time machine's odometer is one of the few persuasive details in the novel. The astronomer's Julian Count (despite its name) is the same idea. But neither of these has the majestic economy of the Long Count, a perfect instrument for reckoning days in nine cycles or wheels, rising by the power of twenty. I needed only its lower gears, but couldn't resist entering them all. Consider the grandeur of the *alautun*, which takes sixty-four million years to move one tooth.

The future was never of much professional interest to us, was it, Bird? Ours is the backward-looking curiosity, the left-hand face of Janus. Prophets and futurologists are invariably wrong. Well, not always: some prophecies are self-fulfilling; luck and inspiration sometimes hit a bull's-eye. HG had the knack, foretelling atomic war in *The World Set Free*. So did William Morris, predicting in 1890 that the worst of times in the fight between communism and the master class would be 1952. And there was that eerie student spoof of *The Daily Telegraph*, reporting that the last council house had been sold off, "Telecom" had been privatized, and Ronald Reagan had become president of the United States. This in 1971.

There's also the matter of "Dunnes," as Anita called them — those glimpses of the immediate future which J.W. Dunne, pioneer flyer and polymath, found in dreams (not only his own) and described in *An Experiment with Time*. I still have the old blue copy she bought in a second-hand shop on Talaat Harb and gave me for my twentieth. You always got upset when we talked about Dunnes, couldn't see why clever people like us would waste our time on such rubbish, etc. Anita thought you protested too much; that you got them yourself but couldn't face the glimpse of the abyss that they implied. I can't say I ever understood Dunne's intricate theory — something to do with eddies in the breaking wave of time, though he doesn't put it quite like that. But I know he's right about the effect; I've had them for as long as I can remember, perhaps a dozen times a year (more as a child), always small inconsequential things, random snapshots of the coming day, never a Derby winner or the price of shares.

The weight of evidence lies on the other side: in unguessed wars and earthquakes, in Bhopal and BSE. Time may be, as Unamuno wrote, "a spring that flows from the future," but the water is dark and we are fish without eyes.

Archaeologists are necromancers, not astrologers; aspiring to hindsight, not prognostication, though like astrologers we scan for patterns in events. And the price, of course, is loss of innocence. Who since Freud can feel anger or joy, love or jealousy — can operate as a social creature — without a chill self-awareness on his shoulder whispering of animal and childhood terrors, of shit and sex and death? So it is with us. The rear-view mirror breaks up the parochial landscape of the present. And our costly reward is to know that no culture is normal or inevitable; that none has a patent on wisdom or a guarantee of immortality; that civilizations, like individuals, are born, flourish, and die; that the very qualities which bring them into being — their drive, their inventions, their beliefs, their ruthlessness — become indulgences that in the end will poison them.

Anita, you, and I — in our different ways — we all chose that narrow band of human time that belongs to civilization: those busy ten thousand years of neolithic revolution. One hundredth of our time on earth, if you grant our kind a million. It wasn't Skeffington's doing, though he reinforced it. *If you want to scratch around for monkey bones, don't come digging with me.* Skef liked the wreckage between one order and the next: Egypt between Pharaoh and Mohammed; Europe between Constantine and Charles the Great. I remember him at Giza, astride a rebellious camel in the shadow of the Sphinx, answering your point about the slaves: *Civilization is always a pyramid scheme. Living beyond your means. The rule of the many by the few. The trick is to keep wringing new loans from nature and your fellow man.*

By mid-November I was ready.

How far to go? Caution recommended a test flight, a one-year hop. But I worried that the machine might work just once and strand me in a time little different from my own, with no miracle cure and no exotica to brighten my last days. So ten years? A century? Or much more? I was like someone who's never left home in his life choosing a holiday abroad. Backpacking in the Himalayas? Diving in the Yasawas? Irian Jaya? Or the Isle of Wight? I needed a good travel agent.

One suspects that the future isn't what it used to be; that I'm more likely to land in Bognor than in Bora Bora. We've been living a long time on nature's savings, and there are signs her bank account is overdrawn. It seems to me that if I go ahead a few decades, or even generations, I run the risk of landing in a mess. So I've made up my mind to follow Tania's clue to the middle of the new millennium. Five hundred years—long enough for a new dispensation; and why be hanged for a lamb?

I want you to know, Bird, as your teeth chatter while you contemplate the muddy scene of my departure, that I thought long and hard about where to launch, for in the same spot I must land. I needed a soft, deserted place. So it had to be the sea, this stretch of ooze and saltgrass off the Essex coast. There'll be minor changes —tides, tectonic shifts—but with luck the worst I'll face will be to splash down or bob up a few metres either way. The sphere should easily take that.

The padding on the walls was reassuring, but I didn't fancy spending five hundred years, however foreshortened, in that dentist's chair. At Fulham Auto Recycling (formerly Hammersmith Scrap) I obtained, from a mountainous docker with Dundreary whiskers, a fawn leather Porsche seat with belts and headrest. The car, he said, had been fatally mauled by one of the lions in Trafalgar Square. *Head on. Total write-off, but the chinless wonder walks away. You won't find a better seat than that, mate.*

I added a flotation collar (a tractor tube), and waterproofed all exposed electrics with plastic pipe and cowls. I bought a Klepper folding kayak, lightweight camping gear, freeze-dried food, water purification pills, instruments for checking weather and radiation, and a case of McGee's Yukon Thaw. I packed: the complete Ordnance Survey maps of Great Britain on CD-ROM and the sheets of the London area; my gun (an over-under rifle and shotgun bought from a yardie on Lavender Hill); a medical kit and manual; a Polaroid for dishing out goodwill snaps to natives; rain gear; rucksack; notebooks and drawing supplies; batteries and solar charger. For trade goods I'm taking Havana cigars, Venetian beads, magnifying glasses, Swiss army knives, bolts of denim and silk, the rest of my money in gold. I decided against the video camera—the one you have—because I'm more likely to be a migrant than a tourist, and it gives me neck pain. I have got a second Oyster laptop, identical to the one wired into the machine.

Such practicalities were obvious, like provisioning a dig. The hard part was the cultural baggage: what books and music, what art? It was fun at first. I could be Photius. I could play Desert Island Discs! But when I began to think more deeply it became a fearsome responsibility. Would I be a bringer of civilization or savagery? What did I owe—and what should I spare—the future? What to do about Clausewitz, Marx, and Machiavelli? What to do about Holy Writ, for that matter? Suppose they have an Inquisition there? Or if the future has forgotten the One True God, do I want to put Him back in business? In the end I allowed the King James Version aboard on literary grounds.

The classics were an obvious choice, but how to define them? For reasons of space and weight, plastic had the edge on paper. But only chestnuts are available on CD, and the Western canon seemed most likely to survive without my help. (What a vestigial thing the canon is anyway: merely the peaks of a continent sunk in time.) Perhaps my duty was to neglected works and lesser breeds — mediaeval romances, alliterative verse, Australian petroglyphs, Peruvian quipus, Meroitic stelae, Polynesian star maps, almost anything by Anon.

Can we even be sure that English will be understood? Who could have guessed, during Skeffington's hiatus, that the dialect of a few blond barbarian marauders would in a dozen centuries become the language of the world? Anyone for Basque, Bauan, Quechua, Quiché, Khaskura, Kichaga?

And music? A half-decent twentieth-century selection would overload the capsule, to say nothing of Andean pipes, Ghanaian drums, didgeridoo, Dowland, Dvořák, and all the usual suspects. What of architecture and sculpture? What of painting, politics, prosody, Pre-Raphaelism, polyphony, pyrotechnics, protocol, and proctology — to list the first things to pop into my head from a single band on the phonetic ether? Of course I took standard references on CD-ROM: Britannica (latest and eleventh), OED, Grove, various companions and anthologies. That left room for a small paperback shelf, from the *Grene Knight* to Graham Greene, and three hardbacks besides King James: *The Time Machine*, my thesis, and the old blue Dunne Anita gave me.

So you see I ended where I started: Desert Island Discs. I won't be able to tell the future much, but I can tell them what I like. And if they know it all and smile at my choices, at least the specimens should be of interest to antique dealers. If the end of History is indeed the Market, I can flog the lot and live a rentier.

What would you have taken, Bird? More jazz, no doubt. And your horn, for you are one of the blest who make their own.

Let's be optimistic: I'll get my medical problem seen to, and earn my keep as a revered authority on late industrial life and letters. I can identify all those things my future colleagues have defined, in the way baffled archaeologists always do, as "ceremonial objects": Rubik cubes, wind chimes, dildos, popes-on-a-rope, Franklin Mint models of the starship *Enterprise*. If they want to know the meaning of *Endgame* or *Krapp's Last Tape* (which you always called *Tape's Last Krapp*), I'll enlighten them. Think of it! I can parse Stein with a straight face. I can account for the fame of Warhol. I can unpack Christo. I can discuss Baudrillard's obscene ecstasy with special reference to Mickey Mouse. I can translate *Finnegans Wake*! It'll be my party. Who'll have the bottle to deconstruct me? And if homo sap has taken a fall, at least I'll be able to poke around in a spirit of leisurely antiquarianism long after the worst has happened.

By the middle of last week I was ready. This is where you came in.

*Postscript. Off Canvey Island, Thursday, November 30, 2000. Noon. Low tide*
All set; the machine on the draining flats, halfway to the shipping channel, attended only by a small oil slick, a few dogfish, some immature coprolites, a thin confetti of gulls. You're in the saloon bar of the King Canute, picking up Scotch eggs and a jug of bitter for a lunch I'll never eat. It's foul and gusty — a brindled sky, rain driving like pins into the face. An easy day to leave England. Though of course I'm not really leaving, just running on the spot so fast nobody will see me. Remember Speedy Gonzalez: *You wanna pay ten dollar to see the fastest mouse in all Méhico?... You wanna see heem again?*

It's cozy in my burgundy leather boudoir, and the green eyes winking around me show that if all goes well I shall soon be in the thirtieth day of the eleventh month of the year of Our Lord 2500; Julian Day Number 2,634,500; Long Count date 14. 4. 15. 0. 17.

Two copies of this letter are loaded on disks. One I'm keeping, Bird; the other I shall put in this plastic honey jar and cast on the waters shortly before take-off. My last deed in my own day, because I don't think I'll be back.

So long, old mate. Thank you. Forgive.

Part II


AFTER LONDON

# — 1 —

A place of light, a sandy plain, a driving wind, a body prone upon the sand. Darkness. A man wakes, stands up unsteadily, touches his eyes. I am blind. Hands mould his face, his chest, his belly, his loins. I am naked. Footsteps hissing in the sand. Dawn. Light; no sun, a hemisphere of brightness, a lid of light over a rippled dish of sand. A woman with fiery hair and nacre skin, naked, her back turned. Who are you? She faces him. I know you! She is frowning, speaking: *So it still works.* Where and when and who are we? *Out here on the rim there are no years or names.* I should have known. *Yes, you should: "Carriages without horses shall go, And accidents fill the world with woe." A driverless carriage, yet you climbed aboard.* Tania!

A half-evaporated dream; or a retinal image of the headlong passage through five hundred years?

There was no way to measure progress inside the sphere, to know whether it spun or leapt or wobbled like a top as it augered through the years, or if it cheated time at all. Yet I was buffeted by forces that felt less like normal motion than distortions in the gravity field. It was as if I became massive, dense, compressed, the matter of a neutron star. I believe I lost consciousness. Then came a dream of myself and Tania or Anita or some figure my mind confected from the two—a vision of symphonic richness from which I have only the lean echo I've just set down.

Transition—though I hardly remember it—from the massy state to its opposite. I grew weightless or, rather, became diffuse to the point where I seemed to make no impression on the upholstery of the seat—a splendid lightness such as you feel in a flying dream, when all you have to do is stretch out your arms to glide above the world, and it's so effortless and natural you wonder why you don't soar that way forever.

This ended abruptly. I was flung against the belts, pressed back, flung out and pressed until I lost any sense of up and down and sank into a second deep of unconsciousness. When I came round I understood that these new inertial forces, which continued though less violently, were familiar: the pitch of a small craft in a storm.

I had "landed"; the sphere was nodding in the sea.

My watch said sixty-seven minutes had elapsed. The Einsteinian paradox? Or had I simply been bottled up inside a sparking, spinning contraption for a little over an hour? I'm not sure which I feared more: the disappointment of opening the hatch to see a disgruntled Bird with his camcorder in the driving rain; or the terrors of an England as unimaginable to me as my England to the Tudors.

But it worked—which is to say I have arrived somewhere strange. It has taken me nearly a day to collect myself and enter these impressions. Whatever I do, I must keep this journal, if only to persuade myself I am alive.

I poke my head out like a hatching chick and this is what I see: a cloudless sky, a molten sun, turquoise water heaving gently to a dark green mangrove shore. And, halfway there, a sandy eyot or cay with a crest of bushes and a spray of palms.

Crawl from my spiny shell, drop anchor on rippled sand and eel-grass five fathoms down. Swim to the cay through glossy water warm as blood.

The jolt of land underfoot after a voyage.

Sit in the sun, toes in wet sand. A lazy suck and hiss of surf, backwash wimpling over stones, crabs running like pianists' hands along the beach. A sky of pterodactyl silhouettes and cries: pelicans and man-o'-war birds. The woman smell of the sea; the fox heat of a rainforest.

A new heaven, a new earth.

But where? Did the world roll beneath me as I spun, landing me in Bora Bora after all? I suppose a part of me had never expected the machine to work. To kill me, perhaps, but not to work as planned (what ever does?). And I think how the Polynesians worshipped man-o'-wars, the sun's messengers, and built stone platforms from which to launch them heavenward with their prayers; and I have a childish urge to build a little *marae* with these stones, an artefact, a human signature to tell me I exist.

Sudden knowledge that the stones aren't stones. They're bricks. Red, soft, handmade bricks, rounded by the sea. A ship's ballast left here long ago? But I've seen such bricks just recently. The King Canute was built of bricks like these.

My God, what happened here?

I swam in a flurry to the machine, exhausting myself, barely able to climb aboard. When my breath returned I got out maps, charts, compass, sextant, put them in a waterproof sack and brought them to the cay. Also the kayak, folded in its bag.

It hasn't taken long to establish that the sun, though it burns with tropical strength, is where it should be for latitude 51°30' North on November 30th. It's harder to confirm my exact position, for it appears that sea-level has risen several metres, drowning Canvey Island except for this small rise on which the pub once stood (if these bricks are indeed relics of the King Canute) and widening the Thames estuary by a mile or so. Thick vegetation along the shore hides all other landmarks.

I assembled the boat — glad of a simple task to stifle panic — and paddled to the bank. The water, high and on the ebb, muttered and gargled between candelabra roots; mosquitoes mobbed me; the knobbly knees of the mangroves nudged me away. Beards of seaweed, the boasts of spring tides, hung from branches higher than my head. I followed the coast for a while, spotting a manta ray, a scuttling lobster, and shoals of sergeant-majors — small fish striped black and white like socks. Here and there I thought I could make out a ridge among the trees, perhaps remnants of a breakwater or sea wall, broken and half drowned, vestigial and nostalgic as an Iron Age fort.

No way in, nowhere to land, no other beach or open ground. And of man and his works not a sign — not a bottle nor plastic bag, no stick of driftwood marked by axe or saw.

I paddled south — frantic now — out into the middle of the estuary where the shipping channel had been. From here I could see north over a fringe of palms to some low hills that seemed to have the profile I remembered. But if they were the hills of Rayleigh, unbroken forest hid the town, and there was no way to get there through the swamp.

The tide was running hard now, emptying from London, the water green and clear — as if no towns or farms disturb the earth. The Thames can't have run this clean since Caesar crossed from Gaul. Am I alone? Or have our descendants solved the problems of existence: controlled their numbers, balanced wealth and commonwealth, and turned our leavings into national parks?

The silence gave no answers and the emptiness was numbing, a chasm without echo. I slumped on the paddles, tired and disconsolate. What now? What would Tania do? What *did* she do? Did she land in this warm and swampy world, jump in for a dip and forget to set the handbrake? Couldn't she have left a warning, a map, a note in the stateroom of her *Marie Celeste?*

I longed to press on westward into London, against the tide, into the sun, as if an effort of will could stop time in its course, reverse the ebb, draw out the day until I knew the best or worst. But already an hour had passed and the sun was low, about to fall behind lobes of thunder flowering in the west. I turned back to the cay, paddling hard across the current; the sky darkened—more with weather than dusk—and a downpour rinsed the Hawaiian colours from the seascape. I left the boat upturned beneath a small tree with leaves like ping-pong bats, swam back to the machine.

I'm staying below for the night, hatch down except a crack, bobbing in the waves like a thorn-apple, wishing for a window or at least a ventilator. The time machine's no place to spend much time.

Bird's already had an earful from me (a copy of which you'll find enclosed; it'll save some explaining if you read it first). So this one's yours, Anita. Your chances of receiving it seem as good as anybody's. Rather depends on whether my transport has a reverse gear in working order, and whether I dare use it.

For ten years I mourned you while you lived; for eight months now I've mourned your death; and here—where perhaps there's a whole world to mourn—maybe you and I can start again. Let's say when I'm finished here I'll come back for you, my love. We'll meet in Aswan, on the terrace of the Old Cataract Hotel, on the evening of your birthday in—well, we'll fix the year later. The sun will be a fiery teardrop soaking into the hills above Elephantine Island, setting alight the desert and your hair, and I shall place this in your freckled hand. And we shall live again.

Did you know I came looking for you once? An impulse, one of my yuletide escapes. I began at Aswan, which is how I happen to know the character of the sunsets viewed from the hotel bar. It was far too late, of course. Your postcard had sat on my mantel for years, curled and yellowed like a leaf.

You were gone and no one in Aswan remembered you or knew where your team might be working. I went out to the quarry to touch the great unfinished obelisk I knew you must have touched, because a love of stones is something we shared. I committed a small act of vandalism there. If you look carefully among the graffiti on the southern side, you'll find the following written neatly in green ink: *I am Yesterday, I know Today, I am the Phoenix who keeps the register of creation and of things not yet created—DL.* You see I looked it up; your quotation was incomplete, the meaning hardly what you'd led me to believe.

I badgered the Germans at Luxor, the Canadians in the Dakhla, the Poles at Heliopolis, the Americans in Ma'adi. (The embassy was closed for the season.) All knew of you, spoke fondly of you, were full of admiration for your work. Several thought they had an idea where you might be. But all their leads ended in dust, at digs either finished or unbegun, at locked offices and empty rooms, at archives ruined by the Cairo fire. My search became impulsive, not to say farcical: I kept running into the same people; I got the trots, requiring sudden disappearances behind boulders and acacia bushes while asking for information. I became careless about my personal appearance. I was stoned by fundamentalists, pickpocketed by children, propositioned by pimps and catamites. Long-faced Copts followed me like wraiths, wailing *Catoliki? Catoliki? Bob Jumble. Very good! Very sorry!* And it wasn't till I got back to Cairo and bought an English paper that I understood: the pope had died.

*December 1*

A pinch and a punch. Dawn's fingernail in the propped hatch, the cloud thinned and carded into herringbone.

A tangerine sun burns slowly into the air, and the clouds begin to fade. I throw some things in a waterproof bag and swim to the King Canute for breakfast: five-hundred-year-old eggs and bacon fried on a driftwood fire. Do you remember those commercials where the city gent, collar turned against the sleet, suddenly finds himself on a tropic isle? Club Med, I think. *That was thirty seconds. Could you stand a week?*

Forgive the gallows humour. If I stop to think for a moment about this place it scares me witless. Early days yet, but it's beginning to look, on the face of it, as though there's no Mayo Clinic here. And I'm stuck till the generator builds a charge: two months to hop another half millennium, four months for a thousand years. How long does a castaway keep his mind?

At least I'm used to my own company. Archaeology's not a bad psychological preparation for the worst. We gave our lives to shards and bones; we chose the skeleton of culture, not the flesh and blood; we were at ease among the dead.

Better after eating. The sun rckindles that holiday feeling of escape and possibility. How long before the warden comes? — a chopper overhead, a speaker braying *Put out that fire!*

I'm staring across the stippled water — the morning breeze still cool — when I notice that my face is burning. So are hands and forearms, any skin exposed yesterday. A vicious sunburn for one winter afternoon. Perhaps beyond this park the air conditioners are humming and the planet's envelope is still an awning gone to holes. I never thought I'd wish it, but just now I do.

Time to make plans. One: disarm the machine and moor it safely somewhere, so it can't do a bunk on me. Two: set up camp. Three: a river trip to London.

*Evening*

Exhausted, a tough day. By ten o'clock the land had warmed, drawing an onshore breeze. By eleven the water was high under the mangroves. I towed the sphere behind the kayak to a small inlet arched by wiry old trees that had seen out many a storm. I secured her with a web of lines lashed to the thickest roots, let the air out of the flotation tube, watched her settle on the silt. None of this easy or pleasant, for I was shrouded like a beekeeper against the sun and flies (and you know how I sweat). If it's this hot now, it must be hell in July.

The rest of the day I've spent setting up camp on the cay: a brick hearth, a soft pad for the tent beneath an almond bush, a plastic sheet for catching rain, a clothesline between two palms.

Whether or not I'm really alone, I've never *felt* so alone. Even on those wilderness treks we did there was always some spoor of the urban world—a cigarette end in the grass, the buzz of an outboard, a jet's scar on the sky. Here there are only these bricks and my things to remind me what species I belong to. And you. And Bird, of course, whom I saw only the day before yesterday on this very spot, though already it seems like years.

Thank heaven for animals. I had a sunset swim and a great sea turtle—shell the size of a dining table—rose beside me with a fishy sigh. She circled twice, dived to inspect me from below, swam with me until I headed for the beach. If I were a Pedro Serrano or a Selkirk I'd have turtle stew and turtle soup, and a turtle shell for a rainbarrel.

Not yet.

Bird was silent most of the way down here in the truck (thoughts of you?), the window open, fire cupped periodically in his palms. We came through Stepney—stopping for his bag, checking the tarp over the "human torpedo"—on through the dismal postwar housing blocks and ranks of garages with broken vehicles in them like larvae dead in a hive, past beaten turf and littered playgrounds full of crippled swings. Occasionally we saw a fragment of the London that had been before the war: a corner pub, the Railway Arms or Lamb and Flag, isolated and shored up with timbers, like a last slice of stale cake.

Night fell as we sat in a traffic jam. We made the A13 and ran east through gravel pits and fens. When we reached the causeway for Canvey Island and saw how busy it was, I began to worry that I might have been too hasty in the choice of launching place. I'd been here only once before — by sea, years ago, with a friend and his father in their sloop, forced into the anchorage by a storm on our way from Brightlingsea to Barnes. Canvey then was marsh and grazing, its village a rather manky resort catering to day-trippers from the East End. The yacht club where we made fast overnight was nothing more than a tidal backwater with a jetty, fuel pumps, and a pub. Behind it I recalled a dairy farm, perhaps a distant clutch of bungalows. Naively, I hadn't expected it to change much. But it had. The fields were a bedroom suburb and an oil refinery. The yacht club was closed up and girdled by a ten-foot steel fence. Worst of all, the entire island had a circumvallation of earth and concrete. Bird and I found no trace of the old launching ramp I'd planned to use, and a long search produced no others that were suitably remote.

It was getting late, past ten. We discussed going back to the mainland and on to Foulness, but Bird wanted a meal and a pint. "Let's stop the night here at the old yachtie pub, Dave. Things'll look better in the morning. We can make an early start." I suddenly felt very tired. The King Canute looked unexpectedly inviting, a low, rambling inn of bricks and beams that must have been an oyster-men's haunt in the days when Thames oysters were fit to eat. Inside was a coal fire and a very pretty barmaid. For the first time since your funeral I saw Bird's posture straighten, his hair spring up. I ordered pints and chicken pies, asked about a room.

"Make that two rooms," Bird said, holding the girl's eye. "My mate Dave here snores like a hedgehog. It's always nice to have a room of your own, don't you think? Nice and...private." He had hopes. She was a looker all right. Not a day over nineteen, wearing black tights and bodysuit under a white crocheted cardigan. Long cornsilk hair was brushed behind her ears, which were edged from top to bottom with gold rings like the binding of a spiral notebook. She had a zircon labret—passé in the West End though not in the East. I never liked the new primitive look much, but she carried it off. Essex woman. Her name was Elaine, and she'd lived here all her life.

Bird said, "Your old man the owner, then?"

I said he couldn't help being nosy; his name was Parker. She had an easy laugh.

"Just work here. Best pub on Canvey. Oldest and highest building on the island. On the highest ground, I mean. You can't have missed the hill." She laughed again. I *had* noticed it, walking up from the carpark, a low meniscus like an ancient barrow—only a few yards high, but conspicuous on land as flat as a lake. My cay.

She pulled a pint for another customer, a regular he looked, an elderly man in an anorak who stared at us. It wasn't the tourist season. Bird ordered more beer.

"That's why it's called the King Canute." Elaine had the art of picking up each conversation where she'd left it, like a chess master playing a dozen games at once. "Used to be the Goat and Boot. Ever heard of the great flood of '53? The whole island was under water except here. Me mum remembers it. Came right up to the doorstep and stopped. Ray's dad—he was the landlord in them days—stood over there in the doorway shouting, 'Go back, go back!' Same fing two years ago in '98. Right up to the step."

"When did they build that wall? I was here a few years ago. I don't remember anything like this." I waved my hand to imply the defences severing the old pub from the sea, threatening my plans.

"Not sure. They made it higher last year, but it was here before. Ray. RAY." She was calling through a low doorway to the public bar.

"RAY!"

"Yeah." (Faintly, over sounds of a video game and a darts match.)

"Ray. 'Ow long's that wall been built?"

"What wall's that, love? The Berlin Wall?"

"The sea wall."

"Must be ten years."

Bird leant across the bar, grinning, his avian gaze on her body like a pair of hands. "Elaine. Another question for you. Where could you launch a boat on the QT?"

"Why would I want to do that?"

I took over, explaining that we had a biggish craft to float. Heavy enough to need a motor ramp. We hadn't much time. Had to catch the morning tide. And we didn't want to be seen because, well, it was to be a surprise for someone near and dear—

"You mean you don't recognize him?" Bird rescued me from what was already a feeble story. "Never mind, love. He likes it better when people don't. You see, it gets a bit tiresome bein' a celebrity like our Dave." Elaine's darkened lashes swept me up and down, puckers of amusement at the corners of her mouth.

"Go on with you!"

"Oh, but he is, Elaine, he is. Cowes, Fremantle, America's Cup —you name it, he's done it." Bird flicked a Camel from its pack, snatching it smoothly in his lips. "So have I, in me own quiet way. I'm his crew." His voice fell conspiratorially as he brushed away the smoke. "We try not to fling it about. You see, it's just we don't want no publicity—paparazzi—all those bottom feeders from the *Sun*. Competition's cut-froat, know what I mean? What we'd like to know is, where could we launch our little craft unobserved?"

"Ray. RAY!"

"Yeah."

"Where could you launch a boat . . . unobserved?"

"Who wants to know?"

"Two gentlemen. Sailors."

"Smugglers are they?"

The sardonic Ray we never saw, but Elaine went through to the other bar and came back with information. The yacht club was indeed closed down, but if you turned left out of the carpark and followed a muddy lane beside a concrete hulk, a barrage boat from the war, there was a way through the fence. "Ray says to watch out for all the scrap round there. And the mud. Wash it off you quick. People have been dumping chemicals and fings, and—" She halted in mid sentence. "*That's* not yer game, is it? 'Cause if it is you can both piss off. This island's my home."

"Fear not, Elaine," said Bird. "Get up early with me tomorrow, and I'll be honoured to escort you round the Ship of Fools." I shot him a frosty glance but his eyes never strayed from hers, and his voice had become as rich and seductive as a late-night DJ's.

"Here. What are you looking at me like that for? Are my eyebrows growing in?"

"Like abandoned railway lines, my sweet." She laughed, and a sleigh-bell sound rang from the gold in her ears.

And after that? Well, you know Bird.

*Thursday, December 2*

Up early to take the Thames to London. An easy paddle at first, riding the flood-tide; wind on the starboard quarter.

The river's artificial banks have long disappeared, and there's no trace of the refineries and power stations that used to greet the seaborne visitor to London like an avenue of sphinxes. Mangroves and palmettos line both shores, and I'm too low in the water to see over them. Occasionally something pokes up temptingly behind—so wreathed in leaves that I couldn't tell a tall tree from a smokestack.

If it weren't for those bricks, I'd believe I'd landed back in the Mesozoic.

It must have been about ten o'clock when I sighted them, two exclamation marks joined by a warped hyphen, black against a Canaletto sky. The Queen Elizabeth Bridge at Dartford. It took a long hour to reach, my messy strokes the only human stir in what was once the busiest water on earth.

I'm trying to set everything down calmly for you, a professional account. I may be this England's only chronicler, and I know how grateful I've been, when searching the darker corners of the past, for an eyewitness careful with the facts. How I felt, how I feel —perhaps you can imagine: as the bridge drew closer, excitement soured to fear, and certainty took root in my innards and sapped me like a parasitical worm. If the bricks at Canvey were a clue, here was confirmation beyond doubt.

The Dartford bridge holds awful proof of age: the concrete leprous, pitted, whittled by wind, warty with cysts of rusting steel. Pelicans line the rods and girders like sailors on the rigging of a shattered windjammer. Cables have snapped and frayed, the roadway seems to hang by magic, and the magic's wearing thin. Whole sections have gone from the raised approaches, leaving piers in the water like rows of prehistoric megaliths.

We made it our business to know what the centuries could do to corbel vaults and marble arches, to the granite slabs of pharaohs' tombs, to Roman concrete and Akkadian ziggurats. We knew the work of seepage on mud-brick, of termites on ironwood lintels, of acid rain on marble caryatids. But how much time would it take to make a modern structure look like *this*?

Time and heat. Your rat is gnawing. *What happened here?*

Warming, obviously, as many foresaw. But for the reasons they foresaw? Or something else, something for which we can't be blamed: an asteroid smacking the planet in the chops; or the world relapsing like a malaria patient into its old sweats and chills?

I remember Skef saying—as an aside in his prehistory lectures—that the ice would rumble south again one day and grind the spires of Cambridge into sand. But not to worry; we'd had a good long run since the glaciers stalled—a hundred centuries in which to tame our food, and tame ourselves, and invent civilization in half a dozen fertile spots from China to Peru—and he saw no reason why the fair weather shouldn't last. Now there's this new evidence from glacial cores—evidence that such long calms are rare, and easily upset. Cycles have changed from ice to heat or vice versa not in millennia, but in *decades*. The boat starts rocking —hotter summers, colder winters, hurricanes, blizzards—and can flip in forty years.

Not proven we capsized it, but the timing is certainly suspicious. A sudden bonfire of the planet's coal and oil and timber can hardly have been a good idea. Or did the missiles fly after all; was the world put to sleep by the one-note sermon of the bombs? Yet the notion that we'd go out with a bang was part of our self-regard, like some twit with a sportscar and a death wish. Revanchist nature may have got us first. Six billion hundredweight of overcrowded ape meat was a free lunch waiting for the wily microbe—as you and I know all too well, Anita.

A good archaeologist doesn't jump to conclusions, so neither will I. What finished Rome? Plague? Soil exhaustion? Goats? Drought? Lead pipes? Mad emperors? Corruption? Barbarians? Christianity?

Distracted by these thoughts, I failed to notice that the only accessible section of the bridge—a ramp ascending from a muddy backwater where the toll booths used to be—had occupants. A brilliantined head peering down at me was such a shock I nearly rolled my boat. The head was joined by others. They swayed and bobbed in curiosity, and soon the parapet was lined with whiskery chins.

When they saw I meant to board their perch, they broke into angry barking, baring teeth and flashing eyes. Luckily I'd brought the gun. I paddled off a little way and fired in the air, raising a blizzard of birds. The sea lions fell silent, as if they couldn't believe what they'd just heard. I fired again, over the head of a large bull who seemed to be the boss, and they dropped from the bridge like grubs from a lifted corpse.

At one spot where the concrete meets the water it has crumbled in a gravelly slope. I landed here, hauling myself up between gaunt spears of steel. The lower parts of the roadway are covered in fish remains, sea lion shit, and tidal ooze (you can imagine the stink). But I soon got above this to where saltgrass and hardy bushes have taken root in guano and disintegrated asphalt. Here I sit, in a welcome wind, nibbling a sandwich, tapping the Oyster's keys.

"In the midst of a vast solitude...on a broken arch of London Bridge to sketch the ruins of St. Paul's." Macaulay was right about the solitude, though this isn't the bridge he had in mind and I doubt that from here one could ever have seen St. Paul's. The odd thing is — or perhaps this is to be expected — it's not silent any more. I hear voices. Or to put it another way, I say things — things we said to each other, word-perfect after all these years, conversations with Bird, with strangers, with myself, fragments of books and poems, both hackneyed and obscure, many of which I didn't know I knew. I catch them starting from me like Tourette's syndrome, or a song you can't get rid of, and my voice sounds familiar and yet foreign, as if I were speaking a dead language.

Our language. Am I alone with all it contains, with the fragments I have by heart and in the sphere? Or have I, like Don Quixote, been driven mad by the wrong books? By all those things you recommended for my thesis — forgotten utopias, dystopias, and romances — by Mary Shelley's plague dogging the last man to the end of the twenty-first century, by Shiel's purple cloud of poison gas belched by a self-fumigating earth, by the "deserted and utterly extinct" London of Richard Jefferies. All those tall tales that bloomed like a cold sweat in the midnight terrors of the Steam Age, when civilization first began to guess that it had found the means to suicide.

But if this empty future is illusory, it is the most substantial of illusions. I have its scorch on my skin and its breath in my face. I feel my body here on this earth. I scratch my bites, taste my own sweat when it runs onto my lips after stinging my eyes. The hallucination is total and consistent. I'm reeling with ontological vertigo. And so once again we're back at the imponderables, back where I started when the machine appeared. How do I know what I know; and what is the *I* that knows it? You used to like that kind of thing, but I (*pace* graduate pretensions) am happy to leave unanswerable questions to the prophets and the French. *"Il n'y a rien dehors du texte."* We'll see.

Among Uncle Phil's bric-à-brac was a pair of Zeiss field-glasses which had once scanned the Atlantic from a U-boat conning tower — clumsy things, twice the size of modern ones that would do as well, but I've always liked them. Looking south through these, towards Sevenoaks and Tunbridge Wells, over a swell of forest hiding the ruins of Dartford, I see the North Downs — distant whalebacks with an olive rime of trees.

I don't think I ever spoke of the farm, even to you. It also has its voices, which have been my silence until now. Otten Hall Farm (in its early days there were otters): a thousand acres in a valley near Tunbridge Wells. An Elizabethan house of chevroned brick in a frame of old ships' oak, each corner braced by a galleon rib, chimneys like ornate cannon aimed at the sky. Odd how a place I haven't seen in twenty-two years is more vivid than anything I've lived in since. It had a long gravel drive, three round oast-houses used long ago for drying hops (windmills without sails, I thought of them), a terraced garden, clipped yew and low stone walls stepping down through roses and fruit trees to a pond dark under the willows.

I've never believed people who say they can remember sitting in their prams, but I remember falling out of mine. There's a chill, a loud wind, a rectangle of cold grey sky, a leafless branch or two, black thorns twitching and scratching at the light; a chill draught of abandonment, of being muted by the wind, the child's cry lost like a gull's on a storm. I sit up and the thorns reach further, the wind louder, colder. But I know how to be warm, how to make this end. Back and forth, back and forth, rocking, the creak of springs. Rocking, and you wake, you sit up and we rock together, together, one rhythm, one flesh. Whoops! How do you sift hindsight from the reptile mind that knew the lonely chill and the rectangle and the sky ineffably? No words: just *feeling*; feeling preserved like something that should not be preserved, like the last meal in the stomach of a bog-man drowned two thousand years ago: a meal fresh enough to eat.

They say there can be no knowledge of the world without language to sort and record it. But I know they're wrong. I remember that chill and that sky, those minatory trees, that hiss and flutter of the wind—even though I can't have had a word for any of those things. Animals remember without words, and we are surely animals. Where to eat, when to run. Anything you teach a horse before he's two years old he remembers all his life. Take Sitting Bull's horse, trained to perform for the Wild West Show in which the great chief spent his failing years. When they shot Sitting Bull near Wounded Knee, the sound of the guns made the old horse do his tricks. On and on he danced while his master died; and the Sioux said he was performing the Ghost Dance—the dance to raise the countless dead; the dance for which the cavalry would shortly kill them all. And I remember, too, the springs louder, the sky jumping, the sky jumping, the sky jumping, the sky jumping. The soaring moment, that cannon-ball release, that freedom as the sky flies away and the earth rears up to strike you, and the wind is buried in a coronach of metal, a landslide of woollies and bonnets and teddybears. And the afterglow, the parents running; worry on their faces; grudging admiration in their tones. *Fancy that. A good pram. And two props! The woman in the shop said one would do. The little monkey.* Carried into the house, away from the chill and the grey, away from the drowning wind, the keening silence. Until tomorrow.

Twenty-two years since the farm came to a dead end (or, if you prefer, five hundred and twenty-two) and I couldn't go back there now even if it were possible to hack thirty miles through these rampant woods. It belongs among two or three places on this island I've never revisited and never will: Otten Hall Farm; the sanatorium at Aldworth Park, where I was convalescing from measles when Mother and Father died; and, yes, the Corpus ballroom. Places frozen in a certain cave of memory, where something bleak is buried; zones off the map, wiped from geography like the sites of Soviet failures. What would I find anyway? Foundations and chimney-breasts among the trees? Roofless oast-houses like broken bottles? Was our house sacked, burned, left to rot away— or do people live there yet? Is England home to a ghastly remnant grubbing in dumps and ruins, or is there somewhere behind the trees a subtle garden of Morrisian aesthetes?

They'd like the farm. It was a good place once.

## — 2 —

*Saturday, December 4, Dartford Bridge*
My halfway house until I find a place in London (assuming I will want to live there). A smelly, windswept spot to pitch a tent, but at least it's high and dry and far from what may lurk ashore. Anita, I've hardly slept since leaving the old world, though I've been drinking myself half senseless before going to bed. It's not the wind

and waves and the sea life, nor the sudden scream in the trees when something eats and something dies; it's the silence that wakes me through the night.

The sea lions, who prefer the lower ramps, leave me alone but the pelicans are bolder, edging along the parapet, clicking their bills and leering at my breakfast with shiny eyes like louche old men at a strip show. It's good to have their company. I've paddled up here to Dartford twice now and seen no trace of cultural activity: no smoke, no noise, no rubbish. Nothing.

If fish and animals can survive, there *must* be human beings. But where; and who will live in such a world? Simple happy folk bopping around in the jungle? Or gastronomes of the old school, famished among all our pasts? I keep looking over my shoulder.

"It was wonderful to see the villages and towns reverting to the earth, already invaded by vegetation . . . the town now as much the country as the country, and that which is not-man becoming all." Shiel, 1901. The perverse fantasy of our age: how good, as we sat in our comfortable houses, to imagine the earth relieved of its human burden, the return of animals and plants, clear water, clean air. My fantasy and yours (how did you stand the warren of Cairo for so long?). I noticed Future Heritage among your charities. I take it you knew they were a store-front for the Earth Commandos, that you weren't bothered by the odd *plastique* finding its way aboard a nuclear ship, by limpet mines on driftnetters, by spikes in redwoods destined for the saw. I too sent money when I could. What was the alternative—look away until the world became at best a cabbage patch, at worst a desert?

But now that the wild has the upper hand again, it inspires in me what it inspired in our first ancestors: dread of the dark beyond the firelight, the world-rim, the wyrm, the trackless weald; the besieging mystery of a creation I can't understand. And what a difference between the barbarism that precedes civilization and that which follows it. This wilderness is no virgin, but old and used, riddled with man-made hazards and abominations.

I am for the woods, but are the woods for me?

Do you remember this bridge, or wasn't it built when you left? Come to that, did you ever return to Britain at all before the end? And if you did, dammit, why didn't you get in touch? I waited like an apostle, wondering what it was I'd done or hadn't done or should be doing. After all, you'd come to me twice—in Alex, in Cambridge—was it so unreasonable to hope for a third coming? (All right, enough. Promise.)

I must have driven over this asphalt and steel many times, heading south on London's orbital motorway. (Northbound traffic used the Dartford Tunnel.) Did Bird ever tell you about the time we got stuck in that with one of his antiques? An Ariel Square Four attached to a sidecar like a caravan, windows opaque with yellow cataracts, upholstery stinking of damp and mice and perished rubber. We ended up spending the night in it, so I remember the smell vividly. He'd bought it from *an old gaffer in Bexley*—I can hear Bird ringing up, asking me to follow him home in case it broke down. I was on his own machine, the wine-red Triumph aptly known as Springheel Jack (you must have had some indelible rides on that).

There was a jam underground, as there often was at rush-hour, and the Ariel's big engine got hot. Oil dribbled onto an exhaust, raising billows of smoke lit by the headlamps of cars behind us. Bird had to shut it down, and of course when the traffic began to move no amount of dancing on the kickstart would bring it back to life.

Somebody gave us a rope, and I towed the Square Four behind the Triumph to a quiet street in Grays. Bird began to tinker, undismayed: *Lovely, innit. Look at those castings! Work of art.* I said I'd rather it just worked. *These things never worked and never will, Dave. Hopeless layout, four cylinders in a square. Back ones always run hot as buggery. But Yank collectors love 'em. Your Yank doesn't expect this old Brit stuff to work. As long as it looks grand, eccentric, and exotic, that's all he asks.*

By the time he gave up it was late and pouring. The pubs had closed, there was nowhere to stay, the Triumph was nearly out of fuel. So we ended up in that sidecar like two bottles in a briefcase, the most intimate I ever want to be with a man. A few days later, when Bird had rounded up some parts, we went back for the Square Four. The sidecar was there, but the grand old bike had been neatly amputated with acetylene.

North of the Thames the land is flatter. The glasses add little detail to glistening swamps and tufts that might contain a relic. To the west, some fifteen miles away, are pillars and stumps of tall buildings in the City—their bases under the horizon. In the quivering noon light, viscous with heat and vapour, it's impossible to see either a wink of glass or the gape of empty sockets. If only I had a clearer memory of how the skyline used to look from here. But the weather was usually foul and the bridge's railing was designed to keep your eyes from straying to the view.

Strange to rest my elbows on a fragment of this rail now.

One thing I do recognize: a great tower, nearer than the others and alone. (*A toure on a toft*—I'll always hear Langland in your voice.) The main building at Canary Wharf, the tallest in Britain when I left, thrown up on the Isle of Dogs during the feeding frenzy of the Thatcher years.

*London's whitest elephant*, Bird called it, *after the King.* One could never be certain about Bird's personal mythology, but he *was* born on the Isle of Dogs, at Millwall—he showed me a birth certificate. Certainly he had an attitude towards the place. *Fucking plutocrat hubris. Serves 'em right it's as empty as the Italian book of war heroes.* According to him, the project bankrupted its developers, who, like so many stern advocates of *laissez-faire*, ran yelping to the taxpayer when the game didn't go their way. They got the government to build a railway there at vast expense, and rented the office space for next to nothing. Even so, whole floors were empty in 2000.

Canary Wharf's worth a visit—it might be a canary in history's mine.


*December 5, Isle of Dogs. Afternoon*
I left the bridge at nine this morning, catching a strong tide, then hugging shallows to cheat a headwind creasing the open water. The cool was welcome; in two hours it would be hot and I couldn't risk stripping off under the caustic sun. (I wished I'd thought to bring a hat. A big straw hat would be ideal; if I can find a suitable material when I get settled somewhere, I'll plait one.)

For long hallucinatory stretches it was possible to forget, to take in only the moment—water, wind, foliage, animals—as I've always loved to do outdoors. Flying foxes, already roosting for the day, were hanging like shabby leather jackets in the taller mangroves. A toucan or a hornbill—a pair of yellow garden shears— sailed across my path. Scarlet macaws swept out of the Erith marshes and screamed over the water to a ridge of high timber covering the Ford works at Dagenham. I considered landing there —the shifting shapes of cars would chronicle our past like potsherds—but factory ruins will be dangerous, and no bodywork could have lasted in this climate.

I need a frozen moment of the crisis: something like the eighth-century frescoes at Bonampak, where a magnificent king announces a great victory and gives the date. But this date is the last the city ever recorded, and the blanks where the scribes were to write the glorious story stayed unfilled, a silence more eloquent than anything they might have written.

The Roding, once hemmed by channels and locks, is free and languid where it joins the Thames, the wind carrying a sulphur

smell from a mudbank where fiddler crabs run to and fro, bran-
dishing their outsize claws. No trace of the City Airport and the
Albert docks. Here and there, where the shore is free of thickets,
I saw a stony ridge, and the stones turned out to be the stuff of
buildings — blocks of hewn granite and poured concrete, gnarled
girders, shoals of brick. The Thames has wiped away our viaducts
and warehouses, and made from them new banks.

You can't see much from a kayak — it's so low — and you feel
trapped like a foot in a shoe. I rested often, drifting, sniffing for
campfires, listening for voices, laughter, dogs, music, drums. But
what I heard was the instinctual clamour of the forest — a skiffle of
buzzing, scraping, belching, and sharp cries — hushing as I passed,
as if to convey to me the dereliction, to say: Your city has been
dead for centuries.

Again and again the enormity of where I am crashes down,
stripping me naked in this ancient monument, my home. And the
next thought: what chance that the rest of the world is any different? The civilizations of the past were local, feeding on particular
ecologies. While one fell, another rose elsewhere. But ours had
wrapped itself around the world, its very scale and complexity
making it uniquely vulnerable to any global change. It isn't hard to
see the droughts and floods, the failed harvests, the end of trade,
the refugees, the desperate measures to control the starving.

Movement beneath a thatch of vines. I froze, but the movement stopped. A heavy shape in the leaves, bulky and grey. Not
human. A hippo, I thought, until I saw an odd-looking snout or
trunk — too long for a pig, too short for an elephant. A tapir come
to drink.

The river opens into steaming everglades and is joined by
the Lea. Beyond this the main channel takes a shortcut through
West India Quay, making the Isle of Dogs a true island, leaving the
lyre-shaped meander of Greenwich Reach quiet and glutinous
beneath flotillas of lilypads and water hyacinth. Canary Wharf was

soon above me: eight hundred feet of tower, tipsy on its feet of London clay.

Hubris, perhaps, though hubris wasn't new here. I remember how Bird used to talk about *Leviathan*, the monstrous iron ship — nearly the length of this tower — built on the Isle in the 1850s and not outdone until the twentieth century. An ancestor of his had worked and died on her. One of the riveters immured in water-tight compartments, whose skeletons were found when she was broken up.

What idolatrous monument defines the apotheosis of the Victorian age, with its terrible human sacrifices? The Crystal Palace? The Eiffel Tower? The Forth Bridge? Or, as I ventured in my thesis, a pair of giant ships: *Leviathan* and *Titanic*? "And as the smart ship grew / In stature, grace, and hue, / In shadowy silent distance grew the Iceberg too."

Whatever bordered Canary Wharf on its northern side has been scoured away. The concrete here is rough and eaten, and the river — near high water — slops into a cellar through a weedy hole and booms in the darkness. High tide is yards above its ancient level, and there are faded watermarks even higher on the walls. Apart from this and its ominous lean, the tower has been well treated by the years. Rags of metal cladding still cling here and there; a few windows even have their glass, though most are dark mouths dribbling vegetation down their chins. The roof — once a glass pyramid which threw the sun like the electrum tips of Egypt — is a tousled wig falling down to a green ruff on a ledge near the top floors.

South of the tower the jungle rambles over mounds and ridges where neighbouring blocks have collapsed. I paddled carefully beneath overhanging branches and beached on a large slab. Noon now, the birds quiet, the Thames flashing like a heliograph beyond the leaves. The ground was a rockery of crumbling concrete, tile, and stone under thick moss and drifts of leafmould —

quite free of undergrowth between the trunks except for philo-
dendrons and other twilight plants. This tropical vegetation is a
puzzle. How did it get here—as seeds in the stomachs of migrat-
ing birds? Or did it tiptoe north, root by root, as the planet warmed?
But if the trees came from equatorial Africa, how could they have
crossed the dry lands in between? The old tropics must have fried
to death long ago, and Earth must wear a ruddy belt like Mars.

I worked my way up a slope, the air soapy with mould and
moisture, loud with a transformer hum of insects dancing in thin
sunbeams. A blue morpho flapped past my head—a butterfly big
as a dove. Strangler figs climb the lower walls, sealing windows
with a downpour of aerial roots. I spotted only one way in, a glassless sill near the top of the ridge.

A slight path led to it, a dent in the moss. What if someone
lived there? But the trail looked like the work of an animal. I paused
beside a large tree to take in my surroundings, had a nervous urge
to pee. At that moment I knew the pale trunk studded with squat
thorns for a *ceiba*, or silk-cotton. I saw tropical cedars, locusts, and
a good-sized mahogany. Suddenly I understood: these trees hadn't
crept north from Africa; they'd escaped from Kew! And the smaller
plants on the forest floor, spiralling trunks, crowding ledges and
sills—these too were runaways from botanical gardens, conserva-
tories, and a million living-rooms. Ficus and avocados, oleander and
epiphytes, orchids and plumerias, brought from Belize to Belsize,
had outlived their owners and inherited this corner of the earth.

I'd just taken a step towards the dark window when the darkness moved. From the black square slipped something blacker.
A large dog? A wolf? Why hadn't I foreseen this? If houseplants
had gone wild, the country could be rife with feral dogs and cats,
and heaven knew what else. My gun and machete were out of
reach, leant against the tree where I'd stopped. I was caught in a
fool's checkmate.

The creature emerged fully from the window, stopped, took

a few more steps down the path. It didn't move like a dog. A cloud quenched the sunbeams; in the thickening gloom I couldn't tell if it had seen me; I still couldn't see what it was. It halted and sniffed. My God, I'd just pissed by its front door! Then the glade brightened.

It was a huge black cat.

The head was compact and powerful, with rounded ears, or rather one rounded ear—the other seemed to be missing. The body looked about a metre from nose to the root of the tail, which was thick, almost as long as the body, slung towards the ground, turned up at the end. The animal kept still, watching me with more curiosity than fear, giving me that cold appraisal you often get from a cat who doesn't know you: *What have you got to offer? What have I got to lose?* But this was no descendant of a fireside tom. It was a puma. I'd never seen a black one before but I'd met a tawny puma, the pet of a jungle hotelier in Guatemala—a playful creature who put her paws on my shoulders and licked my face with a file tongue.

Perhaps because of this memory I didn't panic; and perhaps because I didn't, neither did the cat. It circled downwind and sniffed again. It was close enough now that I could see the nostrils open and the chest inflate with quick, inquiring breaths. It had white whiskers, striking against the black, and a few pale hairs on its chin. It seemed old, but the topaz eyes were clear, intelligent, and deep. I returned its stare (someone told me once that predators will shrink from that) but this cat could have faced down Wyatt Earp. It approached to within ten feet. Again it sniffed, and I could see clearly that its dominant emotion was still curiosity, and that in its stance there was no preparation for a spring. After a very long moment it let out a half-hearted growl—a kind of hail and farewell—and padded into the shadows.

I got in the boat and pushed off a few yards to eat lunch undisturbed by carnivores, my cheddar sweaty and foul in the heat; I washed it down with a few swigs of rum.

An odd calm. That puma told me one thing as clearly as if it spoke English: it had never seen a human being in its life. "And the fear of you and the dread of you shall be upon every beast of the earth, and upon every fowl of the air." I'll leave the rest of the cheese as a thank-you for not eating me. And because the big black beast reminds me of Graham.

One of our neighbours at the farm was a batty old dear who took in strays. Miss Frank. She had dozens. Whenever you passed her house you'd see every windowsill patrolled by tabbies and marmalades, huffy Persians; and you'd often see a big black tom with one ear. She named the black tom Graham—after Billy Graham the evangelist, for Miss Frank was naively devout. About twice a year the RSPCA would come with a red van and take most of the cats away. She'd run amok in the streets for days, half dressed, hair wild, hurling the names of the missing at the sky.

They always let her keep three or four, and Graham was of these, the inner circle. He was well known in the village but not well liked because he "bothered" neutered males, including Merlin, who shared neither his religious nor his sexual taste. There'd be hideous caterwauling, Mother would dash outside, and eventually Merlin would be found, scratched, bitten, drenched with strong urine and glairy secretions. In spite of this, I liked Graham. I sympathized with his outcast status, and I felt sorry for Miss Frank, who, like many a kind soul gulled by a preacher, was blind to his carnal sins.

*Evening, back at the bridge*
Much to report. "Graham" didn't return. After eating I landed again and approached his window cautiously. Inside was a catty scent and the sweetness of rotten meat. It was a puma's lair all right, strewn with rodent bones, long red and green feathers, something that might have been the head of a dog or deer. And a thin forearm, dried up and deeply gnawed. A child's arm—as horrifying as the baby's hand a vulture dropped into Kipling's garden. A child!

I heard a cry, an echo in unknown corridors and rooms, and for a long moment didn't realize it had come from me. Nothing was familiar, least of all myself; to what rough beast belonged these eyes and ears, this weapon-gripping hand? I stood to run, grazing my head, the pain real enough, a welcome slap. I saw you, your death; so many deaths that the greenery outside seemed foul as Flanders mud.

Then I saw abnormally gracile fingers and a patch of fur. A monkey's arm. I laughed—too loud, I think, as though for a hidden audience—and made to leave. But there was a voice, my father's: *If you run now, Davy, you'll never come back.*

For a while I sat, unmindful of the damp earth and fetor of the place, frozen by the thought of Graham, listening to the forest outside—its busy, preoccupied, no-nonsense sounds. And at last I felt collected enough to go on with my exploring.

Graham's den was probably an office five centuries ago, but that's a guess made with inside knowledge (an advantage no other archaeologist has had). You can't deduce much from how it looks today. The original floor lies under a thick deposit of silt and droppings that makes the room low and cramped. The ceiling is white with a pimply rash of small stalactites leaching from the concrete. The walls are also streaked, but here I found human palm prints—oddly like those on the old Arab houses of Alexandria. I examined them closely with my torch. These were done as stencils—more like the ones we saw in the Dordogne caves, made twenty thousand years ago by spraying pigment from the mouth over the hand.

Rock art is so hard to date. But I was lucky. In places a translucent layer of limestone had formed on top of them; they had to be old, probably from the first years of abandonment. This was confirmed by the range of colours; these paints were sprayed from cans.

Beyond the hands was another room, darker, less silted, and

apparently unused by Graham. There was less of the lime deposit here and I could make out stylized lettering—gang monograms, I think—*DROYD, CUCKOO, LEVELLERS*. Also swastikas and Union Jacks, oversprayed with *ARMY OUT!* and *GOD IS WON OF US.* The room led to a passage closed at the far end by a steel door diaphanous with rust. Two strokes of the machete released a flood of light, instantly darkened by a thousand wings. Pigeons!

It was a large suite with glassless windows facing west. The floor was like a chickenhouse—ficus plants feasting on the guano under the windows and leaning out into the sun. If nothing changed much after our day, these were the premises of a newspaper conglomerate owned by a crony of the developers who had located here to help them out. Bird: *The only poor folk that sort ever cares about are the ones whose poverty can be assessed in billions.*

I pictured iron presses and boards of metal type. If artefacts like that survived, I could read the last front page in coppers. But of course the papers printed here belonged to the silicon age; the physical plant would have been off in some low-rent warehouse. I wandered through several suites, all of them pigeon lofts. Remarkable how empty they are. Filing cabinets, desks, terminals, wiring—gone without trace. If there are artefacts anywhere they lie deep in the guano and it'll be a nasty job to dig for them. Lime was leaching from the walls here too, but the concrete underneath looked dark. I chipped off a stalactite with my blade. Soot. The place was swept by fire.

What I need is a view from the top to give me an idea of what I'm up against. We were lulled by lifts into thinking that the juice carton was a good shape for a building. Without electricity you have to walk up, all the way, in the bat-filled darkness of an emergency stairwell. I turned back after a few floors—fifty storeys were beyond me today. I'll need an early start, cold sober. Architects! What a bill of goods they sold us: rooms without windows, windows that didn't open, stairs from a nightmare. As if neon could replace daylight, as if ducts and vents were any substitute for good fresh air. I know you thought I was a bit of a nutter on the subject of fresh air, but what's a room without a window? A cell or a tomb.

Back to Graham's level and on down to the atrium, a hall covering the entire ground floor. Windows and doors were open to the river, the coffered ceiling rippling with waterlights. The floor was hidden under ooze and clumps of saltgrass but I could see patches of green marble on the walls. At each corner a grand staircase descended into unsavoury black water.

Opposite the main door was a stout man in a three-piece suit, about twice life-size, lying on his back. One foot had been planted ahead of the other to evoke progress or resolution, but in the supine position his raised leg suggested a dog at a hydrant or a feeble attempt at some exercise routine. The bronze was verdigrised and caked, but the edge of a hard jaw still emerged from an open collar with a strange cravat (a fashion of the future?) around a flabby neck. Lord Copper, I'd guess: the newspaper tycoon, or one of his successors.

I scraped mud and droppings from his face, to find it obliterated. Not the work of time: you couldn't mistake the hatred in the hammer blows, the flattened nose, the punched-in Orphan Annie eyes. The bronze had been smashed like the stela of an ancient tyrant. I spent another hour probing the ooze, scraping for a name or date, but there was none, nor any trace of where one might have been engraved. This Ozymandias who once favoured the world with his opinions was as enigmatic as an Easter Island *moai*.

The drips and echoes, the sounds outside, the parrot calls and hissing wind and trickling waves fell away. His silence and the human silence everywhere were suddenly as wilting and oppressive as the heat. Dead words rose up to fill it: "Where now is your mighty city that defied nature and despised the conquered elements? Where are your steam-engine, your telegraphs, and your printing-presses.... What use is your Bank Reserve?" Richard Jefferies, 1885: like all true pessimists, proved right in the end.

The sun sank behind a tree and the light inside the tower began to fail. If I wanted to make Dartford before nightfall it was time to go.

A pleasant paddle downriver to the bridge — wind and sun behind me, treetops drenched in the honey light of late afternoon. The fear and melancholy lifted; I felt a surge of achievement: London has begun to yield clues.

*Friday, December 10, Dartford*

For the next two days it rained. A gentle soak without wind, the Thames Valley flowing glacially with mist, the towers lopped by cloud. London's still got her pigeons and her fog.

On Tuesday it cleared up and stayed dry until today.

It's taken all this time to ferry supplies and equipment from machine to bridge. At first the schedule was agreeable — I was catching the morning flow and evening ebb like a commuter. But the tides shift nearly an hour a day; by the end of the week I was coming back in darkness. Luckily, the weather turned fine and the ruler of the tides came out and lit my way.

Soon I must move from here to central London and begin a systematic search — at least while my health holds up. A long job, and risky no doubt, but what's the alternative? Stay on the cay like a cartoon castaway until the machine can fly to another age? No, there must be survivors somewhere, in the hills or further north. There are always a few individuals isolated by chance, or genetically favoured. They will have descendants; I shall find them.

A wrench this afternoon to leave the sphere for the last time. God knows how long it'll be and what will happen before I see it again. Tania's machine seems the only chip off our world not a ruin or a sepulchre, though it is haunted by a ghost: its builder's absence, which is a presence. All week as I paddled back to Canvey I half expected to see her waiting for me on the beach; or, when I was taking out the last things, to find her inspecting the device, frowning at my vulgar alterations, wrinkling her nose at the car seat, the computers. Oh Tania, I said to the empty shell, I can't stay with you here at Canvey; there's nothing for me in these swamps, and I can't tow your chrysalis to London. What are you now, what imago?

— 3 —

*Monday, December 13, Dartford*
The pelicans are getting cocky, drilling open boxes and tugging on my tent to wake me up (it was a mistake to give them scraps). A red sky last night, and today's sun is burning away the mist and a few pink ribs of cloud. I'll give it an hour to make sure, but it looks a good day to climb Canary Wharf.

All right, I'll come clean. I probably could have done it before now. The weather hasn't been that bad. I've been putting it off. The truth is, I'm not fond of corkscrew stairs twisting up into darkness: too much like Mantlow Tower.

We were on holiday in Devon — Mother, Father, and I — renting a cottage for a fortnight, a low, cool place with flagstone floors that smelt of earth and wax. On the hill a mile or so behind stood the shell of a mock-baronial mansion — the sort Victorian industrialists built themselves — burnt out many years before. The country was open and neatly farmed, but in the few acres round that house a forest grew: feral lilacs and rhododendrons erupting over the high garden wall.

All you could see of the house was the silhouette of a gable among redwoods and ragged monkey-puzzles. But from a corner of the garden rose a gaunt shaft, like a factory smokestack, except that it was pierced by small Gothic windows and castellated at the crown. Irresistible to a child of nine. Of course I was under strict orders to keep out. A little girl had died there years before, had fallen from a window and impaled herself on the iron of a rose arbour.

That, said Trevor Penhaligon, the local boy who befriended me, was only a tale made up by grown-ups to frighten wets and sissies. Trevor had a portwine birthmark over half his face, which gave him the look of a spaniel. The village children called him Patch. We made a natural pair, he and I: local outcast; awkward stranger. One evening after supper, when the sun was down and the salmon glow of late summer lit the west, Patch took me over the wall. Soon we were standing at the flared base of the tower. The door was ajar, its padlock pulled from the rotten jamb. It was too dark to make out the plaque. Years later I went back and read:

Erected in fondest memory of Canon Charles Ludley Mus-grave and Emily Isabel Musgrave, née Tunnicliffe, on the tenth anniversary of their tragic deaths, March 29, 1887, by their loving children, Everard, Veronica, and George.

The weight of this sad time we must obey,
Speak what we feel; not what we ought to say.
The oldest hath borne most: we that are young,
Shall never see so much, nor live so long.

No other details; presumably it was the fire.

The spiral wooden stairs were firm at the bottom; it seemed an easy thing to climb, to follow Trevor up and up, our way lighted every third turn or so by the evening in a glassless arch. But the roof must have started to go, for near the top the stairs became damp and slippery, the treads sinking under my weight. I said something about going back, but Trevor snorted in disgust. I was the only boy unashamed to play with him and he was going to make the most of it. Bats began to fly about our heads, diving for the window. Just after that I heard a splintering and Trevor's cry.

It could have been worse—he fell only as far as the spiral below. But a nail caught in his eye as he went down, the eye surrounded by the portwine stain.

I was questioned by police and by my father, who shoved me into a huge wing chair and stared at me, saying he could tell infallibly if I was lying. It had not been my fault, but I could see that neither Father nor the police believed me; they thought I'd taken advantage of poor Patch's need for friendship. And not being believed felt somehow worse than being guilty.

Twenty years later I passed through Mantlow on my way to the BAA meetings. Emboldened by a pint or two, I asked about Trevor in the pub. For six months he'd worn a patch, "a genuine pirate job," the landlord said. "And you know the funniest thing? Nobody ever called him Patch again after that. But he lost the eye."

I asked what he was doing now.

"Who wants to know?"

"Lambert. David Lambert."

The man carried on drying a glass. Then: "My Lord! Weren't you the young bugger put him up to it? That's right. David. Posh little kid from Kent." He put down the glass and regarded me. "Don't you see him in here, sir?"

Farmers standing by the fireplace in jerseys and gumboots, wives at a corner table, three skinheads playing darts.

"No, I can't say I do. But as I recall it was the other way round, I'd never have gone in there if it hadn't been for Trev...." I turned back to see a glass eye on the bar beside my pint, and a pursed dimple of flesh, like an anus, laughing at me mirthlessly.

"Trevor! My God. I'm sorry, I didn't.... All these years. And you've...."

He picked up the eye and reinserted it. (An extraordinary little sound it made.) "Plastic surgery. Marvellous, innit? Compensation like. Gain one patch, lose another."

I wanted to say: It was your idea; you led me on. But it was useless. He had his story; I had mine.

*Canary Wharf, mid-morning*

A good paddle, though I got drenched by a shower not half a mile from here. I pulled in under a tree on the south bank to wait it out, but the heavy drops soon found me and the flies were so bad I had to press on (I've been scratching myself raw). I hadn't gone far when the sky brightened and I caught something flickering in the shade of a broad guanacaste. It was Graham! — his dark bellrope of a tail twitching at the tip, the rest of him reclined leopard-like, chest and belly on a thick horizontal branch, paws trailing luxuriously in mid-air. He blinked at me as if he knew me well and shook his head; he'd had enough of the weather too.

*The summit, early afternoon*

A rough climb. Mosquitoes in the lower levels and bats everywhere, thick as bunches of grapes in the torch beam, to say nothing of their smell — a skunky, armpit reek that took me back to Mesa Verde and Tikal. It was good to know Graham wasn't in the building. He seems friendly enough, but maybe he's just not hungry yet.

Fire doors sealed the stairwell landings, their hinges seized so it was impossible to get out. As I went up I counted floors, wondering if any of the higher ones would be accessible.

Floor 29 was — its door missing, presumably torn off in the disturbances that wrecked the building at the end. I managed to force my way into a suite with all its windows intact. No dirt, no vegetation, no bats or pigeons. To walk in there was to walk back five hundred years. The sun was pouring in, and even though the glass was too streaked and pitted for a decent view I could imagine

I was being shown round by a rental agent. The only mark of the centuries was the usual wino's beard of stalactites and an answering stubble on the floor. No trace of interior walls, false ceilings, decayed office furniture, or business machines. The suite was empty; and it always had been.

The evidence so far — unused office space, an apparent lack of new building on the skyline, the maturity of the forest — suggests that things can't have kept going very long after I left. Was there a military coup (*ARMY OUT!*), a shortlived rally by some would-be Belisarius? Something along these lines seems inescapable. But I still have no inkling of what's happened to the people. Even if the population fell ninety per cent, as it did in the Americas after Columbus, there should still be several million in the British Isles. Where are they?

Warm air and welcome light blew down the stairwell as I neared the top. Rootlets brushed my face and grew thicker until they formed a mass of vegetation gripping a raft of steel rods. The last three or four yards were difficult — like wriggling from a pothole under girders and glass.

The pyramid roof has fallen on the floor below. I came out onto a sort of battlement, a square of blowzy trees inside eroded crenellations that were once wall sections between the top-floor windows. The wind is alarmingly strong up here, sucking and blowing in sudden squalls — the tower yaws and shivers like the mast of a tall ship.

It took some machete work to get a clear view through the tossing leaves around the edge; now London is spread below me like a promised land. Enough down there to keep an entire nation of archaeologists busy for a century, though it's impossible to say where the ruins begin and end. What I see is a rippling forest canopy, broccoli-green in this light, broken by the serpentine Thames — much wider than in our day, lozenged with silty islands

—and patches of moth-eaten velvet which must be swamps. About two miles away the City skyscrapers rear up like super-structures of a battlefleet sunk at anchor, chips of glass and metal winking in the sun as if people were signalling from wreck to wreck with mirrors.

Several of the tallest—Stock Exchange, Natwest Tower, and others whose names I never knew—fit more or less with memory. Enough on their feet, I think, to rule out a bang. But what sort of whimper? Their rotten state, their mad wigs and cavern eyes, the sagging steel and triumphant greenery are a shocking sight—like finding a person you last saw young and healthy dead in the bushes and decomposed.

Stepney and Poplar, almost in my shadow, show a faint pattern under the treetops, a houndstooth of roofless gables. Somewhere down there is Waterloo Villas, Bird's last abode, where I stood a mere three weeks ago; in another world.

His phone was cut off and he hadn't answered my letter. I'd had to doorstep him, taking a bottle to enlist his help with the machine. You know how fond Bird was of smoky malts from the western isles. At Cambridge, when you were away or too busy to see him, we used to sit up in his digs—that attic overlooking slate roofs and a slice of Jesus Green—smoking hash and roll-your-owns, drinking Talisker, listening to jazz, putting the world to rights, the whisky enhanced by a background waft of scorched oil from Dominators and Speed Twins in pieces around the room. (When it came to machinery, Bird was a deconstructionist.) He talked a lot about you in those days, was terrified he'd lose you, couldn't imagine what you saw in him, feared it was only his music. But I think he was wrong there. I remember one evening when we'd been flogging lithos for a fortnight or so and you and Bird had just become a number. He turned to me as you were climbing in the Jag with your canvas bag, jerked his thumb your way and let out one of his tight little laughs: *She's slumming wiv me.*

At that moment a lorry went by, catching your smile in its lights. A drawn smile; a remark too close to home.

Stepney was rough, so I went to see him mid-morning, when the bad apples would be sleeping it off. He had the ground-floor flat, his window fortified with iron bars and a scribble of razor wire. All but two panes were plywood squares. The door was simply a steel plate with three locks in it. On the street outside was a skip full of stinking rubbish and the unredeemable parts of several bikes — bent frames and wheels. I rapped until my knuckles hurt. No answer. I pulled a piece of pipe from the skip and beat it on the bars like an eighteenth-century visitor to Bedlam riling up the lunatics. A wan face appeared behind a pane. A hand made some sort of gesture. I heard bolts being worked back behind the door.

Bird had a towel round his waist. His health hadn't improved in the seven months since I'd seen him at your funeral. His black hair, which used to gleam like the feathers of a starling, was dusty and lifeless. If anything his face had shrivelled, emphasizing the way his eyes were a bit too close together: the pinched, foxy look of the East End, centuries of malnourishment, of watching for others' carelessness. His skin was grey as a cat's beneath the fur. He stared for a long moment, then recognition dawned. "Christ it's you. Come in quick." He pointed to the door of the front room. "Go on in. Meet Moira. I'd introduce you but I've got to have a shit. Moira! Meet David." He vanished down the passage.

The house smelt of old curries, dirty laundry, cigarettes doused in beer bottles, and Bird's signature bouquet of motor oil. When my eyes got used to the gloom, I saw his Parian bust of General Gordon on the mantel and a young black woman sprawled face down on a mattress with purple sheets. Bird came back, picked up a battered sax, and blew a Coltrane riff in her ear. "Moira! Meet my old mate Dave." Moira shuddered, coughed, stayed as she was.

"Let the poor girl sleep. It's you I came to see."

"What can I do you for? Motor repairs? Never did get on well with the infernal combustion engine, did you? After your time."

"You didn't get my letter?"

"Might have. Dunno. Sorry." He waved a hand eloquently round the room. "I've been too fucking busy, and vice versa." His eyes darted over me from head to foot. "Shit, Dave, are you all right? You look like I feel."

We sank into winded brown corduroy armchairs on either side of the gas fire. "Speak for yourself," I said.

"Appearances to the contrary, I'm okay. Basically. Nothing life-threatening. Just booze, bints, brain damage — the usual suspects." Bird found a pack of Camels on the coffee table (a milk crate), flicked up a smoke, shot me an invitation, saw my refusal, lit one for himself. I gave him the whisky. He pulled the cork and threw it away. The same old Bird — never opened a bottle without planning to finish it.

Unlike that evening in April, conversation began to flow. There seemed to be tacit agreement that the unpleasantness over you was behind us; that now you were gone we were linked, not divided, by your memory. I still don't know if you ever saw Bird again. He wouldn't say and I didn't ask. We said very little about you, though you were our toast: *To absent friends.* He talked rather frantically about other women, perhaps as a way of not talking about you — how he'd moved in with a Japanese cellist for a while after Cambridge; how he'd lived with his mother until she died; and a busy little ménage with two Catalan poets, one short, one tall, whom he called Vita Brevis and Ars Longa. I got the impression these women had been supporting him more often than not. I hadn't known about his degree.

"Fourth class, Dave. That's what the bastards gave me. You know what that means."

"Cambridge's genteel expression for a fail."

"Shh! *We* know it. But there's still a few parts of the world *don't* know it. Almost had a nice little thing sewn up in Kentucky. Teaching post at the Jefferson Davis School of Political Science. Yanks still value the classics, bless 'em. And they don't understand our system. They were going to pay my fare and all. But at the last minute somehow the punters catch on this Cambridge bloke's a bit of an artist. Good fing I had the bikes to fall back on. Did well there for a while. You'd be amazed what a clapped-out old Beeza was fetching in the right circles. Never mind a Vincent, and I had one. Some old fart took down a Black Shadow for a winter rebuild years ago, did the work to the last nut and bolt—paint, chrome, new seat, the lot—and his ticker stops before he gets it back together. Picked it up from the widow for a song. Got the beast running—Christ it was a hairy ride—and sold it to a rice king for five million yen. Now all that action's fading away. No one's got the ready any more. Not even the Nips."

Bird's tale ended with teaching music and drama part time in a nearby secondary school.

"You know me, I'm warm, I'm tactile, I'm hands-on. And I've always liked black girls. Can be a problem when you're *in loco parentis*."

I looked at Moira, at the narrow hips.

"Jesus, Bird. Not one of your pupils?"

"Not any more. I got bounced, didn't I? *Qualis artifex pereo!*"

"What did you think you were doing? Don't you worry about the law? They're rough on this sort of thing nowadays."

"Long story, Dave. Boring. Tired of going on about it. Basically, I was in the wrong *loco* when in walked the *parentis*." He sucked heavily on the cigarette, exhaling a blue nimbus in the grey light from the window.

His jazz hadn't gone much better. Bird was never good at stroking the right people, not to mention his temper, and you know how other players resented his easy brilliance—the corrosive jealousy that genius wakes in the merely talented. Kicked out of all the best spots, he'd started playing at the Ramrod, a gay pub off Gloucester Road.

"The front was full of Hell's Queers. Leather boys. You must have seen their bikes outside. Some of 'em had money. In the back was this brilliant combo—two or three old black guys from New Orleans, drummer from Nigeria. I'd go down there every week of a Sunday. Just get up on stage, blow a little horn. Jamming like. Thought we were going great." Bird paused, looking up forlornly at the grimy panes.

"One day I've stopped for a pint. Three blokes come up from the audience. One grabs me sax, another takes the pint out of me hand and pours it down me horn. And the fird one says, 'We'd like you to practise somewhere else, man.' That was months ago. Haven't blown a note in public since."

I gave him my story, parts of it true. The eternal student, a little dealing in scientific Victoriana. I didn't mention the museum job or the inheritance—remember how he used to go on about "those poncey trustafarians" swanning around Cambridge on private incomes? Not that I was in that league.

"You'll like this one, Bird. A prototype human torpedo from the Boer War. I need a hand to get it down to the river and float it. In working order. Mint. Just a matter of winching it on a loader and dropping it in the water. Nothing too hard."

"Why me?"

"Don't know anyone else to trust with this. Somehow I don't make friends the way I used to. London's not a friendly town. Never have liked living in London. Never will." I paused. "It has to be kept *sub rosa* till the right moment. Not even the Imperial War Museum has anything like it."

Bird's head gave a little start. He tapped another Camel from the small hole in the pack and smoked with his jet eyes on the floor, intense, as if hoping to catch a worm. "Where'd you nick a thing like that then?"

He really thought I'd stolen it, reminiscing about some night we'd gone drinking years ago and pinched a cannon from a village green. I told him I'd acquired the torpedo from an American collector who'd picked it up at an estate sale, then decided he couldn't afford the freight to L.A. I'd fallen in love with it and made a swap for some early scientific instruments. I was going to stage a publicity stunt to raise money for industrial archaeology.

"We'll launch somewhere round Mucking or Canvey, somewhere no one's about. We'll make sure it's all right, then tow it up to Parliament. I'll need you to run the towboat and the video camera. Britain's Iron Heritage and all that. Stuff like this is hot right now. Might work into a job eventually. Might be room for two if all goes well. If you're not interested, no problem. But you'll have to promise you won't breathe a word."

"I am so, Dave. I'm interested. I'm your man."

On the following Monday I rented a lorry with a hoist and waited for Bird at the mews. He was right on time and looking better. "Who owns this dump, then?" Eyes bouncing around covetously.

"The Yank. Wait till you see his workshop."

I showed Bird into Tania's room. He let out a low whistle. He walked around the time machine, squatting to inspect details. "If this thing's as mint as you say, how come you've slapped all this junk on?"

"It was a prototype. No one's ever used it. The operator rides inside. I'm not keen on going to the bottom like a stone." That seemed to satisfy him; he stepped back.

"You know what it looks like?"

"A sea-urchin wearing headphones? A chestnut with the King's ears?"

"Nah. It's a virus. Seen 'em on the box. *Weird* fings, mate. Little death-stars."

Time to climb down. A last scan, sketching in landmarks, noting compass bearings for things I might want to visit (I don't want to flog up here again). And no, in all the time I've been up here I've seen no clearing, no boats, no rising prayer of smoke.

But there is one thing rather odd—I missed it until just now—a green line near the horizon some miles to the north. Straight, regular, paler than the forest. I'm fairly certain it corresponds to the position of the M11. Elsewhere, further off and less well defined, are other slim green dashes, all in locations that could be motorways. They seem far too trim—too crisp and straight for all this desolation—as if something were keeping the old roads open to the city's edge.

*December 15*

I wish I'd left things there, climbed down and gone straight home to my blustery camp at Dartford. But there was one more discovery at Canary Wharf, a discovery I wish I hadn't made, though perhaps you'll be able to view it with detachment. After all, you're both a professional and a member of the great majority yourself.

It was on the tenth floor. My eyes were more accustomed to the dark than they'd been on the way up, and I noticed another open fire door, apparently melted by a welder's torch. The suite beyond the door was dark, which was why I'd missed it earlier. The puzzle of darkness where light should have been was easily solved—all the windows had been crudely filled with breeze-blocks. I found a loose reinforcing bar and did a little judicious wrecking in the cause of science, sending blocks crashing through the foliage to the river below. Bats mobbed me like Hitchcock's birds, but as I let in more light they withdrew to the stairs.

They say archaeology's a gift, an instinct; that if you have it you find things, if not you don't. There was a secret here beneath the guano. I poked with the bar at a slight mound. Things inside. I began to dig—slow, filthy work, the fresher droppings alive with golden cockroaches. What I found was this: a group of skeletons, human, muddled together. I exposed five individuals, all adults, four male, all with shackles of rust around wrists and ankles. Prisoners, obviously. Hostages, maybe. Captive captains of the *Daily Trumpet?* That would be going too far.

Among the bones was a coin—a cheap aluminium thing I nearly mistook for a French franc of the 1940s. But the face value was £1,000. Corrosion had eaten into the date—all I could read was twenty-something and part of a Latin inscription on the rim: *Henricus IX D. G. Rex.* Henry the Ninth. What can have happened to William? And the European currency?

In one of the windows a crude stove or fireplace had been improvised, with a smoke-hole to the outside. Charred objects had survived quite well among the ashes; you could see that some of the firewood had been furniture. And I found burnt bone. Like you, I never much cared for bones, didn't get along with old Piltdown Bartle (I wonder if it was true what people said: that he was a surgeon by training who'd lost his nerve on the living?). I skipped a lot of his tutorials, but I did pick up enough to know that this was human. And that the long bones bore unmistakable signs— carving cuts, splits for extracting marrow—of butchery. Canary Wharf was the scene of a cannibal feast.

Perhaps the authorities decided to starve the attackers out, and this was the reply. Elsewhere beneath the guano perhaps lie traces of a final shoot-out and an answer to the nagging questions. Why weren't the victims given burial? Where are the bodies of their captors? Why wasn't the place cleaned up? I've no idea. One can't presume decent or even rational behaviour at the end of history.

Jumping to conclusions? You're welcome to draw your own; I'm merely setting down my findings as faithfully as I can. If you disagree with my interpretations, that's your right and perhaps your duty. Without further digging, digging of forensic thoroughness, I can't say more about what happened in those rooms. And I have neither the equipment nor the stomach.

I haven't set foot there since, and don't intend to. Hardly professional, I know. We were meant to show sang-froid around the dead: we pulled teeth from fleshless jaws, sawed into skulls, tore pelvises in half for the telltale clot of childbirth. Yet I can't face that room again, can't shake from my mind the events we might have seen in England had we stayed and lived.

## — 4 —

In confronting these ruins, Anita, you run the gamut of bereavement. I tell myself I've taken it in, that it's happened and that's all there is to it. And as soon as I think I've begun to accept this, and that it can no longer ambush me, a tinamou mourns in the woods of Rotherhithe and it's as if I'm being notified of the death of everyone and every place and every thing I've loved, for the first time.

Yes, I'm drinking too much, but with only one case of rum in the world there's little chance of turning alcoholic. The best refuge is in keeping busy, leading a full and unexamined life. So what next? Go looking for Tania? Make an expedition to the strange green lines? Or be practical—set up a room of my own somewhere, a base to explore from, to write and work, until I find some people and some answers, or must sail away defeated?

No contest: Tania first. To Midnapore Mews.

This morning—a fine Thursday morning, still and cool, drifts of mist lying thin on the water—I set off at first light, having bivouacked on a sandy island at the edge of the Leamouth everglades. The Thames was quiet, though the jungle whistled and fussed with waking life. I paddled steadily, my chest parting sheets of vapour carrying a faint smell of allspice from the shore. Beyond the Isle of Dogs the river became sluggish and reedy—it has spread over

Limehouse basin and much of Wapping—until it narrowed at the Tower of London. Here I passed a cliff of mediaeval rubble above a shady inlet with a gap-toothed turret back among the trees.

Of Tower Bridge one pylon stands, vined and jagged like a folly in a lake. Near the top sat a big untidy nest. An osprey dropped from it and swooped over the water. I turned the glasses on her just in time to watch a talon graze the surface and seize a fish. It wriggled free as she fought for altitude; the river boiled, and I saw the lateen sail of a shark. My boat suddenly felt thin as a paper bag.

Little of London shows itself through the walls of foliage that hem the river, the presence of buildings merely implied by bulking forms beneath the greenery. All the bridges have fallen, leaving only stumps and cutwaters. St. Paul's, if it exists, was entirely hidden, but the Monument poked up briefly—like a limestone candle melted at the tip. The lovely Gothic face of Parliament has slipped into the water, exposing a warren of chambers colonized by mynah birds and (I think) some trogons. Yet Big Ben still stands —like something from Angkor—huge fig trees in its clockless eyes.

I continued west as far as Lots Road power station, which used to drive the Underground, recognizable as a heap of bricks at the mouth of Chelsea Creek. My flat had been just behind it. I thought I might retrace the familiar route between there and the mews, where I worked so many months in hiding like a saboteur. But this part of Chelsea is impenetrable: a great fen, as it was before London, the mansion-blocks knee-deep along muddy creeks and overgrown canals, the effect serene and eerie, an Edwardian Venice. "Streets full of water, please advise."

It took me half the morning to cut a way in to the King's Road, where the land begins to rise above the tidal zone. From there I continued on dead reckoning, following ridges of fallen brick and long façades running through the forest, porches and bay windows endlessly repeated. It was easier to scramble over rubble than to wade or cut through the rushes and canebrakes thronging the streets. Even so, a mile took an hour. The trouble was fire; the mature forest burned here a few years ago and new growth is rioting for dominance.

At last the Brompton Oratory looked down on me like a blackened Hindu temple. My pulse was racing. Suppose this fire had had human origin? But if Tania or anyone else was living here now, wouldn't there be other clues: a path, an echo of wood being chopped, a feather of smoke, a cooking smell?

That *AD 2500* which so affected me when Powie found it scratched on the brass now seemed a feeble hope. And the lack of month, day, and hour raised a philosophical conundrum I'm not competent to answer: if she's here in this same year but our arrivals were not precisely synchronized (how could they be?), do we exist in the same time at all? How wide is the breaking wave we call the present? Is it generous and forgiving, or as evanescent as a particle of light? Will it be possible for us to detect each other, to meet; or do we inhabit similar but discrete temporal planes, as remote as Hiroshima at 8.14 on the morning of August 6th, 1945, from Hiroshima at 8.15?

Perhaps the best I can hope for is some trace of her, as one finds an empty glass, a fragrance, a warm and dimpled cushion in an empty room.

Map and *A-Z* in hand, I retraced the steps I took that December night a year ago when I first followed Wells's instructions. There's little doubt in my mind that I found number 26. If I didn't, then it lies in a fallen section at the middle of the block. It makes no difference. The ruins are just like any others: a doorway, a chimney, an overgrown scree of mortar and bricks.

No one has been there; no woman-made lightning seared those trees. Mine was the first human foot in centuries. The one thing perfectly preserved was a short piece of the backyard wall, standing to its original height—even to the detail of a bottle stump on the coping where a bird or animal had torn away a clump of epiphytes.

I sat on a stone and wept, unable to believe, still hoping that in reality she *was* here; that somehow we were simply out of phase, hidden from one another by a veil it might be possible to tear aside. This is not the first time in my life I feel mocked by omen or coincidence. So often events seem steered by a hand I can never identify but whose shadow I sometimes glimpse, stealing from the corner of my eye like an assassin. What if I'm dead as a dodo and this green hell of fear and doubt is an undiscovered country of the mind? What then? I do not believe the self lives after death, but that doesn't mean the moment of death cannot, subjectively, be everlasting.

*December 22, Tower of London*

Without the hope of Tania, slim though it had been, London felt even emptier than before, denied any possibility of human presence except the weight of its millions of past lives pressing in on me from the dark banks of the Thames. It was night by the time I got back to Dartford after a four-hour paddle, the last two under the stars. I couldn't stop at the Leamouth sandbank where I'd camped the night before; there were paired rubies in the torch beam — the eyes of dozing crocodiles.

It was high time to find a decent gaff. I decided that it had to be somewhere *old* — already old in our day, some venerable place with honest-to-God masonry and undiminished character. On Saturday, before the sun got strong, I went back to the inlet where I'd seen the Tower of London.

The first thing was the ravens; not the dusty old clergymen who used to dance about like shamans and peck sweets from children's hands (they could hardly claim to have saved the kingdom), but the white-necked raven of the Serengeti. And snail-kites and buzzards living on what the tide casts up each day. They watched me approach between low cliffs of rubble where the river has cut through the Traitors' Gate and outer walls, opening a sheltered inner bay. Here I beached the kayak at the root of the Bloody Tower.

The other buildings — those I've managed to explore so far — are in pretty good shape except for the Jewel House, which lies strewn about the inner bail in suspiciously large chunks, as if it did not expire from natural causes but was blown up by someone with designs on the Crahn Jools.

A choice of lodgings was available. The vaulted basement of the White Tower was whole, but hardly pleasant. I went in far enough to see old cannon lying like crocodiles in ooze and darkness. The chapel on the floor above was more promising, a Norman gem. Light streamed in through high clerestory windows; pigeons streamed out. The trouble, though, was that the lower windows had been blocked with solid concrete.

I thought Sir Walter Raleigh's old quarters might do (they did him well enough for years). I remembered how comfortable they'd looked when Uncle Phil took me there as a boy — fireplace, four-poster, the table where Raleigh wrote the *History of the World*. (Phil was worried about the iron maiden, the rack, the wax heads on pikes — the horrors every boy demands to see. *It's all right, Davy. People don't do things like that any more.*)

Unfortunately the roof and floors, which were made of wood, are gone. But the Wakefield Tower next door — restored in Victorian times with massive if rather *faux* stone vaulting — is nearly perfect. Even the stained glass is more or less intact. I had to smoke out a few squatters: wasps in the ceiling, and a family of large rodents (coypus?) who were keen enough to leave when they saw me. They lacked Graham's cool. Which reminds me that I miss that big black puss. Long may he prowl the Isle of Dogs.

It's taken the rest of the week to ferry my stuff from Dartford and get settled here. I've replaced missing panes with glass from other windows, and cleared the chimney of nests and mortar. I've woven a hat from corozo palm—something between a sombrero and a coolie—and made a cot of withes to keep my sleeping form above the mice. Soon I'll have a log desk and stool. There's comfort in walls a thousand years old when England died; walls to which the past five centuries are merely a quiet senescence after a full career. True, this place has seen its horrors—beheadings, tortures, child murders—but they don't touch me.

The moat is a good spot to fish. Hooked a fat piranha there yesterday—scion of some suburban aquarium—easily caught with a mouse. In short, I'm king of the castle.

My card: David Lambert, Fisher King.

*December 24, 2500*

Christmas Eve: a bad day, as always; as you know. I thought of you pouring whisky macs that night I told you why. Naked on the hearth rug, your hair in the firelight, your pipe smoke racing up the chimney. *Eleven! I can't imagine how one copes with a thing like that. It must have been ghastly. Eleven! You poor thing. How did they. . . . I mean who. . . . How were you told?*

God knows I tried to reveal more, tried to unlock ten years, to answer you with the trust you offered. But the door wouldn't budge. I want you to know I'm sorry, as sorry as it's possible to be. It was that, wasn't it, which eventually drove us apart? The one hermetic part of me I wouldn't let you see. I think at first it drew you—everyone likes a mystery, a sealed chamber, especially an Egyptologist. But a mystery without hope of revelation becomes a mere frustration. You dug and dug and there always remained that one immovable deposit between your curiosity and bedrock. I suppose I worried that if you ever opened the tomb you'd find it empty: nothing but some shards, some dust; perhaps a curse.

This is hindsight; there was no inkling then. We weren't even at the end of the beginning. We were still exploring each other, our pasts, our bodies, a transubstantiation of the friendship and lust we'd had in Egypt into love. *You make me mad. I want to laugh. I want to scream. I want to leap into the air. I can't ever get enough of you. Isn't that what madness is?* And I: Only love and madness stop the world like this.

We'd been to the Hangchow for dinner (you said MSG always made you horny), had had a few before we got there, couldn't understand the waiter. I thought he was asking if we'd liked *Weir of Hermiston*, which seemed odd but not impossible. Then he beckoned you to the side of the room and there was a glass box with a handle—the "Wheel of Fortune"—which you turned and won a free dessert. Later, when we made love, you showed me your new tattoo, your Aten, a sun with hands—a small red sun high in the smooth white vault beneath your arm. How I loved to snuffle there, forbidding you deodorant so I could lick like a calf. The taste of you: salt and sun and sex, a Caribbean holiday that never lasted long enough.

You thought it was so tough, that tattoo. Bird was right about you being a slummer. Bird was dark and dangerous, a sublime fallen angel breathing magic from his horn in smoky basements, and you were tired of white bread and Pimm's No.1 on the lawns of Dominica, tired of haw-haw polo players and tennis pros and fleery laughter.

And I? What was I to you? No jazz, no Cockney; merely the mystery of a sealed tomb? But I know you liked the bit of bent in me. You'd put on that French voice—*Ooh-la-la! You Eenglish man are all so keenky*—and let me bind you with silk and spray my pearls in your hair. Oh Anita! What we have and what we lose.

Christmas Eve: *eve, evil*: a child's etymology that the grown-up can't unseat. And every year gets worse, because the scab on the heart sloughs away and the time-wound becomes more tender, more inflamed. Why let myself be dogged by anniversaries and portents? Why keep a calendar no one keeps, as dead as *ab urbe condita*, the katun wheel? "The years like great black oxen tread the world, / And God the herdsman goads them on behind, / And I am broken by their passing feet."

I blame the Oyster (feeling faintly disloyal as I type this on its keys). I switch it on, and there they are—month, day, hour, minute, second—the last syllables of recorded time, ticking from the life-hoard one by one. A life nasty, British, and likely short; though at the moment I'm feeling better in this London than in mine. I should jettison clocks and calendars, all civilization's miserly accounting, but how do you keep a journal without dates?

As a child, after my parents' accident, I would read and reread famous tragedies—the death of Harold, the murder of Atahuallpa, the knifing of Marlowe, the loss of the *Titanic*, the Crucifixion—and hope that just once the ending could be different. Did the arrow always have to land in the king's eye? Did Pilate always have to wash his hands? Must the drunk start his car at precisely *that* instant on *that* Christmas Eve?

Why couldn't time be halted for precautions and repairs? Why could I rewind a tape but not an hour? Why was the past adamant and the future clay? Was that fair? Time was a tyrant; time was the one to blame. I began keeping a dossier on my foe.

"Time is the devourer" (Ovid). "Time is the rider that breaks youth" (George Herbert). "Time is a great conference planning our end" (Djuna Barnes). Then there were the mystics: "Time is a spring that flows from the future" (Unamuno); the sceptics: "I do not believe in time" (Nabokov); the utilitarians: "Time is nature's way to prevent everything from happening at once" (Anon.); and the hopeful: "Time will run back, and fetch the age of gold" (Milton).

Childish, I know. But it does no good to wear a ghost shirt; the bullets kill you just the same. So I keep track of time. The condemned usually do. He is our jailer and I plan to run.

*Boxing Day, 2500*

A Yukon Thaw got me through. All Christmas Eve night I sat on a parapet above the river, overlooking the finger of Tower Bridge, drinking rum, drinking silence, dissolving beneath Orion, thinking how the lights of the world are out and the heavens blaze unabashed; how silence and darkness went extinct beneath our orange domes of noctilucent cloud, the sirens crying of a thousand private tragedies: an overdose, a rape, a fire, a suicide.

Only stars now, only frogs and crickets and my maudlin songs in this unanimous night. *Stille Nacht, Heilige Nacht.* No illuminations, no carol singers, no last-minute shoppers and hot chestnut stands, no Bing Crosby, no Norwegian spruce in Trafalgar Square, no cold, no sleet, no sermon, no turkey, no King's Speech. No policewoman asking for young David, stammering out her news.

Around midnight a light appeared in the east and moved towards me. (I know what you're thinking.) One or two Flying Dutchmen still sail every night: spies with no one to spy on, Telstars with nothing to tell. It passed over Greenwich, seemed to hang above the circumcised tip of Canary Wharf, then fell from orbit in a last bravura of white and blue and red.

In the small hours of Christmas morning, the rum low and a damp chill rising off the Thames, there came a sound like asthmatic breaths, soft at first, then impossibly loud, from somewhere behind me in the City. Gruff, aggressive barks. Breathing again, urgent, like a pervert on the phone; then a roar from a long throat vibrating through the ruins.

It stopped; the charged silence worse than the noise.

Then an answering voice, miles away—from Westminster or Knightsbridge—and others in a rasping crescendo, as if the dead city had awoken and begun to rage at its fate. I was frozen, as I was when Graham first slipped from his lair. Then, sobering, I knew I'd heard a voice like this before: howler monkeys; harmless windbags.

On Christmas Day I found them roosting in a tall calamander beside St. Paul's, large rufous animals with worried faces and question-mark tails. They could swing freely through the canopy but I'd had a difficult journey along the ridge from Tower Hill.

Anywhere within range of a high-rise is an assault course of fallen debris. Glass shards, embedded in young trees and taken up as they grew, stick out at hand or eye level like the obsidian teeth of Aztec swords. Tempered sheets have shattered into heaps of uncut diamonds, but a few, planted on edge in soft ground, lurk whole among the leaves like giant razor blades. And there are subterranean hazards — the flooded wormholes of the Underground, caved in here and there, and London's natural watercourses breaking free from the tunnels to which they were banished by Victorian engineers. You'll be walking along and suddenly the street drops into a sinkhole or a whirlpool. So much for leisurely antiquarianism. These are not friendly ruins; nothing from antiquity was sown with booby-traps like these.

Cutting my way along Eastcheap and Cannon Street was laborious enough, but Watling Street was blocked off by four or five squat columns set close together: obvious fortifications, tarted up with chevron bands cast into the cement. Beyond these, along both sides of that narrow street with its fine prospect of Wren's dome, were vast concrete slabs, faceless beneath the undergrowth, stepping back and up like Babylonian terraces, without doors or windows or stairs. Bunkers, I'd say, with a Hollywood veneer.

Still, it was worth the trek to have St. Paul's to myself on Christmas Day. Poor St. Paul's, overlooked by banks and trusts, jostled by Mammon. Yet God was having the last laugh: the cathedral is graceful in decay; the parvenus, stripped of their plate and plastic, look like multi-storey carparks from Beirut.

Wren's temple is whole except for the dome, scalped like a boiled egg. Aesthetically this is not disastrous. Light spills in, splashing on marble and mosaic. The smoked colours and gold tesserae; the angels; Christ in his majesty above the vanished altar—even in decay these give the place a Byzantine glow I had forgotten, as if this were St. Sophia, not St. Paul's. It was the private touches brought me back to our London and our time: *TO GENERAL SLIM, 1891–1970, REMEMBRANCE FROM A YOUNG GIRL IN SINGAPORE.*

A cloud passed over; then the sun reached into the broken dome where willowy trees rise like wisps of incense. Seen from the dank hull of the nave, this shaft of light was a Blakean vision—I expected to see the Ancient of Days and to hear angelic choirs. But the only sounds were shivers of wings from martin colonies along the Whispering Gallery, and a drip falling with curious regularity as if from a water-clock.

In the light and stillness and grief, I wished that I believed. That I could kneel this Christmas Day and utter the last prayers in St. Paul's. *God so loved the world. . . .* Did He really? I remember telling Uncle Phil I couldn't believe in a god who'd killed my mother and father and dumped me in the hands of therapists. How can it be, I wanted to know, that one faith is true and all the others lies? For it seemed obvious, even at twelve or thirteen, that religions are artefacts. If there was a universal truth, why hadn't God sent his son (or his daughter, for that matter) to the Chinese, the Tasmanians, the Tahitians? Why leave so many peoples so long in darkness, only to receive the good news from murderous conquerors? How odd of God to choose *only* the Jews.

And Uncle Phil, lubricious vicar: *So, David, you desire to reason with God?* And he answered me with Original Sin and Free Will, all the sophistries spun by theologians to darn their emperor's clothes.

People like us, my faithless love, are too clever by half: too smart to kneel; not smart enough to shape a credible alternative. Off-the-peg comes so much cheaper than bespoke. (Did you hedge bets at the end? Or was St. Osyth's merely a practical choice?) All

I knew was that I didn't know. The best I could say for Jehovah was that he withheld important information and never doubted that his ends were worth his means.

And Phil: *The Jews have a saw, Davy: Man thinks; God laughs. You can take it as a précis of the Book of Job. Where wast thou, David, when I laid the foundations of the earth? Declare, if thou hast understanding. Canst thou bind the sweet influences of Pleiades, or loose the bands of Orion? Canst thou draw out leviathan with a hook?*

The weather stayed warm and dry for New Year, the midday heat intense. The monkeys slept in their trees, few birds sang, and the insects kept up their syncopation, which like the sound of a mountain torrent or the sea becomes the stuff of silence. I explored the riverbanks by boat and on foot, adding crayfish and mussels to my diet. I have a palm-heart salad every day (any young palm will do); also coconuts, dates, bamboo shoots, wild banana, avocado, and an occasional sugar-cane binge. Not bad for a castaway.

The things that I miss don't bear mentioning; the list's too long, beginning with you. It's not even safe to think of cocktail olives, bath oil, shaving soap, a pint and a pork pie. I've thrown my razor in the Thames.

Most days I go for a swim in the small bay below my tower, where there seems little risk of sharks or crocodiles (piranhas, I've been told, don't bother you unless you have an open wound; I hope that's true). Then I sit out the heat on my private beach, shaded by the palm who gave me my hat, listening to cicadas: jets on a runway, ambulance sirens, squeaky tappets: the ghosts of our machines.

I've made several archaeological forays, but with meagre results. More is underwater than I thought; a lot of what looked like forest from Canary Wharf is really swamp. The soil is a web of roots, cables, and reinforcing rod—clotted with glass, burnt plastic, broken tile, corroded engine blocks. I need pumps, coffers, saws, screens, lifting gear, you name it; all I have is my machete, a folding shovel, and a worn trowel from our Alexandrian days. I've turned up two drowned books and some computer files, but the books were like wet bread, the disks blistered and warped.

Fires seem to have gutted every building, probably at the time of abandonment. London must have looked like the Bronx. In general, older structures survive the best. From the Saxons to the Edwardians, architects built for ever, not thirty years. And instead of taunting gravity with composite materials, they enlisted it to keep their buildings up. High-rises, though immensely strong, are being undone by chemistry. Rain and groundwater seep in, leaching minerals, precipitating salts, slowly unfleshing the girder frame of its cement and glass. Several rusty skeletons teeter above the jungle as if abandoned in construction. But some, at least, were not unfinished — for I'm certain one is Centre Point.

*January 6, 2501*
Twelfth Night, when the Santas come down and the tinsel goes back to the attic.

I went to the moat yesterday with hook and line for dinner. It was too early in the afternoon and not even piranhas were biting, but I didn't mind passing a quiet hour or two. After some time there came a muffled splash; ripples spread from under a low branch on the far bank. A rise? But it hadn't sounded like a fish. Solitude was beginning to undermine my wits, such as they are. I'd been haunted again by the notion that things were not as they seemed; that I'd landed not in our future but in something else; that I wasn't alone at all, and even now as I fished I was in the grip of some omnipotent vivisectionist, as obscure to me as the scientist to the white mouse. (And what is that but the human condition?) "The world was not dead, but I was mad...I was labouring under the force of a spell, which permitted me to behold all sights of earth, except its human inhabitants." Mary Shelley. The Quixote syndrome again: madness induced by a diet of tall tales. And what Cervantes didn't see is that the good books drive you madder than the bad ones. Who is sane after Kafka? After Orwell? "If you want a picture of the future, imagine a boot stamping on a human face — forever."

In dreams I see the terror on the faces in Canary Wharf, and all the other faces that I must be trampling every day. And whenever my thoughts run this way they arrive at those smooth green roads. Who goes there?

More ripples spread across the moat, as if from a hidden swimmer. It was silly to feel safe behind this ditch; anything could have escaped from zoos and safari parks. Cats may not like water but they swim; so do bears and wolves. Then movement in the shrubs behind me; and before I had time to react, a dark figure bounded up. No mistaking that truncated ear.

He lay down a length away, his ear swivelling to any sound. I dared not move, so carried on fishing, and soon had a piranha. Graham watched me bring it in. I wasn't sure how a wild puma should look, but he looked hungry — I could count ribs — though his coat was glossy. I clubbed the fish, cut off its vicious head, offered the rest. Here puss, catch of the day, I said in a voice I hadn't used in years, the voice I used for Merlin. Two topazes gave me an idol's jewelled stare, but there was reason behind them, probing my intent. The cat blinked, got up, moved forward casually, stopped short. I laid the fish on a stone. He looked at it, another patient stare. Then a paw stretched, claws came out like blades and sank into my gift. He sniffed it carefully — so like a cat (so unlike a dog) — suspicious, responsible only to himself for every move.

Graham ate slowly, crunching, shaking his head, shooting me glances as if to ask whether I meant him to have it all. I said: You're a panther with manners. He got up, moved closer, flopped down with a sigh, his back almost touching my leg. Without thinking I reached out and stroked his flank, and he turned his head to me and closed his eyes. I worked my hand over the bony shoulderblades and powerful muscles, up the loose skin of the neck, my nails deep in the thick fur. For a while he let me do this; then he rolled over and I saw that Graham was a girl. Or a lady of a certain age.

What could I call her now? Barbara? Helen? Penthesilea? Tobermary? (These were among Miss Frank's repertoire.) No, the world was mine to name; she'd stay Graham. I stroked her chest, the button nipples grazing my palm. She began to purr—a sound so loud and regular that for a moment I thought I heard a motor in this city, and my scalp crawled off and scuttled down my back. What if some intelligence was here, coming for me with a rapture to the stars, to a laboratory, to a small tiled room? This way led to needles and electrodes, to people in smug possession of instruments and overweening truth. A weight fell on my shoulder. *Come along quietly now, Mr. Lambert.*

But it was only Graham's paw, telling me I'd stopped and not to stop. Graham, light of my life, thank heaven for thee!

*Sunday, January 9, evening*
Sunny now for several days. On Friday I went after the big story, a Rosetta stone to break these silences. Where else but the British Museum? You may say I chose to dig there for sentimental reasons and you may be right. The last place we were together. A blowy April afternoon, wet pavements, sad light, car tyres singing in the rain. We met at the cafeteria before I took you to Heathrow, and I snapped a picture of you next your favourite piece, the Sekhmet found by Misses Benson and Gourlay. I have that photo on my mantel in the Tower; they gave it to me at the hospice where you died: a lion-headed goddess in stone like polished ebony, and a pale young woman, her hand fluttering at her throat, her heart already on the Nile.

I reached the BM by paddling to Clerkenwell Road up the

Fleet—a river that's reclaimed its surface rights. This involved a portage around rapids foaming over rubble and girders but was easier than going all the way on foot. I made a few probes in the main galleries on Friday afternoon, enough to show that the museum wasn't holding much beyond debris from the roof and floors. It must have been cleaned out before abandonment. Is everything in some *Führerbunker*? Or was the place privatized, rationalized, made competitive? Perhaps your Sekhmet sits beside an Orange County swimming pool, as desolate now as the sacred lake she left behind in Karnak.

I camped overnight inside the roofless walls—a night filled with every cry and scurry in the hinterland, until I put my headphones on and fell asleep listening to Grieg. Yesterday morning I thought I might try somewhere else (my St. Pancras haunts, perhaps?). But then I had a stroke of luck: just outside the BM I found a tall mahogany that had been downed by a storm some weeks ago, heaving up a great wheel of soil with the roots. A free lunch for an archaeologist. The hole was full of water but not too deep for my shovel to strike a smooth, hard bottom: original pavement. So I had a complete stratigraphic sequence.

The oldest layer was a heavy clay flecked with charcoal and ash. It held chips of glass, the neck of a whisky bottle (Johnnie Walker, from the shape), a flattened plastic jug, a charred piece of motor tyre, several cables, pipes, and architectural debris from the museum portico. The best find was a stack of magazines. Charred and waterlogged, they'd evidently been part of a bundle awaiting delivery or recycling. It took an hour to peel them apart—like trying to separate sodden *mille-feuille* pastry. In the middle was a single legible scrap, with what appeared to be a title. Something on Flaubert? I set the leaf to dry in the sun, and the print became clear: "I am Madame B. Ovary." I'd unearthed the *Reader's Digest*.

Issue of October 2026. The date doesn't prove much—the

magazines could have been ten years old when some dentist threw them out—but it shows that civilization lasted at least one generation after my departure (if you accept *Reader's Digest* as evidence of civilization). I went back to the tree-throw and picked the roots clean. This produced more glass, some corroded costume jewellery, two shell-cases from a rifle or light machine-gun, part of a willow-pattern gravy boat, and the well-preserved sole of a running shoe —a Puma, no less (see what I mean about portents?).

The finds may be unforthcoming and banal, but their very banality is reassuring. There can be no doubt: these are relics of our future. I am no victim of madness or enchantment; there are no lubberfiends following me around. The wigglies haven't munched my logic yet. I'm simply alone in this colossal wreck.

*Tuesday*

Well, not quite alone. Graham appeared within minutes of my getting back to the Tower. Her materializations have become more frequent, often synchronized with my mealtimes, though she doesn't come every day. I always feed her something—you don't want a hungry cat that size. I don't begrudge her; fish are easily caught and it's so good to chat to her. Another *amour fou*, like you and Tania.

I've looked her up:

*Felis concolor*: American panther, puma, or cougar, largest of the purring cats. Weight, to 80 kilograms. Length, to three metres from whiskers to tip of tail. Must make a substantial kill once a fortnight to sustain itself. May range 100 kilometres in a day when hunting. Sometimes seen in suburban areas of North America, due to shrinking habitat. Feral individuals reported in parts of Britain and Europe. Though solitary and stealthy in the wild, captive pumas often form affectionate relationships with humans.

Before leaving the British Museum I'd probed the muddy water in the pit more thoroughly, dislodging a metal sheet on the bottom. It seemed to be galvanized steel, about the size of a wall poster, with a thick plastic coating on one side, opaque and crazed by ancient sunlight. I could see faint letters — perhaps an advertisement — so I thought it worth bringing back here for some restoration. Left it soaking in palm oil for two days, and the text has come up better than I could have hoped. Not quite a Rosetta stone, but — well, what do you make of this?

PROVISIONAL GOVERNMENT OF
HIS MAJESTY'S ARMED FORCES

Emergency Regulations Decree 81
*Summer Evacuation of London Area*

All ambulants with private transport are required to present themselves at ringroad evacuation points (see below for the E-Point nearest you) according to the following schedule: PID cards A-D Monday, April....
[*illegible*]
...ing special assistance telephone 0181-666-5....

E-Point 23: South Mimms. Evacuees will leave their vehicles on the hard shoulder and crawler lanes of the M25 between junctions 23 an....

...minded that no private vehicles will be allowed in the former Welcome Break Services carpark or on the A1(M) north of the M25. Army transport will be....

Embusing times:
Each hour, on the hour, from 0800 to 1800 hrs.

Maddening that there's no date. But Welcome Break! — where we used to stop for cappuccino — the dreadful military jargon — even the same telephone code — these have to be echoes of a time not far from ours. I don't like the sound of "ambulants." What were they fleeing? Heat, presumably, but was that all? Perhaps I'm jumping to conclusions again, but I hear desperation in the tone. Was it really a seasonal migration to the north? Or a final evacuation, the abandonment of London passed off as a temporary measure?

*Friday, January 14*

The diarrhoea is back, and a persistent chill — maybe just too many avocados and wild chillies, but it reminds me I'm on borrowed time. To the green lines soon. I've done enough round here for now.

It's been raining on and off for several days — a brash tropical rain. The sky is blue and hot, then in late afternoon tall clouds pile up like spray above a great waterfall and empty themselves in an hour. I spend these afternoons on my cot, *Temps Perdu* in hand, Billie Holiday or King Oliver on the headphones to banish my imaginings and the sound of the wind scratching itself on the ruins.

Some evenings I light a fire. Graham's lost her fear of it; she lies beside me, stretched out to absorb the warmth, purring like a diesel while the howlers roar from St. Paul's and Parliament Square.

— **5** —

*January 18. Noon, near Walthamstow*

I left at first light and paddled into the dawn's red eye, shooting briskly through the shadow of Canary Wharf, chilled by a breath of fog and the sound of the river slopping in Lord Copper's lair. There was an uproar of parakeets and mynahs feeding in cohune palms, but I was lonely. Graham stalked off abruptly last night while I was stuffing tent and sleeping bag in the kayak, tail low, not a word or a nudge. Packing always did upset the cat.

It was good to turn away from the Thames, north into the Lea. On these new waters—the shoals white with egrets, the wind calm, the river steely beneath the strengthening sun—I felt new life and possibility. Isaak Walton would enjoy a cast today.

I've decided to follow the Lea to its meeting with the M25 ringroad near Waltham Cross. About twenty miles—say eight hours upstream and four back—which will mean camping somewhere tonight. I used to row this river as a schoolboy, further up near Broxbourne. If my memories are relevant at all, it'll be nice and lazy all the way, and I should get a sight of the motorway embankment across the valley some time before reaching it. Just as well.

The countless road and rail bridges that used to span the lower Lea haven't been much of an obstacle so far. Only two above the water—very frail—little more than tissues of rust buckled and sinking under leafy burdens. The Hackney Marshes were more difficult, a scribble of channels, sloughs, and oxbow lakes. Twice I backed out of dead ends, once I had to portage, and several times I was forced to get out and drag the boat through a bog. I've spent the past half-hour picking off leeches.

*Evening*

A bothersome headwind fought me all afternoon, sweeping down the grassy floodplain that was once King George's Reservoir. Here a buck lifted his dripping chin to watch me fearlessly, as if he'd never seen my kind.

Once beyond the reach of tides—i.e. above the general rise in sea-level—I came upon pieces of old weirs and locks. Huge stones from barge canals, some still in place, and a massive iron footbridge fallen on end, with a date cast into the metal: 1835. My job would be a lot easier if the twenty-first century had dated things like the nineteenth. But we rather went off Anno Domini after the

First War. Simply a reflection of the change from stone to concrete, the death of the mason's craft? Or something deeper, all those millions dead; civilization less cocksure than it was before 1914?

The light failed before I reached my goal. I've had to settle for a cold supper and an early night on a hill above the east bank, behind some small remains marked on the map as Pick's Farm.

What a busy, trodden land this was; you have only to spread out the kilometre squares of the Ordnance Survey, and there's hardly a one without a house, a road, a works, a railway, a graveyard, a moat, a Roman road, an Iron Age fort, a Bronze Age barrow.

England hasn't lain this fallow in ten thousand years.

*Wednesday, January 19*

Up at dawn with no breakfast but a handful of rice and a cup of cold tea made yesterday morning. No fires till I'm certain I'm alone.

The suburbs have slipped behind and I'm in Epping Forest now — the first woods that were always woods, though temperate species have yielded to the same tropical specimens that have taken over London. A sad little forest this used to be, diced up by roads, besieged by bungaloid growth, its elms long dead, its oaks and sycamores suffocating in the smog, a dumping ground for murder victims, mattresses, and toxic waste. "The woods decay, the woods decay and fall, / The vapours weep their burthen to the ground, / Man comes and tills the field and lies beneath, / And after many a summer dies the swan."

The woods are tall and stately now. I'm beginning to feel exposed again, a frontiersman on Indian land. A bowman in the trees could riddle me like Saint Sebastian.

*Later*

A fog lay on the river and its marshes for several hours. I was glad of the cover, moving in an envelope of silence. At Enfield Lock were more traces of the industrial past: arches striding beside the water like a Roman aqueduct — the old Enfield rifle works, I think — and on the other bank a few brick houses of the people who had made the guns that made the British Empire. The walls threw back a damp echo of the paddles. I went on through Rammey Marsh, seeing nothing but reeds and a solitary wartime pillbox.

No doubt horrors are hidden all around: beneath those cedars, behind that factory wall, the jungle feeding still on ancient death, recovering the bad debts left by man. "The many men, so beautiful! / And they all dead did lie: / And a thousand thousand slimy things / Lived on; and so did I."

Suddenly it was there: a steel beam high above me like a battleship across my bow. In the soft focus of the mist it seemed untouched by time, and for a minute or so the implications had me shaking. Then I heard a roar ahead, went on into the gloom under the bridge, and saw the river boiling over the wreckage of a fallen span.

Cliff-dwelling birds — a species I don't know, darker and bigger than swallows — buzzed me from a colony beneath the roadway. I drifted back and beached on a sandbank. No crocodile tracks, thank heaven. The concrete piers were blackened (by campfires?) and sprayed with graffiti similar to those at Canary Wharf: hand prints and monograms; in-crowd stuff, the work of gangs who had lived or camped under the bridge.

The moment of truth. Up the embankment through a mass of guava bushes to the motorway's edge, and when I walk onto the ancient road my boots sink into a perfect lawn.

The sun was starting to burn off the mist. Blue showed overhead and heat began to lick my face. The green runway — for it looked exactly like a jungle airstrip, the sort of place suspicious cargoes might change hands — lengthened as a breeze chased tatters of fog into the treetops. I stepped back into the shadows, took out the field-glasses, and scanned the M25. It made no sense. The forest stopped where the shoulders would have been; something prevented it from rooting on the carriageways. Here and there trees were down across the grass, but they were all recent falls. It seemed that as soon as anything fell and decayed, the grass swallowed it like quicksand.

The turf bore no tracks, no spoor, no marks of any kind. Nothing, not even deer or rabbits, seemed to be eating it or using it. Despite its oddness the road had the same air of long dereliction as everything else. I fell on hands and knees to inspect the lawn. This I regretted instantly. The turf was bristly and sharp, composed of narrow tapering leaves, no longer than my thumb, engrailed with barbs. Tiny daggers drew blood from my palms, stabbed through my jeans, and ripped from the cloth reluctantly when I stood up. I walked to the middle and probed; the machete sank to the hilt. I made a round cut and carefully removed a cone of sod. I probed in the deepest part of the hole. The blade sank almost another length before striking an old surface.

The stuff was like peat, only drier—bright green on top, brown and mossy below—if you picture moss compact as steel wool. It seemed to have built up over centuries, to have become so firmly entrenched that no other plants could dislodge or invade it. But what was it, and how had it taken over to begin with? Why was it here? Why *only* here? Nature craves diversity—there's always a community of species, as anyone who's tried to keep a weed-free lawn will know.

This line of thought rang a bell. Ecolawn? Ecoturf? Supergrass, or was it Supersod?

Never mind the name. A notorious scandal in the late nineties, though I doubt you caught it in Egypt. I followed the story closely, a sort of Ralph Nader morality play. Bio-engineering companies had raced to develop an eco-friendly, zero-maintenance lawn. No fertilizer, no weedkiller, no pesticide, no watering, no mowing. All very laudable. The first to patent it would make a killing. The golf trade alone was worth billions. The idea, as I remember, was to incorporate genetic material from nitrogen-fixing plants so the grass could feed itself from the air; to build in pest resistance from natural insecticide producers such as derris; to incorporate the ability of certain trees to poison their rivals at the roots; and to eliminate the need for sprinklers and mowers by including genes from drought-tolerant species and — most controversially — the self-limiting properties of human pubic hair.

There were reports of foul play involving Big Oil and Briggs & Stratton — the sort of thing you used to hear about lone inventors who made cars that ran on tapwater. Only this time there was something in it. Labs were broken into, databanks hacked and destroyed. One of the inventors, an experienced scuba diver, drowned on holiday with empty tanks. Another stalled his car on a railway crossing. An entire Japanese research team died horribly after feasting on fugu at a retirement party.

Despite these setbacks, a successful prototype was produced. But legal challenges kept it off the market. The grass scared ecologists as much as the petroleum and chemical interests. Greenpeace got huge anonymous donations for a Keep-the-Grass-Off campaign. The Earth Commandos, thitherto regarded as the Baader-Meinhof of the Greens, got calls from high-rent lawyers offering to represent Ecolawn saboteurs *pro bono*. It might, they argued, become the most noxious weed in history.

It looks now as though those fears had some foundation. The stuff would seem to be a green desert, shunned by every other life form. Presumably it colonizes any broad, well-drained expanse of paving. (London streets must be too wet and narrow.) Or it may have been seeded here deliberately as a protective cover when the writ of the motorcar no longer ran.

But long live Ecolawn, I say. Instead of having to chop my way through England, I can stroll along these highways like a Monday golfer.

*Bedtime, back at the Tower*

A big black creature was stretched out on my cot when I got home after a stiff paddle. (I discourage this. Her claws have already punctured the air mattress once. Only a cheapie from Britomart but irreplaceable all the same.) She ignored me for half an hour, then looked over her shoulder as if to say, Who the hell are you and how dare you disturb me? Finally she yawned a great yawn — a most alarming sight — and went outside.

*Thursday*

Five weeks now in this unreal city. A downpour the last twenty-four hours. The vault above my bed's begun to drip; water streamed down the chimney-breast and stained your photo, the only one I have. Despite the weather, Graham's staying away as if to punish me for going on a trip without her. As if she knows my plans before I do.

What plans? Stay in London, doing the Flinders Petrie bit until I drop? Go to the time machine and move on? Or follow the green highways to the north? *When you're faced with choices, Davy, and you can't decide, always take the boldest course.* Father's maxim. How do I recognize the boldest course? *Easy. It's the one that frightens you the most.*

So to the north it is. If I'm alone I must be sure.

But how I'll miss my cat!

— **6** —

*Sunday, January 2, Middleton School, Essex*

The days longer now — ten hours of light, yet still mild except at noon.

I left London on the twenty-seventh, after a week of getting ready — drying fruit, smoking fish, bricking up my room in the

Tower. Of the supplies from the old world I still have oats and rice, three dozen packet meals, four and a half bottles of rum. The difficulty will be to carry enough—along with clothes, tent, gun, and Oyster—when the Lea dwindles to a stream and I have to leave the boat. Other travellers to the future were more fortunate: the things of civilization theirs to commandeer, conveniently in working order. Verney took wagons, Jeffson fired up locomotives and rode the rusting rails. But I've only boat and legs to get me around, and a big question-mark over my health.

How was it with you, my love? A steady slide, or did you have periods of remission, when you could believe—as I do sometimes—that the sentence was lifted or had never been pronounced? The experts reckon that life expectancy after diagnosis of CJD is anywhere from three months to ten years, which tells you how much they really know. I've been doubting again that I'm ill at all. It could be psychosomatic, just a way of tricking myself into making this wild voyage. But then you are dead (and Bird was hardly well). If the world's as done for as it seems, I'll fly on and on until I reach a time of gleaming wards and magic bullets and free medical care, and when I find it I'll come back for you, bring you the cure, or take you there; and we shall live again!

I repeated my journey to the M25, doing it in one day now that I knew the route, though the boat was lower in the water. Rain and darkness were falling when I reached the motorway bridge, so I camped where others had long ago, on the bank beneath the span, my firelight playing on faded boasts and fears: *I BEEN TO HELL AN BACK AN DONE IT TRIPPIN; YOUR BORN, YOU WAIST TIME, YOU DIE; LIFE IS A SEXUALLY TRANSMITTED DISEASE.*

In the morning I discovered that the embankment across the valley floor holds back a large body of water. Bridge piers and fallen beams have trapped debris, forming a giant beaver dam of wreckage, silt, and vegetation.

This made for a troublesome portage around uprooted trees and skeletal boats and lorries, but then came an easy glide across a shallow lake among great flocks of waterfowl—ducks, geese, cormorants, several kinds of stork, and sacred ibis. Gaunt walls of half-sunk factories were mirrored on the water, large nests like failed baskets on every windowsill. There was no wind at all, and I remembered you in your pink cap and sunglasses beneath a limp felucca sail at Kom Ombo.

At the head of the lake the forest drew in and the Lea returned to its ancient course—the stretches I rowed as a boy. Well, I coxed. You wouldn't have looked at me twice in those days. I was a shrill little fart working the tiller, yelling exhortations at the galley slaves. *Feather your blades. In! Out! In! Straighten your backs. Pull! (pause) Pull!* It can go to your head when you're fifteen. My own physical culture was confined to the half-hour cycle to the boathouse. I used to enjoy that ride down the lanes through Galley-hill Wood into streets with young mothers, mysterious in their command of procreation. I also did a little sculling (more for solitude than exercise) in a hull no wider than my hips, along quiet reaches where the willows met overhead and private gardens swept intimately down to the banks. I'd glide past lawn swings, upturned dinghies, empty summerhouses—and wonder why their owners never found time to be there.

*Know the trouble with you, Lambert? Your attitude. No school spirit. You don't give a damn about much, do you?* Guilty as charged; especially on school spirit, that fatuous chauvinism they tried to force in our souls like a dark flower. I didn't give a toss whether the school won or lost, but I enjoyed regattas because there was usually a beer tent. In the ivory light beneath the canvas nobody noticed I was under age.

On one of these beery afternoons, my career with the Second Eight ended abruptly. I'd thought we were safely out of the running, but a team had been disqualified and we had to race again late in the day. By then my belly was full of Guinness and my brain circling like a goldfish in a bowl. We were the middle boat of three abreast, a tricky feat of navigation at the best of times. I clashed oars with one team, I clashed oars with the other, the coach livid on the towpath. (Old Spiker: another Phil, though less sanctimonious. He liked teaching juniors to swim, their perfect tummies on his palm. I can see him now, the stoop and trollish grin, skin fiercely browned by a tanning lamp, a leathery ball dangling from his trunks like the nest of a weaver-bird.) We dropped behind but my troubles weren't over. Trying to cut a corner, I swung too close to a jetty. Ours was a lovely old shell of Honduras mahogany, the wood thin as veneer. A submerged piece of iron peeled it like a carrot and we sank to our necks.

Little to see from all those years ago: house foundations here and there, smothered in vervain and wild sunflower; a wall in the varicose grip of a fig; a rat's nest of cables and vines where a power station used to be. The river led a sleazy double life as recreational resource and industrial sewer, water like gravy and a yellow lather at every weir and outfall. Now it has the clarity of jasmine tea. I remember the narrowboats (converted barges, and others meant to look like barges), their TV aerials and frilly curtains, names like *Owlingale, Samoa, Thistle Doo*. I remember the white-faced coots and black-faced swans — the coots' metallic squeak, the swans' tails like white flames on the water when they dabbled — and mallards and moorhens and Muscovy ducks, all of whom somehow managed to scratch a living among chip packets, beer cans, sodden crusts, and iridescent blooms of diesel oil.

Those birds are gone, their places taken by egrets, snail-kites, herons, a morose synod of vultures in a dead tree. Lizards and parrots stir the foliage, the nostrils of floating crocodiles pimple the surface like paired bubbles, and there's a thick fermenting sweetness in the air from windfall mangoes on the bank. You look at this new Floridian Lea and wonder how long it will last. Is this the new order of the next ten thousand years? Or does the greenhouse still run wild, hotter and hotter by the century, threatening an Earth like Venus, where the sky rains vitriol on continents as hot as molten lead?

About noon a shape began moving along the bank, keeping unwelcome pace with me like Spiker on his bike. It followed for a good half-hour, often lost in thickets, given away only by a snapping twig. Then I heard a tributary ahead; whatever it was would have to turn back there or show itself.

A body dived and swam towards me. A black head with a single ear.

I pulled in at a beach, she bounded over, and we rolled together in the sand. Christ it was good to see her, all wet fur and catty smell, her hard pads on my neck, the claws scrupulously withdrawn. I can talk to you and I can talk to Bird; I can hear myself speak and sing and recite sublime poetry and utter gibberish; but Graham is the only living creature I can touch, and who touches me, in this whole world.

I'd hated leaving her behind, unable to explain. For days before I left she hung her head and tail, seldom purred, went off her food, and once she threw up on my floor. It never occurred to me she'd follow. Now that she's here it seems obvious that she would. This is well within her range. No doubt she roams this country often by a web of trails I know nothing of. Maps and memories tie me to an ancient land that's increasingly imaginary. I live in the human shadow; she in the unmanned here and now.

The sun was fierce, the forest and its creatures sinking into midday torpor. I sank into nostalgia, my benign disease. Middleton School, the exile of my teens, had stood on a hill above the east bank. Only a mile away. Why not? A perverse nostalgia, this, because I counted little in the place's favour except that for eight months a year it got me shut of Phil. I beached the kayak securely, took my pack with the tent and other supplies in case Middleton proved a good spot to do some digging. One of the few places the moderns did erect inscriptions was on the self-important walls of pricey schools.

Graham ran ahead along a deer path, stopping every so often to see if she was leading where I planned to go. It was easy to follow with occasional machete strokes. In less than half an hour we came to an overgrown road—too narrow to be carpeted with Supergrass, merely a ridge running through the trees—the back road from Waltham Abbey to Bumble's Green. It was harder to find the drive to the school gates, but ten minutes later we reached a redbrick tower—one half of the Tudor gatehouse. The other half was spread beside it in a recent heap, beneath a stand of glossy-leafed trees.

I used to like this building, all that remained of the original Middleton Hall where Queen Elizabeth had stayed in 1596 to watch the first performance of *A Midsummer Night's Dream*. (Or so they claimed.) The house had suffered the fate of many Tudor halls: pulled down in the eighteenth century to make way for a grandiose Augustan mansion with formal grounds. This bankrupted the Middletons—descendants of the playwright Thomas M—and in the 1820s it became a school.

Graham and I strolled across the old playing-fields, on the leafmould of the forest floor, the trees huge and spaced, nourished by soil never bent to Father's way of farming. The rugby pitch where I'd spent many a cold afternoon in the compulsory cheering claque was ringing with cicadas. *Come On Schooool!* Red-faced shouts and tribal chanting: *Romans came, and passed away, Normans followed, where are they? But here we are, and here we stay. Vivat Middletonia!* But the cheering was jeering (which is all that song deserves) and it came from a troupe of temple monkeys in the chapel ruins. They didn't like the look of Graham, softly softly down below.

Father was a grain grower with an Oxford voice who loved no animals except a pair of Irish setters. He tolerated a small number of stray cats in the outbuildings to keep down mice. Only Merlin, whom I'd rescued as a prickly marmalade kitten, was allowed in the house. Merlin was short-haired, aloof, intelligent—smart enough to avoid the poison that thinned the outside cats during Father's purges of unwanted life. Cats with matted coats, cats strangely contorted by their deaths, accusation in marbled eyes. *One day you'll thank me, Dave, old chap. When you're my age and this place is yours you'll see that what I do is for the best.*

Father was high church, like Mother and her brother Phil, and a true believer in the eschatology of agricultural science. *Don't you think, Davy, that since the good Lord gave us brains he meant us to use them?* Each year brought bigger machines, new seeds, new smells and bells to save the burgeoning world. *Stay away from that stuff, Davy, it'll burn you from bottom to breakfast time.* The man from ICI was a family friend, a confessor, an exorcist of tares. Portentous names fell from his lips like biblical mysteries. My mind construed a mystic link between paraquat and paraclete, Sion and Cygon. By their deeds I knew them, by pious odours and harsh judgements.

As I grew, places I loved were erased: hedgerows shorn, bracken ploughed, streams and ponds abruptly changed—minnows and tadpoles floating like cigarettes, then never seen again. *Don't go in that water, Davy, it's not safe any more.* Victory in the war with the newts. Such victories often took place when I was away at prep school. I'd come home after three months' exile and nothing would be said. Mother and Father would exchange quick looks and whispers in their private code. I'd set off to fish, to net butterflies, to listen for nightjars. And find a wood reduced to an archipelago of stumps, a field thrice its previous size. Another annexation by the Adult Empire: their world larger; mine shrinking away like Indian territory.

I suppose this is how one falls in love with the past, with the perverse desire to arrest time, pluck out death's sting, overturn the victories of the grave. I struck guerrilla blows for the secret places and small creatures that are the siblings of an only child: sugar in the chainsaw, dents in hydraulic cylinders, a cocktail of cement and roofing nails down the red throat of the new combine in whose name so many annexations had been carried out. *David, you're a little Luddite. We can't have little Luddites on this farm. You know we can't. What'll we do with you? Do you want us to send you to Borstal? You know what that is, don't you? It's a prison for bad boys who don't respect other people's property. If you think you don't like school, David, I know you won't like Borstal. Take my word for it.* And I: I wish you were dead! I wish it was you who was dead!

That winter it came true. By the verdict of my own heart I am guilty of parricide, and no one is ever acquitted in that court.

The chapel cloister had had a wall of granite slabs engraved with names: headmasters and head boys, cricket and rugby teams, distinguished scholars, and of course the Old Boys blown to bits in war. Several of these were still in their original position, though the cloister was roofless now, its arches heaved apart by trees. Graham sloped off while I worked, leaving me with the dead.

THE GREAT WAR FOR CIVILIZATION, 1914–1918.
REMEMBER THE SONS OF MIDDLETON SCHOOL WHO DIED
IN THE SERVICE OF THE KING FOR FREEDOM AND JUSTICE.
WHETHER PEACE OR WAR BE OUR PORTION,
LET US SERVE AS THEY SERVED.
THEIR SWORDS ARE IN OUR KEEPING.

Two slabs remained — Able to Babcock, and Richards to Slater — enough to estimate a total of five hundred names.

It took some heavy prying in the rubble to unearth another

inscription, older, from the heyday of nation and school—*Zulu War, Afghanistan, Egyptian Campaign, China Expedition, West Africa, Soudan, Boer War, Tibet Mission.* Scarcely a year without its sacrifice from the 1870s to the 1900s, the tides of empire charted in blood (to say nothing of the enemy). I must have seen all these before, of course, though I can't say I remember them. Who reads war memorials? It's their presence that's important; the content is well known. The idea that they gave pause to the living wore rather thin, didn't it? All those splendid monuments in Flanders, the mortar barely dry between the stones, and Europe wanted more.

Beyond the "Great War for Civilization" was another list for the second act. Another five hundred names.

The day ended before I found what I was after. Twilight began to drown the forest like a fluid welling up from the ground. I'm writing you these notes in the eastern portico of the quadrangle, perched on a fine Ionic capital, Oyster in lap, fireflies winking in the woods.

*Later*

Awakened from an evening doze by frightful caterwauling, the sort that used to come from Miss Frank's unruly garden. I called for Graham, afraid she'd met a rival puma or some other enemy. Or maybe she was getting laid (but surely Graham's a bit long in the tooth for that?). The noise came closer, echoing from unseen walls across the square of forest in the quad. She appeared with a gangling body in her mouth, a monkey. This she leaves at my feet.

"I hope you don't expect me to cook and eat that, Graham." A purr like an idling bus. *Felis concolor,* largest of the purring cats. Exactly what she expects. I've been feeding her for weeks at my home; she's returning the favour in hers, the jungle that is England.

There's nothing wrong with barbecued monkey from a gastronomic point of view. The trouble is moral and aesthetic. Too close a relative. With the hair singed off it looks like a famine child. But it would have been churlish to refuse. We devoured the thing, and I'll say this much for higher primate: it's better than anything I remember eating during the four years I was here. I can still smell the cavernous dining hall, a dank *mélange* of rancid butter, unwashed boys, wet grey flannel, droppings from resident sparrows, and the reek-of-the-day, which hit you in the face when you walked in. The worst was kidneys every Monday: like boiled underwear.

Back to bed with the headphones on. One of Bird's old favourites, Bechet's "Petite Fleur."

*January 30, 9 a.m.*
A night of dreams: the sort from which you wake certain that daily consciousness is a fraud and the real life is the one you lead asleep. Shakespeare was here, directing his own play beneath an oak by the old brick tower, and I was Bottom in a donkey's head—bloody inside and all too real—and Pyramus was singing:

> Now I am dead,
> Now I am fled,
> My soul is in the sky. . . .
> Now die, die, die, die, die.

And then I met Titania in the moonlight, and she had your voice:

> The human mortals want their winter here;
> No night is now with hymn or carol blest. . . .
> Diseases do abound.
> And thorough this distemperature we see
> The seasons alter. . . change
> Their wonted liveries; and the mazèd world,
> By their increase, now knows not which is which.

And this same progeny of evil comes
From our debate, from our dissension.

Titania had an accent, a Russian accent. WS was at my shoulder, shaking his script under my nose. *Don't you see, you Ass? She's not Titania, she's Tatiana.* With that I woke, convinced I had the key to Tania's whereabouts.

My familiar was out hunting while I slept, though she can't be hungry after last night. This time she's caught a — well, either a small emu or a cassowary. I've saved a drumstick for dinner and left her the rest. "So," I say at breakfast, she regal on her haunches, watching me without ulterior motive (porridge holding no interest), "you mean to be my provider, do you?" And she slowly blinks in pleasure. Extra rations mean I can afford another day or two here. A promising site, and I — unlike every archaeologist in history — have the advantage of knowing it in life.

*Evening*

Success! Three fallen slabs and many smaller fragments of a twenty-first-century inscription — with dates. It seems that Latin, and jingoism, came back in vogue:

DULCE ET DECORUM EST PRO PATRIA MORI
Emergency Home Guard
2033 –

There must be a thousand names, though the list is incomplete, the end date never inscribed. They were carved in batches, the earliest in alphabetical order, the latest done crudely in childish letters such as you see on terminal Roman work. Some were women: *Amanda Blackwell 14/5/2020 – 9/8/2036.* Only sixteen years old. The last is an Arnold Wu, who died November 15th, 2039, aged seventeen.

Nothing else came to light in the cloister. All I know is that a war or civil war went on at least seven years and ended badly. Was this Home Guard the work of the same military regime that evacuated London? And against what or whom was it guarding?

*Monday*

Today I had a look at the main building, the eighteenth-century mansion that held the library, headmaster's lodge, and School House, oldest and largest of eight or nine. (Can't remember all the others—Raleigh, Hobbes, Younghusband—a predictable roll of monomaniacs, adventurers, and charlatans. A few years after I left I heard that the old sanatorium, no longer needed in an age of vaccine, had become Thatcher House for girls.)

A storm or tornado downed trees on the cricket pitch in front of the main hall, perhaps a year ago. I had to skirt chaotic new growth, nearly falling into a ha-ha full of bullhorn acacia and fire ants. The building must have burnt long ago with ferocious heat, enough to warp iron joists that carried inner walls, but the shell was complete, even to its chimneys, ornately pedimented like Italian tombs among the treetops.

The house has a central well—a sort of airshaft or pit— dividing the older parts from Victorian kitchens, laundry, and staff quarters. This was faced with white tile, like a morgue, to make the most of daylight draining coldly from above. I remember the way sound rang in there—shouts and oaths and the rattle of delivery carts, shrill and layered, disembodied.

There was nothing here to burn, so most of the tile survives, ringing again when I called out, startling a flock of kites or ravens high in the foliage—their sudden wingbeats loud as helicopter blades. Near the bottom, moss clung to the white glaze; yet I could make out something greener under the green. A little scraping exposed a crude mural in fluorescent spray paint—a parade of human figures in profile. Hard to make out at first, but as more

came to light I could see they were bent, crouched in fear or degra-
dation: women and children menaced by demons, cringing prisoners bound at the wrists, red drops raining from tortured fingernails.
And a much larger seated figure done in red, facing out towards
me, about twice life-size. The Devil.

He had a ram's head, small crosses for eyes, and held a staff
in each hand. His throne was made of human bones — like something from a fourteenth-century woodcut of the Black Death. A
frieze of red pentagrams covered the walls around, strangely bright.
Above was writing: SATAN AWATES; MY ONLY FREIND THE END;
and, unmistakably, NOW DIE DIE DIE.

You will know the vertigo induced by that last line. A "Dunne"
foreshadowed in my dream? Maybe. But let's put this one down to
coincidence, to the local Shakespearean tradition. I have enough
trials without Dunnes.

Despite the quotation, I doubt this was the work of Middle-
tonians — at least, not while the school still functioned. It must
date from the 2040s or later, after the tablets in the cloister fell
silent; after the fire. And that gives these misshapen words a sinister authority, as civilization's last comment on itself.

*Tuesday, February 1*
Very glad of Graham's company last night; she's all the darkness
I need.

The library was a disappointment this morning — nothing but
loam and ash and mosquitoes. The wood that was books is wood
again: bamboos as thick as drainpipes and a banyan like a mushroom cloud above the walls.

My luck was better in the headmaster's study, where my
younger self had several interviews that ended with a caning from
"Half" Nelson (a nasty little martinet with a voice like a peacock's
and the constipated eye of Madame Blavatsky). Some of the room's
contents must have dropped through the burning floor into clay.

This was wet at the time and has remained so, except for a thin layer fired in patches by the heat. We were spoiled by Egypt—if Egypt had been as wet as England, hardly a mummy or papyrus would have survived. But waterlogging in airless mud like this is the next best thing to dessication, so I kept going all day.

At first I found nothing informative, only charcoal, bits of Delft and Wedgwood, a corroded nodule that might have been the movement of a grandfather clock, and an oddly familiar Shiva Nataraja. Nearby, perhaps thrown down during renovations and trodden into the clay long before the fire, were several LP records, three with legible labels: *Best of the Boston Pops, Lawrence Welk's New Year,* and *Zamfir Blows Your Mind.* These can only be from Nelson's personal collection; the school must have inherited it when he choked to death on the dessert course at an Old Boys' dinner.

In mid-afternoon I made a more significant find—several small copper sheets, materials for some hobby or perhaps early photographic plates. With these were traces of a filing cabinet and thin layers of paper debris in plastic folders. Most of the paper is decomposed, but two sheets accidentally sandwiched between copper can be read.

What I have is a handwritten letter (Wot! No e-mail?) to a boy from his mother, who underlined her prose so there could be <u>no</u> mistakes in its reading.

Old Rectory, Whitwell,

HC/143-6553

Mr. Jeremy Unwin,
Churchill House, Middleton School          March 26, '31

Dearest Jeremy,

This is the <u>hardest</u> letter I've ever had to write in my <u>whole</u> life. I want you to know that the news your father and I have to communicate in no way reflects on you. We know you've worked <u>very</u> hard at Middleton. Your results and your captaining of the Second Eleven have made us <u>very</u> proud. Our friends all say how lucky we are to have a son like you. (If we haven't told you so before, it's only because we didn't want it going to your head.)

As you know, I've been out of a job since the Health Service closed. Your father's salary at Landrover is now, in real terms, a <u>quarter</u> of what it was when you started at Middleton three years ago. If it wasn't for Army contracts, they would have gone the way of Hyundai and the rest. The bank now holds a <u>large</u> mortgage on the Rectory, which we used to own outright, and we've had to sell the Patrician. I take the bus into Welwyn now, except when Flo can give me a lift.

Get to the point, Mum. Well, put bluntly darling, we just <u>can't</u> keep on with Middleton's fees. I've already written to Mr. Digby, explaining the situation and asking if there are <u>any</u> scholarships or bursaries for which you might qualify. Apparently Middleton no longer offers them, and of course industry doesn't any more.

So where does this leave <u>you</u>? We think you have two choices, though if you can think of others do tell us. We're all ears. Nothing can be ruled out these days.

(1) We could <u>try</u> getting you into Welwyn Comprehensive. You could finish your exams and, if things improve wildly, go on to pursue your Biology and Medicine.

(2) You could study here at home, sit the exams, and if you specialize more in Physics and Chemistry, your father will use <u>all</u> the pull he has to get you taken on at LR.

The more we think about it, the more your father and I favour choice 2. Comprehensive will be difficult after Middleton. Just the way you <u>speak</u> will count against you. Even if you avoid the worst things that go on there, there's still the violence. Only last year there were those <u>dreadful</u>

needle attacks. The papers said <u>one in three</u> of the children are posi now.

I know it's hard to think of giving up Biology. Even when you were small I remember you saying you wanted to be a doctor. I asked why—you can't have been more than seven—and you said, "Because I want to make people better, like Mummy does." You'll never know how <u>marvellous</u> that made me feel. But now the thought of you going into medicine is simply ghastly. <u>Do</u> read the enclosed leaflet, then burn it. I'm not supposed to have it. Health workers are catching <u>terrible</u> things at a...[illegible]...Labs and hospitals just aren't ...[missing]...misuse of antibiotics over many...[missing]

...home and finish your schooling here. There are several <u>first-rate</u> teachers who are keen to coach. They need the money so badly, poor things, that we can employ them for a <u>fraction</u> of Middleton's fees. Do write <u>soon</u> and give us your thoughts. You're paid up till end of term. I can't tell you how much we agonize...[illegible]...so hard to know <u>what</u> to do. We know at least a dozen young men and women, only a few years older than you, several with Oxbridge degrees, working as cleaners and guards.

Fondest love from us both, Mother

PS. Enclosed is a little something to cheer you up. Take Freddie with you. I'm sure she'll enjoy it, and I know she likes your company (she told me so herself!!). And don't worry about us. We're still among the lucky ones.

Unfortunately the reply to this letter, if a copy ever found its way into Headmaster Digby's files, has not survived. Neither has the leaflet she mentions (perhaps young Jeremy followed her instructions). But I did find, next to the letter, a brochure. Presumably there'd been a pair of tickets with it. The heavily impregnated stock was in remarkable condition. A faded pink elephant adorned the front, beneath the words "BIORAMA! North Europe's Hugest Zooseum!" Very carefully I turned the sodden page:

Come see our star — Jumbo the masculine elephant! Jumbo was acquired by us from Whipsnade Zoo, which stood on this very site! He was humainly [sic] immortalized and now stands before you in all his former glorey. Rent a VR helmet and see Jumbo "stalk the velt"! You'll believe your back in the age of the African giants when you witness this brilliantly taxidermed pakiderm! And half of every pound you spend at Biorama goes to BioDiverCity, our global-class cryogenic animal kingdom where more than 50,000 embryos of Jumbo and his fellow creatures await the day when they can roam the earth once more.

See Nature's World at Biorama!
A division of Vatican Disney
© Biorama 2029

— 7 —

*February 3, near Hatfield. Evening*

Good to be away and heading north. Middleton was too much like rooting in my own grave.

After Hertford the Lea shrank to a chunky necklace of pools and shoals. I stashed the kayak in a railway tunnel this morning, and started hoofing up the A1; or, as romantic Bird would have it, the Great North Road.

With luck it'll be Supergrassed all the way to — where? York? Newcastle? Edinburgh? How far must I go, and how will I know when I've gone far enough? I'm trying not to think too hard along those lines. I've this notion: one day I'll come over the top of a hill and there'll be green fields and a little cottage with a curl of smoke, a red wain in a pond, some quacking ducks and children's voices. What happens after that I'm not too sure. I'm keeping the imagination to a diet of kitsch, or I'd never sleep a wink.

But I do feel fitter than I've felt in years. I bloody well hope it lasts because my pack weighs fifty pounds—and that's after paring down to three shirts, one spare pair of jeans, the thinnest underpad, and a single measly bottle of McGee's. It'll be dry food—oats, rice, packet stews, and whatever Graham and I can purloin along the way. Dumping the laptop and solar charger would save eight or nine pounds, but then I'd need to carry more paper and pens; and I'd have no music, no references, no way to charge the torch or run any disks I may find. So for now I'm staying computerized.

On the outskirts of Hertford yesterday, I passed a spot where the river's cutting through a rubbish tip—a scree of glass, rust, and polythene like bits of loo paper.

All those *things*, Anita—Zamfir recordings, yo-yos, xylophones, weedkillers, video games, train sets, televisions, stereos, snuff films, rocket silos, railways, pinball tables, one-armed bandits, oil refineries, nuclear piles, motorhomes, milk cartons, lipsticks, lawnmowers, lava lamps, Kleenex holders, Jacuzzis, hula-hoops, houseboats, gravy boats, golf carts, footballs, fondue sets, drinks trolleys, cameras, bottles, beds, airliners—all those splendid Things that made up the sum of the world, which we had to keep on making and buying to keep ourselves diverted and employed—were just garbage-to-be. Ripped, smelted, sucked, blown from the raddled earth; turned into must-haves, always-wanteds, major advances, can't-do-withouts. And *pouf!* a decade later, a season later, it's ashamed-to-be-seen-in, clapped out, white elephant, obsolete, *infra dig*, inefficient, passé, and away it goes to the basement or the bushes or the ditch or the bottom of the sea.

"If the earth should again be peopled,"—Verney could boast —"we, the lost race, would, in the relics left behind, present no contemptible exhibition to the newcomers." All very well in 1826, but who could say that now? Our final century has left more of a mess than our previous million years.

One good thing: some plastics are breaking down in aerated soil, leaving a brittle residue which flakes in the hand like fossil shell. You can almost hear the littered globe sighing with relief; maybe this heat is just its way of sweating out the dope.

You're thinking: Why should you care, David? Why give a stuff about the figure we cut to posterity; especially if there isn't one?

I can't easily say. Maybe it's because you and I agreed with Wilde that there's always something vulgar about success. That's why we loved Bird, why you loved me. Why you revered your melancholy ancestor writing at the dead end of a thousand-year poesy—the lovely old loping alliterative line—while Chaucer claimed the future with his rhyme. Why you loved Akhenaten the misfit pharaoh, and the Earth Commandos. And the earth itself. Beautiful losers, every one. But you—you were no loser. Not in the living of your life; only in its loss. And even there you were in the vanguard, among the first to fall as the earth found ways to halt the human infestation.

Now that man has gone—has become perhaps the biggest loser since the dinosaurs—now can we begin to love our kind?

*Sunday, February 6*

Three days on the road and nearly twenty miles a day—not bad when you're loaded like a grunt, terminally ill, and bouncing along on yard-thick turf. At first it was like walking on a bed, but I've perfected a long Groucho stride with a final stab from the ball of the foot, the turf responding with a ripple through its springy skeleton—so that it returns the force the way my expensive running shoes are supposed to do but don't, and I can catch the wave.

Boredom's the trouble: no steep hills, no hollows, no hidden bends, each step and prospect utterly predictable: three miles an hour on a great road built for eighty. And so quiet, despite the cries and hoots and murmurs behind the forest wall—no farting motorbikes and keening tyres, no swish of a Rolls or flutter of a Beetle. The view a tapering greensward between high banks of leaves—the same ahead, the same behind, varied only by the fall of the light. I'm becoming grateful for obstructions, for downed trees and overpasses, twisted pylons. These are crossing points for wildlife—you see hoofprints of pig and deer, dog and cat in various sizes, rodent tunnels through the undergrowth. These punctuate the day.

Graham flows through the bush like a blob of oil, avoiding the turf, which would cut her pads to ribbons. It's even starting to wear my soles. Some hostile genes must have slipped into the test-tube. Children couldn't play on a lawn like this. They should have called it Sod-Off.

It rained much of yesterday and all this afternoon, the road straight and flat over the Roman course of Erning Street, except for a bend at Stilton. What I'd give for a Stilton cheese, a loaf, a pint, and thou beside me. Your ocean of hair in my lap.

Camped in a church at Water Newton, a village of lovely shortbread stone on the first hill I've seen in days. The steeple pokes gingerly from the treetops like a hidden missile, giving a view all round. To the south and east the country has a moth-eaten look, a broken pattern of mossy hummocks and waterlogged pandanus stretching across fens to the risen sea. This looks like crocodile and jaguar terrain—I'm glad of a fire, these walls, and a big cat on my side.

I spent enough time in the old tropics to learn that, unless you're a native hunter or a patient cameraman, a jungle seldom shows its hand. But it seemed unusually silent here while I watched the sunset from the belfry. I haven't heard howler monkeys in two nights now. It was good to see a pair of macaws glide past in the buttery light as the sun slipped below the overcast, flared and died like a struck match.

*Monday, near Grantham*

Dinner at the Ram Jam Inn, if I've correctly identified these arches by the road. A few miles from Sir Isaac Newton's birthplace.

Time to buy your valentine, my unrequiting love.

Which of us do you suppose Bird blamed the most? Shouldn't he share the blame? It got a bit much, being his *nice bit of posh,* didn't it? Often I saw the wince, the sudden collapse in your face when you thought no one was looking. And the pipe; you'd begun to use it as a smokescreen. It was never really you in any case. But Christ it was seductive—the sucking and huffing, your pale fingers in the pouch, the flame between your painted nails. And don't bother telling me that sometimes a pipe is only a pipe.

Water, fire, or earth—which element should we credit with the end of our beginning in the spring of 1988? That bike ride to the Nine Wells? That electrical dinner at my place? Or our escape to the North—our last, incontrovertible betrayal?

Water: the Nine Wells, mysterious source of Hobson's Conduit. Bird wouldn't go cycling. *Wouldn't be caught dead on anything without a motor.* Never had time; thought he could always leave you with a trusted friend. You'd borrowed a man's ten-speed, a sporty one, underswept bars and a saddle with a long leather snout between your legs. A glorious day, you in white shorts with midriff bare, sky-blue shirt-tails knotted below your breasts.

Picnicking under the willows by the springs, the sweat dry on your skin, a filigree rime: *Look at me, I'm all salty.* You stretched out your arm, and I bent and tasted. And you did not withdraw. And you said *I want to kiss you. But I won't.* Why not? *We mustn't. It's not fair to any of us. I may not be a saint, and I'm certainly not a virgin, but I am a Catholic girl—sort of—with a few shreds of integrity still left. With me it has to be all or nothing. I won't go skulking around behind Bird's back.* What about Egypt? Was that nothing? Your laugh. *After a row doesn't count. Out of the country doesn't count. Boyfriend away doesn't count. Sometimes even holding a plane ticket doesn't count.*

It was the first hot afternoon of the year, slicking the cotton to our backs, the seats warm and sticky, the wind cool between our thighs when we stood on the pedals. Back to Cambridge when the sun got low, Hobson's water flowing beside us across open fields, along dark lanes, in its stone gutter down Trumpington Street, a sweet irrigation to the city from the woods. And we at the end of our ride, standing there outside the Rose, panting like racehorses, astride the flow. Got time for a quick one? *A quick what, David Lambert?* And I was staring at your crimson toenails, the mud on your ankles, at the line of dots the wheel had thrown up the bony ladder of your back, at tiny ginger hairs on your neck. *Why are you looking at me like that?* (smiling, glad I was) *What are you thinking?* I'm thinking how much I'd like to be a bicycle seat just now. *Mr. Lambert!*

*Newark-on-Trent, noon, Wednesday Feb. 9*

By the waters of the Trent I sat and fished. The river looked innocent enough — tea-dark and swift through a marsh blizzarding with birds. Soon I had a bottom-feeder, a big, ugly creature of ten pounds or so. Its mouth was strangely thrawn, jaws missing on the bite like twisted scissors. Like the photos of wildlife from the Great Lakes — warped mouths, boiled eyes, sex organs withered by the chemical soup of Love Canal and whatever else North America had flushed into the drink. I felt sick at the sight of the thing — or at the memories it raised. If my lot are extinct, I said to Graham, it's no more than we deserved.

The smell of fish had lured her across a patch of Ecoturf, shaking her paws at each dainty step like a kitten in snow. I was about to throw the foul thing back but she seized it and growled when I made a move. So she ate while I had a lunch of cold rice, palm hearts, and smelly emu. Afterwards we sat together, and I began absent-mindedly to scratch her head. The sun was strong, penetrating Graham's dark fur, which, as on many cats, is thin about the ears. Until today I never doubted that she'd lost an ear in the same way as her charismatic namesake, in some scrap or rut. I don't know enough anatomy to be certain, and my judgement has perhaps been coloured, but it looks to me now as though Graham didn't lose her ear; she never had one. And if this is so, then what does it say about the state of higher mammals on this island? Perhaps she is drawn to me because she has no others of her kind. Perhaps Graham is as rare a beast as David.

We were going to clean it up, weren't we? We put it off and put it off like kids promising to clean their room. Then we went away, leaving our evil to live after us. Upstream in the childless ruins of Nottingham and Stoke and Derby, tanks must have split, drums corroded, transformers ruptured, spilling their immortal toxins. Perhaps it's still happening, old time bombs still going off. "Slowly the poison the whole blood stream fills. . . . The waste remains, the waste remains and kills."

One thing I never understood about the law: if you dumped arsenic into Granny's tea you'd be put away for murder; if you poisoned a whole country with some cavalier industrial process, the worst you could expect was a paltry fine.

Who did time for killing you and me with CJD?

*Near Pontefract, Yorkshire, Friday night*
Beyond Newark the road took me east of the Peak District and the southern Pennines, east of Sheffield, Manchester, and Leeds. The air was drier here; I sweated less. Sherwood Forest is low and sparse compared to the jungles of the south. The trees grow squatter and more widely spaced—eucalyptus, acacias, leafless baobabs with pot-belly trunks and saveloy fruit.

Near Doncaster patches of savannah began to show, and the Supergrass, till now a pale crease on a dark land, became the greenest thing in sight. I'd expected rainforest to cover Britain, to ring this latitude as the old equatorial jungles used to do. Maybe I'm approaching the northern margin of the present woods—a transitional zone equivalent, say, to southern Niger—but it seems more likely that the change is local, a rain-shadow from the Pennine chain.

It was wonderful to see a mob of kangaroos—twenty or more—clear the road in one leap and bounce away through the shadows spread by the evening sun. *Life!*

Graham went after them but soon gave up.

It's raining again, despite the semi-desert, and I'm sheltering under Junction 33, where the M62 crosses the A1 at Pontefract. A dry but dismal place to spend the night, my fire illuminating blistered concrete, rusty stalactites, fading hand prints, and a phrase I've seen a lot of: *HOT WOGS NOT OUR WORRY.*

There are crude walls here, made of rubble, engine blocks, and clay—as if a small band of desperadoes had tried to turn this bridge into a fort. Their work is crumbling and the winds are fierce, twitching the curtains of rain on either side of us. Graham soaks up the fire, flinches at each thunderclap, and when sheet lightning makes a neon ceiling of the cloud she gets up and prowls, a shadow moving in the shadows.

I've been collecting these motorway graffiti, among them some old chestnuts: *Is there intelligent life on Earth? The light at the end of the tunnel is out*, and *Stop the Madness!* (I always did like *Stop the Madness*—you could take it anywhere.) More intriguing is what I call the Watling oeuvre: *WE LIKE WATLING, WATLING RULES, OK? WATLING = LAW & ORDER*, and so forth. I've seen the name in several places. At first I thought it might refer to the bunker complex in the City. But here in the firelight is a *GENERAL WATLING* with a profile silhouette and thumbs-up. So we have an individual, a *caudillo* no doubt, who either named himself after Watling Street or chose that place for his stronghold because he shared its name. These slogans are too well done to be spontaneous, the work of professional signwriters masquerading as public sentiment. Scrawled over them are traces of dissent: *Wally's a Wanker, Army Bastards Out.*

*February 12th, noon*

We set off this morning when the rain stopped, about ten, the road running down to the Aire, and the Aire to the Humber. In the east the valley is barely above sea-level, winding through billows of mangrove and screw-pine to a shimmer of open water. But away from the river the bush is thin and sere, with relics of Victorian industry among the cactus thickets. Graham lay down on a sunny rock, tired after her sleepless night. I picked some prickly pears and ate them in the shade of a textile mill, thinking of the steam dragons that once panted in these walls.

> It was a town of machinery and tall chimneys, out of which interminable serpents of smoke trailed themselves for ever and ever, and never got uncoiled. It had a black canal in it, and a river that ran purple with ill-smelling dye, and vast piles of building full of windows where there was a rattling and a trembling all day long, and where the piston of the steam-engine worked monotonously up and down, like the head of an elephant in a state of melancholy madness. It contained several large streets all very like one another, and small streets still more like one another, inhabited by people equally like one another, who all went in and out at the same hours, with the same sound upon the same pavements, to do the same work, and to whom every day was the same as yesterday and tomorrow. . . .

The French got Napoleon, the Russians gave up, the Americans became the Tories of the world. But the Industrial Revolution, once ignited, burned with an incorruptible logic. You were right about Dickens; in one phrase he had its creed: "Every inch of the existence of mankind, from birth to death, was to be a bargain across a counter."

Could it have gone another way? Is the Good Samaritan always a bad economist? Was capitalism — that "machine for demolishing limits" — a suicide machine? (And was Marxism any different, to say nothing of the struggle between the two?) Or were all human systems doomed to stagger along under the mounting weight of their internal logic until it crushed them? And I think of the Maya temples reaching higher and higher as the jungle died by the stone axe. And I think of Easter Island, and even there — where the limits must have been plain to anyone — the last tree came down to put up the last colossus, the rains washed the soil to the sea, the people starved and ate each other, and there was no escape because without wood there's no canoe.

Fire. It can't have been more than a month after the Nine Wells bike ride. You at my door with three bottles of Australian plonk, *to warm up the new digs*. Where's Bird? *Couldn't come, sends his love.* (Bird would never "send his love.") *I'm afraid it'll have to be just the two of us, Mr. Lambert*. What's all this "Mr. Lambert"? And you laid an oxblood nail on my lip.

You were wearing your empire cotton dress (the one Bird called your fuck-me dress), a wide straw boater with ribbons down your back that matched your hair, and those white sandals with the maddening ankle straps. *What on earth is that thing?* Conversation piece. About 1890. Belongs to my Uncle Phil. It's called a Wimshurst machine — after Mr. Wimshurst, I presume. Makes artificial lightning. When our dinner's had time to go down, I'll give you a demonstration, and you will experience something wonderful.

*Will I now?*

Phil would draw the study blinds, which had been there since the Blitz. He'd command me to take hold of brass cylinders attached to wires with woven insulation, stiff and dry like snake-skin, make me stand on rubber blocks. I'd hear munching gears and a mosquito whine as brass and mica discs counter-rotated between copper brushes at ascending speed. A Catherine-wheel would appear in the darkness. My hands would tingle with electrons flow-ing into me, lodging in my flesh. At length the machine would slow, a mournful descant, and stop with a noise like autumn leaves across a cellar window. I'd hear his stealthy approach, the ster-torous breath, smell the tobacco and drink as he placed himself before me in the dark, the halitosis of his soul. *Put your tongue out, boy, and you will experience something wonderful.* The unsticking of lips, a crusty sound, his tongue darting like a moray eel. Then a burning stab and a bath of light as a great spark passed between us. And his mouth on mine *to kiss the hurt away.*

Fire joined your tongue to mine. In the dark I heard you stamp your foot. *What on earth are you doing? Phew! I've never been kissed like that before. Are you trying to seduce me or electrocute me with this thing? It really isn't necessary, you know. Simpler means will do.* I felt a jolt go through you like a petit mal, and for an instant feared a galvanic spasm in your heart. Anita, are you all right? *Quite all right, thank you.* Ah yes (remembering Egypt), you always did do that. *Only in the right company, Lambert.*

Later in the bath I soaped you, my hands in all the places you said your mother'd told you never to touch without an intervening cloth. *My God you've got a wicked face. You look like the Devil! Or one of the seven deadly sins.* And I: I'm in favour of Lust and Sloth.

*Ferrybridge*

Earth: specifically the Great North Road. About a week later you came again for the night, answering no questions about Bird. We had a breakfast of raw eggs in burgundy and, before there was time for second thoughts, set off for Scotland. It wasn't hard getting lifts with you. A first trip to the North for both of us and, even though I knew the place no better than you did, I enjoyed my native status, showing off the old country to a British girl from overseas: the packed brick houses thinning, turning to stone; the landscape bleaker, the land less spoken for; the dialect thicker at each stop, the Norse and Saxon vowels.

You can't have forgotten this view. We came over the brow and there were the twin carriageways leading down into a valley of concrete lumps and one sad effort at style—a factory like an upside-down grand piano. You said: *The British never did get the hang of modern architecture, did they? Their hearts weren't in it.* The one imposing work was a power station—a dozen cooling towers like small volcanoes, standing on sheets of dark water, steam rising from their mouths in the windless morning, until at a certain height it fluxed across the sky, setting a white lid on the rim of hills.

There it is, near the river—Ferrybridge power station—six towers still on their feet; the rest heroically fallen upon one another in a heap of curves like the Sydney opera house.


*2 p.m.*

*Never forget, Davy, that things can always get worse.* Father was a cheery soul. And they have. Graham has left me. Minutes ago. She's gone, Anita, and I have a nasty feeling she won't be back.

This isn't the time of day she hunts. Not until I looked up from the Oyster did I notice she was missing—I must have been writing for three-quarters of an hour, awash in memory. I called her name, and heard a cry, faint, far behind. Half a mile back was a figure on her haunches in the middle of the road, stiff as a china cat in a gift shop. I called again. Again she answered, but didn't move. It wasn't like her to be sitting on Supergrass. I took off my pack and went to her, afraid she might be hurt. She tossed her head in greeting, blinked her topaz eyes.

What's the matter? I said, and she answered by walking to the bush and giving a brisk little trot south, towards London, letting out an impatient rasp that said, *Time to turn round. Let's go.* Poor Graham! This isn't your mess, and there's no way I can make you understand. Perhaps you should go back to your Isle of Dogs. But I can't give up now. Not when I've come this far. Don't you see? And her answer was another *prrrrp*, another trot, another doleful stare. She arched her back.

She'd been uneasy for at least two days, ever since the forest frayed to scrub. She didn't know this country, didn't recognize its fauna or its smells. We'd passed out of her range. Her pursuit of the kangaroos was half-hearted—for form's sake—she didn't really want one.

I threw my arms around her neck. Slowly she began to purr —a faulty motor, misfiring, stalled by awkward silences. You and I will have to part for a few weeks, old girl. Wait for me in London. Your place or mine. I'll call at Canary Wharf. If not, I'll see you at my Tower. She stayed for a few minutes, licking tears from my cheek with her rasp of a tongue. Then she gave a quizzical falsetto, which I took to mean more or less what I'd just said, and her dark form flowed away from me, tail low among the silver eucalyptus leaves.

— 8 —

*Fountains Abbey, Yorkshire. February 15, Tuesday, about 10 p.m.*
On Saturday, when Graham left, I got no further than the outskirts of Wetherby; slept badly in a church, woke exhausted. The sleeping-bag was wet around my legs—rain or dew had got in. A common enough annoyance, but that morning it seemed the last straw. I lay there utterly miserable; soaked, chilled, and an ache in the muscles as if sickening with flu. Just overdoing things, getting old, stiff in

the wrong places? Or remission coming to an end, the wigglies be-stirring themselves, gnawing new tunnels through my brain? Bad dreams had sapped me; I felt I'd been labouring all night at some fruitless task. It took an hour or more to summon the strength to get up and light a fire.

I looked around for Graham. Remembered. God, I needed her! The life around me seemed so tenuous — its tropical exuber-ance merely a skin of algae on a suffocating pond. Was there any point in going on? Perhaps if I turned back quickly I could catch her up. But she'd probably covered fifty miles already; it would be a lonely trip to London. And then what? I felt stalled in the mid-dle of England. In the middle of Nowhere, without news.

I'd dreamt about the farm, had a long conversation with Mother in the dining-room while she polished silver, showing me her family crest (a boar couchant); a conversation I'd been unable to finish and of which I had only this echo: *a disappointment to your father and me.*

Mary Lavinia Lambert, née Wringham. I hadn't thought of her much on the journey until now. You don't leave room for other women. She's a mink stole, a heady perfume in a bedroom cup-board, a tearful face on a platform, a flute playing in an upstairs room, a certain way with parsnips, a clear voice on the telephone, a shade of reseda in woollens, an old-fashioned manner of speak-ing about England which made it seem a family, a great big family, in which certain things were remembered, promised, and expected. *We* had once had the greatest empire in the world; *we* had defeated Hitler; *we* had the language with the largest vocabulary, the best democratic institutions, the ideal balance between church and state, and a thousand-year monarchy, which was so much better because we wouldn't want a president like the Americans, would we? (And she was right there: it was Nixon.)

This national *we* — usually on the lips of people older than my mother would have been, had she lived — has always reminded me of her. Of a dead woman, of an England that withered on the vine somewhere in the fifties, long before you and I were born. After that *we* became the Brits. And our country—defended by Americans, supplied by Greeks, swept by Jamaicans, fed by Hindus and Italians, bought by Arabs, sold by Essex man—became Youkay, not a people but a place.

One isn't analytical enough at ten or eleven. Not until many years later did it occur to me that the parental front, presented as unanimous reality—*just the way things are, Davy*—was perhaps not monolithic. Did Mother always agree with Father, with the scorched-earth farming, the Marianism, the triumphalism, the taste for beef medium rare, the choice of sherry and schools? His ways or hers?

These were days of loss and absence, silent cries, still branches. Only insect sounds: the endless syncopation one forgets, the shrieking cicadas. I missed the mourning tinamous and flyting parrots; I missed the monkeys. Most of all I missed my big black puss. The country beyond Wetherby was arid despite the rain. A fire had burnt there not many weeks ago. Eucalyptus, a few ironwoods, and century-plants had survived, but the undergrowth was gone, the ground just beginning to send up a boy's beard of green. The motorway banks were black on either side but the turf itself was hardly singed. Evidently the *Übergras* is fireproof too.

Useful though it is to me, there's something horrible about this last functioning artefact, living beyond its time like a zombie, defying a nature that has taken her revenge on its creators.

The Devil's Arrows were not as conspicuous as when you and I were here, but I spotted their dark forms among some chalky ghost gums near the road. We were riding in a pickup with that American, an airforceman about to go home to Cincinnati. If his truck hadn't been left-hand drive we might have missed them: a giant's chisels stabbed in a field of oats, aloof beside the streaming cars. From a distance they looked newly carved by the Bronze Age, but when I got close I saw again how unspeakably old they are; how the igneous rock has guttered at the top like ice in rain, a few atoms each year for fifty centuries, the Buddha's definition of eternity.

Sickness washed over me. I sat down on a fallen megalith. The fire had cleared the brush around; it lay on the earth like a whale, tiny crystals sparkling in its hide. The sun turned black in the cloudless sky and the world began to shake. The sky jumping, the sky jumping, the sky jumping. . . .

When the lights came up I was on my back, paralysed and unfamiliar to myself, just as at the mews. I'd been out for two hours. Is this *it*, my love?

You need to take it easy for a few days, I told myself. Find a nice spot to rest. Do some fishing and gathering, eat well — salads, game — get over Graham's leaving, wash clothes, rebuild body and morale. So I came here to Fountains Abbey, cutting west across burnt ground, relieved to be off the treadmill of unnatural green.

The gardens have fared worse than the Cistercian monastery. Gryphons have flown, unicorns skipped, manticores prowled away. I can't even find the Temple of Piety, where we made love against a wall.

Not much to fear but silences, losses, memories: my younger self and you. *Stop it! It smells funny in here. Not now! Someone might come.* Your hair around both our heads, a shared burnous; the coconut smell of your shampoo. *You're a dirty devil, Lambert, and I'm falling in love with you.* Why do Methodists disapprove of sex standing up? *Tell me!* Because it might lead to dancing.

I'm living in the undercroft, a long stone vault on dozens of thickset pillars; it must be one of the largest roofs in England now. Remember being surprised in here by a busload of Japanese?

I've spent hours bringing this up to date tonight, tapping away after the fire died, staring from time to time into the receding columns lit palely by the life in my machine.

*Thursday, February 17*

Much better in every way. I'm living well, gathering fruit, putting the gun to use (something I didn't like to do with Graham around). Had some sort of jungle fowl for dinner; delicious.

The valley seems to be a microclimate, a finger of the rain-forest. Either that or I'm coming out of the rain-shadow at last. Graham would have loved it here—a leafy fan-vault loud with macaws, toucans, budgies, and white-faced capuchins. Last night howler monkeys roared, and this afternoon I found their roost—a huge *ceiba* fattened on the soil of the brethren's "necessaries."

*"In the latrine deposits was found a mass of senna pods and other purgatives."* You reading aloud from the guidebook to all in the teashop, the grockles choking on their scones, scandalized by our litany of monkish vices: sipping, whipping, gluttony, and buggery. *Did long hours of orison cause constipation, do you think, Mr. Lambert? Or were the brothers merely anxious to (a)void surprises?*

There are buildings in the deer park that I'm certain weren't here when we were. Not impressive but intriguing: four tall chimneys spaced about a hundred yards apart, perhaps factory smokestacks. I wasn't able to get at the furnaces beneath them—too many bricks had fallen—but I could pick out stretches of a footing for a vanished wooden structure. Buildings like this couldn't have been put up here while Fountains was a national beauty spot. These must date from the "emergency" or later.

Nearby was an iron mass—some sort of tracked vehicle—pinned under buttress roots. At first I took it for a tank or a crane, but there's a blade. It was a bulldozer.

*Friday afternoon*

On the road again, the monotonous green conveyor trundling me north. Overhead there's a brassy sun, and my ears are full of Handel and the hissing rain of "Riders on the Storm." No, change that.

Today's a swinging day. Artie Shaw and Goodman are what I need to gobble up the grim green miles.

Three-quarters of the way to Scotland, though the closer I get the unlikelier it seems I'll find an answer there. I've been wondering again whether things could be better anywhere else. Do the machines still hum in Canada, Antarctica, Alaska? Where did America go in her shiny car in the night? And always I come to this: the storms must have raged over the whole earth, and no society as top-heavy as ours could have ridden them out.

But that doesn't mean there aren't survivors; humbled and thinned, no doubt, but carrying on at some pre-industrial, even pre-agricultural level—living again as we lived for ninety-nine per cent of our career on earth.

Or is this state of mind—this *perseverance*, as Father would have called it—mere denial? Unwillingness to accept the fact that all is fordone, that whatever happened was deadly to us, that there's no Shangri-La beyond the hills, no Lost World where human dinosaurs still roam?

Yet Edinburgh pulls, like any goal, like a summit or a sunken wreck. Raise a glass to Auld Reekie, Athens of the North.

— **9** —

*Friday, February 25. Evening, Edinburgh Castle*
A Geordie lorry driver brought us in, his tapedeck playing the sixties. Can't remember exactly where we stayed—in the Hanoverian New Town somewhere—but I still have the moist fetor of the bed, the streetlamp through puce velvet curtains, the shower cubicle like a dank phone booth, the basin of which you said, *Listen to the sound of one hand washing* (there wasn't room for two); and the landlady's grilled kippers after a busy night.

I'd gone out late and brought back Talisker (forgetting it might make you think of Bird) and you said coolly, *Whisky's fine but I want poetry, Lambert*. I looked at you pouting on the corner of the bed, your arms winged to unzip that black French dress, and Wyatt came:

When her loose gowne did from her shoulders fall,
And she me caught in her armes long and small,
And therewithall, so swetely did me kysse,
And softly sayd: deare hart, how like you this?

With such fragments I am shored against these ruins. Edinburgh was a last hope, and what do I find? Yet Edinburgh doesn't feel *quite* as ruined as London or Hertford or Newcastle. I think there may be a ghost of artifice among the plants. Oleanders, frangipani, and bougainvillaea are growing by paths and doors. And on one street near the castle, four or five big tulip trees line up — perhaps the last survivors of a row. If I'm right, people were living here long after the warming began.

I reached the edge of the city yesterday, camping the night on the summit of Arthur's Seat. As you climb there are more subtropical and montane species: southern oaks, deodars, teak, magnolia, Mediterranean cork. I found cedar branches for a mattress and set my tent on them beneath an Atlas pine, the resinous evergreens drowning me in homesickness.

In the last of the light a small fox came to watch me, more puzzled than afraid. I thought of our walks there and the associations of the place that so delighted you: King David fending off a giant stag with a chip of the Holy Rood; the young laird of Dalcastle dogged by his hellish brother. I saw us among the rocks in a hidden pool of warmth, your face above me — those seascape eyes — the sunset clouds failing to outshine your hair.

Okay, I've been a poor correspondent lately, but I thought it better to press on. Only a month to the spring equinox; how long before a heatwave or monsoon?

So I've been hiking like a German — and feeling like one, fingers crossed. I skirted Newcastle on the bypass, and took the low road up the coast. Along the rim of the cliffs from Berwick to Ayton were vast rookeries of seals, pelicans, and man-o'-wars, the droppings so thick and trodden that nothing grows, not even Ecolawn. It was a day of salt winds and wide views of open sea. Not the dishwater sea we knew here, but a paisley silk, turquoise and aquamarine, with a stitch of waves far out on a coral reef.

The rainforest came back in force soon after I turned west into the Scottish lowlands, the A1 cutting cleanly through jungle until it entered the city and shrank to a street. The resiling turf went hard underfoot and died among the shadows. From then on it was machete work through thorns and canebrakes, past sandstone walls and moulting stucco.

I'm dossing in St. Margaret's Chapel on the castle summit, where a breeze keeps the bugs away and I can see the whole of Edinburgh. It's the oldest building and one of the best. Animal bones were strewn about inside, the leavings of a large predator, but all were fleshless, so I assume the tenancy is lapsed. Reminds me of the Tower of London and my absent puss, and how much I miss that bony head butting me in the thigh at dinner time.

*Sunday*

It hasn't been easy taking a look round. Giant bamboo and wild mango choke the Old Town's cobbled wynds. Nor' Loch has returned, drowning the railway station, and half the Balmoral Hotel has slipped into the water, leaving rooms and corridors exposed like an architect's cut-away, some floors tenanted by pigeons and macaws, others by hanumans. The Scott monument keeps upright somehow on its spindly legs, so overgrown it looks like an ornate south Indian temple, especially its wrinkled reflection in the loch.

Two legible graffiti: *WATLING = RIGHT ATTITUDES* and *DEATH TO MACBEATH* [*sic*]. Macbeth?

I've been swimming from a rock below the castle, first thing and late afternoon, drying in the sun beneath a frangipani which is leafless but in flower, a candelabra of pink flames and such perfume!

Fishing's good here. No more piranha; I've a couple of decent bass.

*Tuesday, March 1*

A lot to tell you. I spent yesterday in the Great Hall of the castle palace, turning up a few verdigrised bits of bronze, some glass beads, and two semiprecious stones that might have come from a hilt or shield. All the finds were in or below a layer of ash and charcoal; there was no trace of later occupation. After lunch I took a look at the end wall. Immediately above a great hooded fireplace was a broken area, as if a plaque or statue had been torn away. I uprooted a small tree from the hearth, and here indeed were fragments of a relief.

Made of cast concrete, it was obviously postmodern — which I now define, for archaeological purposes, as anything produced by our civilization after I left it. I managed to reconstruct a cameo of a man and woman, side by side, dressed like the presidential couple of a banana republic, standing above a scroll with the motto of the Scottish royal arms: *NEMO ME IMPUNE LACESSIT*. I'm tempted to call the effigy crude but it wasn't, quite. It was a propaganda piece, like the portrait of any tyrant from Rameses to Mao, and as such it was effective. The decadence was in the message, not its execution. The man had the jutting jaw, craggy features, and benignly vacant grin of a movie star. The woman's face held more intelligence but was hardly benign — a hawkish sneer combined with a cheap hormonal rictus.

The trappings, too, had an epigonal look: loud epaulettes and sash, a vulgar necklace, two Dairy Queen crowns, a cartoon lion and unicorn. The lower part of the scene had shattered in the blaze. The only words I could read were incomplete. I worked long and hard shuffling pieces on the ground, trying to guess the layout and so the missing letters. This is what I came up with:

...TIES KING MALC...

...GARET

...USE OF...ATLIN...

...mini 2...4....

A guess is all I can claim: *Their Majesties King Malcolm and Queen Margaret, [Founders?] of the House of Watling, Anno Domini 204?.*

So it would appear this Cromwell didn't spurn the crown. Malcolm: his real name? Or a contrived echo of ancient Scottish kings? After consulting my Britannica, I think the latter. Which Malcolm would Watling have wanted to evoke: the two who preceded Duncan; or Malcolm Canmore, Duncan's son, who killed Macbeth in 1057? *Never, never, never get your history from the bard!* ("Daphne" Shadwell thundering at Middleton.) Daphne was right: Shakespeare can't be trusted here. To Celtic Scots—as distinct from those mingled with the English epicures—Duncan was the usurper, not Macbeth. And the real Macbeth slew Duncan in battle, fair and square. But Shakespeare carries the day: who wants the facts to ruin a good story? Wot! No secret black and midnight hags; no multitudinous seas incarnadine; no Macduff from his mother's womb untimely ripp'd?

Canmore, the Anglophile, has to be Watling's man. In 1068 this Malcolm married Margaret, sister of Edgar Ætheling, the rightful king of England after Harold died at Hastings. Edgar was here for the wedding, an exile in this castle, dreaming impotently of revenge while the Conqueror harried England.

Strange how the Middle Ages are so much clearer than a few years after our own time. If we'd stayed and lived, we might have been in our sixties when London was abandoned, in our seventies when Watling seized the throne.

There seem to be no more reliefs or other postmodern artefacts in the Great Hall. Ash and charcoal seal a single reign.

No further luck until I turned to the Scottish War Memorial this afternoon. I remember its atmosphere when we went looking for your Forbes ancestors: half temple, half tomb; solemn with Ypres and Passchendaele, with "unknown" soldiers—those blown to smithereens—*THEIR NAMES THOUGH LOST TO US ARE WRITTEN IN THE BOOKS OF GOD.*

Unlike the Great Hall, which was simply burnt, this place had been methodically destroyed, its walls knocked down to the sills, sculptures and plaques pounded into shards. I took this, at first, to be the work of vandals or insurgents. Nothing unusual there. But something made me take a second look in the apse, where those Victorian commemorations had struck us as so vainglorious—*OUTPOSTS OF THE EMPIRE IN THE EAST; OUTPOSTS OF THE EMPIRE IN THE WEST*—as if it were only a matter of time until Britain's imperial jaws fastened on the world forever.

They were gone. And not only were they gone but I could tell from the feeble sculpting and calligraphy that the things which had been smashed and defaced were different. Someone had set up other icons and inscriptions, had bent the shrine to a new purpose. Can you see that happening under a military regime? Something must have happened here *post*-Watling, perhaps long post-Watling.

*Wednesday morning*
A violent thunderstorm last night, the castle ruins drenched in water and magnesium light. I was dry under St. Margaret's vaulted roof, though racked by dreams.

Dreams of the past—of that snug world of umbrellas and taxis, central heating, curry and beer, soft pillows and a woman's touch—from which I woke in terror of my vulnerability. One slip, one accident, one appendix attack, and I shall die like a gangrenous soldier in the trenches. To say nothing of the maggots in my head. Yes, this is cowardice.

One last dig today in the memorial. And if it tells me nothing, then I shall cease these burrowings, close the book, go back to London, and float myself off this bank and shoal of time; return if I can to you, my love, and we shall live again.

*Wednesday evening*

The digging was heavy, especially when the sun began to find me through the thin vegetation that grows up here. Yet I dug hard, for this was the end of the road.

The apse walls had fallen outward, perhaps blown up from within. The rubble I had to shift was mainly small stones and loose mortar from the ceiling vault. At about eleven o'clock I struck a cracked concrete slab below the central window of the apse. A tomb, I thought. It turned out to be the seat of a chair missing its back and arms. It looked more suitable for a bus shelter than a shrine, so I broke it up to see what lay below (even at this distance I can feel your wince). Beneath was only a rough stone block about the size and appearance of a battered suitcase. If I'd not noticed a rusty hole at one end where an iron bar or cable was once attached, I'd have dismissed it as a piece of the building. But the stone was oddly familiar. I'd seen it before. As a child, in Westminster Abbey.

I'm certain it's the Stone of Scone, on which the ancient Scottish kings were crowned—before Edward I stole it and put it ignominiously beneath the royal English arse. But what sort of kingdom could Watling have usurped or founded here? Would they have had electricity, petrol, steam, gunpowder—and for how long? What is the critical mass of a world like ours? If the modern age began when the sum of Western knowledge became too large for any individual to command it—with the birth of the specialist—then the postmodern, strictly speaking, begins with the death of specialists.

Near the coronation stone I turned up several shattered reliefs —like yesterday's but later and cruder, done in a lime plaster. Evidently the secret of Portland cement was lost, and no one had skill or energy to carve in stone. The plaques seem to have been arranged on the wall above the concrete throne, as if the memorial building had been converted into a royal palace after the Great Hall burned. Five or six accessions, including the first in the Great Hall, were immortalized in stucco before the practice ceased.

If we allow a generation to each reign, this rump of the United Kingdom could have lasted until the end of the twenty-second century. One piece bears a date—2167—but the reading's doubtful. If only there were coins. In short, Anita, much what you'd expect: a slide into barbarism. But that doesn't begin to explain why there are no barbarians round here today.

*Midnight*

During wet days on the march I had to conserve torch batteries because I needed all my solar power for the computer. With plenty of sunshine lately, I have the luxury of bedside reading—a real book. Most of the paperbacks are in London. Up here I brought only *The Incomplete Burroughs* (William, not Edgar Rice) and *The Waves* (for its durability; I've never got beyond page nine).

I'm reading *Junkie* with the torch when I recall how artificial light can bring out hidden detail. Back to the apse, so stifling during the day, now cool and camera-black beneath a powdering of stars. I play a glancing beam over the Watling *oeuvre*, piece by piece, from different angles.

Antiquarian's luck smiled again. *Erik wez hier from Cassel*

*Nessie. November 31, 2389.* Scratched on a headless torso. This is no faded spray-paint from the 2040s; this is the presence of another human being in the fairly recent past! Another *literate* human being. All right, Erik could have been more literate (I haven't bothered reproducing his childish mix of letters). And "November 31" doesn't inspire absolute confidence in his timekeeping. But *if* Erik was here just over a century ago, there must be a complex society, Anita—a civilized society or something close—somewhere in Scotland. Where?

*Thursday, March 3, after a late breakfast*
It must have been three this morning when I slipped back into my sleeping-bag. I'd searched until the small hours for more latter-day engravings, but the only new message was a *LANG LIV MACBEATH* scratched on a lintel. No date.

There seem to be no howler monkeys this far north, but other night creatures heard me or spotted the light. A crescendo built and echoed across Edinburgh—wolves or dogs, a large pack on Arthur's Seat and another calling from the little parthenon on Calton Hill.

The Oyster knows nothing of a "Castle Nessie," but surely the name suggests a stronghold on or near Loch Ness, in the Great Glen—that long wound in the earth's crust across the middle of the Highlands?

A big lake makes sense—large bodies of water moderate the local climate. Loch Ness is the largest in Britain, several cubic miles. No doubt its temperature has risen through the centuries, but the rise will have been gradual, giving life a chance to adapt. And it lies among the greatest mountains on the island; there'll be a range of ecologies at different altitudes, ways to hedge bets against the weather. If there are survivors anywhere, the Great Glen is a likely place.

A long way—another week if the road's good—but I must go.

## — 10 —

*March 5, evening. Near Perth*

Travelling light: no computer, just sketch maps of the route and this pocket notebook. Plus one change of clothes, tent and bag, dry food, gun, machete, compass, binoculars, and a single luxury: the last of the McGee's.

The Firth of Forth was to be my Rubicon—a trick I played to get myself started before second thoughts; if I could get across, then I'd go on. Of the great railway bridge built when Tania was a girl only two cantilevers remain, far out in the Firth, balanced on their islands like a pair of pterodactyls drying outstretched wings. The road bridge is in better shape but only just, the north tower sagging at its knees, steel turning to lace in the salt wind. Parts of the roadway have crumbled into the sea, but the girders that supported it still run all the way across. I inched like a kitten along naked lengths of steel covered in nests and guano, hundreds of feet above the turquoise waves. Gulls shrieked and tried to peck my eyes. Good thing there was no rain.

By mid-afternoon yesterday I was across, and from there on the going's been easy—straight up the M90 on a bouncy strip of bright green turf.

Camped under an overpass, a good one with legible advertisements —*FORD BRING THE MOTOR ELECTRIC!* and *SURRENDER TO HITLER! (THE MUSICAL!)* Also the usual palimpsest of hand prints and graffiti:

*Posse Comitatus—We Can And We Will!*
*God Rot Sassenachs*
*Porridge Wogs*
*MacBeath Squad*

Rebels? Pop groups? Death squads?

Just enough firelight to see what I'm doing. The Oyster spoiled me—I'd forgotten how laborious it is to write up notes by hand.

Difficult to sleep. I'm *not* thinking about the reception I'll get from Erik's lot, if they exist.

*Monday, March 7, Lunchtime*

Pitlochry at last, and not a souvenir in sight. Only a stone turret in the treetops, perhaps a corner of the baronial hotel we couldn't afford to stay in. And some miles back an iron letterbox, VR still visible above the slot—Trollope's gift to archaeology.

It took us a while, that spring, to cross these highlands by a chain of parsimonious lifts. Mountains lightly talced with snow; a wrinkle of deciduous trees leafless and dark along the river; conifer plantings deployed on the hills like Napoleonic infantry. And that sheep farmer in a Landrover—whisky on her breath, whiskers on her chin, a hand on my knee—telling us *as a historical fahct* that Pontius Pilate was born here to a Pictish woman and a Roman soldier, and that he ended his days a drunk on Tayside, drowning the fathomless sorrow of condemning God.

*Tuesday evening, Dalwhinnie*

Chestnuts are roasting, a fish is grilling, and down the lake Ben Alder rises against a veined and purple sky. This could be an unspoilt corner of the Pyrenees. I'm pitched beside the distillery—source of a good malt, if memory serves.

Had a hard flog over Drumochter Pass this afternoon—the road buried here and there by landslides breaking up the deathless green. But it's cooler, subtropical, almost Alpine, and the sun is still low enough that little reaches me. (Just as well; I left my hat in Edinburgh.) Around Blair Atholl the jungle trees gave way to ripening Spanish chestnut, so I stopped to gather. Above them came evergreens again, especially monkey-puzzles—araucarias from the Andes by way of vicarage gardens.

There's more wildlife up here, or maybe I'm simply seeing more tracks whenever wash-outs, tree-falls, or bogs force me off the prickly carpet every other living thing avoids. At a stream near the pass this afternoon I got a shock: there, pressed into the clay along the bank, were naked footprints. This quest for humans suddenly seemed unwise. I imagined eyes upon me, remembered that old exhibit in the London zoo labelled *The Most Dangerous Animal on Earth*—a mirror. But the prints were squat and broad, almost like hands. Could the human form have changed that much in twenty generations? Then I saw claws beyond the toes. Bears! I find bears less worrying.

Since then I've kept a sharper eye on muddy ground, seeing more bear, dog and cat (large and small), fox, deer, and the convict arrow of a hefty bird—a cassowary or a wild turkey. Smaller poultry of some sort flit about in the woods, presumably feral chickens reverting to type, the cocks magnificently plumed. Odd that there's been no trace of horse or cattle. Jungle might not suit them, but the drier bush of northern England should, and if there's open country in the highlands there could also be descendants of sheep, goats, donkeys. So far the list of freed domestics is a short one: cats, dogs, chickens, boar, and (?) turkeys.

*March 10, evening. Loch Alvie*

All yesterday and today it's rained, the clouds falling to earth, lifting only to a low, leaden ceiling that dissolves the treetops. Slow going. For hours I was in a cloud-forest, among dripping beards of Spanish moss.

Too wet and dispirited to write a line last night, and not much better now. Nothing to report anyway—the same trudge along the green ribbon of the ancient road, machete work at bogs and streams.

With the muffling silence, and the lack of any living human sign, all my excitement (and my fear) has soaked away.

I have a bad habit of jumping to conclusions: the downside of digger's luck. It was silly to place such faith in Erik. The date has to be wrong. How could I ignore that that fragment was buried under inches of soil like all the others? It couldn't have been lying on the surface only a hundred years ago.

Or could it? To tell the truth, I didn't take much notice of where that particular piece of plaster came from; I hadn't expected it to be important. In short, I committed an elementary sin: inadequate excavation records.

Have just about talked myself into giving up.

*Friday morning*

Saved by the risen sun, at least for one more day. I slept late, until it strode from behind the Cairngorms and across the loch onto the tent, waking me from a sultan's dream — a roomful of odalisques, all with your face, Anita.

The woods were ringing with birdsong. I got out the binoculars and scanned for clearings on the mountainsides, for any clue of Erik's fastness. The pines were unbroken, varying subtly with altitude from Atlas to pitch-pine to araucaria. Some of the highest trees had chocolate-brown trunks with papery red like a moulting cigar on newer growth, and short blue-green needles — at first a few individuals, then a whole stand sweeping up and over the heights of Cairn Gorm and Ben MacDui. Scots pines! Native trees surviving on a portion of their ancient range: what a sight and what an omen!

Porridge with chestnuts never tasted so good, especially washed down with starting fluid — a splash of booze in the last of the coffee. Then I had more straight from the bottle. "Inspiring bold John Barleycorn! What dangers thou canst make us scorn!"

*Evening, the woods below Slochd Pass*

After lunch I reached the River Dulnain and soon came to where the A9 leaves the boggy valley, climbing north over the pass towards Inverness. About halfway, the road stopped abruptly at the edge of a ravine or cutting, resuming its ascent on the far side. I had a difficult scramble through heavy brush to the bottom, where the wrecked bridge lay like a prehistoric skeleton on the railway it had spanned. Getting up the other side was easier technically, but harder on wind and limb.

It was Atlas pine and monkey-puzzle country so far, and I expected to enter the nostalgic realm of Scots pine at the top. But a forest fire passed this way not long ago. The trees thinned, gave way to blackened stumps in a glorious expanse of yellow broom with patches of grass and a brassy tarn. Water lilies were open in the sun, and I heard the plopping of frogs abandoning their pads as I passed. I quickened step, elated by this open land, the promise of a view — a view like the highlands we knew. But at the summit, gusts of fog came spilling over from the other side.

I walked on in cloud — chilly and claustrophobic — the bulb of visibility no more than ten or twenty yards across. Rocks and stumps reared at the edge of this dwarfish world, shapeless and threatening, like hooded strangers on the road. I halted for a fortifying swig.

Perhaps if I hadn't stopped they would have avoided me, would never have come in sight. I thought they were deer. They were indeed the size of large deer, with long necks and fine inquisitive heads turning in unison to watch me. At that instant, while curiosity on both sides outweighed fear, the fog thinned and we got a good look at one another. They were llamas.

No mistaking the haughty nose, the rabbit ears, the long-lashed bimbo eyes. I took this in clearly; my memory of it, though several hours old, seems filmed, no detail lost. Two were brown, one black, the other brown and white. And I'm certain that when they turned and ran back into the mist, I saw coloured ribbons flying from the tips of their ears. They have owners.

Part III

# THE SCOTTISH PLAY

*Edinburgh, third week of May*

A long silence, Anita, but not an uneventful one. First, seven verses to get off my chest, read-only memory; my exercise and consolation:

1: Cracks in the door are my Stonehenge.
    I track the sun and moon across the floor
    and mark the hours with scratches in the clay.
    For when the door swings open twice a day,
    the snapshot of the world's too brief, too bright,
    the aperture too wide, the light so fierce
    I'm blind.

2: They say it's mine, this fetid puddle in
    the dark; they force my face in it and ask
    *Why piss your bed?* But I know it's not mine.
    Rainwater maybe, filtered through the roof,
    through tons of mud. Or someone else's piss.
    They say I'm evil, that I'm mad—I hear
    them quarrelling—but they agree on this:
    that I must die.

3: They say I'm not a man; they call me "it."
    *What does it say? What will it eat? When will it die?*
    No matter that I have two legs like theirs,
    two arms, a face, two ears, a voice, a mind.

No matter that we speak related tongues,
that soon we'll understand each other well.
*A hornie, a hangie, a malkie, a sassenach,*
*a southron, a deil, a kelpie, a gow, a worricow—*
they have a thousand words for fears of me.
They brought me quicksilver, a dish to drink!
(And what an apparition I saw there!)
They brought me seawater, quicklime, some broth,
a llama foetus, garlic cloves, a girl's
first blood, a boy's first milt, a pot of pitch,
and these foul drippings they insist are mine.
Like an old ship I've been up-ended, scraped,
and probed. I'm bitten by their fleas and mice,
infested by their lice, and still they doubt
my kind. *Are ye fantastical?*

4: *Where are ye from?* A far and hot country
   is what I say, a southern place of lakes
   and mountains much like yours. And this
   makes matters worse. They'd rather that I've come
   from Edinburgh, from Perth, the Western Isles,
   or bubbled from the earth, formed in the air
   as a foul emanation of the loch.
   Look here—I say—look at these feet and hands.
   Aren't they like yours? Come here and touch this burn,
   these bones, and tell me: Am I not a man?

5: The things I hear: dawn flint on steel, the suck
   of human feet in clay, and llama hoofs;
   curses and laughter, children chanting as
   they pass my door; the sigh of bowels by day,
   the sighs of love at night. Roosters and owls,
   and in the mortar of my cave, a rat?

And free sounds from beyond the outer walls:
high wind in far-off trees, a parrot shriek,
a raven calling down the glen, and waves
reshuffling the fortunes of a shingle beach.

6: The things I see (if light outside is low)
when twice a day a keeper comes with food:
offal and skinny dogs on trampled ground;
a vulture hopping in a kitchen yard;
wild walls of stone and scrap-iron bricolage —
a misassembled puzzle of our world.

7: Things I don't hear: no bawl or moo, no bray,
no heavy flop of dung, no piglet squeals;
no engine sounds, no snort or neigh;
and on the cobbles and the mud no wheels.

There. It's down on plastic — the scanty word-hoard from my
first days of reunion with the human race. Days, I need hardly say,
of dread. Dread not only of my captors' intentions but of weak-
ness, of inability to speak or act in my defence; dread of the frac-
ture of body and health and mind.

I kept them short, a few lines a day, for I couldn't know how
many I'd have to save against the time when I'd have pen and
paper — if I lived. Such an incarceration seems at best a life sentence, at worst a waiting-room for death.

But I must back up and try to reconstruct the rest for you — from
the moment I saw the llamas that misty afternoon in March, and
soon afterwards became parted from my notebook.

Llama husbandry wasn't a subject on which I was well in-
formed. Would they be left to graze unsupervised? Or were their
herders not far off? With only an hour of daylight left, I decided to

slip back across the frontier of human presence. Contact — the fraught instant when worlds collide — Cook at Kealakekua Bay, Pizarro gaping at the golden temples of Peru — was best left for a new day.

Morning came without sunrise; just a brightening of the fog, a fade of black to grey and grey to white. I spent several hours getting ready, burying gun, tent, and other things I didn't want anyone to find. (I'd camped well off the road, where the woods stood thick and undisturbed.) I brought my notes up to date and buried them too. The danger I'd blithely courted fell on me again. What next? Go up to the first person I saw and say, *Take me to your leader?*

That was exactly what I had to do; that, or turn away forever.

The sun came out at eleven, breathing life into the shadows and steam into the woods. I bathed in a tarn and washed my beard and hair, which had become tangled with swatted bugs and drops of resin. I put on a fresh cotton shirt, underwear, socks, jeans. After a quick lunch I set off, taking only a small nylon bag with some chestnuts, a plastic sheet, one change of clothes, and the very last of the Yukon Thaw. I had no gifts for the locals — the Havanas and gold were in London — but in a pinch I could hand over these trifles. Plastic might be valued here like silk in the time of Marco Polo.

By early afternoon I was back at the pass, marked by a boulder I hadn't noticed the day before. Faded words beneath the lichen: *WITH GOD ALL THINGS ARE POSSIBLE*; and scribbled below: *Without him all things are permissible.* The mist had dropped but not broken; I was above it. The green scar of the old road swept down the hillside, banked above hollow and swamp, engraved into the land where its makers had driven through rock, until it sank into a great fleece of cloud like a child's idea of heaven. Across the horizon stretched an island chain of distant peaks. Beneath lay the Moray Firth, Culloden field, where the clans died, and the mouth of the Great Glen at Inverness, where Macbeth (as Shakespeare has him) stabbed Duncan in his bed. All long ago — perhaps forgotten by the oasis of humanity here now, a strange relict of our kind no doubt altered and deprived in unguessable ways. We had one thing in common, they and I, one thing I could be sure of: we were all survivors of a five-hundred-year voyage. Their genes had travelled through twenty generations; mine had got here self-contained in fifteen weeks. They the tortoise; I the hare.

The fog was thick as the previous day's. Camouflage. But if it hid me, it hid the unknown. After half an hour a silver coin appeared on a pale grey ceiling; a raven croaked and whistled; then the visibility ballooned quite suddenly to several hundred yards. I was in pasture again, mainly grass, rough with boulders and burnt logs, flaming with rhododendron and azalea in fiery clumps on the hillside. There were more llamas — several dozen. And sitting on a rise, their backs to me, three human figures.

They seemed to be wearing coarse cloaks or shawls, of the wool and colour of their flocks; on their heads were wide straw coolie hats rather like the palm sombrero I'd made in London and left in Edinburgh. These rough clothes, the outlandish animals, the landscape changed by fire, brought home to me the gulf between us. To approach in this mist would frighten them out of their minds.

But it was really I who was afraid. *Erik wez hier from Cassel Nessie. . . . Lang Liv MacBeath.* What folk were these? I was caught between panic and compulsion, like a spider at his fatal courtship. I had to retreat, slip away smoothly, quietly, be a peeping Tom. But I have poor nerves for such occasions. My breath came quick and short, and then the inevitable cough. The shepherds turned. And screamed.

They were girls or women — two short and stocky, one slim and tall, their faces dark in the deep shade under their hats. The afternoon light was behind them; all I could see were silhouettes, white teeth and eyes. But they had seen me well.

A sail of mist glided between us. I fled up the hill — tripping on old stumps, on undergrowth — back into the sun above the cloud and on deep into the woods, blindly, until lost. And it felt good to be lost.

I made a rough shelter of sticks and plastic, had a cold and cheerless supper, welcomed the night as it smothered me.

For hours I lay awake, thinking, sipping rum. Twice now I'd run. Tomorrow it was do or die. "To-morrow, and to-morrow, and to-morrow" — *Macbeth* gave me no peace that night, line after line floating up from a school play like bits of something drowned:

To-morrow, and to-morrow, and to-morrow,
Creeps in this petty pace from day to day,
To the last syllable of recorded time;
And all our yesterdays have lighted fools
The way to dusty death.

In the small hours my stomach forced me up. It was very dark, cloudy, moonless. I stumbled some way, squatted, exploded; listened to the woods: the violin creak of a rubbing branch, the washboard of a cricket or a frog; an owl. The fatal bellman.... "Hear it not, Duncan; for it is a knell that summons thee to heaven, or to hell."

Another owl. Strange how the same bird can have such a lugubrious effect on the human mind across ages, across cultures. "*Cuando el tecolote llora, el indio muere*: When the owl cries, the Indian dies." Wise bird, evil bird, always a bird of death.

A blanket fell over my head, a sensation of double darkness and a smell — damp wool and soot, a peasant smell of earth, wood-smoke, dung. I was off my feet. My wrists were seized and bound, and my ankles. A pole was thrust between the bindings. I was slung and borne away like a dead boar.

They carried me for about an hour without a word to one another or to me. Perhaps they feared that I was only one of many. Then I was set down roughly and left on my side, trussed and hooded, while my captors slept. I could hear their farts and snores.

They were up before dawn, eating hastily. They carried me without a halt until about midday, when I heard a chiming of flint and steel, smelt tinder smoke. They cooked—a smell of beans—and sat waiting for something or someone. The heat was stifling. Not once did they remove the filthy hood. Fleas or lice were crawling on my face and down my neck. But I said nothing; I listened.

Remember that pub in Glasgow, where we were both sure the patrons were speaking Gaelic until certain words—fuck this, fuck that, and football scores—revealed that the language we couldn't understand was English? It was like that. They were talking in low, wary voices. They might have been speaking Basque or Hungarian for all I recognized at first, but words and phrases gradually showed themselves. It was a form of Scots, about as far from our own English, it seemed, as Langland's. Or a better analogy would be Dunbar—wasn't he writing here in Scotland five-hundred-years from our time? You would know. I've not forgotten your inspired recital of *Tua Mariit Wemen and the Wedo* at Anna Lau's wedding—the bit where a wife calls her husband: *ane wallifrag, ane worme, ane auld wobat carle.... Ane bumbart, ane dron bee, ane bag full of flewme.*

A bumblebee, a drone, a bag of phlegm. I'm still not fluent in twenty-sixth-century vernacular. My immersion was too brief. I got by (and, for reasons I'll come to, they understood me better than I them). A valley is still a glen, a lake a loch, a house a hoose, a stream a burn. They still have the burr and contractions, the rolled *r*, the long vowels, the lovely survivals of Old English, the craggy loans from Norse and Gaelic. But of course they've lost many words and coined others whose meaning I could only guess.

A young woman seemed to be suggesting that I be given food and water. With hindsight, I think the conversation—much simplified—went something like this:

"What if he dee? What'll the laird say?"

"That kind disna dee." (A gruff, older man.)

"Gi' him some air, for pity's sake." (The girl's voice.)

"Ye'll no look on it. Ye'll no unmask the Malkie."

"Och, he's no hangie. You didna see him yestreen, Kenneth. Awful fair. He looks like Jasus."

"Nae blasphemy from you!"

So the girl was one of the herders who had seen me. It wasn't the first time I'd been compared to Jesus. It happened a lot in Latin America—my blue eyes and blond waves matched every dashboard Christ.

They moved on after a couple of hours. I was trussed again, and later bundled into a dory—a dugout, I thought, from its heavy movement and the thunk whenever a paddle struck the side. We crossed a smooth loch—too smooth and short a trip to be Loch Ness. But they were in no hurry once we reached the other side, as if they felt secure. Just before nightfall we climbed down from the hills, back into the subtropical lowlands or a valley floor. The air was close, the blanket more oppressive. I thought I could hear the swash and tinkle of water on a pebbly shore; I wondered if it was the firth near Inverness.

Next morning there was a man's voice I hadn't heard before —younger, apparently a messenger from the personage they called the "laird." I was weak and very parched, so parched I felt no hunger at the breakfast smells. Hearing the girl's light step nearby, I called for water. She shushed me, but she understood. Words like water don't change. I heard her pleading with the others. About ten minutes later I was pulled to my feet and held roughly from behind—hardly necessary as my hands were still tied.

"So ye're flesh and blood, are ye?" A middle-aged man, in my ear.

"I won't be much longer, without a drink." I tried to speak clearly and firmly, but my tongue was glued in my mouth.

"It speaks!" He almost threw me down in surprise.

"Whaur's Kenneth?"

"Doon by the currach." The girl's musical voice.

"Okay, Mailie. But keep its eyen seeled."

*Okay.* There was comfort in that modern word. For a moment it dispelled the Dark Age ambience beyond the blindfold. Nervous fingers loosened the hood, a corner was pulled up as far as my nose. I drew a splendid draught of morning air. "Still!" the girl said. I did as told and was rewarded with the touch of earthenware to my lips, the water cool and beautiful, leafy and crisp with minerals. How could I ever have drunk anything else—especially that Canadian antifreeze, still burning like gall in my stomach, responsible for at least half my dehydration? And my capture. They mightn't have bagged me like that if I'd been sober.

A whistle came from some way off; my hood was tugged down quickly. The eldest man, Kenneth, had returned.

They allowed me to shuffle downhill on hobbled feet. The fresh air I'd breathed for a few moments told me that we were not beside the sea. There was no hint of salt, of mangroves or shellfish; only the mushroom smell of fresh water. I heard "Nessie" mentioned: it had to be Loch Ness. In retrospect, I must have spent the night not far from the spot where you and I camped years ago beside the old military road that ran along the south shore below the mountain wall, beneath a fringe of oak and beech; where, just as we'd pitched our tent and made a fire, a dour character in full highland fig appeared, straight from central casting, wire-wool hair sprouting from a tam, a villain's beard, thatchy eyebrows, and his hand out. *We charge sax poond fifty for camping.* Even you didn't argue, Anita.

It became clear to my captors that they couldn't get me safely into a currach without my co-operation. To co-operate I'd have to see. The young man, whose name I didn't catch, argued with the one called Kenneth. He had instructions to unhood me before we reached the far shore anyway. The "laird" wanted a bit of a show.

They freed my legs and bared my head, grasping my arms from behind.

We were at the top of a rough stone jetty shaded by coconut palms and several large tropical hardwoods, the newly risen sun behind them. Beyond the trees' long shadows the lake was a smooth aquamarine, scored here and there by the swallowtail wake of tiny craft with scissoring oars. A few had sails but these hung limp. We were opposite Urquhart Bay—neat, cultivated, pale green with grass or a young crop! Above bay and fields, dark wooded mountains lost themselves behind a shelf of cloud, reappearing much higher as a pod of whalebacks. At the nearest point across the water, about a mile away, I could see the great keep of Urquhart Castle, its walls drenched with dawn. And further round the bay, beyond the small river that enters the loch, where you may remember alder and willow thickets, was a suggestion of more building, more stone walls and gables, and little exclamations of smoke in the still air. A living town! I can't tell you what joy—and what apprehension—the sight stirred after fifteen weeks and five hundred miles of ruin. Like finding life on Mars.

All this time—the timeless instant that the view absorbed me—my captors were behind. I saw fishermen on the water, people walking on the far shore, but I did not see an inhabitant of the glen close up until Kenneth and the younger man had pushed me down the jetty and into the boat. I stared at them, and in surprise turned to the woman and the other man, who had stayed ashore. All four of them were black.

For the rest of the crossing it was easier to observe the boat than my boatmates. The younger, whose name sounded like Rob or Hob, took the oars, Kenneth sitting beside me in the stern. Whenever my eyes fell upon either, the oarsman swore and Kenneth prodded me with a dagger he kept in his belt. They abhorred my gaze, and they particularly objected to sly glances I threw at the receding girl. She was the tall one of the three I'd seen with the llamas.

In spite of the rising heat, she kept on the long shawl she'd been wearing in the hills, fastened over her breasts by what seemed an old nickel soup spoon with the handle sharpened to a prong. The men had untailored cotton shirts, essentially sacks with a hole for the head and short, wide sleeves. Both sexes wore a hairy wool kilt which ended just below the knee; they were barefoot. In the shade they'd been bareheaded, but on the lake they donned their coolie hats. I soon regretted not having kept my own; I got the worst sunburn since that first day on the Thames. God, that seemed so long ago, and my hopes of a sleek new world pathetically naive.

The craft was flimsy, beamy, about twenty feet long, its hull made from hides sewn over a withe frame and caulked along the seams with resin or pitch. The idle lateen sail was a reed mat, like that of a Polynesian outrigger canoe. The rough, drab clothing, the crude boat—these were not merely mediaeval; it was as if I'd landed in the Neolithic.

When Hob (this turned out to be the right pronunciation) had pulled about halfway across, there came a bark from Kenneth and he shipped his oars. The old man fossicked in a leather bag, took out a small earthenware cup and a whisky bottle—no different from those of our time, though the label was missing. He poured a tot, muttered a few words, and emptied it over the side. He did this six times to starboard, six to port, and six over the stem. When the lake had received these offerings, the men tossed off a dram each, toasting *Nessie!* as they did so. I thought: six, six, six: the number of the Beast? (For an Anglican, Uncle Phil was unduly fond of Revelation.) Many things had gone in five centuries, but the Monster, it seemed, was not among them.

"What lives in the loch?"

"Fash," said Hob.

"How big?"

"Stop yer widdle!" Muscles rippled under Kenneth's dark skin as he brandished his dirk, though he looked at least sixty. He was shorter than the other but strong, and behind his snowy beard was the set countenance of a martinet, a fanatic. The young fellow had a kind, open face, boyish despite a thin goatee, and I got the feeling he had something going with the girl, or wanted to — he'd looked wistfully back at her as he pulled away.

I am looking up from a book about which I remember nothing, looking out through an oval window in a curved wall of smooth beige plastic. The window of a 747. I look up from the book, through my spirit face in the glass, and am overwhelmed by the *unlikeliness* of flight — saying (to you? Yes, you're there with your food tray down): Who would think that the air is thick enough for thousands of tons of metal to swim like a whale? And you: *Who can expect that this thing's million parts will always work perfectly? They say you land naked if you're blown from a plane. The wind rips your clothes off like a maniac.* Then I see a silver engine blossom in flames, feel the lurching cabin, hear the screams.

The screams and a rough hand on my shoulder shaking me, the fishy smell of the currach, the wet wool and sweat of my captors, their eyes wide as I opened mine (glad, or sorry, I hadn't died?). The screaming — more an ululation — was floating across the still water from a large crowd below the castle on the Urquhart shore. At least, it looked large; I suppose almost any gathering would after months without another human soul. Perhaps two hundred were lining the gravelly beach and a wooden jetty where several currachs and dugouts were moored.

As the crowd resolved into individuals I saw that my captors were typical: all of them were black. A photographic matt, an ebony gloss, a deep indigo — their skins varied. The palest were the colour of a walnut stain. Large hats hid their hair, but it seemed that while some had the mop of Africa or Melanesia, worn in an assortment of springy locks and dandelions, many had straight hair, shaggy or woven in braids. Almost all the men were bearded.

Until the blindfold had come off, my curiosity had been able to focus only on language—and the language of these people did not at all fit their look. Where could they have come from? The number of blacks living in the Scottish highlands in our day must have been infinitesimal. But if the ancestors of these people had fled from city ghettos or burning tropics, why were they speaking like Rob Roys? How had they established themselves here, avoided whatever catastrophe silenced the rest of Britain? And what had happened to the real Rob Roys—the Celtic redheads and Norse blonds, the milky dark-haired Picts?

We landed at the jetty below the castle. The onlookers seemed not merely curious but tense. Dogs were barking, gulls screamed overhead, but the only sound from the people now was a murmur when my feet touched ground. No hat, yellow hair, a reddening face, blue cotton shirt, jeans, running shoes—I certainly stood out from the crowd. The front line wavered when I took a step; there was muttering from the back. A squad of a dozen guards took me from the boatmen. These guys were a bit more impressive. Their kilts had an attempt at a tartan, their hats were leather (oddly like fedoras), they wore wide brown belts and carried wooden staves. I was hobbled again, deprived of my shoes, and frogmarched towards the ancient walls. People pressed after us, but were driven back.

The castle had seen some renovations since you and I scrambled over it—largely *ad hoc*, without regard for period harmony. The keep was crudely roofed with slate and tile from various sources. Gaps in the outer wall were filled with fieldstone, breeze-blocks, pieces of iron, crumbling brick. The most extraordinary feature—one I failed to see until we had made our way through the crowd along the beach—was an avenue of car bodies set on end like ancient menhirs. Perhaps once they served a defensive purpose as tank traps or firing positions, for there's a gently sloping meadow across the neck of the peninsula here, between the castle's jutting headland and the lakeshore mountains. I recognized a Jaguar, a Benz or two, and several American sedans—all large models from the final years of plenty. Some twenty-first-century laird must have gone to a lot of trouble ransacking the garages of Inverness and the U.S. base at Cawdor. I was amazed the cars hadn't rusted away long ago, but it was clear from their daubed look and tarry smell that they were given regular coats of pitch. Three of the best formed a triumphal gate in front of the broken mediaeval towers of the main entrance—two Cadillacs for uprights and a Rolls for the lintel.

We passed through this steel trilithon, then an original stone arch, to enter the lower bail. This area was occupied, as it would have been in ancient times, by a barracks or quarters for the castle staff, storerooms, several small sheds and wooden houses, a dovecot, and a low kitchen with a bulking chimney. My chief impression that day was of a barnyard. Turkeys, chickens, dogs, and cats were strutting and sunning themselves on beaten earth littered with corn cobs and gnawed bones. The place stank of rancid fat, latrines, a compost heap. I was hustled along towards the keep, the five-storey tower-house which so enchanted you with its fireplaces and bedchambers and the spiral stair we climbed to a rainswept view of loch and scowling mountains.

What was the name of that local historian with Mick Jagger lips—like a prolapsed rectum—who befriended you on the battlements? You'd mentioned the Scots in your family, the Forbes line, and he was delighted because some old Forbes had been warlord here back in the twelfth century. I've forgotten most of it—he must have rambled on for an hour—though some comes back in his own words. Colourful names of hard men: the Red Bard, Alexander the Crafty, the Wolf of Badenoch. The Hammer of the Scots and Robert the Bruce, centuries of chaos as Urquhart passed back and forth between Edinburgh kings and the Macdonalds of the Isles, who struck again and again up the natural corridor of the Great Glen "like a dirk atween the ribs of Scotland." (Then came the unpleasantness when the bastard tried to grope you in the dungeon, but let's not go into that.)

Two men were at attention, sort of, beneath a stucco coat of arms. I couldn't make out the heraldic devices on the shield; there seemed to be animal heads and crossed swords or daggers — the thing was crumbling away — but I could read a motto: *Sleep No More.*

We passed into a dark hall occupying the whole ground floor. The squad halted, the leader climbed the stairs. My eyes had time to adjust to the light, smoky with incense and the burnt margarine smell of palm-oil lamps. I saw two field-guns and several old cannon, a big V-twin motor (from a Harley? a Vincent? Bird would have known), and the glassy stare of three or four computer screens or TV tubes. Hanging on the far wall was a life-size crucifix, its Christ blond, bloody, emaciated; blue eyes turned heavenward beneath a thorny crown. He was flanked by oil paintings in very poor condition, perhaps ancestral portraits, and at his feet was a pair of shaggy long-horned heads — from Highland bulls.

On the south wall was a bicycle seat with a handlebar above it, a traffic light, a kitchen clock (upside-down), and a sconce-type porcelain urinal. The assemblage was disorienting, at once too odd and too familiar. Merely a jackdaw gathering of junk? Or the work of some art connoisseur with a taste for landmark modernists?

The officer of the guard returned before I could appreciate the collection more fully. I was hauled and pushed up the spiral stairs, two men ahead of me, the rest behind. We came out into a hall directly above the first, its rough-sawn planks — I could feel them on my soles — strewn here and there with bearskins. The window shutters were closed, the only natural light falling from two or three arrowslits — slender sunbeams blue with smoke from lamps beside a dais. On the dais were a few attendants and a throne, and on the throne was a man. A huge man.

He was wearing a felt Mexican sombrero, moth-eaten and

battered but with all the silver trimmings — a genuine antique from the look of it — a galaxy of a hat that might have adorned a revolutionary hero or a high-priced mariachi singer. Below this, in the moody gloom that such a hat creates, was a puffy face, very dark, with bloodshot St. Bernard eyes floating above a cataract of grizzled beard. The rest of him was covered by a sleeveless jacket made from a black cougar skin complete with head (which snarled at his belly), a tartan kilt (recognizably Royal Stuart), sporran and dirk, and size-fifteen crocodile boots.

This was it: the fraught meeting of alien king and white invader, the encounter of worlds. Would he be florid and obsequious like Moctezuma to Cortés: "My lord, you are weary, you are tired"? Or a disdainful and sarcastic Atahuallpa, flinging down the Bible, averting his nose from the smelly barbarians who dared disturb him at his bath? The deeds of the conquistadors suggest that the best form on such occasions is to be insanely arrogant. I should have begun by informing the laird that I was sent personally by God to tell him that everything he believed in was rubbish, that his soul would burn forever if he didn't do as I said, and that I just might be able get him off the eternal bonfire if he'd allow me to relieve him of his gold, his wives, his kingdom, and his life.

All very well if you're encased in Toledo steel, backed by hundreds of desperadoes with the matches glowing on their muskets, and the natives are dropping right and left from smallpox. But I was trussed like a capon, gagged with a filthy rag, surrounded by a goon squad, and if anyone here was dying of plague it was me.

The guards threw me down and attached my bound hands, which were behind me, to the hobbles on my feet.

"Can it speak?"

"Kenneth says it can, my laird."

The laird had his men ungag me. I was left on my knees, still bound with leather thongs — looking, I imagine, like bottom dog in a homoerotic film. He raised himself from his chair, came within a yard, and shouted something that sounded like *cock-a-leekie*. Whenever he spoke, his beard sprang into obscene life, a small red mouth winking and smacking at the middle of it like the beak of an octopus. I made no reply. He repeated himself more slowly. I began to understand. He wanted to know if I came from "Castle Reekie."

"I'll speak when your men untie me, and not before."

The laird sat down, sighed, gave a low command. A guard lit a torch from one of the lamps.

"Toast 'im, and we'll see if he can sing." (At least, that's what I think he said.)

The guard held hissing pitch-pine to my face. I smelt singed hair and flesh, felt the burn.

I said: "What's Castle Reekie?" At this they all burst out laughing. I considered asking if they meant Edinburgh, then thought better of it. Familiarity with Scottish geography would only make them more suspicious. At a nod from the laird, the man burned through the thong binding my hands to my feet.

I began to give my story. In the long hours since my ignominious capture, I'd had time to decide I was from Llareggub, Wales —the only mountainous part of Britain far enough from Scotland that they would probably know nothing of it. There, I said, a similar community of devout farmers and fishers had survived the catastrophe that struck the rest of the world. We'd survived but we were not thriving (therefore no threat). We were short of seeds and breeding stock, and were ourselves exceedingly inbred. Hideous deformities had appeared amongst us, of which pale skin and yellow hair were but two of the more benign. In short, we were failing. Desperate, the laird of Llareggub had sent out four young men of noble birth to search for other people. One went south, one east, one west across the sea, and I had come north.

The laird listened, eyes bulging like pickled onions beneath his hat.

"We have histories," he said, scanning the room, addressing his companions rather than me. "Histories that were old when ma great grandfather, Erik the Bold, ruled Castle Nessie. And they tell that no one has lived in the hotlands since the Lord God smote the Gentiles. No one."

"Gentiles?"

"Folk like you. I say ye're no freak of birth. I say ye're a Malkie, a spook, a pink, a paleface, an ofay, a gowie, a cueball, a cream-faced loon. . . . How can I put it plainly to ye, man?" He let out a great hiss of exasperation, as if his huge form had sprung a leak. "Ye're a pairson of nae colour!"

He searched me for a reaction and, seeing none, turned to the cross of sunlight in an arrowslit. "Where *have* yew come from? And what the hell do ye think ye're doing, scunging roond our glen?"

A tricky moment. I had to impress them somehow. I began weakly, then *Macbeth* came to my rescue: "In Llareggub there are mountains as big as any here. And lakes almost as long and deep. We know no more of you than you of us. Your people and mine are islands, far over the horizon from each other, standing upon opposite shores of a sea of desolation. Alas! poor country. It cannot be called our mother, but our grave; where violent sorrow seems a modern ecstasy, and good men's lives expire before the flowers in their caps."

Whether or not they knew my lifted eloquence, it seemed to give them pause. The laird puffed himself back up to his normal size and gazed ponderously into the middle distance, the picture of Orson Welles. Behind him on the dais were three others: a woman and two men, richly dressed by local standards. The woman approached the throne, ducked below the hat brim, and whispered in my interrogator's ear for a good five minutes. The laird nodded several times; at the end he smiled.

"Undae him."

And he was holding out his huge mitt of a hand for me to take. "Macbeth of Macbeth."

"David Lambert. . . . Of Lambert."

His bloodshot eyes were twinkling. Suddenly my hand was crumpling in his like a ball of waste paper. The pain so unexpected —such a violation of custom and courtesy—that I heard the cracking bones before I felt the break.

# — 2 —

A soggy floor. Darkness. I didn't know where I was, or when, or whether daylight could find its way in there. I thought it might be the dungeon beneath the keep, where the local historian, having sent his wife to the car for film, pressed his sordid advances on you. But those thoughts came gradually; pain had woken me—my hand worse than the burn on my face—and the first worry was the extent of the damage. I tried to feel the bones, left hand seeking right, the flesh so swollen and the pain so fierce I obtained only more fuel for my fears. To be a prisoner was bad enough, to be seriously injured so much worse. I thought of the empty England that was mine. I thought of the woodland camp where I'd buried my things during the precious hours when I knew of these people but they knew nothing of me. Why had I squandered that freedom, that advantage? I wished the nightmare clansmen away, wished them dead like all the rest and the land empty again. Empty except for me—and I would gladly leave, go back to the machine and sail on to a brave new world without such people in it.

Had this been Tania's fate? It was a long time since I'd thought of her. Her absence no longer seemed so inexplicable: she'd landed somewhere, somewhere like this—or not like this; we are all, as you said, barbarians and always will be—had been stripped and murdered on the spot. Couldn't it have been that simple: Tania killed; her machine spinning its lightning cocoon before her wide-eyed killers and vanishing to rendezvous with me? (Of course this won't quite do: why would they have thrown her clothes back inside? But that didn't occur to me till later.) At the time, this violence brought to mind that other violence, Anita: the night of the May Ball, or rather the morning after.

Wasn't it actually in June? (How we English loved such things: May balls in June; public schools that were private; a Prince of Wales who was never Welsh; and I remember Bird saying how he distinguished British spanners from American: *If it says 'alf-inch and it's not 'alf-inch, then it's a Brit*). The pain you must have felt, the shock, the astounding plume of blood. Was that what killed you, love — not the spilt blood but its replacement, an infusion of slow death into your young blue veins? In my life there've been too many deaths and wrong turns; too many times I've wanted to seize Time by the throat, stop him, make him go back and try again, pause for second thoughts, rewrite his rash and careless history.

Somehow our escape to the North, our naughty fortnight, seemed to have escaped Bird's notice. At least I thought so; perhaps you didn't. If so you kept the knowledge to yourself. And if so, why would Bird have left you in sticky hands for such an occasion? Oysters, caviar, roast boar, a good cellar; a night of dancing to the Organ Donors; a dreamy punt down the river at dawn, a giggly swim in evening dress and out of it, a champagne breakfast — you don't let the love of your life and your best friend have a night like that together if you doubt them.

Or do you, if you're Bird? I never believed for a moment he couldn't afford the tickets. When Bird needed cash he always found it, no questions asked. Was it that cruel streak of his, that need to make a public scene? The dear fellow had his rough edges. Or was it a message for you, a bringing to heel, a letting you know that he wasn't quite stuck to the flypaper?

Did you see him arrive, or was it a surprise for both of us? Did you suspect he might be coming? And — forgive me for asking — but is there a chance you might have been trying to beat the Bird at his own game? Rattle the cage, rouse the jaundiced monster, make him forget his blessed bikes and dismal results, even his jazz, and break into a cold sweat at the thought he might lose you to his old mate Dave?

One day perhaps we'll talk this over, you and I, on a marble terrace while the sun drains into the Nile.

There were two or three different jailers. They came hooded, wrapped like winter shrubs in malodorous rags. I told them apart by their silhouettes, their smells, the sound of their breathing as they went about their tasks. They never spoke. They entered, set down a bowl of thick soup, a corn cob, a slab of bannock. In a corner by the door was a sand basket and some handfuls of moss — my litter box. This was replaced once a day. Don't ask me why they went on about the puddle on the floor; it must have been some sort of mind game to wear me down. These chaps weren't the Gestapo but they'd do until the real thing came along. Doubtless my stool was the subject of faecal divinations by the so-called doctor who tested me from time to time with his array of magical substances.

Home visits from this latter-day Finlay were my only long exposures to any light. He had to see me so I saw quite a bit of him. The fellow was a cross between a shaman and a carpenter — dreadlocked, wall-eyed, half stewed on whisky, dragging around a tool kit that owed more to a garage than a clinic: a rusty coping saw, a chrome-plated claw hammer (his pride), a horse syringe, several crumpled hypodermics that might have dropped from the arms of ancient junkies, a fleam, assorted spikes and chisels, a crucifix, a dog-eared tarot pack, a rectal plug, and a large pair of fireplace bellows whose application I didn't care to contemplate.

He had little interest in my burn and hand except as triggers of pain. The brief given him by the laird was to determine whether I was human. He rubbed at my skin, sniffed my breath, peered down my throat and ears, hit my knees with his hammer, poked a cold chisel up my arse. His efforts to obtain a semen sample excited only himself. In the end he had to bring in a hooded woman — I still don't know who she was — to do the deed. The poor thing was shivering with terror but somehow managed to gain control of her fingers. I considered warning them that my precious bodily fluids might be deadly, but decided against it: such a declaration would only weaken my claim to be a normal man.

I presume he opted for that canny Scottish verdict: not proven. On the seventh night I fell asleep in the vault and woke in a better place.

I was staring up into a small cone of poles and thatch, draped with cobwebs and pimpled with the little brown igloos of mud-wasps. A fieldstone wall surrounded me, daubed with clay and white-wash, the white darkened by mildew. The place, about twelve feet in diameter, resembled an African hut and smelled like a barn. There were no windows, no chairs, no boxes, no furniture of any kind. Daylight leaked in through small gaps between the eaves and the top of the wall, and through a thin yellow parchment tacked over an open panel in the door, which was made of planks pegged together. I was on a lumpy bed of llama skins and reeds over a masonry sleeping platform that filled a third of the room. A brown woollen blanket was drawn over my body. My clothes had been taken off and were not in sight. I'd been bitten all over by insects. Even so I felt rested, hungry. I got up, wrapped the blanket around me, pushed the door. It swung open, giving onto the upper bailey — the oldest part of the castle, an Iron Age hill fort — which I hadn't been able to see the morning I arrived. My hut was one of several; the others seemed to be used as corn cribs.

It was early afternoon. A guard spotted me and shouted something in the direction of the kitchens. I sat down on the edge of the bed, leaving the door ajar. Little eddies of wind were whirling in the yard, twitching long grass and nettles below the outer

wall, wafting Chaucerian smells from the direction of the main
gate and the keep: ageing meat and offal; urine, straw, and dung;
soapy coriander drying beneath the eaves. Intimate stinks spared us
by plumbing, plastic, and refrigeration. Ten minutes later a tall
young woman came. She knocked, took off her hat, hung it on a
peg by the door, entered nervously.

"Yer puir face!" She bent over me.

"I thought they left you behind," I said. "Across the loch."

She seemed pleased that I recognized her. A sting of salt as
she dabbed my burn with seawater. She said the laird's men had
fetched her in a currach "airly this morn."

My relocation from cell to rustic sanatorium was so unexpected and abrupt that the hiatus, I felt, could have been of any
length. Had I been in a coma?

"What day is it?"

She said it was Tuesday.

"Are we still in March?" She made an odd little moue at this,
raising an eyebrow as if I'd asked something inappropriate or
beyond her. She seemed to understand me quite well, though our
conversation was much more laborious than it appears here — broken by hunts for synonyms, mime, roundabout explanations.

She was only an inch or two shorter than I. There was something reserved, even melancholy in her manner. I told her my name
and offered my hand but she kept hers clasped modestly in front
of her. Perhaps it wasn't done for men and women to shake hands.
Her name was Mailie — I remembered that I'd heard the others
call her that while I was trussed and hooded.

"Just Mailie?"

"Just Mailie. Mailie Macbeth." An awkward silence during
which I became aware of the wasps: their heavy drone as they flew
in laden, their preoccupied buzzing as each deposited its clay and
worked it onto the rim of a cell like a potter coiling a vase. I was
reeling again with the fear that I'd utterly misread the facts. Did

you ever meet any Scots named Macbeth? I never did, nor heard of any except a modern poet and a TV character. Shakespeare's villain had done for that name what Hitler did for Adolf. How likely is it, I thought, that the sole survivors in all of Britain are a black clan called Macbeth?

"Is everyone here a Macbeth?"

"Most all of us," Mailie said. "'Cept a few Macdonalds and Grants. And McMalkies up Glen Africa."

"Malkies? People have been calling me a Malkie. Do the McMalkies look like me?"

She laughed. "McMalkie's no the ilk as Malkie! Nivver let anyone hear ye say that! It's just their name up glen. They're like all of us. But you—well I say ye look like Jasus."

Mailie Macbeth was a bright girl, uncowed by the gorgon sight of me and spirited despite her sadness, which did not seem characteristic and which I soon came to know fell on her in spells, the way afternoon cloud-shadows chill a sunny hillside. She said she was seventeen and lived in the castle with the laird's household. She stood straight, a dancer's bearing, hands still clasped, allowing my gaze to roam over her high cheekbones, upturned nose, strong chin. Her face was gentle, slightly pockmarked by a childhood disease but not disfigured. Mailie's glory was her mouth—moist and slightly open—her mouth and her hair, which hung in a single black plait to her waist. (Bird would have got into trouble here in no time.) Naturally straight hair. Not as African as you'd think. These people were mixed.

"Then what *is* a Malkie?" A long silence; I thought she wasn't going to say. But she was thinking.

"An outlander. A waghorn. A sassenach. Kind of a deevil."

"Have you ever seen one?"

"Me? No! It's the auld folk talk of seeing Malkies." She shook her head to change the subject. "Ah'm tae feed you, not chatter."

I asked for my clothes.

She left for about half an hour, bringing back not my stuff but a local kilt and shirt. These I accepted without protest. She also brought a bowl of stew: potatoes, sweetcorn, onions, mysterious salted meat and entrails, presumably bits of llama. "Eat up!" she said when I fished a piece out to inspect it. "Ye're lucky to get thairms in Lent. It's only 'cause ye look sae dwaibly."

Lent: if they knew how to calculate Easter, then the date I'd seen in Edinburgh could be reliable, more or less. The moon had been waxing when I was captured, so Easter would be late this year, the last Sunday in April. I asked why she'd been chosen to look after me; what about her llamas?

"Ma what?"

"Your flock. Your animals."

"The sheep? There's lasses eneuch for them." Her expression darkened, and the lilt died in her voice. "Ang…the laird told me tae come. I'm his…cousin. Hob told him he thought ye might… well, trust me mair than anither." I was burning to know why their behaviour towards me had changed. Why had they let me live at all? Was it politics? While some saw me as a threat, did others see me as an opportunity? Behind her hesitations was a skein of intrigue, but I decided not to pick at it until we knew each other better.

"Are there other kinds of sheep?"

"What kinds hae ye seen? There's brown and brindled, black and ring-straked. . . ."

"I mean smaller woolly animals that go *baa*. " She giggled at the noise I'd produced, then frowned. I said that in Wales we had this different race of sheep, as well as goats, horses, pigs, and cows.

"I've haird of 'em. In the Book. And oxen and asses." She twisted her plait. "We never see 'em here. There's boar in the woods. And bears, wolves, lions." The lions were pumas, I guessed, relatives of the one whose skin adorned the laird. Where there were llamas, there'd be pumas. Graham might have liked it here — though I'd have made a disastrous impression turning up with her.

"Where did those Highland bulls' heads in the keep come from?" I had to elaborate before she understood me.

"Those are no bulls!" She was shocked, frightened. "Macbeth the Great sned those heids frae the Beast." You could hear the capital letter in her voice, the same tone she'd used for the Book.

I got the drift of the legend from her little by little. The Beast, also known as Nessie and Auld Hornie, lives in the loch. Originally it had seven heads. One head would devour a human victim on each night of the week. But ever since Macbeth the Great ambushed it and cut off two heads, one on a Saturday and the other on a Sunday, it has confined itself to occasional feasts of "sheep"—and only on weeknights.

The local clothes were irritating my skin. I scratched my waist and shoulders, thought of Uncle Phil reading John of Patmos aloud in his chair by the fire.

"How does it go?" I said to myself as much as to her. "I saw a beast rise up out of the sea, having seven heads and ten horns, and upon his heads the name of blasphemy."

"Quaiet! Dinna *ever* speak like that ootside the kirk!" She snatched up her things and bolted.

For several days Mailie was my only visitor, though I glimpsed other people—cooks, guards, a few grubby children—when I went to use the ill-smelling jakes in the outer wall. They avoided my eye and quickened their step, but I could feel the heat of their curiosity when my back was turned. Mailie was one of the few not afraid of me. It seemed she had instructions to restore my strength, gain my confidence, and pump me about my identity. I resolved to learn more from her than I gave away, and I began to suspect that she and Macbeth were rather more than cousins.

By the end of another week my face was healing and my hand had started to go down. I could feel the bones now; only the little finger was broken. I wanted to see the town, the former

Drumnadrochit, which they pronounced "Dumnorrit." I asked Mailie if the laird might allow me to attend church next Sunday. She said she'd ask.

On Saturday morning two guards appeared at my door and escorted me to the throne room. Macbeth and his wife were there alone, the woman scowling on a smaller, less elaborate chair. The shutters were open in an east window, letting in a wedge of sunlight and a sultry breeze off the loch. She was younger than he, mid-thirties perhaps, erect, gaunt about the eyes: a handsome woman gnawed by some intractable hunger. Her black hair, etched with filaments of white, was braided and wound Grecian-style around her head. Her shawl was pinned with a large silver brooch worked in an intricate Pictish beast design (an artefact of the eighth century or the twentieth?), and her plaid skirt swept down to a pair of gnarled feet in leather sandals. On her lap, wheezing and snuffling, was an asthmatic Pekinese — a mop with eyes. (A pedigree lapdog *here*? A throwback, I suppose.)

The hall looked less sinister than it had on the day of my arrival. I noticed lengths of broadloom carpet on the walls, a hideous orange *cloqué* that might have come from a hotel bar, so worn and rotten it resembled early mediaeval tapestry. Rows of silvery disks — CDs, no less — were nailed on beams like horsebrasses. Over the throne was a stucco coat of arms and two metal signs with legible writing. One said: *Historic Scotland Welcomes You To Urquhart Castle. This way to* son et lumière *carpark.* The other was a nameplate:

GREAT GLEN RESEARCH STATION
CROP AND ANIMAL DIVISION
DRUMNADROCHIT, GLEN URQUHART.
No admittance. Official business only.
All enquiries from the public to Room 101,
Ministry of Interior, Inverness.

"Ah've decided to give ye the benefit of the doot," came the deep voice from the beard. "Agin ma lady's better judgement." Her scowl was turned on me.

"Ye'll come to kirk as ma guest. If ye say onything at all, or do onything disrespectful, ye're a dead Malkie. But first we must have yer intentions." He leant back expectantly, the wood groaning like an old barge under his shifting load. My eyes strayed to the coat of arms on the wall above him, the stucco much crisper than its weathered counterpart outside. The heads were plainly bull's heads attached to scaly dragon-like necks, and beneath the motto *Sleep No More*, in larger letters, was *LANG LIV MACBEATH*. The same odd spelling I'd seen in graffiti. *MacBeath Squad*. A laboured pun?

Lady Macbeth (or MacBeath, but I prefer the former) fidgeted and sighed. The dog leapt down. I came back smartly to the here and now.

With their lordships' permission, I said I should like to stay a while, learn the secrets of Glen Nessie's success, and return home to Llareggub. If they agreed, I'd recommend to my own lord and lady that communication be opened between the two kingdoms (the grand word seemed to go down well). We could offer a few animals and crops that Glen Nessie didn't have. . . .

"Are ye Christians?"

"Indeed we are. As devout as you'll find. We attend chapel — as we say for kirk — not only on Sundays but every day."

He said he himself held matins every day, and I was welcome to come too, though most of his flock, alas, bestirred themselves only once a week. He beckoned two leather-hatted guards. "Show him the crypt, then tak him hame."

He turned to me. "We're going to begin yer education. Any tricks and ye'll end up like the buggers doonstairs." I assured him there'd be no tricks, adding that I'd need someone to escort me to kirk the first time, to make sure I did nothing disrespectful by mistake. I thought perhaps Mailie. He nodded, turning with a moment's hesitation to his lady. I became aware of a mole on her chin which was bleeding slightly, as if she had just scratched it.

The men led me down to the cellar beneath the keep, their sweat and unwashed wool filling the close air on the stairs. At the bottom of the spiral steps my toes sank into a soft clay floor where the guard in front planted the hilt of his pitch-pine torch (Mailie had not been allowed to return my shoes). Black fumes soon filled the barrel-vault and gathered about our heads, seeking an outlet. I'm sure you remember that unpleasant space, with its sodden tissues and smell of piss in the corners. It was now filled by a neat grocer's pyramid of human skulls, some with a crust of bat guano, others gleaming like ostrich eggs in the resinous light. There was no putrefaction; they'd been here a long time.

"Malkies, I presume?" The guard nodded, throwing me a piratical toothless grin, pride and menace on his hairy face.

"Malkies, aye. And they say a few Macdonalds."

"It must be quite a while since the last one was added?" If they thought I was going to let myself be intimidated by this piece of political theatre they'd be disappointed. This held no terror for me. Keeping skulls was a bit of a cliché even in our day — didn't certain SS officers amuse themselves by swilling beer from enemy noddles? I was merely intrigued by what these relics said about the dark age I'd overflown.

"Aye, a lang syne. Ye're the first one seen roond here since the days of Macbeth the Bold. If ye *are* a Malkie, begging yer pardon."

"How long ago was that?"

"There's no one living noo who saw it."

"But we're ready for 'em anytime!" said the other, clapping his stave.

"Aye!"

A pyramid twelve feet square, say, and eight high. How many would that contain? A thousand? The problem in solid geometry was beyond me. As far as I could tell, the skulls came from robust adults — presumably fighters killed or taken in battle. Most had been caved in by clubs or maces.

That Sunday Mailie brought an old hat to complete my local garb, and off we set to church. It was wonderful to be released from the castle's smelly air and ragged bowl of sky, from the centuries of menace walled up in its old stones; to walk out through the gatehouse and the steel trilithon to the grassy slope below the mountain. I wanted to run like a puppy through the laird's car-henge, never mind my unshod feet.

Mailie, however, set a dignified pace to which I conformed. We passed the jetty where I'd been brought ashore, deserted now except for half a dozen currachs and some hopeful pelicans. House martins began swooping on mosquitoes in our wake from nests under the machicolations of the keep. Banquo's temple-haunting martlet. "Where they most breed and haunt," I said, "I have observ'd the air is delicate." (And I thought just how delicate it was, in a way Shakespeare could never have guessed.)

Urquhart Bay was a shield of light emblazoned with dark boats at anchor. There'd been rain overnight but the sun was already strong, halfway to the zenith and glancing off the water. Upturned dugouts lay like seals along a crescent beach, sweating a fishy tang.

Loch Ness has dropped about three metres — you can tell by retaining walls left high and dry, by new land below the former level. The Urquhart delta no longer has the woods that used to grow around the river mouth, and there's little shade on the path along the shore. The laird wants to see his people, and he wants his people to see him. Apart from an arc of royal palms behind the beach, the only trees here now are avocado, macadamia, and citrus, grown between narrow maizefields which Mailie called rundales. She was unclear whether the farmland belonged to laird or people, to individuals or the clan. The question struck her as odd. I suppose there's no practical difference now: in an empty world the anxieties of ownership have calmed; the machine for demolishing limits is as rusty and forgotten as the rest.

They were growing maize, beans, and squash—the "three sisters" of America—the corn a pole for the nitrogen-fixing beans, the squash sprawling over the ground to keep down weeds. The maize was in tassel but looked poor, only to my shoulder—hardly the tall and generous plant we knew. No one was in the fields that day, and other worshippers from the castle had timed their leaving to avoid us. Ravens called insolently from a stand of redwoods on the mountain, and an eagle circled high above. The wail of a piper came riding on the wind.

After all the desolation I'd seen, Drumnadrochit affected me the way a great city might affect a hermit—closeness and narrowness, the press of people, running children, barking dogs. Macbeth's castle is bizarre but predictable, more or less what you'd expect for a postmodern warlord's lair, but the town is so like the towns we knew, the more wrenching for being half occupied and half in ruins.

We walked through muddy streets steaming in the sun, between garden walls overhung with bougainvillaea, past groves of lime and orange. People were converging on the church, shuffling along quietly on callused feet. In their homespun shawls they looked like woolly Christmas trees with hats. A few grinned nervously at Mailie, took quicker looks at me. Some boys, twelve-year-olds with hard eyes and wild hair, bolder than the rest, began a mocking chant to the tune of "Here We Go Round the Mulberry Bush":

What'll ye dae when the wee Malkies come?
What'll ye dae when the wee Malkies come?

On and on it went, the same line again and again for a hundred yards. Mailie stared grimly ahead, eyes reddening, tears on her cheek.

Most houses are old, and many empty—rotting beams and thatch, gardens overflowing with sunflower, acacia, and century plants. Is the population still falling? I thought so but Mailie denied it, saying that a house is always abandoned when the head of a family dies, to be reoccupied by grandchildren a generation later. All a young couple has to do is gather enough friends and kin to clear the undergrowth, point the stonework, and put on a new roof.

There's certainly no housing shortage.

"Old Griffe's place," she said, as we passed a solid croft of ancient masonry, thatch gone but beams still firm. "Dead at thirty-nine. No wife or bairns. A shame really. He had a...a *growth*. Atween his laigs." She leaned as close to me as our hats would allow. Her voice fell. "They say he had to carry his balls aroond in a bag. For *yeers!* Came summer last and he wadna leave with the rest of us. 'Friends,' he says, 'I want ye to dae ane thing for me. Tear the straw off ma hoose, so I can lie here abed and watch the simmer stars.'" She took off her hat and threw her head back, squinting against the glare. "Four months later we come back and Griffe's still there. On his back. Naething but bones! But they say he was wearing a *smile*."

I thought: old at thirty-nine?

Wild budgerigars were singing in gardens, and from the edge of town came the *chank, chank, chank* of a big cracked bell. I was having trouble reconciling today's Dumnorrit with the straggling Drumnadrochit of our brief acquaintance in the 1980s. The footpaths people use now do not necessarily follow the old tarmac roads, which seem to have been deliberately blocked and torn up long ago. The main road on the hills above the lake must have been planted over with California redwoods centuries ago, many since cut down or killed by the warming, but the survivors are impressive.

Mailie was telling me that after Easter and harvest the clan would disperse to summer homes in the higher glens, especially "Africa," where Macbeth had his "simmer hoose" on an island in a remote high loch. (Presumably Glen Affric, which runs into the head of Urquhart. You and I went there to see a neolithic tomb and the last tatters of primaeval Caledonian forest: Scots pines as thick as oaks, never dragooned in rows.) There, on terraced fields and small plots at different altitudes, the people grow yams, potatoes, and a nutty grain they call *kinoo*, while older children and young adults like Mailie drive their stock to cooler pastures on Ben Attow and Ben Nevis. The floor of the Great Glen gets torrid between May and September, despite the moderating presence of Loch Ness. Only a few clansfolk—mainly the old, who find migration more tiresome than heat—stay behind to keep town and castle free of wild animals.

The "kirk" wasn't what I expected. I didn't remember any church in town except for a small chapel converted into a bed-and-breakfast. But Mailie and other worshippers were converging on a gabled and chimneyed sandstone pile in a commanding site on the north slope of the valley. We came out into an irregular square with some traces of asphalt paving. It was only then that I placed the Victorian bay windows and vaguely Jacobean style: the old Drumnadrochit Hotel beside the road to Inverness! It was the Official Loch Ness Monster Exhibition Centre when you and I were here. If memory serves, we resisted its attractions, scared off by a concrete plesiosaur frolicking in a pond amid the coaches.

The whole northern wing of the hotel has gone, the break sealed off like an amputation scar, so that what is left resembles one half of an unusually grand semi-detached. This has been kept in fairly good repair, with slates on the roof and glass in the main windows—not original glass but a web of whatever pieces they've managed to save or find, held together by lead cames.

The bell, deafening at this range, hung from a wooden frame on the balcony formed by the top of the window bay; it was being struck in the Japanese manner, by a log slung horizontally from ropes. I was tired now—we'd come two miles from the castle and this was my first exercise in a fortnight—but the sight of the laird's mountainous figure working the bell in his sombrero was irresistibly comic. I bit hard into my lip.

People hung back from the door to let us pass. I could read a worn date above the moulding: *AD 1882*. There were no pews or chairs in the kirk, just reed mats and a layer of dry grass on the flagstones. People left their hats in a heap and moved to accustomed places, greeting each other with smiles, nods, quiet words, settling cross-legged in orderly rows. Mailie led me to a place in front. She reminded me to do as she did, giving my hand a squeeze of encouragement when we sat down. Are your family coming? I asked, and she put a finger to her lovely mouth.

There were perhaps four hundred present: men, women, and children, their solemnity punctured by toddlers' shrieks and the whining of lonely dogs in the street. *Chunk, chunk, chunk*—the dull voice of the bell measured the soft footfalls, the children's scuffling, the mindless hiss and gobble of a turkey.

Lady Macbeth and Kenneth, two people I'd come to regard as potential enemies, did not attend. Neither did many others, but this was not unusual according to Mailie—they'd probably turn up for evensong.

It seems that town, castle, and the surrounding district have about two thousand inhabitants. There may be as many more in outlying crofts and clachans scattered over a dozen valleys. Some families stay "up glen" all year, a few spend most of their time in hunting camps, and others have established small settlements on the edge of Inverness, where they mine the ruins—half flooded at high tide—for metal, plastic, glass, and artefacts. Coloured plastic which has not turned brittle is worked like amber. Many women were wearing teardrop pendants and strings of beads. Mailie had on a pair of red earrings of which she was extremely proud—two bottle caps given her by Macbeth.

No more than five thousand people all told. Five thousand from fifty million. If the whole world has fallen proportionately, our numbers are back where they were when we were hunting mammoth.

I suppose I'd expected some dour Presbyterian echo. But the kirk was grandiosely adorned with trappings from a high church: an ornate oak rood screen (quite fine, burnt at one end), a stone pulpit and font with chipped neo-Gothic reliefs, and windows glowing with blue and red rags of stained glass. Most extraordinary was a row of five monolithic columns — great polished shafts of pink granite — marching down the centre of the "nave." They supported a sturdy log trestle needed to shore up the heavy slates and charred timbers of the original roof. These columns must have been brought here long ago, either when machines were still available or when the labour force at a laird's command was far larger than it is today.

"They say we had anither kirk, beside the loch," Mailie whispered, noticing my inspection. "The Malkies came one sabbath day, when all the people were inside, in a big boat throwing fire. The fire went into the kirk and burned it doon. Women and bairns inside! Hundreds! And they say that ever after, when Cassel Nessie went against Cassel Reekie, our men would shout, *For the Kirk! For the Kirk!* each time they clubbed a Malkie."

The worship, too, had its ancestry in a highish church — the "Piskies," I'd guess, the Scottish Episcopalians. The laird began the service by reading from the Prayer-Book, the good old Elizabethan version which Uncle Phil to his credit secretly admired, though his bishop obliged him to use an insipid modern revision.

> I have lifted up mine eyes unto the hills: from whence
>     cometh my help.
> The Lord himself is thy keeper: the Lord is thy defence
>     upon thy right hand.
> So that the sun shall not burn thee by day: neither the
>     moon by night.
> Glory be to the Father, and to the Son: and to the
>     Holy Ghost.

As it was in the beginning, is now, and ever shall be: world
without end. Amen.

No wonder they had little trouble understanding me — every
week they hear the sturdy English of a thousand years ago.

Without his hat Macbeth cut an impressive figure, leading
prayers and hymns, thundering from the pulpit, gripping the lectern, his eyes ruddy and doleful, his voice booming like an avalanche as he read from a King James Bible open upon the spread
wings of a stone eagle. "Isaiah, Chapter Twenty-four," he announced,
and his eyes caught mine before returning to the Book.

Behold, the Lord maketh the earth empty, and maketh it
waste, and turneth it upside down, and scattereth abroad the
inhabitants thereof. The land shall be utterly emptied, and
utterly spoiled; for the Lord hath spoken this word. The
earth mourneth and fadeth away, the world languisheth and
fadeth away, the haughty people of the earth do languish.
The earth also is defiled under the inhabitants thereof;
because they have transgressed the laws, changed the ordi-
nance, broken the everlasting covenant. Therefore hath the
curse devoured the earth, and they that dwell therein are
desolate: therefore the inhabitants of the earth are burned,
and few men left. In the city is left desolation, and the gate
is smitten with destruction. For thou hast made of a city an
heap; of a defenced city a ruin.

Trust ye in the Lord forever: for in the Lord Jehovah is
everlasting strength. For he bringeth down them that dwell
on high; the lofty city, he layeth it low; he layeth it low, even
to the ground; he bringeth it even to the dust.

O Lord our God, other lords besides thee have had
dominion over us; but they are dead, they shall not live; they
are deceased, they shall not rise: therefore thou hast visited

and destroyed them, and made all their memory to perish. Thou hast increased the nation, O Lord, thou hast increased the nation!

At this the congregation joined in, repeating the last verse: *Thou hast increased the nation, O Lord, thou hast increased the nation; thou art glorified: thou hast enlarged all the borders of the land.*

Wishful thoughts.

The laird strode from lectern to pulpit, his breath seething in his nostrils. He stood there, silent for a long time, as if unsure what to say, how to begin—but this was just his way of building attention.

"As some of ye know, and others have now seen, a forwanderer has come amongst us. From beyond the mountains, from amid the clouds. From the South, the hotlands, through the land of trouble and anguish, from whence come the lioness and the lion, the viper and the fiery flying serpent.

"We know only what he tells us. We know nothing of the place of which he speaks—of his home in other hills, beside another loch. Some of ye may say he is sent by our ancient enemy; others will look on his fairness and say to yourselves that here perhaps is the Lord's messenger. For is he not as fair as Our Lord of the Loch?"

Macbeth paused, letting the association sink in, to gasps from the congregation.

"He has been here only a short time. The meaning of his coming is unclear, but I ask you to remember that the Lord has favoured us, has smitten our enemies so that they have dared not come against us in a hundred years. Would the Lord now send an enemy among us, one so weak and weaponless and pale, one who cannot hide his face even in the dark?" Another pause; another collective intake of air.

"Our visitor says that he is, beneath the skin, a man like us, made in God's image, praising the Lord. He says he comes in search of help; that he is a lost brother. Would any man or woman among you turn your lost brother from your door?" Here the laird scanned the nave with his gloomy eyes, waiting until he was answered by scattered calls of *Nae! For shame!*

"And so I say unto you all, the stranger is a guest among us. Let no one harm him unless he shows us harm. Let no one cast the first stone. Macbeth of Macbeth says Lambert of Lambert is welcome here. Here in Glen Nessie with the people of the Lord!"

The laird turned his bloodshot eye on me and smiled paternally.

I had to take communion, a thing I'd never done in my life (in my revolt against Phil Wringham I'd refused to be confirmed). The sham filled me with foreboding. This was tempting fate. But religion was the way to their hearts and, as they say in Nessie, ye have to dree yer weird. Again it was pretty much the Anglican rite, though the wafers were of maize and the wine was watered whisky —a delicious malt, smooth and dark, if a trifle musty. They can't be making anything this good themselves. Somewhere in the Glen there must be a cache of five-hundred-year-old Scotch, unfortunately reserved for ritual purposes.

The oddest thing was the chalice: a long-stemmed Waterford martini glass, *circa* 1950.

— 3 —

It became my habit to attend kirk whenever possible. Mailie usually went with me, and we'd sit in front, which made it hard to see who else was there. Once or twice I felt the hostile eye of Kenneth on my neck, and more often I saw Hob, who'd rowed me across the lake. Mailie wouldn't say if she and he were sweethearts, but he was the only person who looked on her with warmth. Several times, when we walked through town, I asked where her family was, which house was theirs, why she never introduced me to

them or other citizens. She always evaded such questions, prefer-
ring to tell some story like the one about Old Griffe of the herni-
ated goolies.

Through these I formed some notion of her society, so half-
familiar and so strange. You and I didn't go in for social anthro
much, did we? We preferred empty halls to verminous huts, the
clean bones to the flesh. But here in the glen the role of ethnographer, like greatness, was thrust upon me. To survive or escape I
had to master it, and in any case I was so thoroughly bewildered
by the implications of my voyage that I wasn't as dogmatic as I
used to be about distinctions between dead worlds and living ones,
future and past, history and presentiment.

Mailie revealed the glen to be an austere, superstitious, com-
munitarian place—a typical society of the chiefdom type. Only
the laird, his wife, and henchmen were exalted much above the
rest, and this more from tradition than necessity. Centuries back,
when civil wars still raged, the clansmen must have been more
numerous, must have had more need for hierarchy. A long struggle with a ruthless enemy had forged the neo-Macbeths, defined
them, engineered their survival. The laird, like his castle, is a relic
of a martial past, now obsolete but nevertheless the anvil of their
culture. They still fear attack from "enemy country," still believe
that only divine favour keeps the barbarian devils confined beyond the mountains. Small wonder they read more Old Testament
than New.

You and I know there are no more Malkies. Perhaps there are
other human groups in Britain, further north or west, but I doubt
it. They talked about Macdonalds—and one day the laird showed
me pieces of a familiar yellow plastic arch, which he said was the
battle standard of the Lord of the Isles. Did a rival guerrilla band
use that name during the curious rebirth of historical echoes and
ethnic grievance that seems to have marked the disintegration of
the British state? Or is it just that the past is telescoped in their

minds, that ancient Macdonald marauders and the hamburger chain of that ilk are equally remote and thoroughly confused?

Yet though their human enemy has faded away, their embattlement does have more immediate cause. Mailie's tales were full of barrenness, stillbirth, illness, early death, extinct lines, famines. Their lives are the short hard lives of peasants. Few see out their forties, few homes are not in mourning for a parent or a child. Fertility, as you'd expect, is an obsession — so much so that they wink at *de facto* polygamy and polyandry. If a couple are barren, some young man or woman often steps in to do the job. I seldom heard these arrangements between "cousins" openly discussed, but people were certainly aware of the subtly avuncular friendship between a man and his bedroom deputy, a woman and the girl who bore her a child. Mailie would talk about others in this way, but never about herself or Hob. Perhaps it was this that she was hiding: she and Hob were the laird's great hope, but his line could not be acknowledged to need such help. I'd seen no royal children in the castle.

Now that I was allowed to roam around a bit, life at Castle Nessie wasn't bad. Distance from the town suited my reclusive nature — even though it might prove risky in the long run to be so isolated, so unaware of factions. The only physical thing that bothered me much was filth. The clansmen weren't preoccupied with hygiene. I had to ask several times before the laird would allow me to bathe in the loch. He couldn't see why anyone would want to.

One glorious afternoon Mailie took me west along the beach to a shallow bay below the course of the old lakeshore road, where my white arse would attract neither Auld Hornie nor a crowd. The lake was sipping quietly at the shingle, and the mountains of the far shore glowed like ripening apples in the sun. I looked longingly at their palm fringe and mossy coat of forest, at a feather of spray above a waterfall. Over there was freedom, a way back across the

Monadhliath range to Edinburgh and England, to London and Graham, to Canvey and Tania's sphere. The machine would be charged, ready for another voyage. A thousand years?

I stripped and struck out a few yards with a showy Australian crawl. My hand still hurt—it wouldn't cup the water—and my whole upper body was weak from lack of use. Not today, I told myself, not today but one day you'll keep going. I stopped for breath, treading water, and looked back at Mailie. She was screaming and running back and forth.

Such swimming was unknown to her. She thought a crocodile had me by the feet—or the monster. I soothed her, coaxed her into the shallows, showed her the lost art: backstroke, breaststroke, another burst of crawl. She kept her woollens on, which hindered the lesson but was no bad thing as they were overdue for a wash. The sun was setting almost exactly in the west, a great shadow reaching across the loch from the mountain behind us, the apples on the far side gaining a last blush of terracotta light.

When she'd had enough we sat together on a shoal, in a foot of tepid water. Tiny waves slapped and gurgled round our bodies. Soon it was almost dark but the air stayed warm and soft. Mailie put her hand to my face, as she did every morning to bathe my burn, but this time her touch wasn't clinical. I kissed her lightly on the bridge of her nose. Her hand went to the nickel spoon that closed her shawl—forgive me for telling you this, Anita; it isn't gratuitous. She removed the pin and stuck it in the sand. The wet wool fell open and my hand went to her aubergine breast, full and smooth, oiled by the darkening water. Mailie gave a little shudder, a sob. Suddenly she rose to her knees and pulled my face to her nipple. It was long and engorged, a thimble roughened by her homespun clothes. I drew it against the roof of my mouth in a flute of tongue. Another sob of encouragement. And then her warm milk flooded me.

Out of breath, surprised, I tried to pull away—but her fingers had twisted into my hair. My body felt cut off at the neck, adrift, irrelevant, my being compressed between burning scalp and her mysterious fountain. I had no memory of any woman's milk, no childhood echo, no precedent for this muddle of motherhood and lust, forced infancy and grown desire. She relaxed only to transfer me from the slackening breast to the full.

We walked back in silence. We ate in silence. For much of this time she was crying privately.

"Do you want to tell me about it?"

Silence.

"Where is it?" Silence. Then:

"It isna."

"Stillborn?"

"Nae."

"Taken away?"

"Killed."

She uttered the word so quietly between her sobs that I wondered if I'd really heard it. She wouldn't say anything more, neither then nor later. But every evening she fed me—at the loch or in my room. There was no refusing her. She was seventeen and I, nearly twice her age, had become her monstrous infant.

I tried to be detached. Didn't we see an Italian film where some witless old *capo* was suckled like this on his deathbed? No doubt it was good for me, especially since I was by then subsisting on Lenten-kail like everyone else. But it couldn't have been good for her, mentally or physically. I had to watch my teeth. She could have caught Henry this way, or CJD, or whatever it is I have. Biting and scratching, they say, is Scottish wooing, but there could be no fun of that kind between Mailie and me. I was an unexploded mine against their frail ark. They were barely afloat above the chasm of extinction. I could sink them after twenty generations—down to the bottom with the moa, the dodo, and the plesiosaur. The Beast they had to fear was me.

The laird seemed to take my frequent churchgoing as a sign that I was on the side of the angels, as I hoped he would. But what *were* my intentions? In the daily round—matins at kirk, noon siesta, afternoon walk and swim with Mailie (and yes, gently, carefully, we became lovers)—I lost sight of What Happened, let alone my quest for a diagnosis and a cure. I was like a man who takes too long a holiday and loses interest in his life at home: the present was burying the past. Again I doubted I was sick. From this distance my terminal illness seemed suspiciously convenient, little more than an excuse for fleeing a stalled life.

I'd rigged up a hammock in the hut; there I would doze to the drone of mud-wasps in the heat. I was content doing little. It crossed my mind that I might fit in here: marry Mailie, become the laird's tutor, stay on as a bringer of change and renaissance. You can imagine how seductive a thought it was—being a culture hero, a big man in this shrunken place, a one-eyed Leonardo in the country of the blind.

Such illusions were encouraged by a discovery I made at this time. You know how things come to you—insights that have eluded conscious thought—when you're daydreaming in a chair or driving on automatic pilot. You'll be listening to a song you've heard a hundred times, and suddenly a line you've never been able to catch will be perfectly clear. My mind tended to wander like this in kirk. One Sunday I was awash in memory, thinking of Skef and his "pressure of the past" and how you said he made it sound a frightening thing, the dead more clamorous than the unborn. And I remembered that chap in St. Johns who lost his mind after a bad acid trip. I went to see him in hospital, listened to him raving while glucose ran into his arm. He couldn't eat, for every time he sat down at a table it was ringed by the hearty faces of ancestors and dead relations, from his Aunt Mary to grandparents and great-great-grandparents, to people dressed as Regency fops and Roundheads, to Cavaliers and nuns, shorn Normans, bearded Jutes,

Romans, ancient Brits in woad, swarthy little Stone Age farmers, all the way back to hairy half-human creatures ripping into the hospital rations with hands like paws. And then I surfaced in the old language of the Lord's Prayer, and realized the words weren't right. *Our Father whose art's in Heaven, hallo tae thy name. . . .* Just the dialect? I began listening more closely to other things I knew by heart. The twenty-third Psalm, for one, was riddled with childish mistakes: *The Lord is the shepherd thou shall not want. . . .*

Another day the laird read a favourite lesson of Uncle Phil's, a passage any Jew or Christian should have known. *In the beginning God created the heaven and the earth. And the earth was without form, and void; and darkness was upon the face of the deep. . . .* So far so good. He didn't go off the rails until verse five: *And God called the light Day, and the darkness he called Night. And one day there was evening and morning. And God said, Let there be a permanent in the midst of the waters. . . . And God called the permanent Heaven.*

So it went on, a corrupt text. Archaic language they no longer understood had been displaced by words they knew, even when the new words made no sense. But I'd seen the Bible and Prayer-Book: though cracked and delicate, the paper worm-eaten and ink-burned here and there, they were not unreadable.

I watched the laird's rufous eyes, how they moved over the page. They were the eyes not of a reader but of one pretending to read. His services were feats of memory. Mailie had already told me that only the laird's immediate family had "the art of the Book." The trouble was, they hadn't. They'd become illiterate some time ago. And I was the only one who knew.

The honour came without warning, an honour I could have done without. The Macbeths summoned me to their hall and asked, formally and politely, if I would take the part of Jesus in their Easter play.

You'll believe me when I say it wasn't to my taste. Wanting to be God was never among my psychoses. Our asylums were full of Saviours, casting out money-changers from the cafeteria, hanging against the wall in attitudes of crucifixion, yelling the words from the Cross down shiny corridors. And if the real Christ had walked on earth in modern times, no doubt that's where he'd have ended up — at least until they returned Him to the community. I used to pass Him every day on my way to work at St. Pancras; He had a shopping cart, a few carrier bags, quite a whiff on, and a hand out — *Spare chinge, guv? Gotteny chinge?* Not as poetic as the rich man and the needle's eye, but the same idea.

They wanted an answer on the spot. There wasn't time to think it over, to sound out Mailie on what their game might be. I had only a minute or two while the lady petted her dog — it had been sleeping at her feet, making smells, until it woke itself up with a loud one. I agreed, of course. If one must be either a god or a devil, better to take the high ground, though the company's said to be more interesting in the other place.

My stock soared immediately. I was moved to rooms in a guest wing beside the kitchens — early postmodern Tudor, airy mullions looking onto the loch, a fireplace, and a genuine car seat for a sofa. Perhaps, long ago, emissaries stayed here when Loch Ness and Edinburgh sued for peace, if they ever did. It made me think of the Tower and my black puss stretched out by the grate on rainy days, wanting me to do something about the weather.

Now I had Mailie for company, though she never stayed all night. She was my Magdalene, as the laird put it, hinting I was free to interpret her role as broadly as I liked. (Did he want some fresh genes in the family tree, albeit white ones? Or did he think my company might help her through her crisis? She was unlikely to conceive again while suckling.) Lady Macbeth threw a thin smile my way. I had the feeling they'd agreed on this but not for the same reasons. They even gave me back my own clothes. But not my shoes.

It would be easy, they assured me. They did it every year—most of the players were regulars who knew their parts. I asked for an instructor, perhaps my predecessor? Unfortunately, said Lady M, their regular Christ had had a fishing accident last June: his currach had capsized in a storm, trapping him under his nets. But all I had to do was stand trial in the church square and walk a Via Dolorosa from there to the castle, where the Holy Rood would be set up before the steel trilithon. There'd be few words to learn beyond those spoken by Christ himself in the Book; surely she didn't have to tell me those? Rehearsals would start next week. Macbeth always played Caiaphas, Lady Macbeth would be the mother of Jesus, the castle guards did the soldiers, and someone had already volunteered for the role of Pilate. I thought: I hope it isn't Kenneth. It was.

One morning I was lingering in the kirk to talk the laird into further relaxation of my house arrest. What were the bounds? Could I take a hike up Glen Urquhart, or go sailing on the loch? Everyone had left. Macbeth was shutting his Bible when a leaf of paper, a bookmark, fluttered out. I plucked it from the floor to give to him, but in the act of handing the paper over I turned it upright, unconsciously, to glance at some handwriting.

"So ye hae the art." The deep voice made me jump.

"A little. I can make out a few words." He took the fragment from me and replaced it carefully within the Bible. A sharp intake of breath. A huge fist slamming onto the lectern.

"Dinna bullshit Macbeth!"

"All right. I read. Like you do."

It's never hard to tell a Scotsman with a grievance from a ray of sunshine. The octopus beak began working at the centre of his beard, the lips peeling back in a snarl.

"Man! D'ye tak me for a coof?" His eyes seemed to fill the space in front of me. Slowly the anger drained away. He let out one of his great gusts, deflating like a lizard. "Ye've seen me *pairform*."

He'd remembered where he was. I think also that he was a lonely man, glad to break the loneliness of power.

"Ma faither had a little. Grandfaither could do it like you—to himself like. And *his* faither could... could *write*. They say when he was young he went all the way to enemy country, to that accursed Cassel Reekie, and wrote on the walls. I've some things he brought back from there. Perhaps ye can tell me what they are."

"Was his name Erik?" I was lulled by his friendliness. As soon as the words were out I saw I'd given myself away.

"Aye! Erik. Macbeth the Bold. How the deil do you know?"

"I did come that way, through Reekie. I denied it because I was afraid of being mistaken for an enemy. I saw what he put: *Erik was here from Castle Nessie.*"

"Och, it must be a grand sight!" Macbeth turned to the east window with its chips of crimson glass—the hem of a magus's robe—and gazed out, his great-grandfather's triumphal inscription on the mighty ruins floating in his mind's eye as if it were Trajan's arch at Benevento.

When the moment had passed, I said: "Has anyone been there since?"

"Nah. Nae need. Ma granddad said everything there was cast doon, fordone."

"Then why am I still under suspicion of being a Malkie? Why do people speak as if they fear attack?"

"Some things are best kept in the family. It's best that folk have something to worry on. And best tae think they're no alone."

Of course. A warlord needs a war.

"Ye've no spoken of it?"

"Not a word. It's safe with me. Be it thy course to busy giddy minds with foreign quarrels."

"David Lambert!" Another sigh. "David Lambert o' Lambert! Whatever am I gonna do wi' yew?" Then: "Come and see me tomorrow afternoon."

That night I hardly slept. Macbeth knew I could expose him; that I'd been to Edinburgh; that I'd lied. I'd made myself a threat. Was this the time to go—steal a currach, swim the loch? But though I might be able to cross the water, I'd never outrun them afterwards, not without shoes.

Eventually I drifted off, only to wake from a nightmare, sweating like a cheese. In the dream I was God, floating sublimely above the earth, gliding over travel-poster landscapes. The Canadian Rockies were especially vivid—cobalt lakes and jasper stands of Douglas fir. I became aware that a crowd had gathered below, staring up at me as if I were Superman. I gave them a cheery royal wave, a godly wave, and they called out to me, worshipping, magnifying my name. It was then I started to worry. You know—performance anxiety. Perhaps those adoring folks down there expected more than I could actually deliver? As God, or the Son of God (I think I was both, or possibly the whole Three-in-One), what exactly were my duties, what the limits of my power? Were there any?

And I noticed I wasn't flying quite so high. And as I lost altitude the people became less impressed. Soon I could see their faces. They'd begun to frown. It was getting hard to stay aloft. Where I'd been gliding effortlessly I was now flailing and sinking like a wounded goose. The faces became derisive; I heard mocking laughter, jeers, and then they got downright hostile. They felt cheated. This chap they'd been worshipping had turned out to be a charlatan. I saw their angry fingers, their red mouths, little showers of spittle, and sharp white teeth. I fell to earth like a rag, and woke as they tore me to pieces.

The sun rose, shone briefly on my wall, lost itself in a stratum of cloud like poured concrete. The loch turned grey. Rain fell listlessly all morning, as if from a colander—there was no wind. I took the opportunity to avoid the kirk; I didn't want to bump into the laird before obeying his summons. My nerves were bad, my wits slow, I was dog-tired. The dream stayed with me for hours; it seemed obvious that they planned to kill me. Last year's Christ had had no fishing accident: those skulls piled in the cellar belonged to my predecessors in the role. They took their Easter literally.

Fortunately, the warm mountainsides grow a decent coffee, one of Glen Nessie's few luxuries. Coffee was precious here, getting it wasn't easy. Mailie never had any. I'd missed the stuff. The laird's hospitality hadn't stretched to a cup of java until I agreed to be Christ; now I could order it from the kitchen. After two cups I felt better and my worries seemed mere paranoia. The freshest skulls on the pile had to be at least a century old, and there were too many of them to be the relics of an annual sacrifice. Anyway, what could I do? If they wanted to kill me they could do so any time they liked.

Macbeth was by himself when I was shown up. A good sign. He dismissed my escort, heaved himself out of his throne, and walked over to a west window. He bade me sit down beside him in the light, on a bench covered in black llama skin. He went back to the dais, bent down and opened a trapdoor in the planks, wheezing. How old was he? Mid-fifties? But people tended to be younger than they looked. Forty was thought old. Perhaps he was no more than that. A bearish arm retrieved a battered metal trunk—an airtight stainless-steel case, the sort photographers used.

"Ma late faither showed me this, but it didna mean much tae me at the time." He undid the snaps. The rubber seal had long perished, but at least the metal had saved the contents from mice and insects.

"All I ken is what ye see—motty papers and forfairn auld hership from Cassel Reekie. A lot of rottack. Ah've looked at it a dizzen times and it still means zip tae me."

He said Erik the Bold had found this trunk in a castle vault he'd broken open during a trip to Edinburgh. "Tak a look, man. Tell me what's here."

There were letters and legal documents tied with ribbon, files and logbooks, computer printouts and disks, several dozen CDs, other disks in a smaller format new to me, flaky remnants of photographs, audio and video tapes, brown envelopes stuffed with disintegrating banknotes, and several small metal cashboxes. Condition was poor on the whole. Even so, it looked like six months' work. I'd need pen and paper, and the Oyster to try the compatible disks. But what to tell Macbeth?

"This will take a long time, my laird."

"Angus. Noo that ye're one of us, ye'll call me Angus. Angus Kwame Macbeth. Ah'm the only one here with three handles." He chuckled, began to offer his hand, caught my fearful glance, withdrew it with a smirk. "How long? Can we finish by tomorrow night?"

I tried to impress on him the scale of the task. Even a quick run through would take at least a fortnight.

"Nonsense, man! I saw how fast ye read this morning." His great mitt lunged in and snatched out a sheet, tearing it. "Here. Read me this." I nearly choked. This was possibly the best document collection surviving in the British Isles, its importance incalculable. We should have been wearing surgical gloves, separating sheets with spatulas, backing them with acid-free paper, reading by the dimmest light our eyes could stand. The battered case belonged with the Shang Oracles, the Exeter Book, the Dresden Codex, the Dead Sea Scrolls (all of which no doubt had gone; a dismal thought). It cried out to be rescued, conserved, placed in a controlled environment.... But these conservational anxieties begged the question of posterity, of a posterity that cared, that was able to care. When a tree falls in the jungle, who hears?

"Ah'm waiting, David. Ah want answers. And nae fabbs."

*Answer me: Though you untie the winds and let them fight against the churches.... Though castles topple on their warders' heads; though palaces and pyramids do slope their heads to their foundations; though the treasure of Nature's germens tumble all together, even till destruction sicken; answer me....* How to read these things without giving away that I too sprang from the world of the trunk?

The paper was stamped *HMG DSS — SECRET*. His Majesty's Government, Department of State Secrets? State Security? I read silently first, thankful in a way to find little of interest.

"It doesn't make much sense."

"Just read one word then anither. *Ah'll* decide if it makes sense."

Subject met contact outside former Green Pk. tube station, walked to Bridge Street, hailed water taxi No. 2448, 3.23 p.m. Unable to follow (congestion). Subject's partner, Doreen Tubman, held for questioning at Ealing Central, 11/3/35. Update: 19/3/35. Tubman deceased in custody, information obtained from her proved to be inaccurate. Recommendation: No action at present. It is hoped to establish evidence of net or satellite link with offshore entry ring.

"Ye're right. Tubes, nets, rings. Nae sense at a'." He handed me more printouts from a different stack. These were in code, some system of letter substitution. I had trouble persuading him I really couldn't read a word.

Primary documents can be so maddening, can't they? So seldom do they tell you the big things, the things you're after. The great questions of the age are usually commonplaces, which no one bothers to remark. And in official documents, the true crises are so often strenuously ignored. Read the inscriptions of any civilization on the point of collapse, and they celebrate military triumphs, the magnificence of kings, the harmony of earth and heaven — as if nothing whatever were wrong. Then silence. You have to read the silences.

Macbeth picked three manila envelopes, which had turned to flakes by the time he passed them to me. Some of their contents, however, were legible. More files — names and addresses, transcripts of phone calls, downloaded e-mail, reports on the movements of "subversives"—dating from the 2030s and 40s, the time of the Emergency and the Watling regime. Most of the entries were cryptic, the "subjects" identified only by case and file number. I have none of this material with me now. It was sombre reading, along these lines:

Subject abandoned safehouse; last sighted Folkestone 23/9/38....
Subject traced to meeting of Fabian subversives....
Informant no longer reliable in M's view....
Subject believed to have died in '43....
Went missing in '43, believed dead. Foul play not suspected....

So it went on. 2043 came up a lot—a year of war, of plague?

Why these files had been kept was beyond me. Pure accident, most likely. There were reams of the stuff. Early sheets bore London stamps: Metropolitan Police; Special Branch; New Scotland Yard; Box 500, SW1 (wasn't that MI5?). For about four years beginning in the late 2030s the government—these departments, anyway—was based at York; papers after November 2043 were stamped *HMG DSS, EDINBURGH.*

I read in a deadpan voice for half an hour; Macbeth's lids drooped and his beard went stiff with boredom.

"All right, David. We'll do it your way. Ye'll work here every afternoon, waling the gude frae the bad. But nae tricks. I'll come roond frae time to time, and ah'll be a happy man if ye'll be making progress."

# — 4 —

The glen's old King James was a veritable filing cabinet crammed with notes and pages torn from other sources. It interested me far more than the sinister archive in the trunk. Now that the cat of my literacy was out of the bag, I was able to suggest that I really should consult the Book to help me rehearse my role. I reminded Macbeth tactfully that the words of Jesus varied somewhat from gospel to gospel; I'd need to choose the best lines. In Wales, I said, it was unthinkable to perform any sacred theatre without proper preparation. He agreed to let me stay after matins for a few minutes each morning.

My first impulse was to pick the Bible up by the spine and shake it to see what might fall out. But I could hardly do that to one of the last books on earth, quite apart from the bulky and suspicious figure of the laird hovering about, directing sweepers and drapers, getting his church ready for Easter.

For a few precious minutes each day I chased eloquent silences, scribbling notes on the back of a Watling code sheet with a pencil pocketed from the archive, a finger in John 18 in case Macbeth came by. He was moody. Sometimes I felt welcome, sensed an air of companionship; sometimes he seemed resentful, huffing like an aged guard dog, and I would keep my study short.

In Isaiah, marking the passage he had "read" on my first day in church, were a few lines from a translation of "The Ruin." The first English meditation on old stones: the Saxon poet strolling through Roman Bath, down brambled streets, past oozing pipes, carved walls and columns, sculpted heads, and seeing in them not something mute but a society like his own writ large, a place of weapons and gems and beery halls.

> Rooftrees are wrecked,     ruined towers
> fester and fall,     fate fells all.
> What of the craftsmen?     Clasped in earth.
> In the grave's grasp     great men perish.
> Grey lichen grows     on the gore-stained stone. . . .

Leviticus held a page from a guide or manual (for survivors, guerrilla fighters?) printed on paper now little more than tissue:

> Edible roots and leaves are covered in Chapter 1.... avoid tinned goods because botulism may be present. In some areas you may find "wild" cattle. Remember these have been freed by owners defying destruction orders. Don't be tempted! Chapter 2 tells you how to trap, clean, and prepare wild animals for the table. The following species are thought safe: rabbit, badger, hedgehog, most herbivores except cattle, sheep and goat. Carnivores, especially foxes, dogs, and cats should be avoided. A word about horse and donkey: many people are understandably reluct...

With this was a torn menu from the Glenmore Restaurant (undated), boasting: "All our meat dishes are made with finest non-traditional animal flesh, carefully selected by chef from government-certified sources, and deeply irradiated before cooking."

In Luke 10 was a familiar face, some *News from Nowhere*:

> ...sham or artificial necessaries, which became, under the iron rule of the aforesaid World-Market, of equal importance to them with the real necessaries which supported life.... To this "cheapening of production," as it was called, everything was sacrificed: the happiness of the workman at his work, nay, his most elementary comfort and bare health, his food, his clothes, his dwelling, his leisure, his amusement, his education—his life, in short—did not weigh a grain of sand in the balance against this dire necessity of "cheap production" of things, a great part of which were not worth producing at all.... The whole community was cast into the jaws of this ravening monster, the World-Market.

Underneath someone had scribbled pithily: *1890s or 1990s?*

About ten days before Easter, when only the laird and I had been in the kirk—one of the mornings I felt welcome—we were walking back to the castle together in the heat that was building with the longer days. He stopped in the shade of a splendid oleander where the ground was still damp from a thunderstorm the night before, suddenly gripping my arm so fiercely that I thought he might be having a heart attack. But he was bending to pick up a stick.

Macbeth's eyes locked with mine, then returned to the moist ground. Very laboriously and proudly he scratched MACBEATH in the clay path. And he said, "Lairn me the art."

He knew a bit more than he'd let on, enough to make out numerals and the Prayer-Book calendar, though his eyes seemed poor. But why should he want to revive his literacy now? The world of the glen had shrunk to a scale where written records were not needed. Much larger and more complex societies had thrived in the past without them. The laird knew all his subjects personally —what they looked like, where they lived, whom they'd married, their liaisons, their children, their strengths and weaknesses. It was indeed easier to memorize favourite passages of the Book than to keep the entire machinery of pen and paper in working order.

I concluded (and I was half right) that my presence had awakened in him a curiosity about the past. All to the good in one way: if he learned to read again, I'd cease to be a threat in this area. However, I foresaw a serious conflict between belief and evidence should he delve too deeply into the "auld hership"—the booty from Castle Reekie. Oral history is easily reshaped to serve the present, but primary documents, like old love-letters and youthful manifestos, are apt to be disruptive.

The glen's view of its past was mythic, archetypal. Mailie had told me bits and pieces of their legends. Little by little Macbeth also had opened up, and at last I obtained from him the ethnographer's stone: the origin story. Angus said he recited it each New Year's Eve. So had his ancestors, from time immemorial. I think the myth is quite old, even in its present form, for it's in a stiff quasi-biblical English, not the spoken idiom.

Under various pretexts—my research for the play, his writing exercises—I got most of it down on paper:

When the Lord God had made the world, he walked the earth asking his people to tell him whatsoever they lacked. He went first to the Children of Israel, saying unto them, "What do ye need, that ye may thrive and prosper?" And the Israelites asked the Lord for his words, and for the art of reading and writing, so they could set the words of God in a Book and never forget them. The Lord gave unto them what they asked; and the Israelites worshipped and prospered for generation upon generation.

But it came to pass that after a long time they ceased obeying God's words. They began to dispute their meaning, and to fight among themselves, and so fell into the power of the Gentiles. In those days they begged the Lord for one more gift: that he should send his Son to be their King forever. And the Lord did what they asked of him, but the Israelites knew not the Son of God, and they crucified Him on the Rood.

The Lord then went in wrath and sorrow to the Gentiles, to the Romans and Southrons and Americans and many others whose names are now lost, and he said unto them, "My chosen have failed me. Perhaps ye will not. What things do you lack on this earth?" Now, the Gentiles were a greedy and ambitious people, and they asked the Lord God for everything. "We want this; we want that," they said. "Give us all that thou hast to give, O Lord. Tell us thy secrets and we will praise thy name forever. Give us wheels to take us across the world, so we may move as thou movest." And the Lord gave them iron chariots that rolled over the earth, across the plain, above the rivers, and through great burrows in the hills.

"Thy wheels are good, O Lord," the Gentiles said. "But give us also wings, that we may fly upon the air like thine own angels." And the Lord gave unto them silver wings.

"Teach us to build towers that will reach heaven and cities that will stand forever, that we may behold thy glory and never lack a dwelling place." And the Lord showed them how to soften the very stone of the mountains, and harden it in any shape they wished. And the Gentiles took all these things, and for many generations they prospered and multiplied.

Until one day came Satan among them, saying, "Why worship ye the Lord when he hath nothing left to give?" And the Gentiles looked on the Lord's gifts with new eyes, and were unsatisfied. The gifts no longer pleased them, and the earth was no longer to their liking. They turned their iron chariots on one another, nation against nation, and fought like eagles with their silver wings. And they defiled the world the Lord had made.

When God saw this he became wroth. "Have I not given unto you everything asked of me: everything necessary for life and health and increase?" But Satan had hardened their hearts, and they mocked the Lord, answering, "We know thee not, old man. Fall to thy prayers."

The Lord repented that he had made man on the earth, for he saw that all flesh was corrupted and the earth filled with woe and violence. And in those days he set upon the Gentiles a great pestilence, and smote them down while their mockery yet rang in his ears.

"I shall brighten the sun," the Lord said, "to stand as a

fiery sword above the garden ye have spoiled. And I shall sear the earth, that your kind may not live on it again." And men were scorched with great heat, and they blasphemed and died in eternal damnation.

I remember how Macbeth looked as he ended the story: blinking, disoriented, like a man who walks from a dark theatre into a sunlit street.

Whenever the laird tired of his writing lessons or was busy elsewhere, I worked alone on the castle archive. He even trusted me to examine a few things in my room. This made it easier to follow my own agenda, though the pencils and paper I appropriated were so fragile that I worried daily about running out of copy materials before making a major find. I also managed to pocket a few CDs that looked promising—no one but me suspected that the silvery disks were anything more than ancient ornaments or coins.

I found no chronicle, no explanation of the catastrophe, though clues were beginning to appear. It seems the Great Glen station had been set up in the 2020s to find ways of coping with climate change and rising ultraviolet radiation. It had experimented with animals and crops from tropical zones, especially mountain ranges where life was adapted to high UV. The Andes had proved a particularly fruitful source. Maize and beans had ousted oats and barley; llamas had replaced sheep and other livestock destroyed in the losing war against disease.

But mass extermination had not stopped there. Of the papers I saw in the glen, none was as revealing and disturbing as this. I copied it in full:

Darling Loopy,
Forgive the silly name but I have to call you something, and one can't be too careful. You know who you are, as they say.

How I miss you and the boys. Four years! Will they know me? And to think we'll be apart for yet another Christmas. It's too hard. Just remember that I love you and live for the day we're all together again.

Please understand what I'm about to tell you and *why* I'm telling you. The truth is bound to get out soon, and I'd rather you heard it from me. I can't go on pretending I'm patching up Watling's heroes as they fend off swarthy invaders and foil treasonous plots. Like almost every medic in the country I'm in the business of death now, not life — mass euthanasia of incurables at what they call an ASF, "Assisted Suicide Facility." A terrible thing, but we had no choice. Whatever we may think about the Generalissimo, this wasn't his fault. Watling doesn't want to see his little empire melt away before his eyes. It simply had to be done, like the cattle. If the worst happens I shall choose this way for myself and, God forbid, I urge you to do the same. Thanaton-B, if you can get it, is painless and dignified — merely a little ataxia with no convulsions or emissions — *much* better than going like a myxo rabbit.

Oh Loopy, it was so cold-blooded, so much worse than the Home Guard. Did you get any of those letters? I saw hundreds fall in the Westminster riots. With my own hands I tore old ladies from their homes. I saw boat people shot like rats as they crawled ashore. But nothing was as bad as these past months. I don't know the numbers — no one does — they stopped keeping count. Remember the early days, the endless downward revisions of "sustainable demography"? Watling giving the nation his word that if we fell "one jot" below twenty million, he himself would be the next to go? How that seems like another life, another age. It was certainly in the millions for kuru alone, and there must have been five times as many with RISC and heartworm.

Then nothing but official silence, while we laboured day and night.

You must realize, no matter what you hear, that very few medicines are left. Probably none are being produced. I haven't seen morphine in a year. Even the Thanaton's drying up. The thought of running out of gas and having to clobber my patients on the head was another reason to run. I know I couldn't do that.

Don't think me a coward. There's a time when family comes first. The worst is over anyway. We've been over-staffed for the last month. They've reversed the boat-people policy, by the way. Healthy ones are welcomed, but of course they've virtually stopped coming.

Burn this NOW. I'll be in touch. Can't say when or how. I pray every day that you've escaped. Wait for me. Watling can't last much longer. Soon there'll be no "public interest," no "United Kingdom," no "state." We'll be on our own. Get ready in any way you can. Hug the boys.

Love you,

"Josephine"

Comments: File DSS-Inverness 0176-43. Intercepted Lochend 27/11/43. Writer believed to be Dr. Mariana Lockwood, whereabouts unknown since AWOL, Housesteads ASF, 21/11/43. Subject's husband, Anthony Duluth, cereal botanist, Great Glen genetic project, detained 11/1/44. Suspected terrorist sympathizer with links to MacBeath Squad cell operating in Cairngorms.

So a nightmare of the 1940s had recurred a century later — sheds and ovens, chimneys oily with incinerating flesh — as nature foreclosed on our biological debts. (Was that what I saw at Fountains? Had that bulldozer been digging graves?) I found no other references to heartworm. Only dogs used to get it, didn't they? A friend of mine in Houston lost his Alsatian that way. His description was unforgettable—horrible things a foot long living like a nest of eels on the surging blood. Perhaps it managed to jump the species barrier somehow, as temperatures rose. I don't know what RISC was, and I don't think they did either. Another fragment, undated, refers to "human equivalent of mass die-offs of seals, cetaceans, and batrachians," but this could have been something else. I did learn that the acronym stood for Rapid Immune System Collapse. It seems to have spread like flu.

I'd just finished copying this when Macbeth turned up at my door. He made me read it again, tracing each line with his finger so I couldn't suppress one word. His beard was agitated, his beak working away as if demolishing a quid of tobacco. I hadn't noticed my tears. He had.

"Ye're one of 'em, David, are ye no?"

"One of what?"

"A Gentile."

"Well, we're all descended. You and me. . . ."

"That's no what I mean. Ye've come back, have ye not? From the killing-time. Folk are talking in the toun, saying you're nae flesh and blood. That if ye've no come to us from heaven, ye've come to us from hell. Tell me it wasnae the Deil helped you. Can his machines ferry folk back from ayont the grave?" He stopped, regarding me like a father betrayed by a son.

"Look at yerself, man. Look at yer sark and trews. And yer shoes—all the wee bits of tick and brass. Ye cannae tell me they were made by human hands."

"Neither were those guns you've got. Or the carpet on the wall. Or this seat. If machines are the Devil's fingers, why do you keep these things?"

"*Memento mori*, David. *Memento mori*. We look at these bonny things, sae smooth and strong and fine they seem the work of gods, and we say tae oursels, *Those men failed*. It keeps us frae whoring after the like."

"About my shoes. I haven't seen them since I got here. I'd like them back if you don't mind. My feet. . . ."

"Damn yer feet! Dinna deny it. Ah don't have to see you weep to know. You speak the way those papers speak. Ye're kith and kin."

"We have a few more of the old arts — arts you said your own grandfather had. I told you before. But they're dying among us too. We're not half the number you are. We're desperate. That's why they sent me. But I found you — or you found me — by accident. It was a shot in the dark. I'll swear on the Book no one knows I'm here. You have nothing to fear from me. Or my people."

Lady Macbeth had quietly entered the room. Angus was shaking his head. He waved his hand and grimaced, turning me over to her. She approached and put her face right up to mine, a shocking intimacy from one normally so aloof. We were standing by the window. I could see every pore and pimple on her hatchet face. Her breath smelled of whisky and bad teeth. She said something to her husband I couldn't catch.

"Open yer gob," he ordered. "Wide now!" I did as I was told. She inspected me like someone buying a horse. The mole on her chin was still weeping blood and pus.

A guard came in with a bulky object in his hand. Macbeth shot a helpless glance, said nothing. It was a mildewed skull.

"Ye've seen the vault," she said icily. "This was pulled the noo by Doctor from the very bottom o' the heap." She handed it to me, upside-down, tapping the upper jaw. "*Hundreds* of yeers auld." It shook in my hand, but I saw immediately what she was getting at — Lady Macbeth would make a decent archaeologist — the dental work was a lot like mine.

"Dinna tell me," she was breathing hard, her dialect thickening in fear and anger. "Dinna tell me tha' in a glen with twa thoosand souls, ye hae a tooth-dodger as canny as thaat!"

She fled the room in disgust, her dog's claws clicking on the boards behind her. I stood numb, wondering what would happen next. A stake through my heart?

Macbeth lowered himself onto the car seat. I said:

"All right. I'll make a confession — for your ears only." I waited for his nod. "I came here in a boat that sails across the years. Across five hundred years. It's the only one of its kind, and I came alone. No machine can bring back the dead, Angus, I swear. And no one will ever follow."

He had gone so still that for a moment I thought he disbelieved me. But why should a man to whom all machines are mysterious abominations find a time vehicle any less plausible than an aeroplane?

"Where is this boat noo? In Reekie?"

"No. Nowhere near. It's a month away, at the bottom of the island. I came north on foot, through all the hotlands. All the way from London. A month's walk."

"Lunnon!" He looked as I suppose I might look if someone were to tell me they'd come from Belshazzar's Babylon. "Lunnon! Alas, alas, that great city. All things which were dainty and goodly are departed from thee. The light of a lamp shall shine no more in thee!"

"Revelation," I said, catching sight of a possible bolt-hole on his own terrain. "What year is it? Are we not in the year of Our Lord 2501?"

Macbeth nodded. (I hoped he didn't know the adage about the Devil's way with scripture.)

"And he laid hold on the dragon," I went on, "that old serpent, and bound him a thousand years." (God bless that old serpent Phil.) "There are only five centuries between my time and your time, Angus. I am nothing to do with the dragon. The ship that brought me here does not come from the pit."

He gave a little grunt. He was probably too sophisticated to think much of that himself, but it was ammunition he could use —

if he chose — against superstitious murmurers such as his wife and Kenneth. I was thinking: now he'll never let me leave. Why should he believe there's only one machine? If he lets me go, he'll always fear invasion from the past.

— 5 —

Good Friday dawned wet, muggy, and drear — the sky in mourning, as Macbeth put it, for the Son of Man. It had been raining on and off for several days, saturating the clay mortar in the thick stone walls until they began to weep unconsolably behind my bed. Well before daybreak I'd been woken by wind mewling and hissing through the shutters. Dawn brought another sound, an irregular bray of bagpipes from the laird's redoubt.

Do you remember that night at your flat — it must have been one of the last times the three of us were together — when Bird brought some good skunk and we got loaded and watched an Australian documentary on a passion play in Mexico? I heard it now, laughing aloud as I put on my costume, a loincloth and white cotton robe.

*Jesus Chrahst here is the local electrician. In another life he goes by José Fuentes. This'll be José's eleventh crucifixion. He's a natural for the role. They like a gringo Jesus here in Mexico, and he's the only blond in town.* (WIDE ANGLE: emaciated figure staggers along dusty street in noonday sun. Pariah dogs. Huge cross of heavy timber. CLOSE-UP: blood and sweat running like candlewax down face.) *Those whips and thorns are the genuine article. Every year it takes him a fortnight to recover. But José knows the more it hurts, the higher he'll be in heaven when he gets the nod.* (Roman soldiers flogging bony back. ZOOM on welts.) *They love a good crucifixion here in Mexico. The more realistic the better. About the only bit they fake is the niles. But this year José's not so sure. His mates tell me he's looking worried. You see, José Fuentes just turned thirty-three.*

Not long after I'd confessed to being a Gentile, I'd asked Macbeth if he still wanted me in the play. He'd given it some thought, he said, but if he dropped me from the cast Lady Macbeth would wonder why, and it was better she didn't know more than she did. "From lang experience, David, I've found it's best no tae piss on a sulky fire." Half the crop was down in the rain, people were worried about the harvest. There'd be no shortage of murmurers quick to draw a link between misfortune and a Malkie in the glen. "She wants ye in the play, man. Be thankful for small mercies.

"Besides, I happen to know, David Lambert, that for the first time since you got here you're telling the truth. Only a true Christian would tak an interest in the life of Pontius Pilate." He paused, leaking one of his steam-engine sighs while he held my gaze, his eyes animated, amused. Angus was bursting with a secret.

It took me a moment to catch on. Then a sunken feeling of violation and entrapment. His men had found my last camp near Slochd Pass and dug up my kit! He'd wanted reading lessons so he could peruse my notes. (Thank God I'd left the Oyster in Edinburgh!) How much had he been able to understand?

"Now that you've seen it, do you think I could have my notebook back? And perhaps my shoes, while you're about it?"

"All in gude time, David. All in gude time. First we have Easter tae celebrate. Drop it for noo. By the way, ah've been wanting to say I'm sorry aboot yer hand. Ye'll understand that a man in my position has to keep up appearances. It wadna dae to let folk think ah'm soft." He shrugged, oddly like a Frenchman; then: "It's still Lent, but no for lang—will ye tak a dram?"

That night Macbeth and I had more than one dram of his prodigiously aged malt. He was burning with questions about the world I'd left. I did my best to answer them but, even though we spoke similar languages, we had too little shared vocabulary.

Nations, empires, environmental crisis, employment, investment confidence, population explosion, nuclear threat: so many words meant nothing or were limited to a biblical context.

> If I could put you back
> Six hundred years, blot out cosmogeny,
> Geology, ethnology...
> And set you square with Genesis again.

I wished he knew what petrol was, so I could use that famous analogy for the Cold War: two men in a room, knee-deep in gasoline, each with a box of matches in his hand. I wanted to tell him we had seen it coming — a line came to mind, something I'd read recently, "And the price of failure, that is to say, the alternative to a changed society, is darkness." But each attempt to explain raised more unanswerable questions.

In short, I didn't get far in my apology for the Gentiles, even though, like Gulliver before the King of Brobdingnag, I gave everything a more favourable cast than the strictness of truth would allow.

We were, I insisted, a Christian civilization. "Who do you think built the churches and cathedrals and monasteries? The walls must still be standing there in Inverness and Fort Augustus. Look in any town or city and you'll see great monuments to our faith in God." We had merely followed orders. We had gone forth and multiplied. We had subdued the earth. We had taken dominion over every living thing. Christendom had conquered the world. Even Communism had been, in essence, a secular Christianity. "'And they had all things common ... and parted them to all men, as every man had need.'

"Beautiful ideas, Angus. All beautiful ideas. Sacred truths we held self-evident. They may on occasion have led to killing, slavery, and disaster — but you have to concede they were beautiful ideas."

Macbeth wouldn't say much when you scored a debating point. He'd grunt, hiss, ask another question.

"Tell me this, David. What is *civilization?*"

How would you have tackled that one, Anita? Like you I've never attached moral baggage to the C word. The Roman circus, the Inquisition, the Nazi camps, the bomb—the uncivilized did no worse. So I stuck to a technical definition: a society on a certain scale, of a certain complexity. Like the glen, I said, but thousands of times larger. Not one Book but more books than anyone could count. I hinted at cycles of plunder and collapse; I summoned aphorisms, suppressing most of them:

Civilization is plumbing

Civilization requires slaves

Civilization is gunpowder, printing, and the
    Protestant religion

Civilization is arranging the world so you needn't
    experience it

Civilization is the gradual replacement of men by things

Civilization is living beyond your means

Civilization results in deserts

Civilization dies as easily from irony as from debauchery

And Skef, of course: *Civilization is a pyramid scheme.* I added that it was often said by us, to our everlasting credit, that the true test of a civilization was the way it treated its weak.

"No matter what ye say, David, ye must agree that the Lord God in his wisdom did see fit tae smite the Gentiles. Seek anywhere and ye find the trace of his terrible wrath. If the Gent...if *civilization* was as gude as ye say, why d'ye suppose the Lord did that?"

The canny bugger. Even if you left the Lord out of it, Macbeth had us there.

"Let me ask *you* a question. What about Glen Nessie? Why

do you suppose the Lord spared you?" He made as if to reply off the cuff but stopped himself. He poured us each another dram, and his voice engorged with the solemnity he reserved for myth and scripture.

"The Lord came to Nessie in the time of Macbeth the Great, and he asked if there was anything our people lacked. And Macbeth said that we lacked for nothing. We had water to drink and air to breathe; we had sheep for meat and corn for bread. We had the iron and stone of the Gentiles all around us for the taking. There was no gift, Macbeth said, that he would ask of the Lord. And neither did he fear the Devil, for he had met the Beast and cut off two heads, and it dared not show itself again in men's sight.

"And the Lord said to Macbeth, 'The sins of the Gentiles were covetousness, envy, gluttony, anger, lust, and sloth. Thine is the sin of pride. But ye have done well to ask of me no gifts, for the others turned the things I gave them against me and against themselves. Therefore ye shall make no wheels; ye shall have no wings. No horse will carry you; no ox will plough for you. In toil and poverty shall ye live, and the days of your lives will be few and hard. The things that are yours are the leavings of the dead. But ye shall yet have life; for ye are my Remnant, whom I shall never smite.'"

So there it was, the Macbeth archetype: an Adam who asks for nothing, an Arthur who brings his own sword. Self-sufficiency, stasis, survival. The timeless virtues of the Scots.

The play was an odd thing — a pageant handed down through centuries. Rehearsals were held in the castle yard. Not every actor turned up each time. A polished performance wasn't on the cards. Many long passages and minor characters had evidently been forgotten, and much of it was in mime. But some verse passages were literary fossils, in an English archaic to them but not to me. The laird assigned Hob as my coach and director. He was playing a

Roman soldier but, as a former prompter, knew the whole play well; and he was delighted to have an excuse for loitering within sight of Mailie.

She still had not confided in me the details of her secret, but I could see she was frightened of milady and twitchy in the laird's presence. She drew out our walks and swims as long as she could to be away from them. The story wasn't hard to guess: the old man had got her pregnant, and Lady Macbeth, unable to take the long view, had had the bairn smothered in its cot. Where Hob came in I wasn't sure—the lady's stud?

Hob took me through my role with patience and kindness, which seemed his nature, not merely for Mailie's benefit. The flogging would feel real enough, he said, and I could expect some discomfort on the cross, though I'd be tied, not nailed. Once I'd given up the ghost I'd be spirited away in the dark while the crowd was distracted by a "deevil dance" in town; then the Lord of the Loch, the keep's pale and bloody icon, would take my place. I'd have Saturday off—during which I'd have to keep out of sight—and then on Easter itself there'd be the encounter with Mary Magdalen in the garden (among the automobiles outside the castle wall), the walk to Emmaus (along the path to Dumnorrit), and the appearance before the eleven disciples (in the kirk). After that, as Mark and Luke have it, I would ascend into heaven—into the roof trusses with help from a pulley block exempt from the wheel taboo because of its sacred duties.

My last line would be from Matthew: "Lo, I am with you alway, even unto the end of the world."

Hob and I usually went over this in my room. I liked and trusted him, and I believe he had similar feelings towards me. His matter-of-fact coaching allayed my fears of sacrifice; if there was a plan to do me in, he didn't know of it. Sometimes he'd bring friends—one or two of the other soldiers—and I'd treat them to coffee.

If it was a quiet afternoon without orders from the keep, Hob and Mailie would slip off for a walk down the beach. (Her interest in me seemed to be waning, which was just as well, though I regretted it.) On the Tuesday or Wednesday before Easter, the two of them had left and I was having coffee alone with Neil, one of the guards who had shown me the pyramid of skulls in the dungeon weeks before. We'd since become friends. He was a broad man with a frosted beard, bandy legs, and rascally manner. I'd have taken him for a horseman if there'd been any horses. Neil was exceedingly fond of coffee and I enjoyed his easy nature. He'd often become talkative on a second cup.

That afternoon I'd finally worked the conversation round to the warren of relationships within the ancient walls, saying I understood that the laird and Mailie were cousins.

"Cousins! Aye, they are that." He stifled a beaky chuckle. Years of chewing sugar cane had reduced him to turtle gums, despite the dead man's tooth he hung around his neck to ward off dental problems. He swallowed a long draught of coffee, his eyes creased in amusement above the thick rim of the cup—a fine piece of caterer's Doulton marked *Palace Hotel, Inverness.*

"She's the Macbeth half-dauchter. Know what ah'm saying?"

"You can't mean.... He's not her *father!*"

"The laird's her faither richt eneuch. But the lady's no her mother. And that's only the half of it." Neil stopped, peering forlornly into an empty cup, his timing perfect. I wrung the last dregs from the pot for him.

"The baby? You don't mean Macbeth is also the father of her child?"

"If ye can call it that—the puir wee Lot-son."

Seeing I hadn't understood, he put his mouth to my ear: "'And the firstborn went in, and lay with her father....' Know what ah'm telling ye?" Of course: old Lot and his daughters. Desperate for offspring, the glen had taken Genesis 19 as a divine wink at incest.

"And it wasn't right? — the child, I mean."

"Aye. A wee hangie! Wan and heery. And no the first Macbeth to be that way. They say ye couldna tell the laird's uncle frae a bear cub. Sae lazy he'd shit in bed an' kick it oot wi' his feet. And mad as a tree full of budgies. Died in his twelfth yeer, a great maircy."

"So that was why Lady Macbeth had it . . . put down?"

"That's what ah hear. But some say she'd hae done it anyhoo. Tween oursels, man, there's mair milk o' kindness in a witch's tit. The lady's seed-faither was a Macdonald, and them's a hard, hard breed."

Later I thought: "Wan" in the sense of pale? Might Mailie's baby have been done away with because it was too light-skinned? And was that why the girl had been drawn to me? But Neil had said there was madness and abnormality in the Macbeth line. If they were so obsessed with fertility, surely they wouldn't weed out healthy children just for lack of pigment. Or would they? Many clansfolk showed signs of mixed ancestry — straight hair, European facial structure — but I saw no one lighter than a walnut stain.

With no mirror in my quarters I'd begun to take it for granted I was the same as those around me, like a family dog who thinks he's human. The play reminded me of my physical difference: they wanted me because I resembled Our Lord of the Loch. The glen's feelings about white people are complex. Colour confirms their belief that they belong to a creation different from the "Gentiles." Gentiles were white; God's Remnant black. But their Christ is white. So, like anti-Semitic Christians who have to overlook the fact that Jesus was at least half Jewish, they make an exception in His case.

Apparently the Edinburgh Malkies had been white, or mainly so. Those graffiti I saw on my march — *Hot Wogs Not Our Worry*; *Watling = Right Attitudes* — suggest to me that the regime enjoyed support from white supremacists. So does this newspaper clipping in the laird's collection:

... Notting Hill mosque massacre believed to be the work of the Final Solutions. A police spokesman said he deeply regretted the incident, but the force was stretched to the limit and could not be everywhere at once. An FS leader identifying himself only as "Bormann" was quoted as making the following statement to supporters in Trafalgar Square: "We kill the blind. We kill the cripples. We kill the queers. We kill the dykes. We kill the wogs and Jews. And when we've finished killing them, we go to the f***ing graveyard and dig them up and kill them a-f***ing-gain, because they didn't die hard enough."

I'd been thinking about that *Kwame.* Angus Kwame Macbeth. Yet apart from the name (and perhaps the design of the hut I'd been given after release from jail) there was little African about their culture. The black clan's origin was still as puzzling to me as mine to them. They worshipped like Piskies, they wore plaid, they appreciated good whisky, they even played football in a field below the kirk: they were as Scottish as their language.

One explanation that has crossed my mind is that the people of Glen Nessie may have changed colour in the same way as the Black Caribs of St. Vincent. Because intermarriage between runaway slaves and unconquered Indians in the interior of the island was gradual, the slaves' descendants became culturally Carib; but because African genes resisted Old World plagues that slew the Indians, the Caribs gradually turned black.

Something like that could have happened here. The indigenous highland culture—protected by mountains, favoured by the ecological diversity of the Great Glen, sustained by the tropical foods of the research station—had absorbed newcomers: first scientists, then a stream of refugees and rebels from the burning south. What was left of British society had fractured along ethnic faultlines. I'd guess the MacBeath Squad began as a Scots nationalist guerrilla band, operating against the neo-Malcolm dynasty founded at Edinburgh in the mid-2040s, at the height of the RISC pandemic.

As society disintegrated and solar radiation rose, evolution would have smiled on the dark. The cruel triage of natural selection, stalled by medicine for generations, would have resumed. The advantages of melanic skin, especially its protection against immune-weakening UV, could have made the difference between life and death, sterility and reproduction.

This Carib idea still pleases me, but it may not be the whole story. Here's another document I copied, admittedly enigmatic. It was stamped Great Glen Research Station and dated 2035, about two years after Watling's first coup — when I believe he set up the Emergency Government and Home Guard—and a year before the evacuation of London:

From: JKV                                         21/7/35
To: MNR
YOUR EYES ONLY


"Blackface" received in good order. On behalf of us all, I can't thank you enough. Where on earth did you get liquid nitrogen? (Don't answer that!)

Hard at work and early indications are encouraging. Let's hope the Generalissimo doesn't cut us off. All *strictly* on the QT until we see which way the wind's blowing. This material may be our only hope.

Watch this space.

Cheers. And again, a million thank-yous (literally, let's hope).


Why such secrecy and that odd last line? Was this "material" genetic? If so, is it likely to have been for llamas or plants? Your guess is as good as mine, but I believe this may refer to human melanic genes. If so, the clansfolk may not be Hyperborean Caribs after all, but genetically altered Jocks.

The fall of natural man. If I'm right, I'm him.

Rain was still gusting across the loch and the gap-toothed walls when Hob fetched me to the keep. He'd brought a sheet of plastic —my plastic—which he draped solemnly round my shoulders as if it were an ermine robe. He cut a Byronic figure himself, more Greek patriot than Roman soldier, in a guard's uniform enhanced by a red bandanna and a tattered leather jerkin.

The mob in the "Tate" (as I'd dubbed the museum on the ground floor) looked like children who'd ransacked a theatre wardrobe. Every sartorial relic preserved in the houses of Dumnorrit or dug from the ruins had been donned. By the door was a squad of soldiers in cracked hard-hats, scrofulous bobbies' helmets, motorcycle and riot gear. One or two had peaked officers' caps with verdigrised regimental badges. All had their usual kilts and staves, but their upper bodies modelled a range of puma skins, bandoleros, baldrics, home-made chainmail, and ancient leathers, many of which lacked an arm or leg. The room stank of mildew, sweat, and whisky—for the sacred usquebaugh was circulating among cast and pipeband. Alcohol and Christianity: the two great European narcotics. I didn't recognize Mailie until she was standing in front of me, a preposterous figure in a white rayon nightdress over which she'd buckled a Wagnerian bra. "You've got the wrong part," I said. "You should be Madonna." A naked foot, muddy and callused, stamped fiercely on mine. She was *en rôle*; my levity was out of order. What struck me as the makings of a drunken Hallowe'en party was a solemn, indeed sacred occasion.

Lady Macbeth was already praying silently on her knees before the Lord of the Loch, awed at Gabriel's news, her face reverent in the yellow light and honeyed smoke of beeswax candles —reverent and at peace for the first time since I'd known her.

Devotion softened the pinched face into beauty; she'd shed years, had become the Macdonald lass who'd once inflamed the laird.

The whisky bottle made two or three rounds before the rain stopped. We filed out into a muddy yard filling with sunlight as the cloud went to holes and blew away.

Macbeth was reciting something in an orotund manner: "Fear not, sons and daughters of Zion: behold, thy King cometh, sitting on a cuddy." The music drained from the pipes. I could hear another sound—a plaintive, high-pitched *een, een, een*—and in the circle around him I saw a large brown llama. I'd always thought llamas were mute, but the cry was coming from its mobile lips.

Though big as llamas go, it could barely take a rider my size. I sat over the haunches, as one does on a donkey, to avoid breaking the poor creature's back. We left slowly, passing under the trilithon, where two men were digging a hole for the cross. One was Hob; he glanced up and beamed at the radiant Magdalene walking beside me.

A turbulent human river flowed down the path from Castle Urquhart to the town, more people than I'd seen since leaving the past. They must have gathered from the high fields and pastures, from miners' camps at Inverness, from all over the kingdom of the glen. Urquhart Bay was jammed with flimsy leather craft, sails furled like raffia tablemats. A smell of wet wool filled the eddy in which I rode as the crowd opened before me and closed behind, spraying drips from the forest of palm fronds in their hands, like Birnam Wood come to Dunsinane. I passed through the chanting faces in a mellow daze induced by whisky on an empty stomach, by dazzling light and theatrical vapours perspiring from the earth under a sun worthy of the Holy Land.

"Hosanna, Hosanna: Blessed is he that cometh in the name of the Lord, even the King of Israel."

A hideous figure began circling, lunging, spooking the llama, shrinking the crowd, his face livid with berry juice or chicken

blood. He wore a puma's tail, bulls' horns, and what might once
have been striped silk pyjamas.

> I am Lord Lucifer, from Hell I come!
> Prince of this world, great duke of that below.
> The nourisher of sin, the death of man,
> For I began in Heav'n my sin to sow
> Among the angels who with dainty flight
> Flocked by the Throne. In youth did I bestow
> The world with dawn and day and all things bright;
> I was the fairest one, the bearer of the light.

These are a few shards of a monologue that lasted more than
a mile. (What I set down here is merely a Bad Quarto, all I have
left now that the play is fading from my mind.)

The Devil's rant continued until the edge of town. Then it
was my turn, lifting my eyes to Drumnadrochit as if it were the
Holy City, and turning to look over Loch Ness towards Edinburgh,
London, and whatever might remain of the real Jerusalem.

> Jerusalem, woeful art thou. What woe
> Shall fall on those who live within thy walls.
> And they shall curse the day that they were born,
> Run from the fire and sword sweeping thy halls,
> And having fled, look back, and die forlorn.
> Then in those days both meat and drink shall fail,
> Temples and towers shall fall upon the ground,
> The sky will gape and loose a brimstone hail.
> O city! woe on thee when the last trump shall sound.

Mercifully not all the play was in verse. The rest of the morning was taken up with those events of the Passion that still held
meaning for the glen.

I went to the steps of the kirk — below the lintel so proudly inscribed *AD 1882*, as if Victorian civilization had been the beginning of a thousand-year reich of industry and rectitude — and spoke the words of Jesus in Luke:

"Nation shall rise against nation, and kingdom against kingdom: and great earthquakes shall be in divers places, and famines, and pestilences; and fearful sights and great signs shall there be from heaven.... Then let them which are in Judaea flee to the mountains.... For these be the days of vengeance, that all things which are written may be fulfilled. Woe unto them that are with child, and to them that give suck, in those days!"

Mailie was on the lowest step, between me and the crowd, her eyes downcast and red. Thoughtless of me not to cut the last line.

The heat was uncomfortable, for the late April sun was fierce by eleven. Macbeth, magnificently attired as Caiaphas in a flowing robe of white astrakhan llama and his immense sombrero, came out of the kirk behind me and announced there would be an intermission until the shadow of a sequoia on the old A82 touched a certain stone in the church square. This was meant to be a lunchless fast for all, but I suspect most of the citizens had at least some cornbread and water in the cool of their houses to keep them going. Mailie brought me some; we broke it together and ate beneath a bougainvillaea behind the church. She said little and made spaniel eyes, and once she seemed about to blurt something that was troubling her, but kept it in.

At about half past two the play resumed. Simon the leper came to greet me as I returned to the square, inviting me to his house — a stage erected more or less where the concrete plesiosaur once frolicked in its pond — there to sit and eat the paschal lamb with my disciples. On stage was a table spread with bread, jugs of palm toddy (a new one on me; antique Scotch wasn't the only tipple), and a central plate containing a dark trussed object like a Christmas

pudding in bondage. The crowd swarmed at the edge of the platform: wild, eager, fanatical faces, a dark flood from the streets.

In my nervousness, suppressed but not banished by draughts
of usquebaugh, my lines deserted me. My eyes flew around in
panic, alighted on the crowning ornament of the board. Not a
Christmas pud. Nor, exactly, a paschal lamb. It was a haggis — the
first I'd seen in Nessie — and Burns came to my rescue. I got to my
feet, beamed on the crowd with what I hoped was an expression
of Christly *gemütlichkeit*, summoned the best stage Scots I could,
and stretched out my hand to the blob of dubious meat:

> Fair fa' your honest sonsie face,
> Great Chieftain o' the pudding-race!
> Aboon them a' ye tak' your place,
> Painch, tripe, or thairm:
> Weel are ye worthy o' a grace
> As lang's my arm.

Ah, the roar of the greasepaint and the smell of the crowd!
Perhaps they had some racial memory of the Bard of Ayr. Perhaps
they were merely tickled by my camp accent and departure from
the script. No matter: they laughed; their laughter primed my
memory and I was able to dredge up the creaking lines rehearsed:

> In the old law the paschal lamb was for
> A sacrifice. Now the new lamb that shall
> Be killed is me. This is my body, flesh
> And blood, which dies upon the Rood for thee.

"Die, Lord?" inquired Peter. Then came my foretelling of
denial and betrayal. Judas — bearded, shiny-eyed, draped in coarse
black wool — came to receive the body of Christ, ate, and slyly
crept away. The Devil leapt onto the stage, seized the traitor by the

hand, and held aloft his arm like a victorious boxer's, shouting over the jeers and hoots:

Haha! Judas, darling mine!
Thou art the best that e'er was born.
A crown in hell shall soon be thine.
In fire and stink you'll share my throne.

This was what they'd come for: the betrayal, the thirty pieces of silver. Money was not merely Judas's wage; it was an abomination symbolic of the fallen world. Some clansfolk kept a few old coins in their houses, but only as curiosities or, as Macbeth had said, *memento mori*. I'd had to tell the laird what banknotes were when he tore open a rusty cashbox in his archive. They dated from the 2030s and were in huge denominations: *promise to pay the bearer on demand, five million pounds*. "Tell me, David — one says five million and anither says ane million, and aside from that there's nae difference at all."

"It was a matter of faith — faith that you could exchange them anytime for things of worth, or quantities of gold."

"Aye, but can ye *eat* gold?" And I gave him the Spaniard's answer: "We had a disease of the heart for which gold was the only cure."

Judas and Lucifer left hand in hand, closing the scene. Table and haggis were removed. Then, in the church square, we enacted the events of the garden, Judas returning with the high priest's henchmen, coins clanking inside his robe.

"Hail, Rabbi."

"Judas, betrayest thou the Son of Man with a kiss?"

Simon Peter pulled a dirk from his kilt and sliced off a man's ear. I was hardly sober, what with palm toddy on top of Scotch, but it looked too real. Before I could take a second look at the wrinkled flesh in the dust I was haled away to the high priest — back to the stage in the square, where Caiaphas, immense and lugubrious in his dazzling robe, began his interrogation.

"By the living God. Tell us whether thou be the Christ, the Son of God."

"If I tell you, ye will not believe: and if I ask you, ye will not answer."

"Art thou then the Son of God?"

"Ye say that I am."

"Wha' further need hae we of witness?" (Voices in chorus with Macbeth.) "We oursels hae haird it from his ain mouth!"

Enter Kenneth. Short, powerful, mean-spirited Kenneth, who perhaps still believed me to be from Reekie or from hell. He did not make a good Pilate. Not nearly effete enough. He *cared* too much to deliver the Roman's offhand lines.

"Wha' accusation bring ye agin this man?"

"If this man were not an evil-doer, we would not have brought him."

"Tak him yersels, and judge him by yer ain law."

"But under the law we cannot put a man to death."

"Art thou the King of the Jews?"

"Sayest thou this thyself, or did others tell it thee of me?"

"Am I a Jew, man? Thine own priests delivered thee tae me. Wha' hast thou done?"

"My kingdom is not of this world."

"Art thou a king then?"

"Thou sayest that I am a king. To this end was I born, and to this end am I come into the world, that I should bear witness unto the truth."

A hush had fallen, the crowd straining after every word. Pilate then uttered the most subversive words in the Bible, words of civilization:

"What is truth?"

Words that Jesus does not answer.

Pilate turned to the crowd:

"Ye hae a custom, that I should release unto yez ane prisoner. Will ye therefore that I release the King of the Jews?"

And of course the crowd called for Barabbas. Soldiers seized me, whipped me, draped me in purple, rammed a crown of bull-horn acacia on my head. All this was, as Hob had warned, real enough. I moved to the edge of the stage, dropping a spoor of blood across the boards.

"Crucify him! Crucify him!"

"Tak him yersels and crucify him."

A soldier brought a bowl and Pilate washed his hands.

I'll not forget those two miles from kirk to castle gate. It was evening then, about five o'clock, but there was still strength in the sun. I was raw with sunburn, for my only hat all day was thorns. Blood was caked in my eyebrows, behind my ears; with the exertion of dragging the cross it began to flow again. They stripped off my robe and flogged my back, some *pro forma*, others with sadistic glee. Two miles I staggered between walls of noise and swarthy faces egged on by those who loathed or feared me. *Malkie! Gow! Cueball! Spook! Ofay* — the outworn gibes linger in their tongue the way witch and bastard did in ours.

It must have taken an hour and a half to reach my Golgotha. Kenneth was there, watching — watching every flinch and sigh for evil and unearthly powers. The glen's Torquemada, the glen's McCarthy.

The sun was still up, but the castle had been in mountain shade for hours. They laid the cross on the ground, its point by the hole dug this morning, and spread-eagled me upon it. There was a little notch chipped out for my left heel; here they bound my ankles. They tied each wrist to the cross's arms, and I looked up and saw Hob's face above me. He was whispering very softly: *Sorry, sorry.* When Kenneth turned his back to inspect the hole,

Hob raised his voice—*Keep heart!*—but the rest of his words were carried away by an evening wind that had begun to crease the bay.

Sacrifices are best done as the day dies. They waited while the ruddy hem of light slipped up the eastern range across the loch until the hilltops, huddled like cattle above the shore, were all in dark but one. In this way they judged the moment of sunset on the invisible horizon behind the mountains. Then Hob was driving a six-inch nail into my left hand, through the palm, so sudden it didn't hurt. And another into my right, only half healed from Macbeth's handshake, but he ran the nail through the web between thumb and forefinger, and I remember thinking *That will never hold*, but of course I was bound as well. So why nail me at all? And the next thought was that they meant to kill me now. That this was indeed what Lady Macbeth had been up to. Or perhaps this really was the secret of the glen's special covenant with God: a Christ had to die in agony each year to save those with no imagination. Perhaps a crook, perhaps the lightest-skinned. Who knows?

As the sunlight slipped from the highest peak they raised me. The Rood juddered down into its hole, and I was aloft against a crimson sky.

Part IV


TITHONUS

## — 1 —

How do you get attention here without a constant haemorrhage of baksheesh, and who has room for a wad of grotty notes the size of a bog roll? Waiter! Suffragi! What's the use? Yes, your best bottle of Château Ptolemy Fond de Cave and a plate of munchies. Why don't we dine somewhere else later on? There must be a better place. *I doubt it, David. I've been here a year — nearly two — and I've yet to find one. You don't come to Aswan for the food.* Or the wine. *No* (laughing), *certainly not the wine. But don't waste your money on imported — nothing travels well enough to get here in a state worth touching.*

I hope that doesn't include me.

*David! My God, just look at the sunset.*

Dust, I suppose. Or pollution?

*Don't spoil it! Look.*

The sun holds no heat now, no brightness, no pain. Ra, Helios, Sol, Inti, Matahari: you can gaze unflinching into the old god's bloodshot eye. But the size of him! Swollen until he seems to claim all the sky over the desert, burning it up to fuel his waning power; until the sphere on the sand fills the whole earth beyond the Nile: the disk of Ra colossal in his painted barge.

The barge she sat in, like a burnish'd throne,
Burn'd on the water; the poop was beaten gold,
Purple the sails, and so perfumed, that....

Anita?

*Don't stop. Go on!*

Anita, do you think you could bring yourself to...

*Go on! Go on. Give me poetry. Poetry will get you everywhere.*

...that the winds were love-sick with them, the oars were silver,

Which to the tune of flutes kept stroke, and made
The water which they beat to follow faster,
As amorous of their strokes...

I've forgotten what comes next.

*Oh do look! Blood on the clouds. You can't stop now. You mustn't. I forbid it.*

Upon her landing, Antony sent to her,
Invited her to supper....

Age cannot wither her, nor custom stale
Her infinite variety; other women cloy
The appetites they feed, but she makes hungry
Where most she satisfies.

That's all I know. The rest isn't so nice about her anyway. What I'm asking you, Anita, is to call me Mr. Lambert. *That! You came all this way to ask me that?* (Laughter) *I'd forgotten. David, really. You always were so...eccentric.* Do I hear a pot calling a kettle black? Look at yourself. That pipe for a start. People are giggling. Haven't you noticed? Even the staff. *They ought to be used to eccentric archaeologists in Egypt by now, we've been coming here for two hundred years.* Some longer than that; until today I was older than you could possibly believe. *That's what the hungry archaeologist likes to hear! The older you are, Dave — Mr. Lambert — the more likely I am to be interested in you. Eternity was in our lips and eyes. I would I had thy inches.*

The champagne breakfast: people tottering in, men without ties or shoes, girls with wet dresses stuck to their slim bodies (this was you, Anita). Shall I tell you how I remember it?

I hadn't seen him, didn't know he was in the room till someone shouted. And there was Bird, flying on drink, or something, clutching the neck of a bottle he'd just broken on a table: *I've got a bone to pick wiv you.* He always did have a gift for understatement. For a time it looked all right. Max and Peter pinned his arms, someone got the bottle away, Kate Swann went through his pockets. The lad was carrying a flick-knife, one brass knuckle, a length of motorcycle chain, and a steel comb with a sharpened handle. Once they'd disarmed him they let him go — that old school sense of fair play. Someone (you?) was doing Sellers: *Gentlemen! Gentlemen! You can't fight in here. This is the War Room.* And you all stood aside while Bird and I went downstairs to sort it out in the quadrangle.

Max shouted, *Queensberry Rules* (as if Bird ever played by rules). You wouldn't deign to come down. I saw your face among those at an upstairs window. We sparred a bit, bobbing on our toes, sizing each other up, neither really knowing the first thing about boxing; then I landed a lucky one on his chin and he went down like the bad guy in a western. I came back flushed with Neanderthal pride, and all you did was give a frosty glare and say, *You both looked bloody silly prancing around out there. It was like watching two cranes in a mating dance.*

After that we all got maudlin. Bird and I shook hands, the handshake became an embrace, you joined in, everyone cheered. I think they expected the three of us to go off somewhere and fuck our addled brains out. I don't know why we didn't.

Next: you and Bird having an intense conversation in a corner. You slap him and flounce out of the room. Then you and I are sitting on the floor in the passage. Don't remember a word of what was said — by that time we'd been up twenty-four hours, drinking for twelve. I can still hear Bird's shout, a blast of rage. And another voice: *He's got an axe! My God, he's got the fire axe!* Bird advancing down the passage from the head of the stairs, where he'd torn the hatchet from its glass box. *You bastard! You bastard!* We stand up and I say something snooty and provoking—something like, Technically you are, Bird, and I'm not.

I saw him throw, and he was good or lucky—one of those moments you replay in slow motion all your life—straight at my head, a black and red elfbolt cleaving smoky air; and though I could see it clearly—can still see it—I couldn't dodge. And then your pale arm eclipsed the blade.

Without your Navajo bangle you might have lost that hand. In the Möbius loop of film I see the axe strike the wall, the white shower of plaster, the red fountain from your wrist. Not a big cut, but an artery. *Who would have thought the old girl had so much blood in her?* Your joke before passing out. The blood that killed you; the blood you spilt for me.

But of course we didn't know that at the time. I remember visiting you in Addenbrooke's—they only kept you in one night, the nurse said you'd lost more alcohol than blood—and you saying, *As soon as I get out of here I'm taking you home with me. If one's going to get half murdered for something, one may as well do it.* Bird visited you too, a step ahead of the law; they pulled him over later on the London road, though as far as I know they didn't hold him long. You wouldn't press charges, and the cops had had a busy night—a garage suicide, two rapes, umpteen stolen cars and handbags.

Bird and I never spoke again. Not until your funeral.

Pain gushing through me like water from a sluice into a desert field, until the field becomes a swamp, a fiery lake, and then is gone. It was dark when I came round. I'd been dreaming—like the time I fell asleep at the wheel and dreamt I was having an accident, rolling over and over, and was starting to get comfortable in bed again when something woke me. The smell of petrol, the thought of fire. And I was upside-down, still strapped in the seat, roof pushed to the dashboard, mirror against my nose, a lorry engine throbbing nearby and a man calling *Anyone alive in there?* That was real and so was this: I was nailed up like a tigerskin.

Crucifixion has the reputation of being one of the slowest and cruellest ways. That's why kind-hearted soldiers put you out of your misery by breaking your legs or poking a spear in your side. Was that in the script too—the spear? How long would I last if it wasn't? Weren't there Filipino fanatics who had themselves crucified year after year—imitation the sincerest form of worship—and managed to go back to the office after the holidays? If I were a believer this Roman torture might hold such consolations, might be something beyond plain agony and a stagy death.

I had no worship; only pity. I've always felt sorry for Christ, and I've always admired him for twitting the establishment. But I can't believe he was the son of God, except in the sense that we all are, which may be all he meant. Christianity was the work of painfully literal minds. Didn't Freud say, "I am not a Freudian," and Lévi-Strauss deny he was a structuralist? If Jesus of Nazareth came back to earth and saw the quaint Alexandrian tutti-frutti confected from his life and death (to say nothing of all the killings on his behalf), wouldn't he want his name taken off the letterhead? I'll put money on that. Play fair, now; for every visit to Mother Teresa we'd have to include a surprise inspection of a New Tribes Mission, perusal of the *Donation of Constantine* or perhaps *Centesimus Annus*, ringside seats with the Caucasian Christians for Commerce at a Republican convention. . . .

Movement below me in the dark. People there. They sounded fidgety. I couldn't see a thing, but I could feel them watching my hummingbird shape against the stars. Someone coughed. Women were weeping. Mailie? Lady M? A voice hissed *Eloi*... A voice somewhere behind the cross, in a Cadillac, hissing *Eloi*. Eloi? Morlock? No. They wanted me to deliver my line and give up the ghost so they could all go home. I suppose they have this trouble every year. But why oblige them?

The hiss again. Hob's voice. Urgent, kind, implying something more. Trying to help? All right, I'll do it. But which do they want? John: "It is finished." Luke: "Father, into thy hands I commend my spirit." Or Pancho Villa: "Tell them I said something." Hob again: *Eloi!* Of course. They want Matthew and Mark.

With the last of my strength I cried out in a loud voice, bilingually, *"Eloi, Eloi, lama sabachthani?* My God, my God, why hast thou forsaken me?"

The dark mass below began departing to the kirk, where they would see a veil rent from top to bottom; where a glow announced that pitch-pine bonfires were kindling for the devil dance. I didn't hear the last of them go, for I'd passed out again.

The Rood shaking, each shake sending a new flood into the sodden field of pain. A terrible thirst. More shaking and a hand on my shoulder. No! *Quaiet!* Hob's voice. "Quaiet, and we'll tak ye doon." He was on the crosspiece like a cat, stretching a crowbar to the nail in my palm. "This'll hurt. But mak nae soond. An they catch us, we're twa dead men." It hurt all right, but he hadn't driven the nail deep and it came out in one tug. The same with the other. He began to untie the ropes. Cut them! I said, but he ignored me. Later, when I was shivering, hunched upon the ground, he explained that it had to look like a miracle: an angel would untie ropes, not cut them. Don't ask me why.

"Where's Mailie?"

"At the dance. She sent ye these." The gibbous Easter moon hadn't risen yet but had begun to wash away the stars above the eastern mountains; in the cold light I could see a shiny bundle. Plastic! I started to speak; he ordered me to hold out my hands. The right one wasn't bad, but my left was warm and sticky, still flowing.

Suddenly it stung and I caught a gust of whisky. He washed both wounds from a small bottle, bandaged them with cotton.

"D'ye think ye can swim?" No way; I'd have to steal a boat.

"Aye. Better for you, but less of a miracle. Anyhoo, the wind's agin ye." I could feel it on my face, chilling my whole body, even though it was a warm easterly sweeping down from pastures and valleys folded in the Strathnairn foothills. The currachs couldn't tack against the wind because they had no keels or centreboards; if I could get across the loch I'd be safe from pursuit until the weather changed. But there was no chance I could row.

"Ah cannae linger." Hob repeated his warning about what would happen if anyone found us. His orders were to split my side with a spear. Mailie had talked him into this mad rescue, saying she had secret instructions from Macbeth. He gave me a last swig and put the bundle in my lap.

"Dinna undae it till ye get across. It's waterproof—a wee bit of food and some of yer things."

I was thinking about the boats and the wind. In getting me off the cross, Hob had knocked down the superscription, *Iesus Nazarenus Rex Iudaeorum*. It was a teak plank, old, finely planed and carved, about a yard long and a foot wide, less than an inch thick.

"Will you do one last thing for me, Hob? Help me to the dock with the bundle, and bring that board?" He slung my better arm across his shoulder and we wove through the night to the water's edge below the castle. The keep was near but empty and unlighted, a black slab of missing sky. Everyone was in town for the strange dance. A dance on the night Christ dies? Irregular, but no doubt it made sense to them. A kind of exorcism perhaps—the powers of death and evil exulting for a while, only to be vanquished on Easter morning—something like that. Well, they'd need an understudy for the Resurrection.

Hob soon grasped what I wanted, and he was good with his hands. He lashed the board to the gunwale of a small sailing curragh so that it knifed into the water. It wouldn't work too well on the opposite tack—I should have had one on each side—but I could keep it to leeward most of the way if I held a diagonal course across the loch.

"Say goodbye to Mailie for me. No thanks are enough for what both of you have done." I threw my arms around him feebly. "What will happen to you? Shouldn't you both come away with me now."

"Whaur would we go if we did?"

"South. To Yorkshire, or Wales, or London. We could find somewhere to live." (To the future, I nearly said, but there's only one seat in the machine.) His answer was firm. They preferred the devils they knew. He was sure the laird had given the nod to this escape. It was the lady wanted me dead. If they kept out of her way for a while—went hunting and herding on the far slopes of Ben Nevis—they'd get by. After all, I'd be gone; the official version would be a miracle or the Devil's work or some such.

He undid the painter, gave the boat a hearty shove into open water. I raised the sail, picked up some headway, left Urquhart Bay and its flotilla of skin craft behind me in the dark. I looked back twice, wanting to wave. But all I could see was the dark void of the keep and, in Drumnadrochit, a bonfire blush on the erstwhile hotel and Official Monster Centre.

That night's longueurs and reveries of pain are deeply incised, yet much of the escape from Macbeth's kingdom is already indistinct: ten days compressed to a continuum of hiding and running, light and dark, heat and rain. I suppose it took about two hours to make a southwesterly tack in the clumsy vessel by the rising moonlight to the wild shore beyond Foyers, where no road has ever run and shale cliffs drop thousands of feet to the loch and another thousand to the bottom. I remembered the place from our walks, but got there more by luck than judgement, as wind and leeboard took me. I saw a pale froth in the darkness, heard lumpy waves on shelving rock.

The frail boat struck, filled instantly, its belly torn.

I remember nothing more until the sun spilled from behind the mountains. Somehow I'd wormed ashore like a primordial creature laying unconscious claim to the land. Somehow in that first dawn I retrieved my bundle and sank the wreck with stones; somehow I climbed the scree, a panicked hare weaving between lianas and fig roots, beneath leaves like shields and umbrellas, between writhen trunks and glowing flowers that seemed to want to love me or devour me — heedless of dangers, terrified only by man.

The sun climbed behind a broad anvil of thunderhead. Loch Ness smoothed, turned orange, and boiled with heavy raindrops like machine-gun fire. No boats could sail that day.

A cave: perhaps the corrie we saw, where Bonnie Prince Charlie hid after Culloden. It was large and dry and dark, the entrance among elephant-ear taro and splinters of rock encrusted with swollen roots. At the mouth was a bed of straw, half rotted away, and scattered bone and charcoal beneath a smudged ceiling. Others had been here, but not lately. I threw myself down and slept for a night and morning, waking in perpetual twilight.

A sunbeam told me it was close to noon. I crept out, checked for signs of fresh activity — tracks, fleshy bones — sat on a boulder, unwrapped Mailie's bundle in a rippling pool of sun.

Hob was right about the laird's connivance; here were nearly all the things I'd brought to Nessie and those dug from my last camp: nylon bag, shirt, socks, jeans, fishing line, tent, machete, and at last my notebook and my shoes. The laird had kept the torch and gun (perhaps they hang now beside his Duchamp urinal in the Tate). Mailie had wrapped several food parcels in banana leaves and sisal — toasted kernels, dates, dried fruit, a small pawpaw, and half a dozen young green oranges. I ate the oranges on the spot, all six. I towelled down with the loincloth and, for only the third or fourth time in two months, put on twentieth-century clothes (I'd thought it unwise to go out in them at Nessie).

The tailoring felt like armour, a defence against this savage future. Shoes were odd and constricting on my toughened feet, but they too gave a sense of power and fleetness, of advantage. If I'd had matches (the laird had not returned my lighter, nor replaced it with tinder and flint), I doubt I could have resisted the temptation of a fire, for I still shivered with shock and exposure.

Spells of delirium or nightmare in which I was back on the Rood, at the threshold of death, or believed I had stepped beyond. Several times in my life when I've had such brushes with death the feeling has come afterwards that perhaps I didn't escape, that the sickness *was* fatal, the Mantlow stairs *did* fall away beneath me, the motorbike slid under the lorry and the huge wheels did not miss my skull. My earliest memory of this is the December I fell ill with measles. I'd got it badly, was kept behind in the school sanatorium after term broke up. I was about to go home on Christmas morning when the policewoman came with the news about my parents.

For some time I believed that it was I who had died, not they. That the rest of the world had carried on without me; that the story I'd been told was merely the stuff of hellfire. The adult mind employs more sophistication but it tells the same fables to itself. The sensation of having escaped and lived on becomes a solipsism, a trick of evaporating consciousness or, if you like, an anodyne from a loving God to spare you the blow of your extinction. And it follows that one may *never* know when one has died, may go on living an echo, like a player performing to the darkness of an empty hall he thinks is a full house. And the ever-running play you write and act is your eternity.

For two or three days I rested, sleeping, eating, anointing my wounds with pawpaw and lichen, binding them with spider's webs and strips of cloth, and in lucid moments pondering different plans. Only two seemed possible and both were mad: a blind hike over the Monadhliath Range through jungle and pine to the Edinburgh road near Dalwhinnie; or a skirting of the glen's frontier along the edge of the high pasture until I reached the same road near the scene of my capture. Hobson's choice. The first was shorter but harder, and I could more easily get lost. The second was riskier — if they'd caught me once they might again.

Both plans required the same beginning, a southerly scramble up the mountain rim of the loch. I left the cave on the third or fourth day, making no decision about route until I'd had a chance to test the going and myself. I had no compass, no knowledge of the land. All I could do was guess direction from the sun and stay high above slopes and valleys burnt for pasture. Once or twice I saw a lonely clachan far below. No signs of life, no smoke. The people were still at the Easter festivities in Glen Urquhart. Perhaps that's why Lady Macbeth didn't find me — her men weren't looking yet.

The supplies didn't last long, but despite larcenous thoughts of corn and eggs I kept away from crofts. I rationed myself severely, spent hours gathering chestnuts, unripe guavas, palm hearts, even grubs and ants mashed with berries. What bears eat, I ate.

Luckily the forest here was part of the glen's hunting land. Each year they fired the undergrowth to raise new shoots for deer — so the trees were spaced, the floor open. If it hadn't been for this I doubt I could have got away before food and energy ran out. The easy woodland drew me on, encouraged me, until I thought it better to stick to the shorter, higher route. I pressed on through mist and cloud; I stumbled, slept where I fell, under plastic in the rain, too tired and too afraid to pitch the tent.

And one morning I awoke and saw that I'd left the kingdom of the glen. The forest was different: wild, tangled, not burnt or trodden by man in centuries. The only trails were the ways of deer, and a wolf came boldly to snuff the air downwind while I was eating. The mountains were trending lower now, towards the Spey below the Cairngorms, where back in March I'd first seen bear tracks and Scots pines.

With the wild came that racial fear of the wild: a grizzly bear is no less frightening than a crucifixion.

On over Drumochter Pass, between the sunset shadows of the Boar of Badenoch and the Sow of Atholl, down the ever-green highway, until a few days ago I reached the Firth of Forth, saw Edinburgh Castle in the distance, and knew I'd neither strength nor hands to climb the slimy girders high above the water. But I could swim. I swam from one pier of the old railway bridge to the next, resting in the pterodactyl shadow thrown from its girders by the moon (for they say sharks never hunt at night), swimming on and on, a bladder of air trapped under my plastic sheet. How precious that silk and amber of our times. And what I would have given, in those damp nights and mornings, for a butane lighter. Ten thousand years of civilization to make each one of us a blithe Prometheus. My God, what we threw away!

And so, my love, I'm back in the ruins of Castle Reekie, which on second acquaintance seem to stand for all ruins, for Ur and Thebes, Manhattan and Tenochtitlan; all proxied by the vacant Athens of the North.

A strange proprietorial glee: from here to the south coast, Britain is mine. I am pharaoh, fellah, king, citizen, chairman, comrade. And I have answers now to fill this silence, even though my answers may yet kill me.

One thing seems clear enough: nature didn't clobber us, except in self-defence. There was no *deus ex machina*, no cosmic foot. But *when* do you suppose an end like this became inevitable? I can't help playing "What If" a lot—as we used to do in The Wise Monkeys:

What if the cave bears had eaten all the cave men?
If the lions had eaten all the Christians?
If Charles Martel had lost?
If Moctezuma had won?
If Hitler had been admitted to art school?
If Gorbachev had been a movie actor?

What if we'd come to our senses in 1945, when Little Boy made war obsolete? We were a mere two billion then; could we have bought a future for the price of the Cold War?

Shall we go for the "great villain" school of historical blame, or must we concede that the enemy of the people was the people? How many politicians were willing to tell the world that four billion, or six billion, or ten could never live the California dream? How many of those billions would have voted for them if they had?

This I do know: by the time the world agreed on the presence of icebergs it was far too late for *Leviathan* to change her course.

But did the smart ship ever have a rudder?

— 2 —

*Edinburgh, May 20th, Friday*

There. Ten days typing to bring you up to date. One finger, then two. The hands are healing now. Life is free and ample. I have light and heat, fish and fruit, hat and music, the Oyster with its fossil words and winking eye for company.

I've had to forsake St. Margaret's Chapel, all venerable piles: too obvious if the men of Nessie come after my white skin. So I've moved to the fourth floor of a block of flats near the docks in Leith —a stack of kennels, ugly, brutalist, fledged with a dozen kinds of epiphyte and creeper, entered by a tidal lobby and a flight of dank back stairs. But what a grand view of the Firth of Forth—both bridges, Inchkeith Island, and a clear run to where the Firth curls into the sea.

You'd love the weather—every day in the thirties, the nights seldom below twenty—the weather of Dominica, I dare say. A sea wind comes each afternoon, drawn by the heat of the dead city at my back; and each morning, when the land cools and the water holds the warmth, the wind makes its way back through these glassless rooms. I make fire only for cooking and only after dark, in a pit of a yard where they used to keep the dustbins. No one will find me here.

In truth, Anita, I'm hoping that one day soon I *will* see a sail out there, for it'd save me a lot of bother to steal a boat. Steal a boat and sail down to the Thames, to the time machine, to you. Otherwise I'm rather stuck. The walk down England will be hungry and hot with neither gun nor Graham to feed me. The sea's the thing—I can fish the reefs, find crab and lobster, cut coconuts and palm hearts all along the shore. Each day I look at that turquoise water and white stitch of reef, and whisper to myself *a sail, a sail.*

You may think this feeble, this failure to improvise, but remember my condition. These are not carpenter's hands. I thought of building a light kayak from bamboo and plastic but such a craft, even if I could make it, would not survive one scrape over the reef. I've already combed the beaches at low tide, and there are sunken vessels here—waterlogged timbers and flensed ribs of iron. A small fibreglass hull, smooth and blue as a mussel shell, got my hopes up—but she was only half a boat, flushed from Davy Jones's locker by a storm.

My condition isn't simply a matter of wounded hands. Cleopatra's revenge is back, a sign that the hourglass is running low. I felt so much better at Nessie that I could believe I was cured or had never been stalked by your patient killer. Perhaps Mailie was my cure—perhaps the clansfolk have some immunity and I drank remission with her milk. There'll be no more of that, and dammit I miss the girl. I even miss that old grizzly bear Macbeth; and Hob and Neil.

This being moved after the event: Why is the echo richer than the source, and time remembered always grief? People come and go, and you hardly notice how they feel, what you feel. Then one day when you least expect it remembrance slips like a blade into the heart: what you did and didn't do, said and didn't say; and suddenly you fall down into a cold and sunken place with only your regrets for company, there gutted by sorrow and remorse and left to die.

If you think me gloomier than usual let me tell you why. So busy was I retrieving the things I'd left at the castle, finding this new gaff, entering the account you've just read of my weeks at the glen and my escape, that not until now did I go through the pockets of my dirty clothes—those returned me by Macbeth. It seems he hadn't gone through them either, for they still held some things I'd filched from his trunk: pencil stubs, wet paper, and three CDs. Two have a playing surface good enough to raise an image. One's an *Oxford English Dictionary*—I was hoping for a future edition with new terms and definitions. But it was published in 2008, so there aren't many. I knew that the other was something to do with the London police—I'd picked it out because I thought it might have information on the decline of the old capital—but couldn't read the full title until now: *Metropolitan Police Violent Offenders Files, Decennial Database 2000–2009*. Disappointing: not even ten years, a mere toenail in our future's door. I was about to eject it when a thought occurred. I entered *PARKER*, C.G.

PARKER, Charles Gordon
ALIAS: Frank Tite. A.k.a. "Bird" to close associates

DATE/PLACE OF BIRTH: 4/9/67. 23 Harbinger Rd., Millwall, Isle of Dogs

LAST KNOWN ADDRESS:14 Waterloo Villas, Stepney

CHARGES AND CONVICTIONS:

(1)  11/8/86 Burglary, Tony's Two-Wheelers, 186A High Street, Walthamstow. Sentence: 18 mos probation.

(2)  5/6/88 Arrested on suspicion of assault causing grievous bodily harm after an incident at Corpus Christi College, Cambridge. Police summoned to ballroom early on June 5 by anonymous telephone call. Caller alleged that Parker "went berserk" with a fire axe in a crowded room, severely cutting the wrist of one Anita Langland. Parker apprehended speeding in the southbound carriageway of the M11 the following day; released from custody when Langland refused to testify.

(3)  16/07/95 Receiving. Using Tite alias, Parker acquired antique motorcycle parts stolen from National Motor Museum, Beaulieu, by persons unknown on the night of May 14. Sentence 2 years; served 15 mos Wormwood Scrubs, early release for good behaviour.

(4)  19/12/00. Charged with the murder of David P.W. Lambert.

*Click box for case summary.*

CASE SUMMARY: His Majesty v. Charles Gordon Parker, Old Bailey, commencing 09/03/01.

CHARGE: That on or about the 30th of November, 2000, the defendant did murder Dr. David Philip Wringham Lambert.

PLEA/S:

(1)  Not guilty.

(2)  Guilty to manslaughter by reason of diminished responsibility.

SYNOPSIS:

Dr. Lambert was said by two neighbours to have disappeared from his home early in 2000. As it was not unusual for him to travel abroad, they did not report him missing. Later interviews with another neighbour, Mr. Calixto Pool of Mérida, Mexico, established that Lambert had falsified information concerning his absence at that time and had gone into hiding for several months.

Prof. C.V. Skeffington of Cambridge University, former tutor of both Lambert and Parker, who had been undergraduates together, testified that Lambert had announced suddenly that he was leaving for South America in January 2000. This was supported by a letter on file at Lambert's place of employment (The Museum of Motion, St. Pancras) requesting an indefinite leave of absence on family grounds.

No further sightings of Lambert are known until November. Parker's live-in girlfriend, Miss Moira Austin, testified that she saw Lambert visit Parker on November 21.

Miss Elaine Vinney, employed at the King Canute public house, Canvey Island, Essex, testified that Parker and a man answering Lambert's description had stayed at the premises on the night of Nov. 29, 2000. Lambert was never seen again. Parker was brought in for questioning when it became known that he was the chief beneficiary of Lambert's will, which had been changed in Parker's favour one week before Lambert's disappearance. In discussing additional motives for the murder, Mr. Julian Avery, for the Crown, suggested that Lambert and Parker had been confederates in some criminal scheme for approximately a year and had then fallen out.

Parker's statements to police were inconsistent. At first he denied any recent contact with Lambert; later he admitted that he and Lambert had stayed at the King Canute on Nov. 29.

Acting for Parker, Mr. Vikram Chatterji (Legal Aid) produced in evidence an amateur video purporting to show Lambert boarding an unorthodox watercraft on mud flats near the former Canvey Island Yacht Club, and the craft subsequently exploding. Parker stated that the vessel was an antique human torpedo acquired privately by Dr. Lambert in the course of his professional activities. He further stated that he had made the video himself, and that it accurately recorded the events as he witnessed them. An intensive search of the estuary produced no trace of vessel or occupant. Lambert's body has never been found.

Lambert's flat was searched for evidence relating to the case, but a forced entry had been effected by persons unknown, apparently soon after his departure for Canvey Island. Several rooms were in a disordered state. Items of value and personal papers appeared to be missing. Nothing was found to corroborate Parker's version of events. The defence's videotape was examined by experts, who pronounced it an ingenious forgery making advanced use of computer-generated images.

Mr. Justice Sir Raymond Tether ordered psychiatric assessment of the defendant. Mr. Chatterji withdrew the not-guilty plea, entering a defence of diminished responsibility. The jury deliberated approx. 3 hrs.

VERDICT: Manslaughter by reason of diminished responsibility.

SENTENCE: Parker confined at Elm House Psychiatric Facility for the Criminally Insane, Walthamstow.

RELEASE DATE: Indefinite.

NOTE (18/02/10): In '07 Parker was moved to the new Southeast Facility at Romford. He has never wavered from his story, maintaining to this day that he is innocent. There are at present no plans for his release.

Oh, Bird, I'm so dreadfully, dreadfully sorry—believe me I never thought anything like this could happen. It did occur to me that you mightn't find the honey jar. But who could have foreseen the flat being done? With my papers there to back it up, they might have believed your video. Even if they didn't, they would have got Dr. Six's name. She would have told them I had reason to believe myself terminally ill, that I was taking Anita's death pretty hard. It would have looked like suicide, not murder. Why didn't you show them the Mews? (No, that wouldn't have done any good. What would they have seen: an empty stable with a few bits of tack and no inkling of the bolted beast?) The previous convictions can't have helped. You never told me about those. Vincent parts, was it, Mr. Tite?

So now I have both your lives on my conscience, Anita: a slow death in Egypt; a living death in Walthamstow. Do you think poor Bird ever forgave me? Could you have forgiven such a thing? I know I couldn't. Thank God I'm alone in this world and the only life left to ruin is my own.

But I can hardly leave it at that. I make a solemn vow before you now, in the summoned presence of both your shades, that I shall do the decent thing—do my damnedest to get back to the machine, fire it up, confound our enemy, send him back to unbend his bony finger and rewrite his heartless works. As soon as that bristled sphere is bobbing there before me on the tide, I'll slip into its hatch, buckle myself in, reverse across time's banks and shoals, run back and fetch the age of gold: the time when all of us had options left to play. And we shall live again, my love. We all shall live again!

*Edinburgh, Thursday, May 26*
A hard week since I learnt the fate of Bird. Hard to get up each day, go on the food quest, make departure plans. More than once

I climbed to the jungly roof of my block and thought perhaps it was time to end it now. And one morning—Monday—the old incubus was back. I couldn't get up. Paralysed for an hour, shaking like a Parkinson's case for two hours more.

On Tuesday I rallied, and lucky that I did. Things are moving faster than expected.

My wish has come true. I look out over the Firth and there it is: a sail. An odd sail rigged like a junk—one of those reed table-mats, but larger than those on the loch—with a billowing black emblem, crossed daggers, and a red burgee.

Not a currach. I can't make out what she's made of, but it's something pale and smooth—certainly not hides. She comes slowly, for the wind is from the west, and there's a clumsiness about her seamanship.

*Same day. 7 p.m, off Bass Rock*
It took them all morning to beat feebly against the wind, so I had time to go to the castle and light a fire I had prepared—a smoky, lazy fire, the sort an unwary resident might keep alive to save on matches. I returned to the flat, gathered my things, and left them on a bank where a loading crane nods over the channel, stooped and netted with vines. I climbed up and hid among the leaves, watching the invaders through binoculars.

It was the lady's men, all right: her bandog Kenneth and two others. They tied up half a mile away at some mangroves near Harry Ramsden's, "The World's Most Famous Fish and Chips." They spotted my decoy fire. Off they set, all three, leaving no guard, thinking they'd nab me at siesta.

It was so easy—though I burned enough adrenalin to last a year—like nicking a sportscar with the keys left in. To reach the castle would take them at least an hour, even if they found the best route, so there was plenty of time. Sailing the thing was another matter; if the wind hadn't been with me I don't know what I would have done. It was touch and go picking up my gear.

The Macbeths' royal yacht and navy, now under my command, is a glorified currach made from the ivory hull of a motor launch, presumably dredged from the loch or the mud of Inverness. She has no centreboard, keel, or rudder, being steered by a pair of long trailing oars lashed to pegs at the corners of the transom. In all but the best conditions it would take two men to keep this tub on course. But I mustn't grumble — the wind's been fair, the weather fine.

Anchored for the night inside the reef but a good way off-shore. Already twenty miles between myself and Reekie. I doubt Kenneth and co. will think too seriously of coming after me — there's no road here, and they should be more worried about getting home. "Thou hast conquered, O pale Galilean!"

*May 27, mid-afternoon*
Heading southeast today, beyond Dunbar. The weather holding. A tattered ribbon of the Great North Road in sight along the cliff-tops. I put in this morning to gather shellfish and coconuts at Tyninghame (it's nice to have maps again), where a river breaks the reef. Also tried some modifications. The long steering-oars do give a certain keel effect, and they are easily raised to pass over the reef. The rationale for two, I suppose, is that when the boat heels one of them will always bite. By lashing a tie-rod between them I should be able to hold course with one hand in most weathers, leaving my other free to trim the sail.

I've named this delightful craft *The Laughing Falcon*. I heard that fowl on a trip to Central America during my Houston years. (Until then I thought you'd made it up.) Exactly as you described: *Ha! — ha! — ha! — ha! — like someone trying to come in the room next door, and never quite making it.* Not like you, my love.

297

*June 2, near Scarborough*

I feel blessed to glide along the silent shore of England, to look into deeps where the young reef falls away and stingrays flap in the indigo void like sheets of news. Dolphins follow me, uttering quizzical squeaks that seem to say, *You? You! We thought we'd seen the last of you!* And while I was swimming from the boat this morning an extraordinary sound reverberated my whole body — a single pulse loud as a giant bell — and a blue whale rose in a boiling tumulus and lay on the sea, its eye intense and microscopic above the hinge of a striped jaw.

The largest creature ever to live on earth, the Oyster tells me, a creature whose lifespan was thought by some to be five hundred years: a life as long as my voyage. So I like to think it's not impossible that this leviathan was a calf while Herman Melville sailed, that it saw each nightmare come and go — the whalers, tankers, and torpedoes; the nylon nets and brown cascades of waste; the white atomic blooms on South Sea atolls — and heard the last propeller die away.

A week now of sun and steady westerlies, the weather enchanted by some friendly god, an easy twenty or thirty knots a day, the *Falcon* brushing aside medusa fleets and eel-grass meadows. I'm visited by turtles and sharks, by flying fish who net themselves in the sail (and soon are frying fish), by a phosphorescence that ignites at the bow in the evening water and smoulders as if another moon were shining up through fissures in the seabed.

It's all so lovely that I catch myself thankful for the warming and the plagues, exulting with a terrible *Schadenfreude*, a Noah dancing in the rain.

*June 9, Yarmouth*

The Wash has grown into a shallow sea, drowning the Bedford Level and the Lincoln fens. I had trouble here (where King John lost his treasure), running southeast by dead reckoning, grounding on banks and weed-encrusted ruins—but the long oars are good for wriggling off.

This large river I presume to be the Yare. If so, I'm within a hundred miles of the Thames. The East Anglian coast is a wild Florida of dunes, lagoons, palmettos, and a mangrove beard that may once have been the Norfolk Broads. My maps could be of Roman Britain for all their relevance to this corroded shore. I came here once from Cambridge. Even then whole towns had fallen to the sea since Tudor times, and people said you could hear the chimes of Dunwich underneath the waves. I heard them, love, I swear I did.

A day and night of thunderstorms. I huddled in a windmill on a bubble of land near some sunken village with a name like Rooting Abbots, where a single pylon stood and the wind sang like a bullroarer in the wires. At least I had music of my own: Stones, Marley, who remind me of you pulling pints at the Loco, and Purcell, whom you played while cooking in your flat. And the only Sinatra Bird could stand: Sid Vicious singing "My Way." Bird gave me that on the day I left.

Poor dear Bird. My God, what have I done?

*June 14, off Clacton-on-Sea*
Whenever the sun hides, the palms turn into dirty feather dusters and this becomes a low Conradian coast, dreary and sinister and unforgiving. All its buildings have been swallowed, from the Norman tower of Orford to the Edwardian towers of Clacton.

All gone except for Sizewell power station: a great cracked dome like an Ottoman mosque, the sea washing its feet and the screw-pines driven back in awe. No, that isn't quite right—in the lee of mounds and outer walls the bush was creeping in stealthily, an invasion force getting ready to storm the main redoubt. But it was held at bay, crouching—the ground swept clean, no gulls or birds—the dome still blasting radiation like a dying star.

There's no reef there; the swells were rolling in from the

North Sea, into the reactor chamber through some underwater rift, for after every seventh wave or so I heard a dull boom deep inside and the dome spat a geyser at the sky.

*Off Shoeburyness, June 16. Breakfast time*
Travel's a drug and I'm high as a kite. Canvey Island's just around the head, and I'm drunk at the thought of running back to you and Bird and the 1980s, perhaps to that summer we met in the South African's old car.

Think of it! The Soviet Union's still on its feet, Thatcher's in Number Ten, Ronnie's in the White House: the world is right for Manichaean certainties. Climate change, poverty, plague, the population time bomb — all the circling fates still have, in a word, *deniability.*

And Bird hasn't yet done Tony's Two-Wheelers. Not a bad place to go back to, 1986 — a favourite restaurant where the food tastes good even though it may be lethal. *I* will know that certain dishes must be avoided (and so will you if you believe me), but we needn't let that ruin things. We can enjoy the party while it lasts. For all my hostility to progress, I am its child and don't want to live a peasant. I like clean sheets and hot water. I like shampoo and contraception. I like books and photographs and music on the button. I like being able to believe anything or nothing without the Inquisition dropping in. I like knowing that the world is round and very old; that the sun is a star and the stars are suns.

In short, there's a lot to be said for civilization as it was before the Enlightenment got vertigo, communism shot itself, and capitalism ran amok through the last unrifled pockets of labour and resources. The end of History! The divine right of Things! Couldn't they see they needed one another — that the reds needed the blues to keep them eating, and the blues needed the reds to keep them honest? Couldn't they see it would never do to pretend the twentieth century didn't happen; that if they mistook the 1990s for the

1890s, then all the blood from Sarajevo to Sarajevo would have to be spilt again?

You and I will have to hold our tongues as the new feudalism hoists itself into the saddle. You and I will know the planet is too worn out for one last gallop. But let's feel the wind in our hair until the old nag drops. And to hell with "Never gallop Pegasus to death."

All right, one gets a little dotty out at sea, to say nothing of the radiation dose I got at Sizewell (let's hope it shrinks my wigglies). The sight of the time machine itself will doubtless be quite sobering. *An ugly thing, as massive and forbidding as an armoured car.* Deliverer or executioner? I've been having nightmares again.

I drop anchor at the edge of the swamp. I wade waist deep up the inlet where I moored the device. But everything has changed. Mangrove knees are everywhere, new shoots rising from the mud as thick and fast as bamboo under a POW. And then I see something blue around a stem: a bit of mooring line. And another bit, and another. But no time machine. Panic. Despair. I examine the ropes. Not frayed but melted: it hasn't gone adrift; it's flown.

The next thing is a glimpse of something caught in a thicket, an unusual colour that is nonetheless familiar. I hack and squelch my way, a journey of ten yards and half an hour. A straw hat. But not my straw hat, nor the sort worn in the glen. No. It's a neat straw boater with a heliotrope silk scarf, such as a young woman might have worn in 1899. And the scarf is soaked in her floral essence, and under the hatband is a note.

Good Morning, Mr. Lambert,
I have been watching you. I visited your rooms in the Wakefield Tower, and read your notes while you were away. I feel I know you, Mr. Lambert, and I feel you will forgive what I have done. It was not an easy decision. No doubt you think it unjust of me to strand you in this age of heat and desolation.

But you should know that you, by your actions, stranded me. I know you meant no harm. Neither do I. You are right in thinking that flesh and blood cannot go back.

Goodbye, Mr. Lambert. Forgive.

Yours sincerely, Tatiana Cherenkova (Miss)


Good morning? How could she know what time of day I'd get here? Or even if I'd get here at all? Sometimes in dreams your reason can step in and say, Come off it now, this is absurd — change the plot to something less implausible. But my mind did not perform these lucid duties. I woke in a running sweat, and again I was pinned like Gregor Samsa on my bed.

The nightmare held me long after I awoke — like those air-crash dreams I'd get before I flew somewhere: the sustaining magic gone from the sunny tube, the sky jumping, the earth rising, weightlessness, tall buildings shouldering up outside the oval windows, the wings torn off, the screams, the lurching cabin filled with fire.

What logic can one apply to a device that undoes all our notions of effect and cause? It makes no difference where the thing came from, whether it was the work of earthly genius or unearthly science, or even where Tania is marooned. I am only a primitive who found a car and turned a key. If I say I understand the laws that govern it, my understanding isn't even Ptolemaic in approximation to the truth. But that's hardly reason enough to turn away. We gnaw our way through life not knowing (or kidding ourselves we know, a purer and more consoling ignorance), and if ignorance were cause enough to give up we'd all be virgin suicides.

What if the time machine really has flown, if my precautions were inadequate? In a few hours I'll know. What then? Will I have the strength to flog up to Hatfield for the kayak? Bugger Half Nelson's records and his Nataraja, but if I'm condemned to the Tower of London for the rest of me days I'll want the kayak.

Lying here this morning I've been scribbling obituaries in my head. Who doesn't want to read his own? That mix of admiration, intimacy, and wit; the pat on the back for jobs well done; the sense that all is forgiven and posterity will care. If the machine is gone or doesn't work I'll not wait long for the skinny bloke with the scythe. I shall go to Canary Wharf, drag these bones up that accursed tower, kick out as many of the remaining windows as I can, and take a dive into Father Thames. Probably the drop will do it; at a height like that they say the water hits like concrete. Just to make sure, I'll bring a little meat along and scatter it for the sharks — monkey meat, if I can get it, to sharpen their tooth for higher primate. Of course I could ask Graham to do the honours, but somehow I don't think she would. I've never doubted that most housecats, if the size ratio were magically reversed, would devour their owners the instant they got hungry; but big cats, having no chip on the shoulder, are apt to be more honourable.

My notices. As the last postmodern in England, surely I'm allowed a pair of incompatible obits?

*The Times:*
LAMBERT, David Philip Wringham, museum curator, on Thursday, by his own feet while vandalizing the premises of the *Daily Trumpet*, aged 533. Only child of the late Montague Jason Lambert and Mary Lavinia L., née Wringham. In his long life Dr. Lambert became a noted scholar, reading Archaeology at Cambridge (Downing 1985-88), staying on to earn his Ph.D in 1993. His thesis, *Mechanism as Meaning: A Portrait of the Engineer as a Young Man*, attracted international attention and secured him a post-doctoral fellowship at Houston in the U.S.A. In 1995 he returned to Britain and became Head of Acquisitions at the newly founded Museum of Motion, St. Pancras.

On Nov. 30, 2000, Lambert became the first man (though not the first person) to travel in time, following his discovery of a late 19th-century device built and abandoned by one Tatiana Cherenkova, a student of Nikola Tesla. Mr. Lambert is perhaps best known for his book *A Scientific Romance*, an account of his subsequent voyage in the device, and for his generosity to animal welfare. He leaves the largest estate of recent times, though it must be said that the properties are in need of restoration.

*Daily Trumpet:*

LAMBERT, David P.W., Ph.D, suddenly on November 30, 2000, at the age of 33. In his tragically short life, Dr. Lambert had already become a noted scholar, reading Archaeology at Cambridge, 1985-88, and earning a doctorate in 1993. His first academic paper, "Invisibility as Metonymy in the Discourse of H.G. Wells," was widely recognized as a landmark in its field.

Prof. C.V. Skeffington, Lambert's former tutor, remembered him as "a dear friend, a stimulating colleague, and above all a brilliant, unconventional mind. But poor David had a difficult life. His parents were killed when he was ten or eleven, and he never got over his first real love affair. As Dryden said, 'Great wits are sure to madness near allied.' Had it not been for this tragic instability, I feel certain he would one day have accomplished major work." Prof. Skeffington also recalled having to discipline David for keeping a "non-approved pet" in his rooms, an American panther which the tender-hearted Lambert had freed from a circus.

In April 2000, Lambert admitted himself to Elm House Psychiatric Hospital, Walthamstow, where he had undergone several courses of treatment for clinical depression as an adolescent. His final outbreak was believed related to the untimely death of the young Egyptologist Anita Langland. She and Lambert had been close during their undergraduate years.

On November 30, an equipment failure during a course of electroconvulsive therapy induced Dr. Lambert's sudden death. A hospital spokesman expressed "profound concern and sympathy," attributing the fault to an unexplained power surge known to have occurred at that time through-out the southeastern sector of the National Grid.

Does the second one strike you as more plausible? Am I mad as a March hare? Trapped in echoes at the stroke of death? I don't think so. I may have been flat on my back while I composed the above, but I could still feel the bake of the sun through the tent. I could smell tropical flowers—almonds and banksia. I could still hear the silence of England. And now, as I fry shaved coconut in turtle fat for breakfast (yes, I did it: had turtle stew and turtle soup the other day at Gunfleet), this world around me is as palpable as any I have known.

I remember you telling me when we met for the last time, when we'd just broken up and you were leaving for Egypt and I was in one of these moods, afraid of losing my mind, *You'll be all right, David. I don't think you're crazy for one minute. Really mad people never worry that they're mad. They think they're perfectly sane.*

As promised, I'm coming back to you and hang the risk. And not purely from altruism or remorse. I've seen enough to know that I could make any number of hops into the future and never find another aspirin, let alone what we need.

The Glen Nessies of the earth may survive, human numbers may eventually rebuild, we may with time and luck climb back to ancient China or Peru. But the ready ores and fossil fuels are gone.

Without coal there can be no Industrial Revolution; without oil no leap from steam to atom. Technology will sit forever at the bottom of a ladder from which the lower rungs are gone. And how heavily the fallen knowledge will lie upon any who hope to resurrect it! Remember what Skef used to say about digging up the past—that there's only one chance to get it right because excavation is destruction? I'm sure the same is true of progress. A civilization such as ours ploughs up the rails behind; we had at best one chance to get it right.

The most we can aspire to now is a Scrap-Iron Age: old girders beaten into swords and ploughshares over charcoal fires, stainless steel more precious than gold. Not for a hundred million years will the earth become gravid with new coal and oil, and Lord knows what will have evolved by then.

Still, let's keep the bald ape's reputation in perspective. Even if our peculiar gifts were ultimately fatal, nature will make the best of the mess we've left behind. She'll make a new creation, a new race that *needs* a pinch of PCBs to thrive. The shrunken roll of creatures in our wake will ramify and replenish the earth. Time will exalt new rulers of the planet who, aeons from now, may look back gratefully on us as a blue note in the music, a supernova burning bright and brief to cook new elements for future life—like the first plants, which filled the air with a poison gas called oxygen. If a dinosaur can become a hummingbird, all things are possible.

*Evening, off Canvey Island*
Back at last on the spot where I began, on the cay that was the King Canute.

*Friday afternoon*
Dog-tired. I've had the devil of a time locating the machine in the mangroves without the kayak. The *Falcon* can't get in between the

knobbly knees. I was up to my chest in roots and mud, slashing at the shoots and vines that choke the inlet. Yes, I panicked, afraid my nightmare had come true.

Then I saw it—not the newly riveted device that appeared before me in the mews, but scabbed and pitted now, belted like Jupiter with tidelines, its copper needles green as lightning rods—more than ever like an unexploded mine.

Again a slight hiss when I undid the hatch, but no feminine perfume. Only a musty smell of bilge. I feared a leak, short circuits, a dead generator. I wiped mildew from the leather, sat down, tested instruments and switches. The moisture on board was only condensation, an inch or two of slopping rust. One by one, the green eyes came to life around me.

A few days' preparation and the thing will fly.

*Sunday, June 19, Evening*
Today I sailed to the Isle of Dogs, riding the tide with an easterly behind me, to say goodbye to a dear old friend.

I hardly dared scan the shore for that shadow in the shadows, those topaz eyes, that single ear. And climbing the ridge to her front door in Canary Wharf was one of the hardest things I've done since coming here. What if she was sick, or mad, or dead? What if all I found of her was a matted corpse?

She wasn't there, and in a way I'm glad, for parting yet again would have been so hard on both of us, and she might have followed me back to Canvey somehow, only to be hurt or frightened by the launching sphere.

But I know that Graham lives. I entered her den and all looked well: meaty bones by the door, some macaw feathers and deerskin, a soft depression where she sleeps. I waited a couple of hours, fishing from a concrete slab. She didn't come home before I had to turn back with the tide. I left two piranhas (beheaded as always) for her dinner.

And I took a keepsake which I'll show you—a hank of jet-black fur.

*Off Canvey Island, Tuesday, June 21, 2501. Noon. High water*
The solstice and my thirty-fourth—and hot enough to fry bacon on my hat. This is the last dispatch from the future, love. The machine is ready and I sail this afternoon.

Will it be as I dreamed on the Rood: an earthly paradise of bad wine and good company beside the Nile? Was that a vision of the future (or more precisely an amended past)? Let's hedge our bets. I've not forgotten the possibility that though the machine may be able to travel back through time, its occupant may not. I'm still inclined to believe that this was Tania's mistake. She took a peek at this age, didn't like what she saw, slammed her device into reverse. . . . So you may find nothing but a hollow shell, while I am cast adrift with her far from the shining archipelagos of gravity, where those who try to cheat the writ of time must swim forever up that dark stream flowing from the future.

Common logic, for what it's worth, says something like this must be so, for if I could go back, I could meet myself (or not quite meet myself, always entering a room as my original is leaving it), and it must be impossible to become a double, for duplication is creation and, though we clever apes may juggle the exchange of energy and matter, creation from whole cloth remains the last prerogative of God. So I shan't be surprised if I join Tania on an endless river flowing against us just as fast as we can swim; or lie withered yet mindful in an icy night, a Tithonus doomed to age but not to die.

Still I'll climb aboard, for I'm condemned, with little to lose and much to gain, and my return is the only hope for you, for Bird, for my mother and father.

If Tania could scratch a date, I can at least write a warning:
*For Ms. Anita Langland, Girton College, Cambridge, 1988.*

*Don't go to the ball, don't raise your hand, don't go to hospital, don't let them put a needle in your arm.*

Or, better:

*For Ms. Anita Langland, Malvern Hills, Dominica, West Indies, 1984.*

*Don't go to England, don't eat the food, don't fall in love.*

And of course I already know that the me who is writing did not return, because the you that I know did not become a vegetarian, did fall for Bird, did fall for me, went to the ball, was given blood, and died. And the me that I know did not pull a wire from the car to keep his parents in on Christmas Eve.

But what we know amounts to a hill of beans. So I'll entrust my failing body and eternal soul to this gilded gear, cast off, and steam into the shadowy silent distance, looking all moon-eyed fishes in the eye, and to hell with icebergs, for the smart ship is unsinkable.

One last thing. If this arrives with nothing of me but a heap of sweaty clothes, would you arrange an epitaph? Anonymous, if you like, To an Unknown Sailor. I thought *Tithonus*:

> The woods decay, the woods decay and fall,
> The vapours weep their burthen to the ground,
> Man comes and tills the field and lies beneath,
> And after many a summer dies the swan.
> Me only cruel immortality
> Consumes; I wither slowly in thine arms,
> Here at the quiet limit of the world.

# ACKNOWLEDGEMENTS

My thanks to the following for generosity with their time and many help-ful suggestions: David Young, Shirley Wright, Anthony Weller, John Saddler, Bella Pomer, Farley Mowat, Alberto Manguel, George Lovell, Lois Hill, Antony Harwood, Maureen McCallum Garvie, George Galt, Henry Dunow, and Julie Anderson. Thanks also to Marian Fowler, Eric Wright, Andrew Tidbury, Emily Zarb, Joe Fisher, Tom Brown, and Michael Coren.

I am grateful to the Canada Council and the Ontario Arts Council for their support; and to Mike Poole for material inspiration.

Special thanks to Janice Boddy, Louise Dennys, Diane Martin, and Gena Gorrell.

Books particularly useful to me in my research included: *The Invisible Man: The Life and Liberties of H.G. Wells* by Michael Coren; *Tesla: Man Out of Time* by Margaret Cheney; *Loch Ness* by Richard Frere; and *The Passion Play from the N. Town Manuscript*, edited by Peter Meredith. Among the now-obscure catastrophe fiction of the last century, I found *The Purple Cloud* by M.P. Shiel, *After London* and *The Great Snow* by Richard Jefferies, and Mary Shelley's *The Last Man* especially interesting.

# PERMISSIONS

p. 126 "The years like great black...": from *The Countess Cathleen* by W.B. Yeats in *The Collected Plays of W.B. Yeats*. © Michael Yeats. Reprinted courtesy of A.P. Watt Ltd. and Michael Yeats.

p. 129 "How odd / Of God / To choose / The Jews": from "How Odd of God" by William Norman Ewer in *The Week-end Book*, eds. Vera Mendel and Francis Meynell (Edinburgh: Harrap, 1924).

p. 165 "Slowly the poison...": from "Missing Dates" in *Collected Poems* © 1955 by William Empson (Chatto & Windus, 1962). Reprinted with permission of Curtis Brown Ltd., London, on behalf of The Estate of William Empson.

p. 223 "What'll ye dae...": from "The Coming of the Wee Malkies" by Stephen Mulrine, in *Scottish Poetry 3*, eds. George Bruce, Maurice Lindsay, and Edwin Morgan. © Edinburgh University Press, 1968. Reprinted courtesy of publisher.

p. 245 "Rooftrees are wrecked...": from "The Ruin" (anon.), trans. Peter Reading in "Three Versions from the Exeter Book: Fragmentary."

## SOME OTHER SOURCES

p. 55  "Unseen maggots...":  from Conrad Aiken's novel, *Blue Voyage*

p. 66, 126 "Time is a spring...": from an untitled sonnet by Miguel de Unamuno, in *Poesia: Obras Completas* (Madrid, 1979), my translation.

p. 90  "Il n'y a rien...": Jacques Derrida

p. 139, 309 "The woods decay...": from "Tithonus" by Tennyson

p. 258 "If I could put you back...": from *Bishop Blougram's Apology* by Robert Browning

p. 258 "And the price of failure...": from Eric Hobsbawm, *The Age of Extremes* (London: Michael Joseph, 1994).

p. 259 "Civilization is...": I have no sources for "plumbing" and "living beyond your means." The other definitions, somewhat loosely but in order, come from Oscar Wilde, Thomas Carlyle, Max Frisch, Ernst Jünger, Donald Marquis, and Joseph Krutch. "Pyramid scheme" is Skef's.

p. 281 "quaint Alexandrian tutti-frutti": Norman Douglas

p. 297 "Thou has conquered...": from Swinburne, *Hymn to Proserpine* (words attributed to Julian the Apostate).

p. 301 "Never gallop Pegasus...": from Pope, *Imitations of Horace*

*Every effort has been made to contact copyright holders. In the event of an inadvertent omission, please contact the publisher.*